Joy

&

Murder at Misenlake Manor

STEPHEN BEGG

ISBN: 978-1-9998982-6-7

DEDICATION

Mum. For the gift of books and the love of all things sleuthing. Thank you.

The difficulties which this boy experiences with himself, as well as with his relationship to the world, are the price he has to pay for his special gifts.

Hans Asperger 1938

ONE

ENGLAND. DECEMBER 1898 – The last meal? How could it matter? Bring along what they would. As it was, it inevitably arrived with a clumsy clatter. A sulky looking egg and a slice of blue-tinged ham, and as an accompaniment, an afterthought, a blackened banana.

In her early twenties, the young woman retched back another sprig of fear. How could this be happening ? A governess at a substantial country house with just two six-year-old girls to chaperone, heady days, and such memories, long days with the heat of summer fading and the sunny squeals, the welcoming crunch of autumn leaves, and those carefree rambles with their soft feather-grip hands. That was before it had all gone wrong.

And as the Christmas season had announced itself; there'd been him. A delectable sexual frisson, an intimate tingle of closeness, suggestive glances, the verve of his touch and his whispering breath on her neck. An eruption of emotion brought such an unbridled affair of lust; he was everything to her.

Neither of them had attempted to stem the inevitable. They hadn't needed to; it was love, all encompassing, eventually proving to be as fragile as a flutter.

He'd forsaken her at the moment of truth. She tried not to think on it, to blame him would only deepen the misery. She loved him so even unto death.

A sob tried to breakout as her legs again began to shake. She pushed away the chipped china plate, the greasy breakfast at home within this horrid and dank cramped cell.

The look he'd given her – did you – could·you? The grey-smudged pockets beneath his red-rimmed eyes had quivered as he shut his tenderness away forever.

On the unsteady bed, the scratchy blanket reminded her again of her hell. She was to be executed – hanged and in so few hours, for a crime that she didn't commit. Where was justice? But crucially, where was little Ceccy? It had been too long now still to hope, but an accident – what else?

The fir trees had smelt so fragrant that day, slick with the stickiness of a newly-iced cake, a frostiness coating the air, screaming – wrap up warm! She could see her two little charges now, Dotty and her twin sister dressing the Christmas tree whilst the lady's maid, Chantrey, sorted through the odds-and-ends chest.

'Too fine for the poor box. Seems a shame, but mistress wants rid, these old scarves and gloves have to go,' Chantrey had said. A wizened-faced lady, but even-tempered and not one to fuss others with her thoughts.

The girls had whirled and paraded, throwing tinsel, juggling baubles. Ceccy had been so excited, the frail mite so different from her boisterous bouncing sibling. The pink shawl had dwarfed her, but Ceccy wasn't for giving it up despite Dotty's pulling and snatching.

'That's Mother's shawl. You have no right to it.'

But Ceccy had been steadfast so the girls had settled on a brooding war of tetchiness.

And it was time at last – the divine moment arrived. He was coming home from town. A week's business had seemed an eternity. The scribbled note; how she'd indulged herself, holding it close as if to smell his scent. The express train would have him in his carriage and at the gate anytime now. She looked at the Bavarian cuckoo clock. Twenty minutes perhaps.

'I have a parcel being delivered – a Christmas surprise. I want to meet the postman at the gate,' she'd gabbled. 'I'm ever so anxious to keep it a secret.' A half-truth, but it would suffice. Chantrey had barely glanced up.

To snatch a moment alone with him – to break her news before the manor and his family enveloped him once more. Her insides had tightened. She recalled the rip in her belly the day the doctor had confirmed her fears. But now, the moment had come. What would he say? His reaction would be everything. But he loved her so. It would work out.

Chantrey had sniffed at a tatty hat.

'You'll keep an eye on the girls for me?' she'd said to the huffing maid, attempting to calm her breath and conceal her excitement. 'I shouldn't be long. If you could …'

'Just don't dawdle,' Chantrey had chided. 'The master's due today and he won't thank you if he hears the girls whooping and dashing about the place unattended.'

And with an uncertain smile, she'd stolen away. Escape. Anticipation. Tripping through the well-trodden path dodging the grabbing brambles, not minding the spraying branches as her heart whistled bliss for what would be the last time.

'Got to turn your light out, I'm afraid, miss,' said the guard through the grate. His footsteps faded, almost as if they were relieved to flee the condemned woman; released from the agony of a last errand and the possibility of the whimpering cries for mercy.

Now as the darkness enfolded her, with an effort, she lay back and tried to think of her God. She knew she was innocent. There had to be a reprieve coming and this horror would fade into an appalling remembrance. But would he then come back to her? Her mind tossed raw memories. Oh, Ceccy, where did you go?

Back then. Standing at the gate she'd been so desperate for a sight of the carriage, then came the sound of the cart's wheels as it slashed through the mud. And he was there, leaping down, an unsure look as he'd spotted her. Then, an enquiring smile almost a rebuke, but with a reassuring tip of his hat he'd led her back toward the manor. 'I'll walk the rest of the way with Miss Ines,' he'd shouted back to his driver.

As they were encased by the iciness of the scrub, she'd batted away his half-hearted remonstrations and circled his arm, relishing their closeness as they cosied up and made their way back through the trees. But it had been less than brief.

A crackle then a faint yap had risen to a yell of panic.

Something was horribly wrong. He began to run before her; a parent's instinct perhaps. And then suddenly there was Chantrey clasping Dotty's arm, as the child tried to wriggle away.

Ceccy was gone. That was all she'd said. Chantrey's reproachful eyes had burned out at her as the guilty concord was sealed between them.

Dotty gushed tears and fell into her father's arms, swooning, her eyes wet and fretful. He'd lifted her up with soothing words and mellow questions. But Dotty had become hysterical and then fainted again. The child was helped back to the house by Chantrey, leaving them to search. But Ceccy was nowhere. All the usual hideouts and play spots, not a sound or sign. He'd remonstrated. She'd forgotten a special place? Somewhere they'd rambled? Somewhere forbidden?

Then the doctor came, followed by the police, who stirred the villagers, enlisting all help in the search for the missing child.

Back at the manor the policeman were all about them and the grilling had begun. 'Why had she left them unattended? The postman? He wasn't due until later in the day.' The interrogation went on and on. But she wouldn't give their secret away.

'Now, miss, the maid informed us that as soon as you left the house, the girls upped and raced after you. There was no stopping them. You were barely out of sight so she assumed that they'd caught up with you. But you're telling us this never happened? But how can that be? It's but a short stroll. You were only going to the gate!'

How she'd rifled through her memory bank. Recalling their walks. Their hidey-holes. But all had been raked over and re-examined. The detective had become sterner. His eyes more and more distrustful.

After another sleepless night, more fruitless combing there'd been still no word. Summoned to the drawing room; *he'd* been there, but wouldn't hold her gaze.

'Did you ever take them to the cove?' the detective had asked.

A flash of surprise. But no, of course not. The rusted railway track in the tunnel was all twisted and bent and even if you managed to pick your way through the metal maze, there followed a perilous climb down to the old hauling platform. She recalled the dismal place. A lone visit to assess the fuss. The way the sea funnelled into the inlet, no benign blue ripples, just a harsh greyness battering the rocks below. Dotty had frequently whined and wrangled – take me there, she'd commanded with her grim little face. That one was born to command, always the adventuress. 'Why not? I want to throw pebbles off the cliff. I want to see the water spurt.' But no had always been her firm answer.

That fateful day, the sullying of their bond. The room had held a chill, a dismal silence. She'd seen his hands make a fist, a red tinge blossoming on his cheeks, but when she tried to make eye contact, his features had swiftly darkened, and she knew their love was ebbing away.

'I'm sorry, Miss Ines, but why then would Dotty tell us different?' The detective had struggled to contain an agitated sigh.

That's when the world had begun to spin out of control. Told to keep to the study while they'd searched her room. Their letters discovered – their candid words of love. His words: *'I adore you my darling, but the girls are everything. We must find a way to halt this madness. If only I could turn back time.'* His writing so upright and bold, just like the man she'd come to adore.

And her own scrawl, unfinished and unsent now that she'd heard he was his way back to her. *'They will soon be gone and we can be together.'*

Undoubtedly, she'd meant the children's annual trip to Wales. They always spent New Year with their godmother – a tradition. And the mistress had been forthright. 'Miss Ines, you will not be required!' Chantrey, and the servants at Colwyn would suffice. And he? He'd made some plausible excuses. Said he'd follow on after tidying-up some business ends. It had been arranged. An entire luscious week to themselves. Such a heavenly dream. But these words, written so plainly, she could now see held a more sinister bent, their naivety twisted.

And then by chance, on top of the wardrobe, shoved to the back – they found the pink scarf. Ceccy's shawl, ripped and ragged.

The tale was then spun. The evil temptress leading her charges to the cove, appeasing their longed for foray, ending in a watery death. Slipping from the outcrop as the little sisters had made their stuttering and tottering descent. A story of horrible chance as one girl almost fell saving the other.

But Dotty had defied the danger and had scrabbled clear, running frantically back to the house.

The story was of course nonsense. Although Dotty had been ridden with shock, why hadn't she spoken up for her governess? They'd always been friends. Now this made-up mess. And what had really happened to her sister? Had she been taken by somebody? It made no sense?

And with the damning note went any remaining sympathy she'd hoped to garner. She was now the vixen; entrapping her prey – reaching above herself with morals rent aside.

Dotty became bedridden and nobody would press her. The likely conclusion had become obvious. The governess sacrificing her lambs due to the obsessive lust for her master.

The kindly sergeant had tried to reason with his superior. No body. No evidence. But at the trial – the love-notes, and the tattered scarf were all. The jury glared their disgust at the wanton woman in the dock. The judge's black cap and barely an intake of breath, let alone a gasp. And her love? He'd cruelly averted his eyes as he'd helped his wife sobbing from the court. That was how she came to be condemned as a murderess.

'Sergeant Coupar! Come in and stand easy.' The chief constable fingered some papers on his cluttered desk.

'I can get the midday train, sir? It's a bit of a hike from the station, but with luck I may reach Misenlake before dark. Time's short, and as I requested, I just need you to sanction the chitty for the cost of the trip and I'll be on my way …'

'I have received your latest medical reports, Sergeant. It appears these visions, these intuitive instances that seem to plague you …'

'Beg your pardon, sir, but can't this wait? If I can be allowed to have another sift through the place. I have a hunch, you see, that could just dig up the truth of what really became of that child.'

The chief constable exhaled and interlocked his fingers. 'I know you to be a good policeman, Coupar, but this last case has been so high profile, well, quite frankly, you've hardly enhanced our reputation. These insights that you say come to you, they gainsay your superiors. I know the detective in charge of this latest case is most concerned that you have become a bit of an oddity; this unconventional obsession has become a blessing to our rabid paper men.'

'But without a corpse, sir – Lord bless the wee mite,' said Coupar. 'There has to be more to it. I am sure if we were …'

'Enough, Coupar.' The chief constable held up his palm. 'Ines has been convicted and tomorrow justice will be carried out, as is right. As for you, I'm sorry to have to tell you that I'm recommending you to be retired on grounds of mental health. Over the years, your foibles – shall we call them, have been indulged. But these broadsheeters need no more encouragement. Ten years ago, we had mediums hunting the Ripper and the Force being derided as incompetents. We won't go there again. Now, your badge, if you please.'

'What? If you'd only allow me one more recce. I felt this presence, you see, of this young woman and she has to be there for a reason. I feel really strongly that Miss Ines didn't do it, and on the gallows tomorrow, there'll be a terrible miscarriage of justice.'

'I'm sorry, Sergeant, that it's come to his. A settlement of two months' pay in lieu has been agreed. But you must get some rest, man, or I fear the worst for you. They will lock you away in an institution.'

Coupar studied his badge; it had been his life, but sad as it was, there was no time to dwell on his own torments. He had to go back. With or without the help of the law, he had to find a way. And there might be just enough time. Would *she* be there again? Would *she* lead him to the answer?

TWO

ENGLAND. DECEMBER 1948.

My name is Joy. They say I'm different, that I'm not the same as everyone else. They say all sorts of things – the people who buzz around me. They talk a lot, too much I'd say, all kinds of nonsense as if to fill their time, it's mainly hopeless prattle. It doesn't really get them anywhere or mean that much, well not to me anyway. Everybody seems to want to put things in a place where they sit neat and snug, trenches where they can be covered over. But it sort of suits me as I detest their waffle. It so hurts my ears and often gets in my way. I used to ask myself – in my head of course – why is everybody shouting so much? That's when I learned to remedy it by slinking off to my place, with all my things, ordered to my design, and best of all, where I can shut all their noise out.

They made me see a doctor, well my mother did. Serious men dressed in white coats with hairy faces and plump plum noses. They asked me lots of questions and wrote things down. Possibly they wanted to catch me out. Obviously, I gave them my 'I can't fathom you' face, and wheeled my eyes, before gaping into the distance in that wayward fashion that always works. And it did, a treat, even on those cleverest of fellows.

When I was seven I got in a lot of trouble. I think it was then that my mother gave up on me for good. The stress and shame of having a child so different had become too much. You see, I've always had this thing about fire. I did not think much on it beforehand, but I suppose setting my wardrobe alight was always going to end badly. I was intrigued to see how the smoke would billow out. Would it writhe and roister around the room, a very different beast to the spirals of blackness that followed every German bombing raid? Would it smell cleaner somehow? The singed clothes and burning leather would have a sweeter pong, more wholesome than the bitter tang of brick, wood and human remains that simmered away in the streets? My mother had screeched, then sobbed, her features sagging with all that sighing and huffing, tutting and scolding, dog-tired by my very existence. It was inevitable that one day she would send me away. But you see, as I have mentioned, fire has always held a fascination for me, its might and unpredictability. It's the same with the sea. Although for a long time I had never experienced the warring waves and the crashing ocean. I wanted to test myself, learn the knack of not being able to control everything around me. These sort of thoughts would normally send me running, but somehow in the rowdiness of the flames, and the majesty of the rushing swell, I found a spirit, an unrepentant force that held such an attraction for me, much more precious than anything man could invent. To me they were both like a herd of wild horses that had to be allowed to gallop freely, not leashed or corralled; the same as me.

And you have to know that it was in those mesmeric blazes, those licking tendrils of fury, that lit the way and finally illuminated the riddle that had baffled everybody up until then. But then, those busy people at Misenlake did so wrap their baggage in such tight bundles just like the Christmas gifts that were placed underneath that oh-so splendid tree. That Christmas at Misenlake Manor was so full of hints and strands, all thrown together in a maddening tangle. But I have never let my head get fuddled that way, nor will I ever, let's pray, after all, how can you see, if your mind isn't given the chance to believe?

1898 – The day before the execution.

'The major and the mistress have gone away,' said a well-wrapped Chantrey as she stood firm at the gate. 'And all the staff have been moved on. I'm to see to the house and then join them ready to sail. India no less. I can't say I'm ever going to warm to the idea, but my mistress needs me and I'm not likely to find a position elsewhere after what happened hereabouts on my watch.'

'But I just need to take one last look around, something has been …' Coupar's features dropped.

'I thought the investigation was done. Can't be right hanging the wretched girl, but setting your cap to catch your betters, and that poor bairn, well, it's rough justice, I suppose, but necessary nonetheless.'

'Look,' said Coupar as the teeming rain ran down his nose. 'If the place's empty, who will know? I won't be but half an hour. My instinct tells me we've missed something – something vital. I would never forgive myself if I didn't have one last forage.'

Chantrey looked unsure, but eventually with a clang of keys she opened the gates. 'Be quick, mind, and make sure you take those muddied boots off at the porch.'

Coupar wasn't listening. He hurried down the drive and running up the stairs, headed straight for the nursery

Joy wasn't keen on trains. It wasn't their grunginess or all that bothersome smoke, or even the spluttering passengers, it was the fact that with all the right and properness, printed timetables, finely tuned engines there was such disorder where there should have been – order!

People lamped cases, barged through crowded doorways, all last-minute rushing and scurrying. The steaminess of the carriages with their threadbare seats wallowing in their scruffiness. Even the rain trickles on the windows had a sullied tinge and seemed to want to mock the passengers' boredom with their unruliness as their droplets mischievously darted right then left before being flicked away by the whipping wind.

Joy straightened her checked skirt and pulled out her knitting. The clicking needles levelled her and drowned out the snorting sideburns opposite.

Aunt Clarice was next to her and also asleep with her usual hazy smile of indifference, oblivious to the troubles of the world; scrubbed and starched every bit the midwife – if only all were as she.

As the train plundered northwards, Joy's life came at her in fragments like the darkness of the approaching tunnels. Memories in snatches trumping those that warranted no more than a second thought and moulding others that might help in the future into edible segments to be gorged on in good time.

The war itself had of course, along with everyone else's, touched Joy's life. It had finally rid her of her mother and robbed her of her father. Joy's peculiarity, her own way of dealing with things, had always seemed to whip up uncalled-for storms that would rampage about her, whispers and sighs and those aggravating looks that her mother couldn't resist sharing with her hard-nosed confidantes.

Neighbours tittle-tattled: 'She ain't right.' 'Almost childlike.'

'Feel for the parents, but blessed that the girl is happy enough.'

'Simple soul! Lives in her own world.'

Mother had been so ashamed to be the focus of their hollow charity. Was Joy to blame? Mum had never grasped that some saw the world through a different lens. But why would she when her own life was such a chore?

But Dad had been different. Always there with a joke and a smile. To Mother's fury he'd named her Joy; his bonny sparkler. Then came the war. Dad went, of course. He was of an age where he could have chosen to stay safe, but the guilt and pain of training such innocents – how could he keep on sending them to their deaths? So, he signed up and with that special grin handed Joy a jangle of coins, medals from WW1. 'These will help you remember, and be sure to look to your mum, it's not her fault.' And with a final hug he'd marched to his death; a tank assault in a far-off land.

Mum wasted no time after the ghastly telegram. Packed Joy off to Aunt Clarice in Yorkshire. Safer there, away from the doodlebugs. She got that one right. The air raid shelter at the end of their street took a direct hit a month later, and finally put an end to Mother's troubles.

Arriving in windy Yorkshire, Joy had sat on her case and waited in the school hall. It was full of children, perhaps the eldest around fourteen. The whimpers and sniffles had grizzled on and on. Boys chased each other mimicking Spitfires, until one by one, family by family, the melee had dissipated and had left Joy alone. Two tyrannical looking women had muttered and grumbled until, at last, Clarice had come galloping in. Her hair was as higgledy-piggledy as her breathlessness, camphor and lavender was everywhere, that and a hacking dredged-up cough.

Joy had scurried out behind the bustling skirts, dodging the half-smiles and uncertain assurances of the two grumps. But she'd been blessed as she took to Clarice instantly. After the harshness of her mother it was with a relish that she learned to be with another, someone constantly harried and busily harassed. A swashbuckling nurse and bustling midwife, Clarice had had the sense to leave Joy to poke and prod around the house, allowing her without rebuke to meld her caves of safeness, those simple niches of comfort living in her own world in her own way.

And thereafter? For Joy, the war soon evaporated into the rain-sopping dales. Life with Clarice, who wasn't really her aunt, but was her mother's cousin, proved to be flawless, a clean break with the past with no blame nor remonstrance. In fact, Joy had barely noticed the war until it abruptly ended.

The only rumple in this exact but contented existence was the express train that had always been Christmas. The time of false merriment. Clarice imbibed all that came with the season and invaded the house with holly and alien smells, and as Joy saw it, over-the-top disarray. It not only disturbed her equilibrium, but shattered her painstakingly constructed neat lines.

Clarice could be an odd egg. She never talked of her life, of her parents or of family. In truth, it suited Joy's sense of detachment. Then last year, in the run-up to Christmas, something altered. A shift in Clarice's mood. Insisting a change was necessary, to begin with she suggested a visit to the poorhouse, succour for the unfortunate orphans of which there were too many, she'd said. Years were passing and she longed to revisit her roots, memories to disrobe before it was over and done.

This had been a disaster for Joy. The orphanage with its grungy sombreness, with the proximity of so many youngsters bowing deferentially to her ladle, others slathering at the pot. Joy had run for the gates and hollered to escape. It had been awkward for Clarice, Joy had been aware of that. But there had been no admonishment, just a worried smile from her sort-of-aunt.

This year, Joy had feared the same, and as Christmas had crept up, Joy's anxiousness had grown like a tumour. Summer's glossiness had waved them goodbye, passing them onto autumn in an indecent hurry, and just as the trees were robbed of their orange glory, the subject of Yuletide loomed large like a stodgy Christmas pudding at the breakfast table.

A ruffling newspaper and a ringed advertisement in the personal column were thrust in Joy's direction.

'This could be just the tonic for us,' Clarice had said with a rosiness that wasn't to be dampened. 'Sea air and a right champion house full of history and log fires.'

Joy glanced at an advertisement. A week away on the east coast for the festive season. A gathering of strangers, but as Clarice reassured her, a mansion large enough to hide away if needs be, and the clincher: the sea within hiking distance.

Clarince twinkled. She knew Joy always pined for the sea. A sole trip to Scarborough and the rolling white-tips stretching as far as the hazy horizon had hooked her the previous summer.

'You have to try to be in my world sometimes,' Clarice had nudged her. And then in a more sober voice, 'Perhaps you could try a little? For me? I don't know how many more years I can continue to pretend my work makes up for the past. In reality, it deters me from seeking all that I had once hoped for.'

It had been quite a speech, well, for Clarice anyway. And this time, Joy knew a cunning trance or conjuring up a frightened glance wouldn't deter her aunt. The bumps were coming and she would have to withstand their judders.

Clarice said plainly, 'There's an address in York to apply to. I'll get a reply sent by the next post.'

*

'Miss?' The warden clumsily plonked down the cup, the steaming brew creating a muddy moat in the saucer. He was gone in a second. The condemned young woman was glad. Without his consoling eyes and awkward glances, she could still cling to hope. They didn't execute decent people in England!

Tidying her hair, she tried to think of things long past as if it would somehow reverse the future. Her mother, so proud of her learning and such a position, to be governess at Misenlake Manor.

The train's steam had veiled her mother's tears and flapping hanky. That had been the last time she'd seen her mum, tuberculosis finally releasing the frail woman from her battle against ailing health. At least she'd been spared the trial and the scandal.

But there had been the ragging remorse. She'd written so rarely, after the initial flurry. When she'd fallen for him, her past life seemed a world away, a different time, in a way sullied and crude. And the funeral, if she was honest, had been an incumbrance. Up and down in a day, a guilty dash back to get a glimpse of him before bedtime.

After the arrest, out of pity, the men that mattered had cloaked her condition from the public. They'd delayed the trial despite the clamour. The searing pain of childbirth had followed, but such love. And then inhumanely, after three short days, they'd wrenched her baby away to be cared for by some unknown hands, a upright family she'd been told. She'd believed them. She'd had to. And what from him? A short note – *'For the best!'* How could he?

But as she recalled the gurgling softness, she'd vowed she'd always be with her angel, in one way or …' She stopped herself short.

The door opened and a round-faced man in an oversized suit filled the doorway. Slicked-back hair, a jowly jaw and wishy-washy eyes. Her heart flipped. A civil servant – the reprieve!

But from behind him stepped the priest, like a carrion all in black his blinking eyes ready to transport her to his God.

She stumbled, spinning the chair. As she bent to right it, her legs folded and bile rose in her throat. Two guards lifted her, the priest murmuring some indistinguishable words.

The corridor was even colder than the cell, and the echoes of the footsteps seemed to grow louder, more menacing. The pungent smell of dampness and carbolic reminded her of hospital and those visits to her father, those journeys that had also ended in death.

Oh God! I don't want to die. Please somebody save me from this. Lord, let someone come. She looked at the suited man for reassurance, but he just strode on ahead, down the never-ending scrubbed passages.

And then they were there. More men, more suits, more bland, but discomfited faces as if voyeurs ashamed to be prying. Two traps were inlaid in the wooden floor with a simple catch and the noose hanging above like the devil ready to drag her to hell.

The priest touched her elbow. She almost hit out. How dare he? How dare all of them – she was not guilty. She didn't deserve this horror!

The hood was hastily slid over her head, ruffling her hair. It was white, not black. That seemed odd. Then as firm hands grasped her shoulders setting her straight, she suddenly saw it all. But why? She could hear the words thundering in her head over and over – '*ding dong bell, ding dong bell …*'

But it was too late. Breath was swept from her belly and such incredible pain, her lungs burning, hotness slipping down her legs, and then a swooning darkness until death came for her like a coiling snake

From the train Joy and her aunt decamped to a private bus which they surprisingly found they had to themselves. Joggles and jerks threw them about as they left the town behind. Litter lay everywhere. Newspapers soaked in rain, the forlorn twinkle of feebly lit Christmas trees behind net curtains. A new Britain.

Supposedly no longer a child, but now a young woman, so Clarice often told her, Joy would need to be polite to her fellow guests, and not dismiss their kind attention with that face.

Well, Joy wouldn't promise. Old enough to vote, but still young enough not to care fitted her nicely. Forging forward now that the war was done, that's what had been said. The crumbling buildings on the newsreels had been cleared and those gaping craters had been dredged of people's pasts and filled with prefab dwellings that emerged like housewives waiting patiently in line for anything to be had. We all should smile a bit more, and be grateful, or so they kept saying. But of course, the carping had been irresistible: rationing and shortages, scrummages and queues had continued and the drabness of life now naked before the masses, so a clever man had written in the newspaper. And now, there was no real point to it all. But as far as Joy was concerned this emergence of the Labour Party had mainly ruined Dick Barton and the many more thrills offered up by the wireless.

Joy's grouchiness finally slid away as the sullen driver barked that they'd arrived. Hunched in the driving rain, he'd rung the bell on the imposing iron gates: Misenlake Manor was carved into the galvanised iron. Clarice grinned like an excited child. They'd arrived for their most singular Christmas.

THREE

JOY TOOK A BREATH. The room was almost as she wanted it. The washstand needed to be shifted a bit, in line with the painting above. And the door had a mind of its own and kept clumping shut. Joy wedged more card, and measuring a fingers length was relieved to see that it remained ajar, not touching wood, just how it should be.

The bed was a neat white apron, all-tucked, and the runner rug beside it was reassuringly worn flat with the boards. The mirror on the wall above the dressing table was clean of smudges. Joy studied her freckled face and hastily turned away. It would only lead to the inevitable tedium of trying to order her straggly auburn hair, best left to its own invention, or better still plonk on her flower pot hat.

There were indents in the floorboards over the far side of the room. Another bed had held the wall by the window; two cots in one room, perhaps this had been a nursery once. Joy sniffed deeply, almost expecting the waft of child's play, of paints and sweet things.

The wall opposite was covered with three crudely brushed watercolours; all dull greys and off-whites; scenes from the coast possibly close to Misenlake, one with a cramped strip of sand and thereafter the sea stretching away to an indistinct horizon.

Behind this wall was a bathroom which Joy shared with Clarice, Jack-and-Jill style, who'd been berthed in the adjoining room.

Joy could hear her aunt's gentle snores. The journey had exhausted the purposeful woman. A nurse who'd put so much vigour into the war years, her own health now seemed less sure. Only a croak, but always followed by a rattle, at first it had irritated Joy, but as time passed, she'd become rather concerned.

Clarice had always been reassuringly where she said she'd be, well mostly, but certainly never where she said she wouldn't be. Reliable and holding Joy's life with a levelness that cushioned her over the lumpiest of lumps.

Someone cleared their throat, and with a knock the door creaked open. A downcast-looking man in a white shirt and long coat nodded his head and set a card on the fire mantel. 'Downstairs at six sharp, please, miss. Thereafter the mistress begs an initial audience with all of her guests.'

The embossed card set out: 'Cocktails in the Drawing Room'. They were to be followed by supper and a welcoming address in the library. All clearly written and precise. Joy liked that. Seeking out Clarice, she shook her from her reverie and they enjoyed a conspiratorial giggle. Clarice thought it all so deliciously mysterious, Joy not so much.

'There's only to be ten others excluding the staff and the lady of the house,' Clarice rather unnecessarily pointed out.

Joy had other thoughts. She was going to wear purple. Her indulgence, her favourite colour. No annoying trinkets, just a pretty frock, a short cardigan and her brogues. The suitcase she'd been told to pack was scant. Two identical checked skirts and too very similar ribbed cardies, and her slippers. Those and her knitting bag of course. And tucked away safely in her handbag were her fidgets, as Clarice annoyingly referred to them.

*

The stairway down was bedecked with swags of green, twists of ivy, berried holly framed paintings, and there was a delicious and intoxicating smell of spices. Despite all this effort the house itself still struggled to repel the cold, almost as if it was ill-prepared for the winter frost, as if it had been locked away and not been inhabited for a time.

Clarice plodded on boldly and Joy, sensing warmness, forged ahead through the main reception area. As the air began to radiate a more cosy glaze Clarice gestured to a door to the left, a hum of voices coming from within.

Joy took a breath.

It appeared they were almost the last, as a smattering of guests were dotted around the room. A fire flickered in the grate, its hissing helping to check the curbed silence that greeted them.

Clarice nodded and beamed to all. An older man, balding, with a spongy face, stood up and gestured to a sofa. They sat down in his place and the man shuffled to a nearby chair.

'I'm Barasch!' he told them, stretching out his ageing limbs.

'Well, that's all of us, I guess,' said an American man, sweeping back a thick brush of black hair.

The room again fell silent; nervous smiles and self-conscious adjustments seemed to be the order of the day.

An immaculately turned-out man emerged from a side door carrying a tray of coupe glasses with bubbles. 'I am Monckton. You will find that there's also sherry and fruit punch if you would prefer.' He bowed and left his pasty-faced replica, who'd handed Joy the card earlier, to rearrange a gleaming trolley full of decanters and shakers.

'What do we call you?' asked the American, downing his champagne.

'Sir, I've been engaged as the footman, but as there'll be only two of us along with the cook, I am to see to all that you may require. My name's Drabble.'

The door reopened and Monckton entered with a tray of tasty bits. Joy was impressed by his aloof manner; every inch the butler. She studied his face. It was terra-cotta coloured and pricked with red dots and dashes, veins sprouting beneath his leathery cheeks; his nose was a bit of a lumpy pudding and the hint of wheeziness fired from his lips.

'Dinner has been held back, but in any event will be served no later than seven-thirty.' he stated to nobody in particular.

'We are waiting on someone?' asked a plump lady stuffed in a gold gown. She looked overdressed and her make-up was thickly painted, very shabby-grandeur.

'Yes, indeed. Miss Royce has been delayed. She telephoned to say not to hold dinner on her behalf, and she will put her foot to the floor and be with us in a jiffy. Her words not mine.' Monckton almost smiled.

'Oh!' said the American.

More sipping of drinks and polite conversation followed.

Joy stared at the clock. It was a remarkable invention, and totally absorbing. Stuck to the wall, perched almost like a birdhouse, it had a sort of train track to the front that formed a crescent leading from two doors either side of the bronze face. In the centre to the front was a woodland scene with a block or severed tree trunk.

The clatter went on around her and, as usual, Joy tried to syphon out the noise. The other guests held little interest. Joy sat deeper in her seat. There was a heaviness to the décor: the voluminous green drapes flowed like an ill-fitting robe, the clumpy mahogany furniture formed divots in the faded well-worn rugs. It all made the clock seem somewhat frivolous and out of place in all this formality.

'I'm Grauler,' volunteered the American with a friendly grin to the room.

More tongue-tied silence.

'Gee, this is some place. Must be worth a packet,' he added.

'Indeed,' came the sole reply from the stuffed gown.

The room once more descended into the tinkling of glasses and shifting of seats.

It was a great relief when at last dinner was called by Monckton, and they filed across the hallway through some double doors into the dining room. It was an exceedingly long room stretching the entirety of the north side of the house.

A card had been placed at each setting and Clarice grabbed Joy's arm as they eased about.

Jostling Joy into a chair, Clarice lurked uneasily; she didn't seem to want to take her seat.

A sallow man approached, possibly in his early thirties, but his sunken cheeks and a dullness to his eyes suggested he'd survived some sort of illness or misfortune.

'Herr Claube?' asked Clarice, gesturing to the card on Joy's right.

'That is correct,' the man answered stiffly.

'I wondered if you wouldn't mind swapping places? You see, my niece is not used to this kind of thing and I …'

The man replied coldly in a German accent. 'I am sorry, but if this is the place that has been set for me by our hostess then I consider myself duty-bound to honour her request. I am sure your niece will manage.'

Clarice stuttered. Joy looked to the table. Claube took his seat as another man limped over. Leaning on a walking stick, he smiled faintly. 'It's fine you can have my spot. I'll shuffle down.'

Clarice coloured. 'Thank you … Mr Scanner,' she said, eyeing his card.

'Please, no need for thank yous, this is a rum old do for all of us. It's been a heck of a time since Perry Scanner has tasted the comforts of a house such as this.'

Claube seemed self-absorbed, unaware that the table had disapproved of his curt manner. He twiddled with a cufflink.

They all settled and again an uncomfortable silence simmered. Drabble filled water glasses then wine goblets. Joy swapped over her knife with her fork and unfolded and refolded her napkin.

'Our hostess? She's not joining us?' Grauler, the American, asked Drabble.

'I couldn't say, sir.'

'Unfortunately, the mistress of the house will not be attending.' Monckton had taken command. 'She is unwell and therefore will dine in her chambers. It is most inopportune as she was hoping to greet you and make an address in the library later. I understand her lady's maid and her companion, Miss Crabb, will now take up that mantle once she has settled her mistress down for the night.'

Soup arrived. Then fish, and the supper rumbled along. An edginess prodded at Joy, her eyes struggling to find a place to rest. In desperation, her hands massaged her forehead as she attempted to thwart the sniping stares from around the oval table.

Thankfully Claube's dark reticence meant he offered little more than polite snippets, and they were infrequent and always directed to the lady to his right, a Mrs Sands, a dour Scottish woman in her fifties, who informed them with a forced smile that she preferred to be addressed as Gracie.

This Gracie advanced to the gathering that she was a nurse and revealed that she'd heard that Misenlake Manor had been commandeered as a hospital during the war.

Joy sort of listened. She wasn't good at paying much heed to others. Her brain seemed to always shy away from the bumbling banter that they seemed to relish in.

Naked without her things, she thought she would pass the misery by attempting to tidy the other guests into pods. Her likes and dislikes and first impressions. Joy adored lists. Without her jotter for the moment, she would have to satisfy herself with a mental register, tidy up the strands when she was alone a bit later.

Next to Gracie was another man with a foreign accent, but his was hazy as if he'd lived in England for some considerable time. He had a youthful face framed by a mop of floppy blondness. Introducing himself to the portly lady in the gold gown on his right as Kosik, he explained that he was Polish and had been a fighter pilot in the RAF.

This impressed the golden lady, who smoothed down her curls and offered up that she was Mrs Pomp. Mrs Pomp was chirpy and irrepressible. She twittered aimlessly, filling in every pause with intelligence of her late husband, the Brigadier, and his exploits during the war. They were told, and it appeared expected to react to his rank and that he'd passed away whilst in India in the heated run-up to the Mutiny. Not on the streets that were now a battlefield for independence, but sadly of cholera. His health weakened by the strains of authority during the war years.

Next to her was Barasch. He was the gallant old man who'd given up his seat in the drawing room. Next along was a waspish-looking lady who sniffed into her hanky every minute or so. Her grey frizzy hair was yanked back into a tight bun and she had the hint of a moustache. She said little and seemed a bit prickly. She mentioned the East End of London several times and the Blitz and how her nerves had been shot! Many of her neighbours had been blown away, a horrible sight to see. Her name was Nan Biddle.

Mrs Pomp had looked aghast as the woman jabbered on, painting a lurid picture of her background. Miss Biddle, had been sure to tell them all that she'd never married, but had ran a boarding house for sailors and other serviceman near the docks in London, 'all right and proper, and no mucking about,' they were all to understand.

Barasch had listened courteously to Miss Biddle and had volunteered that coincidentally, he had been a near-neighbour and seen the aftermath of the Blitz. This revelation had spawned questions of 'do you know such-and such or hear about all the immigrants that had taken over this or that street?'

Barasch's tired eyes had just politely blinked.

Simon Gloss sat beside Biddle. He revealed he was almost local. He had been the estate manager at the manor for the duration of the conflict, but had gone away at the end of the war. He'd journeyed back on a whim, to see the old place and joined this unconventional gathering.

Kosik fingered the rim of his glass as Mrs Pomp silenced the table by asking why a man of Gloss's age hadn't gone to war.

Gloss stammered, mumbling indistinctly about a medical condition.

The seat next to Gloss was vacant: Miss Royce's place. In the adjacent chair was Grauler the American and next, completing the circle, was a distant-looking man who murmured that he was Melville. A professor of something that nobody seemed to make out, he appeared to be more uncomfortable with the proceedings than Joy and keen to get the stuffy occasion done with.

As the dessert plates were cleared the door swung open and in breezed a brash lady batting away Monckton's offer of food. Joy could smell her before she could see her. The scent smelt sickly, heady and although Joy had no experience of these things, probably expensive.

Confidently offering her sparkle to the table, she sat and gestured with her glass to Drabble. 'Any champers? Fill her up, this one will do.' She pulled a wine glass close. 'I have had one lousy journey.'

'And who might you be?' asked Grauler.

The painted lady sniffed at him. 'A Yank?'

'Steady on. Name's Grauler, but most call me Fuzz.'

Slurping down the champagne, she gestured for a refill. Although dressed to standout, on closer inspection she was clearly past her debutante years. Her scarlet nails clutching the glass couldn't hide the wrinkles on the backs of her hands or the blue risen veins.

'What a trek! I'm lucky to be here with this beastly weather drawing in.'

The group instinctively looked to the curtained window.

'The snow started coming down when I was just outside Doncaster. I almost gave up as they say the forecast is for a week of this horrid stuff.'

'Do I detect the smidge of an American accent yourself …?'

'Royce. Rebecca Royce, and it's Canadian actually. I've lived there since I was a child. Miracle I still hold some of my original patter although it's been such a time. Seems my Yorkshire drawl has decided to resurface now I'm back.'

'You're from these parts?' asked Gracie.

'I was.' Rebecca Royce sniffed up and set her elbows on the table. 'Anyone have a cigarette? I'm exhausted, but ever so relieved to have made this little party back in the old country.'

She stared po-faced at Joy, but was rapidly distracted by Drabble. 'If madam doesn't require dinner perhaps everybody will retire to the drawing room. The fire has died in the library and Miss Crabb thought we'd be more comfortable in there.'

'You wear too much make-up!' Joy blurted out.

Somebody choked back a cough.

Rebecca Royce tilted her head on one side and pursed her lips as if to reply.

'This way if you please, ladies and gents,' Drabble hurriedly said.

Chairs scraped back, and Clarice chivvied Joy along as they all filed out.

'Wild goose chase,' said Rebecca Royce, throwing Joy a sharp glance and taking a light from Grauler. Puffing smoke, she went on, 'Received a note in Liverpool saying my solicitor needed to see me urgently down in London. Hot-footed it down there and was told they'd shut up for Christmas. With these itsy-bitsy roads, it's a fluke I made it here at all. Back home we're all set up for the snow. A feathering here and the world comes to an end.'

Mrs Pomp sniffed.

Everyone had found a chair in the drawing room excepting Grauler who seemed happy lounging on the arm of a sofa.

'I was lucky that a chap I met in a roadside inn just north of Hull who was heading out this way.' Rebecca Royce flicked her hair. 'Name of Vince. He knew the roads. Said the coastal route would be impassable. Took me via York, led me straight here. Civil of him. If it weren't …'

She was interrupted by the door opening and a slight woman, probably in her sixties and looking underdressed in a knitted cardigan, padded into the room.

The lady cleared her throat and with a quivering hand put on some dark-rimmed glasses. Reading from a notebook, she started rather robotically,

'My name is Martha Crabb. I am engaged as a lady's companion to Miss Dorothy Gwynne. To begin with, my mistress and your hostess wishes to apologise for being incapacitated and therefore unable to greet you herself.'

She pushed her glasses back. 'This gathering, as the Gwynne family have grown to call it, is the third of its kind. Major Gwynne, in his Will, stipulated that every Christmas twelve deserving souls were to receive seven days' hospitality at Misenlake Manor in recognition of their services during the war. Being a military gentleman, and seeing first-hand, how here at Misenlake people were not only physically mended, but also had their spirits raised, garnering a togetherness that he was eager to ensure would continue on.'

Miss Crabb took a breath and briefly regarded them over the top of her spectacles. 'For those of you unaware, the manor was utilised as a hospital during the conflict. The late major was explicit that this invitation was to be extended to all those who may have suffered, or indeed made a difference over that catastrophic period.'

Joy tapped her nose with her forefinger. It was another go-to habit. Sometimes she poked it again and again, always fearful that one too few taps would bring forth some disaster. This time it'd been more of an involuntary motion brought on by fretfulness. This Crabb, her eyes had a blackness to them, glassy and impenetrable, as if guarding her thoughts.

'There are no organised activities other than a visit from the local choristers regaling us with festive carols on Christmas morning,' Crabb eventually stammered on. 'There are to be no formal introductions as the late master felt it politic to let his guests decide whether to unveil their wartime experiences or keep their counsel as they would see fit.'

Several peturbed glances skimmed the room.

'Guides can be engaged from the village if you would like to walk. Robin

Hood's Bay is particularly beautiful even at this time of year, even if a bit of a hike. Boots and capes are also available and absolutely advisable as the coastal path is not a sheltered one.'

'Will Miss Gwynne be well enough to join us on the big day?' Mrs Pomp enquired eagerly.

'I am not certain that will be possible. Tomorrow being Christmas Eve, the day may arrive just a little too soon.' Miss Crabb smiled thinly.

'May I ask what is wrong with her?'

Crabb's eyes shot an uncertain look. 'Mental fatigue has brought on a wasting malaise. She needs complete quiet and rest. This gathering has come at an inconvenient moment, but she is most determined to honour her father's spirit.'

'Has the doctor been? Must be difficult to get anyone to venture out here in these conditions.' It was Barasch. 'If I can help? I am a physician.'

'Do not concern yourself. This is not an unusual occurrence.' Crabb clasped and unwound her fingers. 'Well if that is all? I will be about if required. It would appear nobody will be going too far if Miss Royce is correct about the forecast. You have met Monckton and Drabble. They are new to Misenlake, but they appear most able. Our new cook will hopefully provide, as her references attest to, an exceptional fayre.'

Monckton nodded and followed Crabb from the room, which then descended into gushing chatter, but Joy had managed to down the volume.

Rebecca Royce's smoke had formed a swirling mist that clung to the ceiling like a hanging fog. Joy had become fascinated by it whilst Crabb had made her stuttering speech.

But as time had gone on, rather than dissipating, it had become denser, somehow viscous, engulfing and clouding the entire room. None of the other guests seemed too bothered. Joy waved the worst aside and took a step back as the clock chimed nine. The resonant clonk of the strikes drew Joy closer. The gloss of the smooth wood brought a warmth to her fingers, a momentary calm, but then its two small doors flipped open.

What followed was a bit bizarre. On one side an aproned lady scurried out, dashing to the tree stump. From the other door emerged a rather ludicrous bearded figure in short dungarees wielding an axe which he brought up and down repeatedly, savagely attacking the block as he jerked to a halt. It could not have been the makers intention, but it gave the look of a primitive execution.

The clock clicked, its dong silenced, and as the swirls of tobacco finally cleared Joy's disbelieving eyes met three emerging figures.

Joy blinked and batted away more smog as she attempted to focus in the rapidly emerging light. Where had everyone gone? As she squinted a shimmering shadow surrounded a seated figure that was possibly a young woman who was crying into her hands, and beside her were two larger blurs, their gruff burble suggesting men, and as the light brightened further, one was revealed as policeman in a dated uniform.

'Hem!' At this point, I took a moment. I was confused, bewildered and bemused all at the same time. Then, as I realised that the whole room had emptied and been replaced by these rather vague and unclear images, I became shivery with fear, a cramping iciness gripping hold of me.

I grabbed at a sideboard, grasping its sturdiness in the hope it would bring back Clarice and the others, and that I could shrug this oddness off as some sort of demented daydream.

But the room sharpened into focus, and it became clear that these figures were actually real-life people. But where had they arrived from? My thoughts drifted to my mother, and her cocksure insistence that I had some sort of brain-wasting malady. That image brought a stubborn fortitude and a determination to keep my senses under as much control as I could muster.

Looking about the room, the next thing I noticed was that it was much altered although it was clear that I was still in the drawing room. I squeezed my eyes into a squint and could just make out Clarice and the other guests, but they sat vaguely in the background, their outlines no more than shades clinging to the periphery, their forms a blurry paste of shapes and colours.

Muffled voices came and went. The myriad of lights that had greeted the vision had finally flown, and despite some wooziness behind my eyes, the picture had positively settled.

The seated figure was absolutely a young woman, probably in her mid-twenties, and dressed in a simple twin-set, a bit dowdy, her hairstyle even by my reckoning, hopelessly out of mode.

I edged closer, attempting to part the frothy haze with my hands. But it evaded my efforts, always lifting and shifting like a too-quick fly.

The seated woman's shoulders were tilting, and although I couldn't hear her sobs, I could see that she was crying. And to add to the strangeness of the moment, a lightness came over me, almost lifting me from my feet and then an enhanced sense of being, heightened emotions almost dragging tears from my eyes. I could taste their saltiness on my cheeks, but somehow I knew they weren't my own. I felt sorrow and anguish so crushing my stomach curdled as if I'd eaten something bad. But again, it wasn't my sadness, or my desolation.

One of these men who stood to the side was explaining something, his voice authoritative although difficult to understand. His tone was bullying and badgering, but I felt it was directed at me, not the woman in the chair. I flushed and a piercing spasm shot through my head and brought the giddiness back.

The furnishings of the room juddered and shifted, slipping in and out of focus like a subject under the lens of a microscope.

I tried to narrow my gaze, but the figures began to mist as if they had been coated with a spray, and the picture faded to darkness just like one of the new-fangled television sets being turned off, its screen dimming to a pinhole light.

'Joy?' A hand tugged at her arm. Clarice's concerned frown regarded her. 'Are you well?'

Everyone in the room was staring. As Joy's eyes scanned the room, one by one they looked away, excepting Mrs Pomp. 'Does she need a doctor?'

Barasch was quickly on his feet.

'No, no … it seems to have passed,' said Clarice doubtfully. 'Steady now, Joy, let's get you to bed. It's been a impossibly long and exhausting day. Just a bit overcome, I suspect. Come along.'

Joy took an arm and was led from the room. Glancing back, the three shadowy figures had all but merged with a cloud of tobacco smoke, and as Rebecca Royce puffed circles once more, the quirky clock woke up and chimed the half hour, and this time its funny little figures stayed firmly hidden behind their closed little doors.

FOUR

JOY WOKE to a feathery patter on the window pane. Pulling aside the drapes she looked out onto a snowy landscape. The yews held boughs of fluffy whiteness, branches open-armed like salesmen flourishing their dubious bargains. Tumbling petals fluttered to earth as the sky above slopped what appeared to be the final dregs of its load. A flimsy sun peered through the greyness as the stinging morning awoke; nature was going to be give them a respite – for now.

The geometric paths within the parterres showed flecks of gravel, but the rosebeds were blanketed white, only brutalised stems of the sheared roses poking through the snow. A set of steps framed by urns was being cleared by a hunched man labouring with a shovel. A wheelbarrow beside him was heaped with his efforts.

A tap spluttered next door. Clarice was clattering about in the bathroom, tutting and huffing and then butchering a melody.

'Joy, are you awake? I'm afraid we have barely a trickle of water with which to spruce ourselves. The pipes must have frozen.'

Joy methodically tidied her medals on the bedside, George V's face-up, gold to the top, bronze the base, as always. She checked and double-checked, then set them straight twice before dressing hastily, stepping into her ribbed stockings and skirt.

The traumatic fainting fit or seizure had hounded Joy until a swamping sleep had eventually doused her anxiousness. And she had awoken sporadically through the night. The nagging doubts that had chased her out of her slumber had been of her mother's unhelpful invention that Joy's so-called ways were purely medical and it was criminal that the doctors would do nothing for her. A fever of the brain, she'd called it, and if Joy didn't want to try and be a bit more normal, fit in a bit, this unholy affliction would lead to her being taken away and locked up for good. Joy knew her mother had been ill-informed and had been wrong to harangue her with these unforgivable threats, but Joy had been hounded with this same horrid tale so often that this latest crankiness, these apparitions had revived the gnawing dread that her mother had been right after all.

Fears of dark rooms and white coats, of straps and buzzing machines, had always been the thing of nightmares. Joy tapped her nose and attempted to force back the dread. Her mother had been wrong. There had to be a more obvious explanation. Joy hummed to herself. Perhaps the house was haunted? They always were in the films. And would that be too awful? Rather that than the horrific thought that she was cursed, fated to lose her mind.

Yet, could these visions really be ghosts? Joy felt a zing of exhilaration and instantly knew it would be addictive. She scolded herself with another tremulous poke at her nose and pulled her skirt to the front – easier to flee from the subject, dismiss the bizarre flit from her thoughts. A blip. The essential explanation that would for now allow her to embark on the day ahead.

She wouldn't spoil Clarice's treat. She wouldn't mention this ghoulish nonsense to her aunt. Her secret. Another added to the cache she kept locked away from prying eyes.

Joy sighed. A daunting week lay ahead. Ducking these strange somebodies and all their made-up merriment was top of her list, and then a breakout to the coast and the enthralling thrill of the sea. She would be home soon enough. Back to her own world. And all would be as it should be.

There were few at breakfast. The scarred buffet suggested plenty had already come and gone.

Clarice helped them both to porridge and they joined the table.

'Are we the last?' Clarice asked Perry Scanner.

'No, no. Not at all,' he replied devouring a sausage. 'We've not as yet had the pleasure of Miss Royce's company nor our American GI's.'

Joy rearranged the cutlery and lifting her eyes, sneaked a look along the table.

The man Kosik glanced back. He had a handsome face in a disorganised, almost piratical sort of way. His long nose was bent to the right and a raw scar marked his cheek. But Joy saw no fun in his cobalt gaze just bolted doors. She could sense a hatred that he couldn't keep locked away; a man who looked like he had no time for love and held no remorse, in all, a man to be frightened of.

Further down the table Miss Biddle was eating like a bird, her body-pose tight and defensive.

'Is the young lady recovered?' asked Barasch.

Joy dropped her eyes and muttered, 'This porridge is horrid. It's too wet!'

'She's fine,' Clarice interrupted hurriedly. 'It was a long day.'

'It was for us all,' answered the doctor.

'Well, it appears not so for the German or the mad professor,' interrupted Perry Scanner.

Barasch frowned.

'Blinkin' kraut!' chirped Miss Biddle, forgetting herself.

'The oh-so-cheery Claube was a POW. At a camp down near Hull,' Scanner explained to the table.

Miss Biddle moaned. 'But what the 'eck's a German doing here? He ain't got no right. We were told the gathering was for folk who'd done good deeds and that kind of thing.'

'That, my dear Miss Biddle, I can answer that for you.' It was Gloss. 'You see, during the conflict, Misenlake was also home to several German airmen. The family's train of thought was that it was inhumane to disallow the most badly afflicted, even if they were POW's, even if they were the enemy. There weren't many, but yes, we did have Jerries here for a time.'

Kosik dropped his fork.

'Really? How appalling,' said Mrs Pomp looking put out.

'It was in the local rags at the time. The family took a lot of heat and the experiment was rapidly discontinued.'

'This England, huh!' Kosik's features had darkened. 'Even your royal family has links with the Nazis. And squirreled away in these country houses, who knows?'

'How dare you!' Mrs Pomp pushed back her chair and threw her napkin down.

'We should be polite. This is not a good beginning, no?' said Barasch standing up and shepherding Mrs Pomp back to her seat.

'This Claube? How do we know he was a genuine German POW?' asked Miss Biddle after a pause. 'He could be one of these fleeing Nazis.' Her eyes flitted around the room.

'It's my job to know stuff,' answered Scanner hastily. 'I'm a journalist, freelance these days. Was a war correspondent during the conflict. I've a schnozz for digging.'

'And you say the old fellow, he is some sort of a professor?' asked Barasch changing the subject.

'Professor Melville, or so he says. No need to burrow so deep this time, we came down together from Whitby station,' Scanner explained.

'And why do you doubt the veracity of the man?' Mrs Pomp asked.

'Probably harsh.' Scanner held up his fork as if to aid his response. 'It's just his accent is a bit clipped. You know, the sort where you can't quite light on its origins.'

'But Melville is a very British name, no?' Kosik queried.

'Yes. Probably my snooping nature. Plenty of our aristocracy have similar overtones.'

Kosik frowned at Scanner.

'What's he a professor of?' Barasch enquired, picking at a pair of kippers.

'Archaeology, apparently. Up bright and early stalking some ancient Saxon hoard somewhere hereabouts. During the war years the auxiliaries dug out an old mine shaft, a sort of underground safe haven.'

'Auxiliaries?' asked Kosik

'Yes. You've not heard of them? Then again, you RAF lot never paid much heed to the rest of us I suppose. They were disbanded in '44, a sort of elite homeguard. Last line of defence, sabotage, prod the enemy in any way they could if the Bosch ever made it over here to Blighty.'

'And this interests our professor?' Barasch pushed his plate away, picking fishbones from his teeth.

'Well, the tunnel doesn't, but it seems they found some sort of chalice whilst they were digging them out. The papers that ran the story reckoned that there's likely a Saxon burial ground in the vicinity. Probably the reason he responded to the advertisement. Suspect he's trudging around in the snow trying to locate it.'

'Would be worth a tidy sum, eh?' Grauler bounded into the room.

'Guessing so,' answered Scanner.

'And what was our professor's claim to fame during the war?' Kosik asked. 'Wouldn't have been much call for archaeologist. Unless they used the shovels and picks to dig out the rubble during the Blitz.'

Scanner laughed, but Miss Biddle scowled, murmuring something about foreigners under her breath.

'Of that I have no idea,' answered Scanner, limping to the dresser and refilling his plate. 'As Miss Crabb told us last evening, secrets can be kept or let out of the bag, as suits the individual. Our professor has been very tight-lipped.'

'And your leg?' asked Gloss.

'Took a bullet from a sniper at the Anzio landing.'

'It gives you much pain?' asked Barasch

'The torturous twinges are never far away. Damned nuisance.'

'The nerves – they are mending, that is all. It is sign of improvement, but it is a difficult one to gauge. Let us hope it may improve for you in time.' Barasch scratched his wrist unconsciously. Possibly a habit.

Scanner grimaced a thanks.

Drabble appeared and began to tidy the plates.

'Made it just in the nick of time,' said Gloss. 'Wouldn't be a great start to the day – missing out on my snaggers.'

Barasch looked confused.

'The others not joining us, eh, Drabble?' asked Grauler.

'Miss Royce does not eat before midday apparently. Professor Melville, Herr Claube and Mrs Sands breakfasted earlier.'

Joy's eyes were drawn to the door. Something urged her to go back to the drawing room. Partly to reassure herself that all was as it should be, that her way of life would remain unchallenged. And in small part, perhaps to prove to herself that this unwelcome fuzziness, those visions that had intruded upon her peace, were some sort of daydream brought on by a nervous exhaustion, borne by all this newness, the anxiety of meeting all these unknowns. But more significantly, to eradicate this creeping concern that these were not the seeds of her mother's premonition becoming a reality.

And on the fringes a part of her felt a thrill, a fascination with this strange old house and perhaps a glimpse of those who had once inhabited its murky corridors. A power to see what others could not.

Clarice followed her eyes, but before they both could escape, Monckton reappeared.

'If you would all be so kind to make your way to the library once you have finished. Miss Crabb has some further information to impart. Then the day is your own. A luncheon buffet will be available in this room every day from one p.m excluding Christmas Day, when you will dine in the Great Hall.'

'Not much to do in this lousy weather unless you're fond of snowmen and frozen toes,' joked Grauler.

'Drabble, perhaps you can ask Slack the gardener to track down the Professor and Herr Claube. Miss Crabb is most particular when it comes to punctuality.'

The library was beside the drawing room, an uneven and tapering passage separating the two chambers giving the entrance the feel of an add-on or a knock-through. Inside, through the unusual circular windows you could make out a cobbled yard below and the scatterings of a stable area.

Rebecca Royce lay across a chaise longue wearing dark glasses. Most of the group were toying with books. Joy buried herself in a leather chair by the fire and pulled out her knitting. Opposite her, Mrs Pomp was scribbling in a diary.

Crabb's announcement was brief and did little to lift the strained mood. 'We apologise for the lack of running water. It is most tiresome. At the start of the war when the house was converted to a hospital new pipes were laid. But even modern engineering cannot defeat such foul weather it would seem. The roads are blocked and the surrounding countryside is treacherous. But we will stoke the fires high and …'

'A physician has come since yesterday?' Barasch enquired.

Miss Crabb looked peeved. Their hostess had been advised to keep to her bed and it was unlikely she would be joining them anytime soon she again firmly retorted.

'But he came?'

Crabb ignored him and carried on.

'If the doctor got through perhaps we could manage a trip into the town. I hear there's a couple of dandy pubs and a quaint old church,' said Grauler enthusiastically.

Crabb snubbed him also. 'As I have said …'

'The roads will be impassable I'm afraid.' Gloss interrupted helpfully from the gallery above. 'You see, the manor lies in a dip, so whichever way you take a turn, it's an uphill haul. Even with chains on the tyres, it's the devil of a job. I should know, I've been stuck often enough.'

The faces of this gaggle of strangers clouded, lapsing into their own contemplations. Thrown together by their own design, they were briskly coming to terms with the stark fact that in this snowbound wilderness, within this desolate house, the only respite open to them would be the amity or otherwise of their fellow guests.

Interview over, Crabb turned to leave.

'One thing I don't understand, if I may, Miss Crabb?' questioned Gloss. 'Why has Miss Dorothy taken up the old quarters at the rear of the house? I find that most peculiar.'

Crabb glanced upward, but didn't reply.

'When the army commandeered the place,' Gloss continued, determined to explain his random musing, 'she turned those particular rooms over to the nursing staff and they were never renovated after the terrible fire. I suppose, being untouched by the flames, there was no real need to erase a lot of family history.'

All eyes were on Gloss excepting Crabb's.

'Fire?' Scanner quizzed.

'The north wing and the chambers to that corner were all damaged. Our over-boisterous squaddies accidentally set it aflame when celebrating VE day. Too much hooch and hullaballoo in what is now the dining room, but was then a communal space. Anyway, the point I'm labouring is that the tower apartments that lay directly above the fire were spruced up, almost completely revamped. Miss Dorothy personally oversaw the refurbishment and then took those rooms as her own. Fabulous views from up there. So why the change of heart? Nobody cared much for the musty staterooms strung along the back. There's no view to speak of, the sea is obscured by rising land which is pitted with scrub.'

Without turning Miss Crabb muttered, 'Miss Gwynne has her ways. She considers the apartments at the back of the manor to be more private.' And before Gloss could grill her further Crabb withdrew.

Gloss tripped back down the stairway. 'Such a treasure, isn't she? I swear she smiled once, but it may have been wind.'

Mrs Pomp tutted.

'You seemed to know her well?' asked Perry Scanner.

'No, not at all really. She was not here during my stay. After the war, a lot of changes were made. It was a busy time. But then as things calmed, I became restless and took a fancy for a break from Misenlake and all the wartime memories. I took a myself to London. It was agreed by the family that they'd hold my position for a few months. But as it was, I was told that the major's health had fallen off a cliff, and I'd only been away some weeks when I learned he'd croaked it, poor devil. Decent fellow, the major, if a bit of a duffer.'

Rebecca Royce's chest rattled as she spluttered and massaged her arms. 'Can somebody stoke up the fire. It's getting chilly in here.'

Grauler obliged, and with a wink settled himself on the pouffe like a grinning Buddha.

'I was setting myself to head back for the funeral,' Gloss continued, 'when I received a missive terminating my employment. Tad harsh I thought as I'd always rubbed along pretty well with Miss Dorothy or Miss Dotty as she preferred us all to call her.'

From somewhere between the bookcases, Professor Melville let out a cry. He emerged entangled in the folds of what looked like a map and a metal ruler. 'If you would all excuse me. I have some research I am anxious to catch up on.'

'I also am requiring some air.' It was Claube as he trailed the professor from the room.

Barasch's eyes followed the German out.

'Something I said?' Gloss said with a smirk. 'Anyway, where was I? London, as you know, is a bustle of industry, rebuilding and plenty of opportunities. It worked out well for me for a while, but then I grew a bit sentimental, got to hankering for the brisk winds around Misenlake, after all, it had been home during the war years.'

Grauler offered Rebecca Royce a cheroot from a silver case.

'Finally pitched up a week ago,' Gloss went on. 'And then as luck would have it I met the butler fellow in the pub in town.'

'Monckton?' asked Scanner.

'That's the chap. Told me about this rum do, this gathering. That it was in the major's Will – a stipulation. Thing is, they had a last minute cancellation, chap rang the house to say that he'd had a change of heart. Well, I was in the right place at the right time – Johnny-On-The-Spot, I suppose. Monckton gave me the number to ring, and bingo, I was in. To be honest, the lady at the agency appeared especially relieved. Was in a funk about some travel arrangements or something. Anyway that's my little tale.'

'Has Monckton been with the family for a long time?' asked Perry Scanner.

'No. That's another little mystery. All the old staff, those that were here during my days, have all been dismissed. The new cook hails from the next village but one. Monckton and Drabble are as fresh to the place as you bunch.'

'But Crabb has been with Miss Gwynne for many years?' Again Scanner spoke.

'Not a bit of it. Crabby is also local. Her father was the gamekeeper way back when Miss Dorothy was a youngster. From what I've gleaned from the gossip in the village, she was only taken on last summer. Again fortunate to be on hand.'

'So perhaps a new beginning for many of us,' said Barasch.

Gloss frowned. 'The locals said Crabb left the area when she was a teenager, and was rarely seen back here until her father passed. She then came back, but quickly rented out their lodge to a doctor.'

'So, just like you, her timing couldn't have been better.' Scanner seemed to enjoy the chase.

'Some might call him a smart alec,' Clarice whispered in Joy's ear.

'Was Miss Gwynne surprised to see you again? Bit awkward, having laid you off?' Scanner was in full newshound mood.

'Suppose it is, but we still haven't crossed paths. Potentially a bit embarrassed – I thought possibly money problems – death duties, the scourge of many. And the war, well, it scarred us all, didn't it? People find their own ways to settle after all that upheaval.'

'So you've not actually caught up with her yet?' To Joy, it appeared that Perry Scanner's continual probing was becoming a bit too intense for the other guests and the group had begun to splinter off, meandering amongst the bookshelves.

'No. Not set eyes on her since I left. Can't believe she's feigning this illness just to dodge me. But I've known odder things.'

Mrs Pomp pushed back her chair and grabbed her bag. 'I will not sit here listening to this tittle-tattle. Miss Gwynne has kindly offered us the hospitality of her home for a week over Christmas and this is the thanks she receives – and from loyal staff members as well. There's no integrity these days. People have soon forgotten how the war brought us together, and how that fortitude and spirit eventually won the day.' And then she duly marched out.

'Staff?' said Gloss, blowing out an exaggerated sigh. 'Formidable lady that.'

'Widow of Brigadier Randolph Pomp, Commanding Officer of the 36th Brigade,' Perry Scanner informed him and a dozing Rebecca Royce.

'Bit of a come-down for her, what?' said Gloss with a cheesy smile.

'Time for that chess match, Kosik?' Barasch enquired.

The Polish man nodded, and helping the old man to his feet, they both also left the room.

'Dropping like flies,' said Gloss, whistling a tune.

Rebbecca Royce dumped herself in the chair Mrs Pomp had vacated and stretched out in front of the fire like a cat. 'How does one get a drink around here? It can't be too early for a festive sherry.'

'Rather! A hot toddy. Just the ticket.' Gloss tugged on a pulley by the door. A faint ringing sounded somewhere within the house.

'I think we will manage a short walk around the grounds before we're properly snowed in,' said Clarice gesturing to Joy.

'I'll join you,' said Gracie Sands. They were the first words anybody had heard her say for a bit. Her accent was soft, almost sing-songy.

Miss Biddle followed them out, leaving the journalist and the former estate manager to entertain the Rebecca Royce at the fireplace.

'So who was this unfortunate chap who decided to cry off …' They heard her voice trail away as Clarice sought out Drabble for wellies and some capes.

The sky was darkening and was plump with hanging clouds. Another snowstorm looked imminent. Joy watched as the gardener shovelled yet more sludge into his wheelbarrow. Toward the treeline Joy spotted another figure, hooded and in a mackintosh pacing wide steps. Stooping, he looked back at the house as if measuring distance before striding another half-a-dozen leaps.

The wind had died and the snow was chunky and compact underfoot. The gardener had been hard at it as only a scattering now covered the crunching gravel.

Joy stood and looked back at the manor as Clarice and Gracie trudged toward some steps that led to a frozen-over fountain.

The grey flinty brick of the house melded with the misty sky and the speckled lights shone bright from within. It was a tall house, but hardly sprawling, with its irregular tower making it appear a little lopsided. The way it sprouted up from the surrounding bleakness gave it the look of a rogue thistle, almost a scruffy schoolboy lounging where he oughtn't.

In fact, Gloss had been incorrect. Misenlake didn't so much sit in a dip, but at the bottom of an incline. It was true that grounds that lay to the front undulated unevenly, but it was the steepness of the hinterland that made it appear dug-in.

The escarpment that lay beyond the manor, sloped upward reaching out to the rocky coastline where the ragged scrubland was dotted with sprigs of gorse. Above, mewing gulls dive-bombed the tower as they took a ride on the blusters, roared on by the slashing currents of the North Sea. Joy sniffed in the saltiness and suddenly yearned to see the squall thudding up over the rocks.

She wondered if there was a hidden way to the coast; there always was in novels, a secret valley or suchlike. Joy futilely perched herself on her toes as she tried to see more, and turning toward a wall for a better view, she almost collided with a young man of a similar age.

'Steady there, miss. It's slippery enough without you bounding about.'

Joy cast her eyes to her feet. 'A boy!'

'Sorry, miss?'

'Ernest, stop mithering the guests and get on with you.' It was Slack the gardener.

'I've done what I can with all this mush, Mr Slack, t'aint much else …'

'We've wood to stack and the main gate to salt as the choristers are coming from the village this evening. So we'll have none of your malingering, my lad.'

'I thought our God-squad weren't due until the morrow,' Ernest chirped back.

'You know what thought did?' growled Slack, approaching and feigning a swipe at the young man's head with a glove. 'Been brought forward on account of the weather, not that it's any business of yours. Go stack the firewood and fill the barrow with salt and I'll meet thee at the gate.' He then turned to Joy. 'Sorry, miss. He don't mean 'owt. He can be cheeky, but he can't help himself, you see. Been brought up with seven elder sisters. That spoilt he's been.'

Joy pulled at her woollen hat and kept her eyes fixed on the manor. It sounded horrendous. She never thought much of having a sibling, let alone seven.

Slack tracked her gaze. 'Drab old place, aint it?'

'I want to see the sea!'

Slack took off his wide-brimmed hat and swiped some sweat from his brow. 'Well, you can, but not that-a-ways. The terrace over there that you can see stretches around the house, but the outbuildings and stable block prevent a complete loop, if you've a hankering to investigate.'

Joy was still curious to see if there was a trail leading up and over the cliff. She fancied it would be an exhilarating and romantic climb, something out of *Wuthering Heights* or the like.

'Centuries back, there was a saltwater lake here, mainly during the winter months. It were an overspill from the sea. Then when the Gwynne's bought the place, they reinforced the headland and extended the old house to make it a bit more grand. A bit more becoming.'

'Those overhanging rocks are man-made?' Joy asked.

'That's right. Odd place to want to settle, but I'm guessing with the encroaching sea, the land was cheap enough. And of course, the alum industry was up and running and there were plenty of good tenants to be had – steady payers and the family soon profited. Worth the stench, I suppose.'

'That's why it's known to the locals as Manky Lake,' Ernest shouted over, pinching his nose and laughing as he dodged another assault from the gardener.

'Get on with your work, ya daft beggar.'

Joy thrust her hands deeper in her pockets as a knotty pause followed.

'I'll leave you to it then,' said Slack at last. 'If you need help, just holler. I'm supposed to be the gardener, but with so few staff about, I tend to turn my hands to whatever's needed.'

Joy was left standing as Slack dragooned Ernest toward the main gate. She was miffed after all his chuntering that there'd still been no answer to her question. There had to be a way to the sea.

Hurrying after her aunt, she spotted the two diminishing figures tottering through an arch and into a walled garden.

'Be careful not to stray beyond the vegetable plots,' Slack shouted after her. 'That field's a mudbath. 'Twas dug out for latrines by the army. Lot of loose earth still ain't settled. Darned dangerous. Almost lost the mutt there a few weeks back. Blinkin' squaddies!'

Joy scurried down the steps, her wellies being a couple of sizes too big making her feel that she was waddling like a duck.

Clarice had heard her and turned. 'Slow down, silly, or you'll have a fall.'

'Holes in the field. Dangerous to go much further,' Joy said panting.

'Yes, dear, we heard. Now, stop puffing like a dragon and introduce yourself to Mrs Sands here.' Clarice put her arm around Joy's shoulder.

'Please call me Gracie,' the woman replied, her full lips widening into a smile.

Joy hid behind her scarf. She thought this Mrs Sands' face looked interesting. It was a real jumble, and almost masculine; rectangular in shape with a long nose and very dark eyebrows which were way too far above her eyes as if somebody had stuck them on hurriedly as an afterthought.

'You don't smell like a nurse,' Joy stated simply.

'Joy!' admonished Clarice.

'Do I look like a nurse?' Mrs Sands retorted batting away Clarice's apologies.

'No, you don't.'

'Joy!' Clarice scolded her again.

'It's all right. No harm done.'

'Hem!' said Joy, prodding the snow with her foot and taking umbrage at a half-formed snowball. She definitely wasn't a nurse. She didn't know how she knew – she just did. It was always this way!

The two ladies continued chatting as they made their way around the wintry garden.

Joy's mind turned to the funny clock and the clouded images. In the past she had often seen things others hadn't noticed. Just like knowing this woman wasn't what she said. It sort of came to her. Joy put it down to the fact other people were easily distracted, too caught up in their own troubles to see what was going on around them. It was easy for her to watch diligently, cocooned in her own space where she delved through the clutter at will. Her mother used to give Joy such looks. 'In her own world that one,' Mum liked to grumble.

But like the bizarre episode from the previous day, life sometimes came at a rush. On more than one occasion Joy had been aware that somebody was at the front door before the knock came. She didn't know how. Perhaps she'd heard the footsteps or the gate tapping. Another time she'd seen a man on his bicycle and the word 'crash' just shot out of her mouth. Moments later he swerved a pothole and collided with a lamppost. Her mother had widened her eyes and bustled them home. But these odd little moments had never been a hindrance to Joy. Why would they be?

But this latest happening? Perhaps just a dream, or had the house sought her out? Was it opening up to her, showing something of its past? She wouldn't countenance that this was the next step towards madness. Her mother had been a stupid woman. She'd always been wrong about everything. Joy prodded her nose. Well, Misenlake Manor could keep its secrets. Only a week. Hug that thought. Easier that way.

As the three of them made their way back to the house, the two women wittered on, Clarice doing most of the talking, rambling about their humdrum village and the boys who'd never come home.

'You have family?' Clarice asked Gracie Sands.

'I lost my bairn and husband to the war,' Gracie declared.

'Any brothers and sisters?'

'Nay. My parents were the wrong side of fifty when they had me. I lost them both before I was out of my teens. Then in my twenties the Great War arrived. I moved around a bit. All those wretched laddies needing help.'

'And this fancy? What brought you here?' Clarice wiped away a falling trickle as the brackish wind again gusted hard from the sea.

Gracie thrust her chin deep into her scarf. 'Nobody likes to be alone at

Christmas.'

They made it back to the house, and on entering, found it was broiling within, the windowpanes wet with steam; a heady mix of woodsmoke and Christmas odours coating the air.

Not being hungry, the three of them made their excuses. Joy fancied that like her, neither of them was overly keen on mingling with the other guests – it was a bit of a trial.

As the two women ascended the stairs, Joy hesitated, and peeling off, made for the drawing room. Her fascination to see the clock again was all-consuming, and like a frozen pond, although she was aware that to tread the ice would be foolhardy and dangerous, she could not resist the rush.

Unfortunately, on opening the door, she found the room busy with bodies. A tenseness was brewing, the conversation appeared stunted and the flushed faces combative.

Miss Biddle had immersed herself in tea. She seemed extremely fond of slurping her cuppa, as she called it, and had more or less commandeered the pretty posy patterned teapot.

Barasch looked annoyed and was manhandling the newspaper, wrestling the sheets into order.

Scanner was fiddling at the chess board and humming tunelessly.

Claube and Kosik appeared to be having a stand-off near the window, Joy could hear the sharpness of their tones, but not their words.

The clock chimed half past one. Joy turned away from the scanning eyes and marvelled at the intricately carved wood. A beamed wooden hut with green firs either side. The face was unspectacular with Roman numerals, but Joy was fascinated by the swinging pendulum and again became immersed in the wonderful rich-sounding clump of the tock, so much so she didn't hear Barasch padding up behind her.

'Black Forest, I would say. Exquisite craftmanship,' he said, peering over her shoulder.

'German?' Miss Biddle sniped from her chair. 'More foreign muck.'

'Muck?' Claube hissed from the window.

'You must not forget, Miss Biddle, that it was us 'foreigners' who saved your precious little island from invasion.' Kosik was also getting involved. 'Without us Poles, and the Czechs, Canadians and so on, the Battle of Britain would have been lost and your cherished way of life would have been commandeered by the Nazis just like the rest of Europe.'

'The real German people were manipulated by the Nazis,' Claube rallied.

'Ya-di-ya,' countered Kosik, his face showing a tinge of pink. 'We have heard it all before. Just like those death-camps that never existed. Everyone always just obeying orders.'

Barasch marched to the fireplace, his hands twiddling behind his back.

'I see debate is pointless with small-minded people like you.' Claube's own face was scarlet.

Miss Biddle mimicked him scornfully.

'You know much about clocks?' Kosik asked Barasch, pointedly turning his back on Claube.

'No, but I know that area of Germany well enough. The dense evergreen forests that hide away those lost villages, untouched by the war, nestled in their shadows.' Barasch caressed the wooden clock.

'Your home is Germany?' Kosik probed.

'Home? Huh! We, who have never had somewhere of our own until now. Perhaps this new land will bring hope. A place to settle. But will the future finally take us to peace, allow us to set our roots?'

'Israel?' Kosik asked.

Barasch dipped his head.

Joy found a chair next to the clock. Without her knitting, she felt she had no place to hide. Fortunately everybody as was usual, ignored her. It happened a lot. People never seemed to understand how to approach her and generally took the easy option, which was total disregard. And that had its advantages and sometimes threw up some interesting consequences. It was as if people would forget she was there or that she spoke a foreign tongue, or was deaf and that she didn't hear their conversations, treating her as if she were invisible and thereby unwittingly letting her into their confidences.

Joy sat patiently trying to blot out all the strained politeness. She stroked the lush wood and slid into her own repose. She wanted to hear the clock chime two and watch the mad-looking figures emerge from their house and carry out their ceremony. She wanted to see them race back to their little hut, and most of all, be reassured that yesterday had been a one-off, a glitch within her brain.

Rebecca Royce flounced in, followed by Grauler.

'I keep telling you, call me Fuzz.'

'Fuzzy Grauler. You've got to be kidding? Is that a stage name?' she asked acidly.

'Hey! What's eating you? And it's Foozee Grow-Lay. And I ain't never been on no stage. Man of fortune until the war caught up with me, and sent me to this godforsaken postage stamp of an island.'

'And what was your contribution to the mighty struggle?' Scanner had finally beaten himself at chess and joined the party.

'Acquisitions, procurement, that kind of thing.'

'So you were a spiv? How vulgar!' Rebecca Royce rent out a throaty laugh.

'I got intuition, that's all. I know what folk want and I know where to find it. It's a skill. The army's no different.'

Rebecca Royce popped a cigarette into her mouth and leant in to Grauler for a light. 'Well, it appears the old country is still sunk in austerity and rationing,' she added puffing out spirals. 'Coupons for everything. There's even a fuel crisis. It's such a crushing bore as in Canada you can get whatever we need.'

'You need nylons? I still got plenty of stock, reasonable price,' Grauler babbled on.

The room seemed to choke with embarrassment and an uncomfortable silence followed.

'And what convinced our mysterious hostess to invite you to this gathering?' Kosik asked the American.

'Regular GI, that's me. Invalided on the eve of D-Day. Falling container smashed my foot almost to a stump. But I did my bit.'

Claube snorted. 'You seemed to have recovered moderately well.'

'And you, Claube?' asked Kosik, 'Luffwaffe?'

Claube almost clicked his heels. 'We were shot down on a bombing raid over Hull. I was held captive in South Cave camp for the last two years of the war.' He spoke with a mechanical stillness as if he'd been asked the same question many times before.

'A bomber?' Kosik asked.

Barasch shifted in his chair as if tired of the ragging. But rather than leaving the room he just repositioned himself beside the fire and pulled out a small leather case, possibly for his spectacles.

'A Heinkel.' Claube turned his back and went to the window, peering into the swirling greyness outside.

'A murderer of innocents,' murmured Kosik.

'I had you down as some sort of officer. More infantry than a flying wallah,' said Scanner with a teasing smile. 'POW? Cave Castle looming over you, eh?'

Claube swept back his hair. 'You English are fond of your medieval fortresses.'

Scanner's eyes glinted. He appeared to be enjoying the German's discomfort. 'But you must have plans to go home – back to, how do you call it – Das Vaterland?'

'Getting fat on our rations, although they're scarce enough,' Miss Biddle niggled, her face chewing itself up. 'I would have told Germany to lump it.'

'This is becoming impossible,' Claube blurted out. 'I will not stay here to be scorned and interrogated. The war is over, if you were not aware.'

'For those that survived it,' observed Barasch, squinting and fingering some implements within his compact leather case. Inside were a set of syringes, presumably some sort of medical kit.

'I knew this would be a mistake. I was naïve enough to think that I'd find some peace and perhaps some Christian charity in this backwater, but you people, crowing of victory, you will never let us forget.'

'Forget? You're having a tin bath,' Miss Biddle yapped scornfully. 'Never heard such rudeness. They should have kept you in prison or made you clear up all the mess you made with your flaming doodlebugs.'

Claube clenched his fists and looked around the room for support.

None came, just a simmering hostility.

'Ignorance!' Claube shouted, and ramming a fist into a palm, he muttered something in German before storming out.

'Good riddance to bad rubbish,' yelled Miss Biddle after him and turned to the room with a grating giggle. 'Blinkin' cheek!'

'It's hard to forgive,' whispered Barasch his eyes fixed to the door. 'And impossible to forget.'

Again the room fell silent, excepting the constant puffing of Rebecca Royce and the slurping Biddle.

The clock struck two. As before, the mechanical figures scurried out and performed the same ritual, chopping and bowing over and over, then lingering before racing back to their dens.

As Joy stood entranced, her surroundings again began to blur, the room tilting as if her head had lost contact with her body. The cigarette smoke thickened, billowing up, swirling over the ceiling until a shaft of light speared through the murk, cutting through the haze.

Another scene began to emerge, again imprecise, its lustre cloaked with a halo like a radiating moonstone.

'Hem!' Unfortunately it had been no fluke, as here I was, and it was happening again. Therefore I could no longer hide behind the pretence of some sort of weird one-off fit. And this time, I found I was clenching my fists rather too brutishly, digging my nails deep into my palms. But I was determined to be strong, find out for certain whether this fantastical experience was spawned by my heightened emotions or was in fact just as it seemed, a passage back in time. Conquering my fear, should I reach out to this semi-reality or else shy away and continue to learn to live with the horrific paradox that I was going slowly mad?

As before Barasch and the others seemed to slip back into the murk of the room, their hazy figures somehow intangible, a heat-glow, but nothing distinct.

But what I had worked out was that the more composed I became the clearer the objects in the room appeared. The colourful silkiness of the drapes suddenly seemed richer, the polished furniture shone, thrusting itself at me, and emerging as if to an opening sequence of a play was the same young woman. But this time there were no sobs, just unsettled hands and an imploring look, pitiful to witness, as the bullying official loomed over her.

He was pacing back and forth as if trying to contain his frustration. As before the words were almost unintelligible and as I strained to hear, the faint smell of hair cream washed over me. I was suddenly even more aware of all the things around me. For some reason my nose was suddenly that of a bloodhound as I could smell all sorts of subtleties, musty whiffs like mothballs, then peppermint, the acrid tang of beery breath followed by a disconcerting tickle licking the back of my neck.

I instinctively twisted around and met the eyes of an equally startled man. He tottered back a step. The wispiness of his moustache caused me to sniffle, such was his close proximity, and then it was my time to draw back as we both took stock of each other. He reached out to me, his fingers trembling.

Excited, fearful, inquisitive, transfixed, I was all those things, and more. This sense of superiority, of holding sway over the past had swamped me until this moment. I almost shrieked out loud as the middle-aged man before me cowed back, a hand flapping and waving as if to sweep me away.

Had I been born to this? I was always told I was different, or peculiar or both. Now this unnatural power had been released, to be able see what others couldn't, it raced around my body like a potent drug.

But I had run ahead of myself. The fuzziness arrived again, and with it a shroud of blackness. I reeled. The room flipped then jolted then tipped again. I was going to vomit. I lurched forward onto my knees, spitting and drawing in breath. But the wooziness won and I collapsed. Two strong arms caught me.

'Hey. Steady there, young lady.'

Joy's head cleared as she squinted up into Grauler's face. Beyond him, the room was as it was. The ghostlike man had vanished, as had the others and now her fellow guests zoomed into focus. They all stared at her quizzically.

'You OK?' Grauler's boozy breath asked again.

Joy scanned the room. All eyes were upon her and there was a pause as if they all expected some sort of explanation. 'Ghosts!' she announced.

And before anyone could answer, she straightened her skirt and bolted from the room.

FIVE

'DING DONG MERRILY ON HIGH …' The local choristers were good. Joy began to join in, but her squawks were curtailed by a rebuking shush from Clarice.

The spangled tree was magnificent and everyone had made a real effort to dress for the occasion. Even Monckton's stony features had eased as he handed out steaming goblets of mulled wine.

The carol singers had lined themselves in the main reception hall. It was a masterpiece of planning as it meant wherever you lingered, in the drawing room, the dining room or hovered on the stairs, even in the gallery above, you had a unrestricted view. The milling from room to room added to the party atmosphere with the guests finally warming to the season.

Joy stuck close to Clarice and they were soon joined by Gracie. They found a spot just inside the dining room door.

Rebecca Royce was flanked by Grauler and Perry Scanner in the drawing room opposite, and on the stairs was Miss Biddle along with Kosik who'd slicked his hair with cream making him look quite dashing, or so Joy thought.

The gallery above wasn't quite visible from Joy's vantage point, but she could make out a pair of gleaming shoes and the turn-ups of a set of pinstriped trousers.

Mrs Pomp emerged from behind Rebecca Royce and joined that group and seemed in fine spirits as she lifted her sherry glass in salute to them.

Finally, with a haunting *In the Bleak Midwinter* the glorious affair was done and the carol singers trudged off into the night singing *'We wish you a merry Christmas …'*

A gong sounded and they all filed into dinner. This time there were no place settings, but as seems to be human practice, and gladdening to Joy, everybody made their way to the seats from the previous evening.

Red-tinged cheeks and well-spirited guffaws filled the room. Eventually, a settled chatter hung over the table.

'Where are the others?' enquired Mrs Pomp, glancing over at the door.

Barasch bustled in. 'Excuse me. Nature catches you so often as your age races on.'

Mrs Pomp looked horror-struck.

'Where is our German parachutist?' jibed Perry Scanner, enjoying his weak joke. 'Not fluttered down yet?'

'And our mad professor?' Grauler enquired. 'Fallen into a pit?'

The alcoholic playfulness was in full flow.

'Yes, where's he got to? I haven't seen him since breakfast.' Gracie concerns failed to cut through the party spirit.

'Probably cooped up in his room, more maps and research chasing fool's gold,' said Scanner. 'Well this soup looks too good to spoil, so if you want to wait for the old boffin and our sensitive German then I'm afraid you're on your own.'

Aside from Mrs Pomp, who started to say something then thought better of it, everyone took this as the signal for dinner to begin.

Raucous banter of Christmases past raged, and talk of how the war had temporarily destroyed so many traditions, that were now being reinstated.

'The world is back on track and I toast all you fine folk,' Grauler declared, wielding his glass.

'No little lady in your life, Gloss?' asked Perry Scanner, spooning up the last of his soup.

For once the former estate manager's beaming smile subsided.

'Sorry, old man, didn't mean to pry.'

The chatter died. Scanner's knack of asking awkward questions was becoming vexing.

'No, it's been a while now. You see, my Gladys bought it at Dunkirk. She was a nurse on a ship sent over to help evacuate the troops. Big red cross yet the filthy Bosch didn't let up. Took a direct hit. Some survived, but not my best girl.' Gloss wrestled with his napkin, and downing his wine, looked up with brimming eyes. 'Come, enough of this talk. It's Christmas Eve, not a wake. Let's all have a refill, Drabble! Drabble? Where is that infernal man?'

Soup done with, dover sole followed.

Clarice mouthed 'Better than the dreaded snoek' to Gracie. They both grinned.

The fish speedily despatched, it was to be venison for the main course.

'Come now,' said Mrs Pomp. 'Even if we can excuse our ill-disposed German, shouldn't somebody go check on Professor Melville? He may have dozed off after all his exertions. I'd hate for him to miss such a first-rate feast.'

Drabble was sent scurrying to check.

'So what are we going to do with our big day tomorrow, folks?' Grauler's voice was slurred. He looked sozzled.

'Parlour games?' suggested Mrs Pomp. 'Or cards?'

Rebecca Royce yawned. 'How about we strongarm old Crabb to let us sneak up and visit our hostess? We could cheer her up a bit. She must be browned-off stuck in bed on her own over Christmas.'

'That's a delightful idea,' said Mrs Pomp.

'Or something a bit more energetic to make space for the turkey?' Gloss's eyes twinkled. 'There's a huge crater beyond the line of oaks over by the main gate. Auxiliaries again – bit of sabotage practice – way too much TNT. Always full of water. Anyway, with this beastly weather it's probably iced over, always did during the war. How about a spot of figure skating?'

'Now you're talking.' Grauler gestured to Monckton for a refill, his lips stained with red wine.

The door opened and Drabble came in, and standing close to Monckton, whispered in his ear. Monckton raised his eyebrows.

Joy felt a chilled shimmy run down her before the rest of the room had noticed the murmured conflab.

Monckton made a polite shushing noise. 'Ladies and gentleman, I'm afraid that neither Professor Melville nor Herr Claube are in their rooms. A cursory search suggests that they are not anywhere obvious within the house.'

Eyes darted to the window and ears couldn't fail to hear the manic yowls of the wind.

'But surely they aren't out in this? Do you think they have made a dash for town, that this gathering didn't suit them?' Gracie's voice quavered.

'The German may have – surly sort,' Gloss remarked.

'On foot, sir?' Monckton arched a brow. 'No vehicles have left and I'm afraid if they are out in this storm they are unlikely to have made much progress. More importantly, they could have fallen foul of the mounting snow. The drifts will be perilous.'

'I don't know about parlour games,' said Rebecca Royce. 'It seems we're heading for a manhunt.'

The room descended into an unruly hooey.

Remain calm, please.' Monckton held their attention. 'Drabble and I will scout the grounds. Unfortunately, Slack has left for the evening, and I do not want to waste time tramping to the village to fetch him.'

'I'll help,' said Gloss. 'This is my terrain. I know it better than you two. You've only been here five minutes.'

Monckton bowed. 'I'm grateful, sir.'

'I'll come with you.' Kosik said, pushing back his chair. 'I'm not sure one less German is ever a bad thing, but this professor may have injured himself.'

'Count me in.' Scanner was next. 'You can't keep the newshound out of a hunt. I've dodged all over northern Europe ducking bullets. This will be a piece of cake.'

'But your leg …' Barasch started.

Scanner shot him a bad-tempered look.

'I'll hold basecamp.' Grauler hiccupped, drawing disdainful looks from Rebecca Royce and Mrs Pomp.

'Perhaps we could find Miss Crabb and ascertain what medical supplies there are here in the house?' suggested Gracie.

'Good idea,' said Clarice. 'No way an ambulance is coming out in this.'

'Look old man,' said Gloss tugging Kosik aside. 'Shouldn't we keep this to the two of us? It's pretty nasty out there.'

Kosik pursed his lips. 'As you wish.'

'I'm sorry, everybody,' interjected Monckton, who'd left briefly, but had now returned. 'Miss Crabb insists that nobody is to venture out in this weather. It is far too dangerous. I know you all mean well, but we wouldn't want to lose anymore of you. I will take Drabble and we will cover the land between here and the main gate.'

Gloss coloured. 'I don't agree. I know my way about and we'll have torches. No offence, Monckton, but I'm going to give it a go.'

'I can't stop you, sir. And as you say, you know the ground better than the rest of us. But you are taking an unnecessary risk. However, I would beg you to inform Miss Crabb beforehand.'

Gloss softly punched Monckton in the arm. 'Don't fret, old man. I think it's for the best. What she don't know won't worry her.'

Barasch touched Clarice's elbow. 'I'll come with you two ladies. I'm afraid I will more use sniffing out supplies than sliding around in the snow.'

'Joy dear?' Clarice nudged her. 'Don't wander off!'

Joy had no intention of wandering anywhere. The clock in the drawing room had become an unhealthy attraction. This sensation of power, almost of being able to control a supernatural energy coupled with the burning curiosity to see who she really was, or even could become, was drawing her in. This kick was impossible to shy away from, this icy frisson had hold of her. The sense that she was some kind of chosen one, her specialness a conduit to souls from times long gone, and that the manor was unfolding a story, uncloaking the past for a reason; she was scared, but it was a good scared.

On cue, the wind battered the house, the windows rattled and juddered. Joy hunkered down into her cardigan. The sergeant's disbelieving eyes again jumped into her head. If he was some lost spirit, some apparition in time, how had he been able to actually see her? Had she appeared to him as some vaporous ghoul? She couldn't shake off the impression that the manor had been anticipating this moment, had been waiting for her and was now relieving itself of a tortured past.

Joy tilted her head as again the shutters shuddered in the storm. With these men now missing, something inside her told her that the sought after medical supplies would not be needed. They were gone for good.

SIX

'THOSE CAPES ARE DRIPPING!' Scanner observed as they approached the porch.

'Perhaps the two wanderers have returned. Snuck back in whilst we were having the inquest in the dining room,' suggested Gloss.

'Check their rooms again if you will, Drabble.' Monckton rifled through the pockets.

'But there's three of them, and they're drenched.' Perry Scanner peered over Monckton's shoulder. 'Has anyone else been out?'

'Not on a night like this, sir. Miss Crabb and the mistress dined upstairs. Cook has her snug adjacent to the kitchen and rarely ventures out. Has all she requires. She's rather partial to the wireless.'

'Could they be the gardeners?' asked Kosik.

'No, these are for sole use of the guests. Slack and his boy keep their bits out in the old tack room.'

Drabble came plonking down the stairs. 'Still no sign, Mister Monckton.'

'Then it's a mystery.' An unsteady Grauler shot Kosik a blowzy look. 'Perhaps we should ask the ladies if they can shed any light? The two nurses and that potty girl did go for a stroll earlier. Maybe they were crazy enough to go out again. How do you limeys call it?' Grauler mocked an upper-class accent, 'a breath of air before dinner.'

Clarice halted in her tracks and scowled.

Joy watched the drips fall to the floor from the oilskins.

'Now let's be clear, we never set foot outside in this foulness.' Gracie warded off an approaching argument.

'I'll get the torches. They'll be plenty in the army surplus stores in the stables.' Gloss donned a cape and ran outside.

Joy skirted the group. She wanted to tell them all that they were wasting their time. Those men were gone. Hazarding the glacial darkness would achieve nothing.

Gloss was back in minutes and passed Monckton a torch. Handing another to a stooping Kosik, he pulled back.

'Force of habit,' the Pole explained as he thrust a bayonet down his welly. 'I always keep it close – from my flying days. Insurance against becoming entangled in the parachute. Crashing and burning is a horrible a way to die, but even worse, there's no honour be in being trussed-up like one of your Christmas turkey's for any filthy Nazi to take a pop at.'

With that the door was dragged open and the sweeping chill bundled in. The hovering servants along with Gloss and Kosik dipped their heads and shot looks of farewell.

Joy lowered her eyes and slipped away.

Inside the drawing room the fire had long since died and the boards and rugs had already acquired a dusty, chilly and inhospitable edge.

'Gone,' Joy muttered to herself over and over as she pootled around the room. It was as quiet as a public library; there was no presence, no spirits, no vibrancy or colour. The room felt lifeless.

Dragging a chair over to the clock, Joy peered at the time. Nine forty-five. A door banged somewhere and running steps sounded on the stairs adding to the feeling that it was going to be an unsettled night.

Battling a mixture of pimply impatience and chafing anxiety, Joy continuously poked the tip of her nose. Three times. Then five then three again. Perhaps she should run out, stay out of this beguiling room and stop this nonsense right here. But something inside her head told her that this was critical. It was as if her presence had riled the house, woken up the manor as it had realised that she could be an outlet to release its stewing humors.

The clock seemed unbothered by all her fuss. It gave the impression it was aloof, as if Joy's scent was an unwelcome intrusion. Its two tiny doors were like eyes, looking on scornfully, and its lofty casement haughtily regarding her as if she were a mischievous child.

A vague whiff of tobacco wafted up from the rug. The clock tocked.

Joy's fingers were running amok, a pianist without a piano, so she clasped them to her lap.

Reaching out to stroke the wood, Joy jolted back as the minute hand finally clicked, the bell clanged and as before the doors spang open. The two figures sped out like Punch and Judy dolls racing toward one another.

Again the room seemed to shift, a sideways lurch, the furniture furring in and out of focus. Joy blinked and tried to hold herself. At last her head caught up with her legs, and with a retch Joy opened her eyes to a picture settling with its tremors.

'Hem!' On this occasion I held myself together quite well and therefore felt not only rather proud, but also steadfast. I was getting the hang of this jiggery-pokery. Learning to suppress my fear, albeit just below the surface, was a new trick I hadn't realised I was capable of. Again, the more I managed to quieten my doubts, the more distinct the images and their voices became. As my tenseness eased, well just a tad, the entire room began to bloom, as if washed down, touchable and alive.

I could see minute particles swirling around the chandelier. I could feel the coarseness of the woman's woven skirt. But with this increasing impression of alertness came another oddity. I had absolutely no spatial awareness. I was there in spirit, but my body felt unencumbered by the need to dodge the furniture or step aside as the smudged figures glided around me. It was as if I was drifting on currents that were giving me a grandstand seat, that is if I could just manage to plonk myself down; I was like a bee buzzing and butting my nose wherever the mood took me.

I hesitated a bit at first. The hanging sensation was more than a little disconcerting, but I finally charged myself and stepped down to earth and set my face as if entering the stage.

The young woman from before was sitting upright in her chair, her hands toying with the hem of her tweeds. She appeared more composed this time, but her face was sheet-white, and the shallows of black-blue that were smeared beneath her eyes had deepened.

Pacing beside her was the same tall man; he had his thumbs in his waistcoat pockets. He was still in charge.

I became braver, inching closer, half expecting them to turn and ask me my business. But the man didn't appear to notice and began to drone on. The woman mouthed something, but I couldn't hear her. It was frustrating as I could smell the lemon tea on her breath and when she lifted her cup my own upper lip smarted as if scalded by the liquid.

The tall man scratched his nose, and I could see the flecks of dried skin flick to the shining tabletop.

My heartrate had evened, and as I relaxed further I found that the voices became even more coherent as if these passages from another time had finally accepted my presence.

'So you maintain, Miss Ines, that you have never taken the young ladies to the cove,' said the tall policeman. 'Indeed, on the day Miss Celia went missing you were heading for the gate, and were quite alone. This is what you contest?'

'Yes, inspector. I have told you a dozen times. The first I heard of Ceccy's disappearance was when we … when I bumped into Chantrey running towards me in the wood.'

The Inspector turned his back and pulled out a pocket book and tacked towards me. He halted just in time as I dipped back, swerving like a boxer. Aniseed was on his breath and I could see the claggy hairs hanging from his nostrils. He sniffed, licked the end of his pencil, and noted something down.

I took a chance and leaned in. The Inspector didn't flinch. He just twisted around and paced about a bit, finally rejoining the young woman.

I gathered myself. I was tempted to shout out, something irreverent, interrupt them to see if they could hear me. But I didn't. I felt a little cocky, but not enough for that.

Over the inspector's shoulder, the uniformed sergeant was sitting at a desk, his face was almost resting on the polished wood. He was scribbling notes.

'Can I go now?' asked the young woman. 'I need to pack my things.'

'Pack?'

'Yes. It is understandable I suppose. I am to be dismissed – let go.' The young woman's shoulders shook and tears once again began to fall.

'I'm afraid you won't be going anywhere, Miss Ines. Not until our enquiries are completed or the body of this unfortunate child is found.'

The woman started to cry out loud.

'Strike that, Sergeant Coupar – the bit about the body. Bit clumsy of me.'

The sergeant glanced up and his glare stretched across the room. He'd spotted me! There was no doubting it. He baulked a bit, steadied his pen, and with a pluck at his earlobe, squinted as if he was trying to re-focus.

I wavered a bit. For the first time, I began to be unsure of myself. If this man could see me, was it proof that I had dabbled in something that would have been well left alone? What If I became stuck, like a gramophone needle in a groove of the past? Panic then arrived in a hurry, for both of us.

This sergeant got up and started to lurch toward me, a finger waggling as he started to point me out.

'Coupar? What ails you man?' The inspector's eyes flared.

Again the sergeant gestured towards me. For a moment I was sure he was going to scream – *'Ghost!'* But then, his features relaxed as he seemed to decide to hold back. 'Sorry, sir. Just … err … my mind racing as usual.'

'Coupar, you really need to pay more attention,' grumbled the Inspector. 'You and your damned intuitions. You'll end up in the nuthouse.'

'Yes, sir. Sorry, sir. It's just that …'

'Just what, Coupar? Just nothing. Sit down and finish your blasted notes.'

The clock then chimed the half hour and the swinging pendulum suddenly froze. The room followed suit. The Inspector was stuck in a pose, with his hand on his hip. The young woman's hanky was tight to her nose and the sergeant stood open-mouthed, reaching for his chair.

As I could feel the dizziness looming, I was tempted to drag myself closer for a final look. But a slight movement spooked me. Those eyes! The sergeant's weren't glazed like the others, they shone, as if a life was attempting to escape, leave the past behind and come along with me.

And then the scene wobbled and a slip of wind bothered the drapes and reality was chased back into the manor. The drawing room door opened behind me, and with a rasp, a drenched Drabble appeared with a basket of firewood.

SEVEN

'GET THAT FIRE STOKED,' brayed the venerable Monckton, as he barrelled in behind Drabble.

'You all right, young miss? Looks like you've seen the ghosts of Christmas past, present and plenty of more yet to come,' said Drabble with a jaunty grin.

Joy slid her eyes to the left.

Monckton huffed, and left the room.

All of a sudden there was a crowd of people. First Rebecca Royce strutted in with Grauler close by; Mrs Pomp shadowed them.

Clarice and Gracie soon followed, with Barasch wedged between them.

With a worried frown, Clarice grasped Joy's arm. 'You look a bit peaky.'

Miss Biddle appeared in a worn red dressing gown, fluffy slippers and a dowdy coloured headscarf. Then with a hullaballoo came the others, Gloss cupping his hands, zipping over to the fire. Kosik swept the snow from his hair and dried his hands on his trousers. Perry Scanner collapsed into the nearest chair and flexed his knee, wincing.

Monckton materialised again, this time with a tray and a decanter. Having seen to most, he doffed his head to Miss Biddle and sent Drabble from the room. 'Drabble is making fresh tea. I apologise for this inconvenience. It is very late, but having reported to Miss Crabb, she would have a word before we retire.'

'There really is still no sign of either of them?' Mrs Pomp asked Gloss.

'It's pitch black out there and having no moon isn't helping. In this foul weather we could barely see six feet ahead of us even with the torches.'

'I'm afraid it was becoming too dicey to continue the search.' Perry Scanner seemed in considerable pain.

'We'll try again in the morning, if only for the old man's sake,' said Kosik throwing back his glass in one hit.

'But where can they have got to?' Mrs Pomp's eyes searched around the group.

'Claube probably made off. Realised he wasn't welcome and did a runner.' Gloss topped up his glass and refilled Kosik's.

'But how?' Rebecca Royce face crumpled in disgust as she attempted to shrug Grauler's lolling head from her shoulder.

'Perhaps jetted away on his doodlebug,' joked Scanner.

'Who cares, one less German can only be a good thing, no?' Kosik stared down the aghast Mrs Pomp.

'But what about the prof?' asked Miss Biddle, coddling and blowing breath on her tea.

'I can only think he was fool enough to head to the coast. It's precarious at the best of times, but in this muck? He could easily have fallen and just as likely ended up in the drink.'

The room stopped breathing. Nobody thanked Gloss for this insight. Then the fire crackled it back to life as a backdraught rushed down the flue with a whoosh.

The clock ticked, but nobody spoke. There was a strange atmosphere as if this rising emergency was an inconvenience, an annoyance met with false concern. After all, nobody really knew each other – did they?

Joy lifted her eyes as Miss Crabb entered the room.

'Thank you for waiting,' she began. 'My mistress is more than distressed to hear that two of her guests remain unaccounted for. However, she would urge against any further searches tonight. Unfortunately, to add to our problems, the telephone lines are down.'

'Really?' Gloss interrupted. 'I thought the army tidied up the old cables. Although I don't suppose it matters much, nobody likely to get out to us in this out-of-the-way spot. The roads will be a proper jumble.'

Miss Crabb shot Gloss a grateful smile. 'Monckton has suggested that it is probable that Herr Claube decided this Misenlake gathering wasn't for him after all. As to the professor, that is obviously more of a worry and we can only hope he made for the village and has found shelter until the weather relents.'

'Why would the prof go to the village? He seemed hellbent on searching for this buried treasure of his,' Scanner said, smirking, but nobody joined him.

'It is hard to say,' Miss Crabb reflected. 'All that is certain is no more can be done tonight. Hopefully the telephone will be restored in the morning and we can alert the police and perhaps the coastguard. It would be foolhardy to make for the cove in this weather, but as you so succinctly put it – our professor was rapt in his quest.'

Miss Crabb nodded to Monckton and withdrew.

A din of chatter followed. Joy hummed to herself, hoping they would soon be able to go to bed.

'So we're supposed to leave the man out there to freeze to death?' Mrs Pomp's eyes implored the group. 'The Brigadier would never have countenanced it.'

'Who knows where those maps could have taken him? It's unimaginable,' Barasch said, shaking his head.

'As Crabb said, the cove would be foolhardy in this stew. There's a man-made gash in the land that leads to the coast, the scar from an abandoned alum works,' explained Gloss. 'In Victorian times boats came down from Newcastle laden with their rancid cargo and it would have had to be lugged up the cliff face, thus they dug out a rail tunnel. The coastline here is merciless and the sea worse yet. There were smugglers in times of old, so there's possibly caves and other passageways that lead up onto the bluffs. If he's had a fall, and the sea hasn't taken him, then he may have holed-up in one of them.'

'The water would be freezing, no? In the unlikely event you could battle the sea, all would be lost on a night such as this.' Barasch looked genuinely sorrowful. 'And all for a buried treasure! Being alive should be treasure enough for us all.'

'*Stille Nacht*, indeed,' Kosik added.

A brief silence followed, broken by Rebecca Royce 'No blower? What next? How am I to ring friends back home and wish them a Merry Christmas? This country is so primitive.'

The clock chimed twelve.

'Bed,' Joy announced and hurried from the room.

Behind her she heard a brief respite from the excited chatter, then some machine-gun laughter.

Mrs Pomp's high-pitched tone rang out. 'Well, Christmas has come. Let's hope the Lord's gift of life comes to the professor and Herr Claube on the morrow.'

And drifting somewhere around the corridors, '*Stille Nacht … Heilige Nacht … Alles schlaft …*'

*

'Happy Christmas, Joy.' Clarice popped her head around the bathroom door. 'You decent?'

Joy had been up for hours, staring out of the window as the blackness had eventually dispersed leaving blue-grey shadows that stole over the powdered lawns, flicking at the house like evil spectres before reluctantly slinking back to their dens.

Sleep had come immediately, as it mostly did, but then a clock had chimed somewhere and startled Joy awake. Her mind was probably where the others were roaming, choked with the two missing men, as sadly, Joy knew they were gone, swallowed by the troubles that held this house. Misenlake was attempting to shake off past sorrow, redressing a tragedy and with that, firing new miseries into the present. Joy could feel its shifting tensions.

On waking, Joy had groped inside her darkest segments. Her specialness was at the core of these flits back in time, of that she was certain. The real conundrum was what on earth was she to do?

Once starting down this course, her churning brain had known no let-up. It had chugged and clanked. This was not normal. To organise was essential. Why had this sergeant been able to connect with her? The others were clearly unaware of her existence. She had grappled and sifted through her thoughts, over and over. Shouldn't she be consumed by the desire to find out who these people were, the young woman and the anguish that was devouring her? And what had happened to bring such unhappiness? After all, it wasn't a play put on for Joy's benefit; these people had led everyday lives, these were their histories.

But for whatever reason, Joy always came back to the same spot. She had been chosen, fated to be the audience that Misenlake Manor had longed for. This unhinged Christmas was a performance of its contrivance. Patience, nerve, and reason were required. Suddenly, Joy felt very grown-up and responsible. Not in charge, that could never be, but these hapless houseguests were a part of something of far greater import, and like players on a stage, the fiendish author had them lined-up to be saved or cast aside. This was the mind-shifting Christmas that was untangling around her.

And then to the easiest and most ridiculous solution: what if she just asked this sergeant, straight out – *'Who are you, please?'*

Would he reply? Would he be able? Would he sputter – *'Yes, miss, I'm a hundred-year-old ghost, and this is what happened here way back then?'* And what would that do to her sanity? Joy's mother's fraught features had again loomed large. Would Joy be stuck in this hazy parallel world slowly going as mad as her mum had always predicted?

As was usual in times of stress, Joy had turned to structure. Her dad's medals. They were always, of course, neatly stacked – bronze at the bottom then silver then gold. And obviously George V's head was never hidden, never underneath, proud on top.

She'd checked that the door had been ajar and steady. Everything that was within her control was as it should be. She'd checked and rechecked, straightened the watercolours, patted her hairbrush, and touched the wood of the bedstead. Then she couldn't desist. Over and over, forever. To stop would bring worse than disaster. Until Clarice came and announced Christmas had begun.

'A present,' she said holding out a parcel.

Joy ripped open the parcel. A musical box. A ballerina. A nondescript plinking tune, but the dancer was elegant with her toe neatly pointed as she twirled and whirled. Joy loved it instantly and didn't pull away when Clarice hugged her.

'Breakfast? I'm famished. Let's hope there's word on our two escapees,' Clarice burbled with misplaced merriment.

Bacon wafted everywhere as they hunted down the dining room. It seemed everybody was up early, excepting Rebecca Royce. Mrs Pomp was attacking unfortunates with pronounced air-kisses. Joy ducked and dodged under her arm.

'Plaintive young woman. Barely utters a word!'

Joy sat down and waited. Gracie squeezed her shoulder and shimmied in her seat. 'Merry Christmas, Joy!'

They ate. Nobody mentioned the absent souls. To Joy it seemed they were almost ashamed of their cosy slumbers. And now, sitting in this opulent room, warm as toast, tucking into mountains of grub after such a snug night, the reality of the situation had to be doused by piping cups of tea and coffee. To talk of the strays would mean they had to do something, or at least show some concern, especially now the snow was at last beginning to relent.

It was Monckton who broached the subject. 'Ladies and gents, I have news, some good, and I'm afraid some not so keen.'

Everybody looked up, and Grauler's pained eyes looked fearful that more would be demanded of his pounding head and bruised body.

'I'm told that Slack, the gardener arrived at dawn and is shortly to make a thorough search of the grounds. He knows the lay of the land, so there will be no need for any further search parties. Miss Crabb has given him his orders and requests that we leave him to it. Indeed, her preference is for all of us, including the servants, to keep to the house until the weather brightens.'

Grauler looked relieved, others put out.

'As you no doubt have noticed, alas the pipes seem to have frozen once again. More inconveniently, and on investigation, it seems we have a cracked pipe. It is beyond my or Slack's ability …'

Groans rumbled around the table.

'But there is a man in the village we expect can rectify the problem,' Monckton went on, raising his voice and gesticulating with his palm for calm. 'But this will obviously not be happening on Christmas Day.'

'No running water, I hear!' Rebecca Royce strolled in wearing a silk kimono.

'Perhaps not today,' said Gloss in reply. 'However, there must be something we can do with all this snow and ice. I'll have a think. I will confer with Monckton and Slack and see what's to be done.'

'And the telephone lines are still down I'm afraid,' Drabble added.

'Are there no phones in the village? If Slack can reach us, couldn't we take a shot at getting there?' Scanner winced as he lifted himself from his chair.

'Miss Crabb has said that the drifts between here and there are at least chest-deep. And in actuality, Slack arrived on horseback, and even then, I understand he almost turned back.' Monckton seemed to be growing in authority; people appeared confident to trust in his words.

'That is correct,' added Miss Crabb stealing into the room. 'My mistress again begs your pardon and wishes you all the season's greeting. In the Great Hall at the rear of the house, she has laid out some gifts, as is customary. You will find them under our wonderful tree. They are just trinkets, but she hopes it will add to your day. There is also a piano if anybody is able? Otherwise there is a brand-new Sobell wireless which will of course bring us the speech from our King. The fire in the hall will be well-stoked, and I suggest it is in there that you will be most comfortable as with the paucity of staff, it will be difficult to keep all the hearths burning throughout the day. But to reinforce Monckton's words – please keep inside, stay warm as we do not need any more guests going astray.'

She left to a few mutters and moans.

'Super! A day listening to some amateur plonking on the ivories whilst we all imbibe each other's rankness.' Rebecca Royce wasn't impressed and took her ire out on her boiled egg.

'Well, you knew what you were signing up for.' Mrs Pomp set her knife and fork straight and left the table.

Rebecca Royce appeared not to hear her. Joy studied the lady's face. 'Yellow teeth,' Joy muttered. Indeed they were grungy against the thick white foundation which concealed most of her blemishes, but not the crevices around the mouth nor the sagging skin under her chin.

'What?' Rebecca Royce's features sharpened.

'Why did you come back to England?' Gracie butted in hastily.

'Lure of the old country – roots – curiosity, I suppose,' Rebecca Royce replied eventually, softening her glare.

'How long ago did you leave?' Gracie had begun to awaken the spindles in Rebecca's brain, but she still seemed languidly distant.

'I was six or seven. The new world, opportunities. I barely recall.'

'I want my knitting,' Joy declared.

'She speaks. Oh marvel of marvels – it is a Christmas miracle!' Rebecca Royce said caustically, appearing to be pleased to avoid any further interrogation from Gracie.

Clarice threw her a look and ushered Joy from the room. Gracie joined them in the hallway.

'Don't mind that painted hussy,' said Gracie. 'Quick spruce-up, eh? And then let's take a gander at the gifts our bonny hostess has for us.'

*

The Great Hall stretched across the back of the house, directly below the old quarters where Miss Gwynne had taken up residence. A series of concertina doors led out to a raised patio that offered a grim view, a bluff of tangled gorse and weeds.

The rich wood panelling within the hall added a lavishness, but the high beamed ceiling was a blemish on its grandness as it was thick with grainy paint, a dirty burned amber colour.

'Yuk!'

Gloss followed Joy's gaze. 'Nicotine. Dirty stuff, never start or you won't be able to kick it. This was the mess during the war. One thing our injured boys craved – a puff on a Lucky Strike. Yanks had bundles of 'em.'

'Not much trade in tobacco. Too many stogies to hand.' Grauler had livened up, a coupe glass of bubbly in his mitt already. 'Now bananas, they were the real gold dust, proper currency.'

'Yes, we have no bananas!' sang Perry Scanner. A few chortled.

'Is it time for presents?' Mrs Pomp's gusto addressed the room.

'Hold on two minutes Miss Biddle isn't here,' Barasch replied.

'I overheard that hideous woman insisting on a needle and cotton,' drawled Rebecca Royce. 'Darning most likely. Horribly common, of course. It's too doleful, but I'm not sure she has much of a wardrobe to fall back on.'

'We can wait,' said Barasch with a pronounced sigh.

Miss Biddle arrived some fifteen minutes later and directly behind her came Monckton. His face was drawn. He was clearly shaken.

With a quaking voice he addressed the room, 'I'm afraid, I have the direst news. I have found a body.'

EIGHT

'OH MY!' Mrs Pomp shrieked, her hand drawn to her mouth.

Gracie crossed herself and Grauler shakily refilled his glass.

'Unfortunate wretch. He must have frozen to death.'

'Did he have a fall? Was he found on the rocks.'

'Would it have been quick? To think he was outside all night whilst we were here jollying it up in the warm.'

'Where was he found?' asked Gloss, cutting through the clamour.

'We are assuming it's the professor, not our sensitive Nazi,' observed Kosik, casually peeling an orange.

'Why, yes. How unpleasant of us. Is it Professor Melville?' Mrs Pomp asked, sitting forward in her chair, her hands on her knees.

'It can't be Claube, he was fit as fiddle. Too much meat on those bones for a POW if you ask me,' Scanner pointed out.

'It's neither of them, I'm afraid,' said Monckton.

The room gaped. Bewildered looks, mouths ajar, some audible gasps.

'Neither of them! How can that be?' Gracie asked, a hand hovering over her mouth.

'It's Slack, the gardener!'

'Slack!' A few of them shouted in unison.

'Yes. And he has been murdered!'

'Murdered? How? Why would anybody kill the gardener?' Gloss's features tensed.

'Where?' Kosik asked.

'Draped over his wheelbarrow like some slaughtered beast. His head ...' Monckton gulped, trembling hands clenching in and out of fists.

Barasch offered him a tumbler of whisky from the sideboard.

'His head's been staved in with his own shovel.' Monckton swallowed and massaged his shaking hands. He was blowing hard. 'If you'll beg my pardon.'

'We should ring the local constabulary immediately.' Mrs Pomp had assumed command. 'The Brigadier would have ...'

'If we had a telephone that worked.' Rebecca Royce lit up another cigarette.

'Surely in the village …' Mrs Pomp realised her mistake.

'Who is going to make it through now Slack has copped it?' Gloss jumped in.

'But who could have done such a thing? A simple man. Could he have such enemies?' Barasch queried.

'There's a lunatic on the loose.' Grauler had taken the opportunity to glug a glass of whisky on top of the champagne. 'First the old prof, then the Kraut and now this gardener guy.'

'His snow clearing was a bit laboured, but even so …' Scanner held out a palm. 'Sorry. In bad taste, I know.'

'But Mr Barasch is right. Who would want to kill the gardener in such a brutal fashion?' Mrs Pomp's gaze ran around the troupe.

'Perhaps Claube has gone crazy,' Kozik observed as he helped himself to one of Rebecca Royce's cigarettes.

'But why him? He hadn't even met the man,' said Gracie.

'As far as we know,' said Scanner.

'What does that mean?' asked Gloss, and the room erupted in theories and accusations.

'Now please, let us be as calm as we can manage in this dreadful situation.' Barasch had panic in his voice, but obviously found some solace in keeping others steady. 'Perhaps it would be wise for me as a doctor to examine the body. Then if, as you say, it is a crime scene we must preserve the surrounding area and then ask a volunteer to try to make his way through to the village.'

'Are we not forgetting that our vengeful German could still be out there?' Scanner said with a twinkle.

'Yes, you're right, but we will still need to organise a search for the professor.' Mrs Pomp was eager to regain some sort of authority.

'But is it safe? And are we even secure in this house? It's so remote.' Rebecca Royce for once had a serious look on her powdered face.

Joy got stuck into her knitting. Sometimes people would guess – a scarf, a jumper, a shawl. She never really understood why. Did it need to be something in particular? Knitting was all it was.

The door barged open.

'Mister Monckton, sir … you have to come.' It was Ernest the apprentice gardener.

'Who gave you leave to enter the house?' Monckton's consternation was interrupted.

'But Mister Monckton. I've found a body.'

'We know. Poor Slack …'

'No, sir. Another. On t'other side of the walled garden, stuck fast in one of those old latrine potholes. 'Orrible it is. Arse up like a duck fishing in a pond.'

'But who is it?' Mrs Pomp shrieked.

'Now, Doctor Barasch, I don't think you are thinking clearly. Slack is dead. I was out on the terrace and there was no mistaking it. I was in the forces, I know a dead man when I see one. Flopped over the barrow like an animal. His head battered to a pulp. Beg pardon, ladies.' Monckton inclined his head.

'Are you suggesting I am not to examine him?'

'Your phrase, sir – a crime scene. Best left to the police. Now, whether it's Claube our German or the professor stuck fast in the bog, there's a chance they may be still alive.'

'Dead also.' It was Kosik. He seemed nonplussed by the whole drama.

Barasch's head spun from Monckton to Kosik.

'I tend to agree. Last night the temperature dropped way below freezing,' added Gloss.

Monckton put his arm on Ernest's shoulder. 'Now, laddie, did you see if he was still breathing? Did you recognise the body?'

'No, Mister Monckton. Like I said, proper glued in it was. And I didn't want to get too close. Slack said that field is a deathtrap this time of year. I didn't want to risk it and end up like him, up to my noddle in sludge.'

'It is definitely a 'him' then?' Scanner ducked the filthy looks.

'Whoever it is, we need to do our best, and if there's the slightest chance …' Gracie began.

'There isn't!' stated Joy

Monckton shot them all an admonishing glare. 'Mr Gloss would you know if there is any rope handy?'

'Of course, in the garage. Always had a stock in case the cars came a cropper.'

'If you would be so kind.'

'Now Doctor. If you accompany me and Mr Gloss, we will ascertain if our body is still alive. We will be steady and take rope to yank us out if one of us finds trouble.'

Barasch hesitated. 'But should we not see to the gardener first?'

He was shouted down again.

'Now, Ernest, if you can accompany Mr Kosik to the village. Take Slack's horse and when you get there knock up the postmaster, and tell him to contact the constabulary.' Monckton held everyone's gaze. 'If the rest of you stay here in the hall, I will lock the main door behind us.'

'Are you suggesting we are really in some kind of danger?' Mrs Pomp asked. 'If the Brigadier was here, he would have organised a watch.'

'Well, there's been one murder, perhaps two, and we also have a missing person. Something horrible is going on, and until the police arrive, I propose we all stick together.' Monckton gave a hesitant bow and left the room.

The gentle tinkle of the piano added to the sombre mood as the Great Hall suddenly seemed vast, its cavernous ceiling as far away as the stars.

Joy enjoyed Perry Scanner's easiness on the ivories. He was well-skilled and the lulling tunes glossed over the stunted conversation. Grauler, had remained, obviously, and as was now his habit he was fawning over Rebecca Royce.

Gracie and Clarice had settled at a corner table and were flicking through the family albums that presumably had been left out for guests to browse.

Joy stood by the Christmas tree staring at the silver baubles as they twisted on the boughs. The gifts, all shiny reds and golds, lay unopened. It had seemed inappropriate to unwrap them, especially as the name tags of Melville and Claube were clear to the fore.

Mrs Pomp was twittering to nobody in particular, regaling the room with tales of her husband's chivalry and how she wished they would have seen how easily he would have assumed command. When he barked people shook a leg, she told them.

'Half-a-tick, I need my woolly,' said Miss Biddle. 'I can't shake this chill no matter how close I stand by the fire.' She made for the door.

'Should she go alone?' asked Mrs Pomp.

'Grauler will go with her, won't you, Fuzz?' said Rebecca Royce, desirous to be rid of the American's attentions.

'As you wish, sister,' he replied.

'Hem!' Murder and more than one. Sometime in the past, something bad had happened in this stale old house, and I could sense it had never settled since.

And these horrific killings, as that was what they surely were – were undoubtedly connected. So here I found myself wedged between the now and then, within a complacent present that was overlaying a pestilent past. Was it down to me to unstitch these tangled threads? And could I shake up these unseeing houseguests and make them realise the fraught danger they were in? Or should I just shout out loud – run away – get out while you can – otherwise Misenlake's going to grab each and every one of you and create another treacherous tale for others to witness sometime in the future? I felt a trifle silly. I was becoming rather hysterical if only inside. I scolded myself that I had to hold on tight as this was just the beginning. 'Hem!'

Rebecca Royce stared over at Joy, a drowsy look sizing her up as if she were a scruffy street beggar. She puffed smoke toward her; orange lipstick tarnished the butt of her cigarette.

Joy snorted loudly and walked out of the room.

The fire hadn't been lit in the drawing room. The staleness of tobacco was being fanned by the whipping draught that swept along below the floorboards. The manor felt suddenly neglected, less resplendent, more like a shifting animal staving off the cold, pining for respite.

The clock showed five minutes before eleven.

This time Joy wanted to confront the past; have a word and hold eye contact with the sergeant. He was the only tangible link. Somehow she'd decided that by bringing the past and the present together then these apparitions would skulk back into the fabric of Misenlake's history. It would be over and the murders would stop.

Joy caressed the wooden clock. The tock of the clock chimed eleven, and as on the previous occasions the wooden figures came hurtling out. The temperature rose in the room, the nip in the air sucked away by a crackling fire as the room brightened.

Joy stumbled some steps and groped thin air, reaching out for a table for support. Her misted breath added to the cobwebby vapour that slipped down from the ceiling like a veil.

The warmth from the hearth breathed holes in the mist until the room finally cleared, and as before, the tall inspector was asking his questions as he towered over the tearful young woman.

'Hem!' I steadied myself, determined to puzzle out how to communicate with this sergeant's shimmery world. I immediately looked for the him, but with a flutter I saw that he wasn't in the room.

Instead, at his place at the desk was a pimply-faced young copper in an oversized uniform, probably a PC, chewing on a pencil and taking notes.

'Now, Miss Ines. Do you recall what the young ladies were wearing on the day Miss Celia disappeared?' The inspector's voice boomed in my head.

'You have not questioned Chantrey?' the young woman answered. I felt her sullenness.

'We have, but we like to double-check, to be sure.'

'Their red dresses with the yellow collars.'

'They were identical?'

'Yes, excepting in size, of course.'

The inspector pulled out his notebook. The flicking of the pages went tap-tap-tap in my head. 'Yes, here we are. You told us that although twins, they were in looks very different. Your words – Miss Dorothy is sturdy, full of vim and into everything, auburn hair with freckles – just like PC Ritchie over there,' the inspector chuckled to himself. 'Whereas Miss Celia was olive-skinned, of much slighter build and had straight black hair.'

'That is correct,' murmured Miss Ines.

The inspector walked over to the PC and nosed at the page. Seemingly satisfied, he banged a pipe on the hearth.

The noise hurt my ears.

He then stood sucking on the wood before approaching the rear of Miss Ines' chair. 'Was either of the girls wearing anything that would distinguish them apart? Perhaps a hat or …?'

There was a pause. I wanted to mark the page and have a think. The sergeant being absent had scuppered my madcap plan to try and converse with these phantoms. Perhaps if I made myself busy, leapt about a bit, picked up a vase, be a bit like Elvira in *Blithe Spirit*, then my presence would be signalled to these others. I stepped closer. My shoes woke a creak in the floorboard, but nobody turned.

'Hello?' I offered.

Nobody moved or showed any recognition. I stood behind the young woman, so close that I could see the red blemish on the nape of her neck the result of her continuous and agitated plucking at her skin. Her hair was pulled in a bun; her trembling fingers brushed a stray from her collar.

I reached out to touch her shoulder, but bolted back as she shrieked, 'A scarf! That's right,' her face brightening. 'It was a long pink one with so many folds it was more of a shawl to Ceccy. She and Dotty were fighting over it, but bless Ceccy, she wouldn't give it up. It was one of their mother's, but had been discarded. Chantrey was preparing to give it with some other bits to the local Christmas fayre.'

'A scarf,' the inspector scribbled deliberately in his notebook.

I was now so close that I could almost feel the heat radiating from the young woman's reddened cheeks.

'A long pink one …' The inspector dictated to his constable, as he rummaged in his ear with a finger. Flecks dropped onto his shoulders.

I nudged past the young woman's chair and provocatively perched myself on the arm of a sofa immediately adjacent to her. I sat forward and studied her face. She had freckles like mine, but finer. Her lips were cracked and looked sore.

She coughed and I jerked back, spittle flecking my cheeks. It was all surreal. As if I was at the theatre in the front row willing the heroine to escape from a tight spot.

The PC began to chew on his pencil again.

An unsettling silence was filled by the inspector once again leafing through his notebook, and sucking on his unlighted pipe, and the young woman fiddling with the hem on her skirt.

The clock ticked and tocked behind me, as I switched my thoughts back to the present. If I got up and high-tailed it out of the door, then peeped back, would these people have been sucked away, syphoned back into the spirals of the yesteryear? Or would history just continually repeat itself over and over, always waiting for me to dip in, insist that I redress some awful injustice before Misenlake could be reset. It was all too hard, and a bugger's-burden. But now was not the time for some over-fussy experiment or pathetic self-indulgent squealing. I needed to pay attention. I was sure I was here to help somehow.

The clock chimed the half hour and the door behind me groaned. The sergeant entered. He twitched and shot me a rattled glance as I shifted from the arm of the sofa, keeping his distance as I drifted back toward the doorway.

'Sir, you better come with me,' he said, his eyes darting from me to the inspector. 'We've found something!'

The inspector nodded and they both hurried from the room.

'Hey!' I meant to offer, but the words wouldn't come. I then thought to follow, but immediately the essence around me shifted and again a jerky sickness came over me. The room began to darken as if somebody had snubbed a candle, then trails of smoke and the fire was abruptly extinguished with a jet of steam as if someone had thrown a pail leaving the solid cold slate of the hearth.

A woman's voice, nearby, grating but firm came to me. 'Hem!'

Shutting and reopening her eyes, Joy shook off the dizziness and, swallowing back the sicky sensation, was confronted by Miss Biddle. She was standing over by the window, and beside her, tinkering with the chess pieces, was Grauler.

Joy stumbled to a chair and slumped down into its lumpiness. A drift of sandalwood, rich and spicy wafted up from somewhere.

The conversation by the window continued unabated. They clearly hadn't noticed Joy. Was it possible she was still partially cloaked within the illusion?

'Run it by me again, old gal. You're being a bit cryptic.' Grauler was almost shouting.

'All I was saying, is I wanted a word. Me and you, well we aren't like the rest of this lot with their airs and graces.'

'Steady on. I don't see it that way.'

'Please yourself. But you need to know that this murder business ain't all it seems, that's all I'm getting at. Somebody might have seen something. At the front, where our rooms look out, well, they're right above that path where the old gardener copped it. Don't you see?'

'See what? You cockneys speak the dandiest of language But yeh, I suppose. But what's your point?'

'I don't want to live in a prefab all my life, that's all.'

The clock struck the half-hour and their words were lost in the chimes. When it had quietened it was clear that the parley was over, as the two of them began to leave the room.

A chair scraped back. It was Miss Crabb. With a groan, she levered herself up and out of an armchair. 'I must have nodded off. Do forgive me. I came to check on the fire and must have passed out. With all this business, sleep is not a willing bedfellow.'

Miss Biddle's eyes slid to Joy. Joy turned away.

'After you,' said Grauler as Miss Biddle pulled her cardigan tight and scurried from the room. Grauler followed, but Miss Crabb loitered by the clock.

'You are fond of clocks?' she asked Joy.

'Not really,' Joy replied, her eyes stuck at her feet.

'Such an odd child. Wrapped in her world. Perhaps for the best.'

Crabb threw a graceless smile and left the room, and Joy, with three taps on her nose, made for the stairs and trundled up to her bedroom.

'Dead? Not a surprise really.'

When Joy entered the hall she noted that the piano was hushed and that Perry Scanner was quizzing a damp-looking Barasch.

'Was he drowned or suffocated or …?' asked Scanner.

'It's hard to say, exposure perhaps. The mud had sucked him up. As the garden boy so succinctly put it, stuck fast.' Gloss helped himself to a drink.

'Where have you put him?' asked Scanner.

Barasch demisted his glasses.

'You haven't left him there, popping up like some mole in a fairground game?'

'The butler insisted we were not to move the corpse.' Barasch warmed his hands at the fire. 'And of course, he is quite correct. If the police are on their way we shouldn't disturb the body.'

'Well, it's obvious how it happened.' Scanner joined Gloss with a whisky. 'Claube clonked Slack for some reason only known to himself. Then scarpered and got dragged downed into the quagmire. You would have thought the army would have done a better job tidying up after themselves.'

'So it is Herr Claube?' Mrs Pomp asked.

Gloss nodded. 'Rum way to spend Christmas Day.'

'I'm sure the unfortunate Slack would agree,' Scanner remarked.

'Is there a Mrs Slack?' Mrs Pomp enquired.

'No, thankfully not. Lives all alone, apart from his beloved horse, and always has, according to Drabble.' Gloss fingered the rim of his glass.

'Aren't we all forgetting something?' Gracie gave Barasch a hanky from her bag as he struggled again with his steamed-up specs. 'Professor Melville?'

'Well, the police will soon be here. No doubt they will arrange a thorough search of the area.' Mrs Pomp's eyes scanned the group. Her voice quivered faintly. It was clear she was trying to curtail her own growing anxiety.

'Perhaps, Melville is the culprit. On a murderous rampage to keep his treasure trove secret,' Scanner suggested.

Nobody laughed.

'Maybe Slack was a witness to the prof's murder. And Claube, whilst making off with the Saxon booty, got into a struggle, and bam!' Grauler said, again rather too vociferously.

'Excepting there was no treasure-trove by Claube's corpse, old man,' Gloss pointed out.

'Baloney! It could have been sucked down in the bog. What are we waiting for? That loot will be worth a packet,' Grauler cried in jest, punching the palm of his hand.

'How splendidly American,' said Rebecca Royce with a sarcastic snort.

The intrigues were halted by the double doors swinging open. Kosik trampled in looking like a snowbeast. He shook himself by the fire, spraying wetness like a soggy dog.

'Had quite forgotten about you, old chap. You've made it there and back?' Gloss asked.

'Are the police on their way?' Mrs Pomp asked.

'Better than that. They have returned with me,' said Kosik still drying out. 'They are with Monckton. The detective wanted a word with the mistress of the house and then no doubt he will wish to examine the bodies.'

Gloss handed Kosik a glass.

'Has our mad professor turned up?' Kosik quizzed.

''Fraid not,' Scanner replied.

'Then it appears we will be all destined to battle the elements once more. The policemen will no doubt organise a search party before the weather closes in again.'

'But surely the police should take care of that?'

'That is the problem, my dear Mrs Pomp. There are just the two of them, and even so, it is only due to sheer luck that we have them at all.'

'Just two?'

'Yes. I'm afraid the phone lines were down in the village. But luckily, this Constable Nouse is a local man and was up from London visiting his mother. The other is a Detective Sergeant Prim; being a bachelor, he'd tagged along for the season.'

'Oh! Well it's good to have the police on the premises so promptly. We should be thankful.' Mrs Pomp took a seat and blew her nose.

'Yes. The weather is only going to get worse. We would have been stuck without them.' Kosik flicked more wetness from his hair.

'So we're to be holed-up here for a time until they can call on reinforcements. Merry Christmas indeed.' Scanner traced his eyebrows with his fingers.

Joy felt the house groan beneath her. The wind joined in, rattling at the casements. The elements seemed to be mocking them.

Sinking further into her seat, Joy knew there was worse to come. The past was gobbling up the present and there would be no respite until

Misenlake had showcased all the wickedness that had once found its home here in this maddening Medusa of a house.

NINE

DETECTIVE SERGEANT PRIM wasn't as expected, indeed a much younger man, perhaps thirty with a fresh complexion, cloudy blue eyes that peeked out of an almost feminine face. His sleek swept-back locks, were black with a flick of grey, and his thin moustache was a smear, a touch to lend maturity to his otherwise youthful features.

From behind her knitting, Joy imagined that he would have been considered terribly dashing by the young girls from her village, that is, if it wasn't for the one fatal flaw; he was only five and a half feet tall.

Addressing all the guests in the Great Hall, he'd made up his mind to not only introduce himself, but give them a potted history of his life thus far.

Prim had explained that he'd been a detective before the war interrupted his career and threw him into the Military Police. On resumption, he'd distinguished himself cracking the infamous smuggling ring at Liverpool Docks; forty thousand pairs of nylons confiscated on the cruise liner *Hollandia*.

Nobody spoke up although Grauler had spluttered a bit.

His sidekick and festive host was Constable Nouse. He nodded continuously during the monologue as if adding weight to his governor's address. Nouse was also rather short, bent over, and stipple-faced with a crooked nose and wrinkled forehead. Around sixty, he had the look of a clown; hardly ideal, Joy had thought, in a policeman.

'To begin with,' Prim went on, 'whilst it is important that we find the whereabouts of the missing professor, I must insist that nobody attempts to leave the house until I have taken full statements and made contact with my superiors at the Yard.'

'But he could be hurt,' Gracie piped up.

'And I'm not sure how anybody's in a hurry to go anywhere in this storm,' Kosik observed.

Prim spoke firmly. 'If the man is injured, it is most probable he will not have made it through the night. If, however, he has just lost his way then I'm sure he will soon turn up and perhaps has stumbled along the coast to …'

'Robin Hood's Bay!'

'Thank you, Nouse.' Prim clicked his fingers at his constable and they made a huddle away from the group, muttering for a minute or so.

A few tutted. Joy frowned inside. This policeman appeared rather caught up in his own self-importance.

'Otherwise, I cannot discount the possibility that he could be our killer and has made good his getaway,' Prim suggested grandly as he returned to the fold.

'The professor, the murderer? But why?' Gloss's face creased in incredulity.

'Well, with two corpses already on my hands, he is the obvious culprit, and if not him, then who?' Prim flourished a hand dismissively.

Nouse wagged a finger as if to add weight to the statement.

Prim meandered amongst them. 'It would lead to the only obvious conclusion any capable detective would arrive at. That the murderer is still here within this house.'

Prim paused for effect. Joy almost expected a fork of lightning at the casement or an appropriate drum roll to follow.

'Miss Crabb has made the drawing room available for my purposes,' Prim went on, weaving his around the room. 'I am well aware this is Christmas Day, but policework takes no holidays. I have proposed, and Miss Crabb has agreed, that dinner should be delayed until later this evening.'

The room held its breath. Rebecca Royce even put out her cigarette.

'Before I begin the individual cross-examinations, I have a few questions I would like to ask you whilst we are all here together.'

Nouse nodded and crunched his knuckles.

'Herr Claube was a German gentleman, a former POW. From what the servants have told me, he wasn't the most popular of house guests.'

'Nobody's too fussed with the Bosch, old man, after all we've been through. Are you suggesting one of us did away with him because he was a German?' Gloss continued to look bewildered.

'Somebody did,' said Prim.

Nouse nodded again.

'But he probably drowned, well, didn't he?' Mrs Pomp looked around the room for support.

'That is what we were supposed to conclude. However, once Monckton and the other …?'

'Drabble, sir,' said Nouse.

'Drabble had carried the body to the stable area, which we are utilising as a temporary morgue, I spotted an almost indiscernible wound on the nape of our German's neck. It was only a prick, but it ran very deep. It could easily have been missed by the layman, but I noticed it nonetheless.'

Nouse again gestured with his hand as if to encourage and endorse his boss.

'I am no medical man, but such a thrust could potentially have killed him instantly.' Prim glared at them all as if waiting for a response.

'A narrow aperture?' Perry Scanner eventually queried.

'Indeed.'

'Like a stab with a spike or perhaps a bayonet?' Scanner's eyes slid to Kosik.

'Yes, that sort of thing. Anyway, where was I, yes, thank you, Nouse, I can manage. So, all this talk of an accident is bunk, I'm afraid. Herr Claube was either murdered and dumped in the bog or fell in the slurry and was killed by an assailant as he floundered for a foothold. Either way, it's a nasty business.'

'He was a strong-looking man,' said Gracie. 'Not many here could attack him successfully then drag him into that field.'

'That much is clear, my dear lady.'

Gracie's face went pink.

'And then we have our gardener. He was, as far as I'm aware, unknown to all of you, so why was he killed? This was an even more unfathomable incident.'

Nouse tapped his temple.

'Be still, Nouse. You'll make me lose my thread.'

'Unfathomable? Surely his head was crushed with his own shovel,' Scanner stated glibly.

Prim balanced on his toes, flexing back and forth as if indulging in some sort of gymnastic exercise. 'Can we all agree that we have been fortunate enough to have had no further snowfall since last evening?' he lectured them.

They all nodded and Nouse smirked.

'Slack was found slumped face down over his barrow. It is clear the murder weapon had been a shovel?'

'We know all this, Inspector. Where's the mystery? Other than who did it, of course?' Rebecca Royce quizzed.

Prim sighed. 'Monckton, your most observant butler, informed me that when he discovered the body, looking down from the terrace above, that something most peculiar struck him.'

The group all stared at Prim as he stroked his ratty moustache.

'You see, this is where things become a little befuddling.' Prim hesitated, leafing through his pocketbook. 'I took great care when I went to survey the scene that I did so from the exact same vantage point as Monckton. This view threw up a peculiar and immediate problem. There was only one set of footmarks leading to the body.'

'Should make it a breeze then,' said Grauler. 'Match the prints and we won't need to call on Charlie-darn-well-Chan to solve the mystery.'

'One set, Fuzz, my slow-witted American.' Rebecca Royce lit a cigarette.

'Huh?'

Prim gave Grauler a pronounced glare. 'Exactly. And beyond doubt these trails were made by the gardener. You see he was wearing snowshoes and they gave out the most distinctive prints. The only other indentations were the furrows made by the wheels of the barrow.'

The room frowned as one.

'How could that be?' asked Gloss.

'Could the killer have been clever enough to use Slack's prints to cover his tracks?' queried Gracie.

'Nope. Slack's footwear had left a particular print, and the footmarks were unblemished. So no, I'm afraid that is implausible.'

'So are you saying he was brained by some sort of missile? Or hit from above? Some sort of flying machine perchance?' Scanner smirked.

'Either that or he committed suicide,' said Kosik.

'That is such bad form,' said Gloss, suppressing a smile and shaking his head.

'Could someone have covered their footprints over with snow?' suggested Gracie.

'The path was a picture of virgin whiteness.' Prim smiled to himself. He appeared happy with his attempt at poetic prose.

'Then how is it possible?' Barasch popped the question.

'It is a troublesome tic that I cannot yet get the measure of,' said Prim. 'But I will get to the bottom of it. I always do, don't I, Nouse?'

Nouse nodded right on cue, and for good measure, tapped his forehead in salute.

For reasons known only to Prim, the one-to-one interviews were to be conducted in a random clutch, a muddle of sessions that dragged into early evening.

The troupe all shuffled about in an anxious funk waiting to be called. Joy sat with her knitting as the others grumbled impatiently.

'What a way to spend Christmas Day.'

'I wish I'd never set eyes on that advertisement.'

'At least there's lashings of hooch to get us through this hell.'

Mrs Pomp had been the first to be called. She'd seemed pleased. Ten minutes later it was Gracie, then Clarice. Scanner was next and after him, Barasch.

'This is insufferable,' whined Rebecca Royce. 'I haven't bathed. I haven't eaten, and my head's splitting. How much longer is this charade going to go on for? If the promised weather holds off, then tomorrow I'm off and away. The Austin Seven might not be the prettiest, but she's proven to be a game old bird.'

Drabble called Rebecca Royce next.

It appeared that immediately after their interviews, most decided to head to their rooms as the only two to return to Joy were Gracie and Clarice.

The room continued to empty and Joy still waited her turn as she clicked away. Perhaps, as was customary, she would be an afterthought and therefore be excused the interrogation, but then Drabble called her name.

In the drawing room, Prim had bizarrely formed a crescent of three stiff chairs, all facing a ladies' writing bureau. The diminutive detective had squeezed himself beneath its veneer. He gestured for Joy to sit in the middle chair.

'Hem!' I had begun to find this decidedly comic individual rather irritating. He was a most unlikely lawman, or so it seemed to me. Murders, missing people, my heart told me that Misenlake had worse in store for us all. It was as if the house was heaving on its foundations, yanking up its secrets by their hair and waggling them in full view. The answer lay in the past. A history the manor was eager to spit out, regurgitate, and to me. And now this Prim? He just wouldn't do. We needed better.

He began to warble. My presence was secondary and to listen was pointless. I switched off and eyed the clock, idly wondering how long it had been on the wall.

Prim's wittering rattled on. 'Did you observe anything from your bedroom window? You are one of the four that overlooks the terrace and the steps down into the knotted garden where Slack was found.'

'Have you asked the others?' I asked in a sulk. This needed to be over. I had other things to get on with.

'Of course! Miss Biddle couldn't offer anything up, and as for our American friend, Mr Grauler, well, he said he'd slept in late.'

Not a surprise the amount of liquor he's been guzzling, I thought.

'Unfortunately the only other rooms that have a similar view belonged to our missing professor and the unfortunate Herr Claube. So you see, you are my last hope, a potential eyewitness.' Prim accidentally knocked aside an inkwell with an errant hand.

I slid my eyes as far to the left as I could and then started to hum. This worked most of the time.

'Well?'

I made a grunting sound.

'What was that?'

Just a few more moments.

'I'm sorry, I don't understand what …'

From behind, the clock began to chime. I could hear the figures clicking on their tracks.

I snorted loudly. Then again.

Prim was swished away as the room dimmed. And as I stood awaiting the next incoming emotion, I was pleasantly surprised as despite an awful cramping and breathlessness in my chest, like a mild bout of indigestion, I found myself welcoming the oncoming experience, and the chance to escape this prissy detective. I was ready and felt almost composed.

Then, steam slipped from my mouth and my fingers began to prickle. As I coped with these latest manifestations, I was engulfed in pipesmoke that whirled all around me, and cutting through the veillike mist, I found a drowning graveness held the room, just like the moment the sombreness of a funeral is signalled, as the black cavalcade arrived.

The tall inspector was seated this time. Prim and his twee little desk had been ushered to the fringes, shrouded somewhere in the folds of the present.

Then, most oddly, a new perception, a piping heat as if I'd been caught short, running up and down my legs, tingling my toes. This sensation then started to coat my insides. As if somehow I had offered shelter to another soul, and it had climbed inside, trembling at first, but then with growing confidence, zipping itself up, like a too-tight cardigan.

The burning sensation in my chest immediately relented, but in its place came a sort of a wobbliness as if the possessed being began to settle, followed by a daub of emotion as if my feelings were merging with another's.

A tickle, a splurge of silliness, like a shot of adrenaline, then foreboding and most of all a sapping miserable ache behind my eyes. And then at last I had arrived. I was there in the room.

'Now, miss, do you recognise these?' I heard the inspector address me.

A garbled splutter choked in my craw. A bundle of letters bound in lilac ribbon was dumped on the table.

'I do.' Words blurted out of my mouth. But they weren't mine. The murmurings were soft and timid. The voice was that of the young woman. What was happening to me?

'For the record,' the inspector motioned to the young constable, 'I have shown Miss Ines some letters written in Major Gwynne's hand.'

So, this is Miss Ines! That had been the name of the sad young woman.

'These are letters from a sweetheart, miss.'

I felt a rush of shame, a hotness rise over me. It was followed by a defiant flame of anger. But not my own – hers!

I'm not giving this patronising man the satisfaction, the voice thundered within me. It hadn't been sordid. Benjamin's wife didn't love him. She wanted the position and the house and obviously to be known as the lady of the manor.

I must say at this point panic had begun to take over. Being there, plopped down in the past, was surreal enough, but these voices, these unburdened feelings; I was another living, breathing human being. I fought back. I suddenly wanted this horror gone. I needed to banish this tortured young woman from me. But I was pincered. I couldn't shift the sensation, the impression I was in her grip. My insides tightened. She wasn't going anywhere.

'Well, Miss Ines, do you care to comment?'

I felt hatred. And a sarcastic voice gabbled in my head. *"I do a lot of work for charity. Somebody must. These dreadful times with so many in want."* The mistress did not care for Benjamin or her two children. It was a tragedy, I blurted out.

'And this one letter in particular, the one you now have in your hand?'

I could see the blue smeared squiggles and somehow a long cold night full of tears came to me.

'It appears not to have been sent?' The policeman's eyes were all over me. It was as if he was just about to triumph in a fraught game of chess.

The young woman's thoughts had taken over mine. Say nothing. You have done nothing wrong, nothing to be ashamed of. He loves me. He will always be there for me.

The inspector tossed the letter. 'You can see what some may think these words suggest.'

Fear gripped my chest as my heart turned over. Her words – I did not mean that. How could they think …?

'Miss, miss? Drink some water and compose yourself.'

I slumped in the seat, and yelped as I felt a pinch at the back of my foot, a chafing blister that had suddenly sprung up.

Then, without warning, the springing energy, the light-headedness subsided, drained away, and with a sucking motion, I deflated like a balloon, a great stress having been relieved.

And waking, through gathering light Joy saw the rubber-faced Nouse.

'Perhaps the doctor should see her or perhaps she needs to be restrained…' began Prim.

'I will be fine in a moment, thank you.' My head was settling, almost recharged.

The house was letting me delve deeper, beginning to show me things that might make all this go away, at last unpick some of its knots. The sense of euphoria of being the one flitting from this world to the past filled me with energy.

Prim brought me back to grim reality.

'Well it seems you have nothing of worth to tell me. If that is how you …'

'You should ask *her* again,' I interrupted.

Prim looked at Nouse, his features creased in bewilderment. 'Who?' Prim's features blackened. 'It is a skill of my job to be patient. Unlike others, I do not dismiss you from my suspicions due to your condition.'

Nouse went pink and lowered his eyes.

'Now, I should ask who again? Please be explicit. You are not some amateur sleuth – a would-be heroine that no doubt you have read about in one of those fantasy detective novels.'

Prim came closer. A nutty whiff on his breath. 'You need to realise this is not a game,' he snarled. 'It is deadly serious and …'

'Sir! I don't think it's appropriate …'

'Be quiet, Nouse.' Prim turned his back, his fists clenching. 'Pah! This is going nowhere. Go for now, but I will want further words.'

And so I left, but hesitated for a bit in the hallway, gaping in the mirror as if to check I was really myself again, and that my girlish features hadn't been taken over by the wan-faced young woman.

You see, these methodical policeman always start from the beginning and like a game of snakes and ladders nudge onward and upward, taking great care not to stumble and slip up. Fair enough! For them crime is a formula, a series of happenstances linked by human behaviour. But sometimes, I would suggest, it would possibly be more helpful to begin at the end and envisage the journey that had been undertaken to arrive at that point. It seemed obvious to me that the piece of the riddle they were most wanted to nail down, the mysterious footprints, would potentially cloud the reason why. And thereby make it harder to ascertain, well – who did it? Most are too fussed with trying to prove what their mind can comprehend rather than concentrate on what they have really seen. And as for this one, Prim, well, least said the better.

For now, a list was required. 'Hem!'

Clarice and Gracie were in cahoots in the Great Hall when Joy shimmied in with her notebook.

'All went well, dear?'

Joy nodded and found a spot beyond the piano, hidden away, and opened her jotter. Drawing or doodling was not Joy's thing. Her fingers never seemed to be able to declutter themselves. They were always messing about. That's why she enjoyed knitting; amongst other reasons it demanded their strict attention, routine and rhythm or else a bloodied fingertip.

But writing had always been a challenge. If Joy wasn't so in love with the starkness of her thoughts being there in bold type, she'd have foregone the misery years back. She had no other reason to write.

This arriving novelty, the power to transcend time had given her an increased sense of worth. The incongruity of being someone else, not in body, but in a sort of wrapped consciousness had surprisingly invigorated her, given her a sense of responsibility that made it more essential that she set things down.

Prim was starting at a disadvantage. It was obvious that he'd become obsessed with the peculiar circumstances surrounding Slack's murder and was intrigued by the impossibility of the crime. As if he'd been challenged, his intellect prodded. This could be his big case; the world finally realising what a great detective they had in their midst.

Joy chewed her pencil. In Prim's defence, Joy guessed everyone had that inner confidence bordering on arrogance within them somewhere. It just needed nurturing by overt success. Some believed in themselves enough. Others would push themselves forward. And many others were just happy getting up, doing bits and going to bed with no gnawing sense of what might have been!

Taking up her pencil, she cursed her fingers and painfully started to write, willing her digits to take up the challenge. It was hard work and a mess. But after thirty minutes hard scribbling she was happy with what she'd managed. She had written down all the names of her fellow guests. Next to each of them was either a tick or a cross, excepting one that had a question mark next to it.

'You and your lists, Joy dear, there won't be enough lead in the world if you carry on this way.' Clarice smiled over at her.

Joy grinned back. It was nice having such a decent person to look after you.

'We should change, dinner is nearly upon us, and I'm famished. Let's make a bit of an effort, eh? After all it is Christmas Day. Hopefully for a couple of hours we can all forget this nastiness.'

Gracie had left them alone together. 'I don't believe this puffed-up inspector.' Clarice had chivvied. 'A murderer amongst us, huh! I suspect the German fellow came across the professor and well ... poor Slack must have seen something and that was his undoing. Then fleeing, Herr Claube gets trapped in the mire. That has to be it – horrible, but now at an end. Don't you think?'

Joy did not reply. But she didn't think so, no!

'Hem!' You see, Clarice wanted it all to go away. She couldn't see what I could see. The German man had been lost when he'd arrived at Misenlake. But wherever he'd chosen as his final battlefield, his war had been fought, that was for sure.

Drinks were served in the library.

'How much longer are we going to be without running water? It's intolerable – it's so damned primeval – and I am beginning to pong!' Rebecca Royce railed, crinkling her face as she sniffed vaguely at an armpit.

'I agree, my dear. Something has to be done. We cannot spend an entire week without bathing, and this weather forecast!' Mrs Pomp plumped up her curls.

'Monckton thinks he has a solution,' Gloss chipped in.

'Thank the Lord!' Rebecca Royce exclaimed.

'Thank Pears!' Scanner laughed loudly. 'Make a great billposter, don't you think?'

Gloss shook his head. 'Seems the prof asked Monckton if he could make head or tail of some of those old maps he was studying – you know searching for clues as to possible whereabouts of the lode he was so sure was about here somewhere. But Monckton, being a bit of a new boy, couldn't help much.' Gloss refilled his own glass with champagne and waved the bottle in invitation to the group.

Simon Gloss seemed to be enjoying being the old hand, in the know. 'As it is, if he'd sounded me out I couldn't have been much help either. It seems Melville was trying to track an underground stream of sorts. He thought that once upon a time a brook may have run through the land and the Saxons would have settled alongside it. Monckton tells me that some of the maps are still in the prof's bedroom.'

'Personally, I'm not sure I believe all this guff about buried treasure. If there really was anything to it, why hadn't the British Museum or the like pitched up?' Scanner took a tome down from a shelf and flicked through the pages.

'It's all very noteworthy, but how does that solve our water problem?' Rebecca Royce pulled at her hair.

'Monckton thinks it worth a punt, to see if the source of water was tapped into a well near here.'

'Great, so a freezing bath drawn from a well to cheer Christmas – we're not penguins!' Rebecca Royce gestured for a top-up.

'Here's the thing,' Gloss continued. 'I happen to know that the old hay barn was converted into a laundry during the war. I had a peek and the vast tubs are still in place. We have plenty of firewood. Hey presto – hot water, even if it means a bit of lugging and hauling of buckets. There's plenty of us and will work off a bit of the Christmas spirit, eh?'

'Seems a long shot,' said Scanner. 'Couldn't we just shovel up the snow? This mysterious well, if there is one, could be frozen over as well.'

'Possibly.'

'Clean water from a well sounds more in my line.' Grauler had woken up.

'Better than stinking,' Rebecca Royce declared.

'So when is Monckton going to set off on his water hunt? Don't tell me he has a diviner. What next, a druid's cape?' Scanner's foppishness was beginning to grate.

'First light, he tells me. If he has success, he'll enlist a few of us to help do the heavy work. We pile up the fires, and with a bit of luck we'll all be clean as whistles by breakfast.'

Dinner was goose. The food was good. Everyone was ravenous. Joy tackled her meal as was her custom – chomping her way methodically from stodge to the choice cuts.

Concentrating on her grub, Joy drowned out the festive gaiety. She didn't find it so obscene that the ensemble had shaken off the death of these two men so effortlessly, or that they appeared to find the professor's disappearance as more of an inconvenience than a tragedy, but to her it was beyond belief that they had so little interest in who had committed these atrocities or to consider that there may be a murderer among them. Clarice's assertion, Joy sensed, suited everyone. The dastardly German had done it!

Food devoured, chairs had been placed in front of the huge hearth. The fire was leaping and logs cracking and collapsing into the blaze with a whoosh of fireflies. Parcels were retrieved, excepting the two which were a distasteful reminder of the horrors that had occurred. The image of the two men prone in an outhouse leapt into Joy's head, and scanning the other faces, it was clear their memories were dousing the enthusiasm for this most festive of moments.

But Rebecca Royce swept past everybody in her silky Christmas number and seized her gift. Unfazed she was about to rip open her parcel when Perry Scanner held up a hand. 'Steady on there. Have none of you noticed something rather peculiar?'

All eyes ran to the tree. A few frowns and scratching of chins and their attention snapped back to Scanner.

'Count the parcels. Are we not supposed to be twelve – just like the days of Christmas?'

Rebecca Royce replaced a stray tress, and held her gift limply.

'Well, I count thirteen, unless I've made a mistake.' Scanner watched on as they all began to count.

Barasch won the race. 'You are correct. This is indeed most odd.'

'I think I may have the solution,' offered Clarice, cutting in tentatively. 'When I replied to the advertisement I asked if it would be permissible for me to bring Joy along. That must be it.'

'Possibly. But Crabb, in her initial address, said we were to be twelve – following the tradition as was set down. She made a particular point of it.' Scanner rapped the presents with his stick.

'Something may have changed,' said Mrs Pomp. 'As you say, there are thirteen parcels, and presumably thirteen bedrooms were prepared. You are making the humdrum appear sinister. We are all a bit spooked, but let's not make it worse. Let's open them up and enjoy what's left of the day.'

'Gloss?' Scanner turned to face the estate manager. 'You told us somebody had cried off – last minute and you were on hand, a ready replacement.'

'That's correct.' Gloss tightened his gaze. 'Hey, what are you insinuating?'

'Nothing, old boy. But it would be easy enough to add an additional parcel. They're all bound in an assortment of wrappers.'

'What a load of baloney!' Grauler exclaimed with a flourish. 'Why would anybody bother? And what about the rooms?'

'Easy enough to pitch up and find a spot. Plenty of beds to be had here.'

'But they were all made ready … somebody can't have …' Miss Biddle chipped in.

'Not difficult to pop your head around the door and find a berth. Although the keys were in the reception hall, the rooms weren't locked. I'm sure most of them will have been made up.'

'Easy enough way to sort this. Crabb must have a list.' Grauler downed his brandy. 'That's the rub. She probably forgot young Joy here made us a baker's dozen, easily done.' But he looked unsure.

'I suggest we inform the inspector. He needs to be made aware of this. It could, as Scanner suggests, be important.' Kosik was idling in a chair, his flinty eyes regarding Gloss keenly. 'And as Mr Scanner has noted, although bold, it would have been easily achieved.'

'What are getting at, Kosik?' Colour again rose in Gloss's face. 'Why are you all staring at me?'

'It occurs to me,' said Kosik, his words precise, 'if our German is not the killer, then it's possible that there is some other motive that as yet we are unaware of. Our murderer could have used this ruse to be a needle amongst our haystack, to infiltrate the party, and as we are all strangers to one another, we would be none the wiser.'

The company seemed to hold their breath.

'But the table placements,' gibbered Gloss. 'You're not telling me that our murderer added a card, a set of cutlery and glasses, well, it's preposterous.'

'Of course you're right, Mr Gloss. It's obvious Miss Crabb will have the solution.' Mrs Pomp said in a soothing tone.

Drabble, who was standing by the door, coughed for effect. 'Err, excuse me, ladies and gents. I'm afraid I'm not so sure that will be the case.'

All eyes turned to him.

'You see, Mister Monckton noticed this very issue when you all first pitched up.' Drabble's voice had a break in it. He was flustered. 'He spoke to Miss Crabb, but she told him that this year they'd left the invitations, the organisation of the thing, to this agency in York. She said that that's where the error was likely made and not to fuss, just to make up an extra room. With Miss Royce running late, there was time enough.'

'*Stille Nacht* …' Kosik sang in a whisper.

'We had better inform the inspector,' said Gloss, hot-footing it to the door. 'He will contact that damned fool agency and sort this out in no time. I won't have people casting doubt!'

'It's late. Can't this wait until tomorrow?' said Gracie, stifling a yawn.

'An agency open over Christmas? Snow laying all around and no telephone line to be had?' Scanner said with a faint smile. 'I suppose we could just open these.' He lifted a parcel with his stick and passed it to Gracie. 'Who knows, what is inside may make your enquiries redundant and it obvious who our so-called impostor is.'

As it turned out the gifts were tokens, clumsily made wooden boxes, some carved photograph frames, knitted scarves, bobbly socks and a couple of watercolours similar to those in Joy's bedroom. They all came with a note explaining that this homecraft had been the product of those invalided at

Misenlake during the war. Names that no one knew, but each gift bringing back the feeling of empathy and togetherness that the horrific conflict had blossomed. Individually, none of the presents stood out, but Joy was happy with her woollen mittens. They were useful and smelt warm.

And thereafter, after some false Christmas spirit and alcohol-driven sentimentality, Misenlake finally slept.

Joy, unusually, did not. Normally, her head dumped on the pillow and then the morning arrived. But this house was enclosed within a storm. It was refusing to be still. Joy listened with bedclothes high to the creaks and gurgles below the boards as the pipes thought it fun to join the fray, bellyaching about the cold.

Joy reached out for her medals as reassurance, but one dropped to the floor, running across the boards and tinkling against the wall underneath the watercolours. Groping about, there was a lot of dust, somebody hadn't been thorough. She came across an odd series of scratches right up against the poorly-fitted skirting. Beyond was the shared bathroom. The marks looked like an animal's clawing, some sort of rodent, or perhaps a cat, had been trying to get at something.

Reclaiming the gold medal, Joy padded to the window. The wind seemed to be in fine fooling. Working itself up, free from restraint it was doing laps of the manor, rushing past and goosing the shutters before moving on only to return within minutes. The pitch outside had slipped to a purple-blue that patterned the seeping snow, giving the light an unreal smear of colour and creating shadows that sank and rose like waves on the sea.

Joy's eyeline traced a beam of light that jogged and bobbed along a pathway flanking the main drive. A shining flicker momentarily lit up something slick, possibly an oilskin, as the jigging spark moved further from the house.

The indentations beneath her feet welcomed her toes as she traced out the shape of an imaginary bed. This had been a place of rest, for a child's head to sleep the slumber of the unconcerned. Innocence was all! Joy awoke from her trance and again cleared the window of the moist mist that threatened to dribble. The zipping light had been eaten up by the darkness and the sky had now turned to a swollen grey. Petals had begun to flutter, at first as if they'd been scattered by some nymph above, then the flurry increased, and the snowstorm was caught by the winsome wind driving the blades of frozen chill at Misenlake as if would-be invaders were laying siege.

Joy straightened her coins and laid down her head. The sergeant from the past's face came into her head. But tonight she could do nothing, only huddle down into the covers. What had happened to the young woman all those years ago? Such betrayal, so much anguish! Joy's rattling mind eventually eased. Tomorrow would come soon enough and with it, perhaps another step forward. The house wanted her help. She was sure of it. Joy slid off her coat of duty and slipped into her dreams, her snores and snuffles blotting out the churning pipes, and as always, even now, she slept without a thought.

TEN

STANDING GUARD, the jovial Nouse informed them on their way into breakfast that they were all to bring down their gifts, Detective Sergeant Prim's orders. They were made to lay them on the sideboard before seating themselves as usual.

Joy was reluctant to give up her woolly comforters, but was told by Clarice that she must. On entering the dining room, Joy almost collided with Prim, who was lurking behind the door beginning another lengthy speech. From what Joy could gather, Miss Crabb had been responsible for the presents, but was unable to recall much about them. However, Prim appeared to want to have a gander anyway, which seemed a tad over-the-top, his investigations inching forward, it would appear, at a snail's pace.

Miss Crabb came and went. Prim informed them that he was to quiz them over breakfast. Miss Pomp thought it very irregular, and Gloss thought it dashed bad form. But the policeman pointed out, rather theatrically, if he wasn't among them, he wasn't at all.

Uncharacteristically, the buffet stood bare. Gloss sniffed at the empty trays, appearing miffed that he was being made to wait for his customary full plate of sausages; musing that Monckton would be out tracking down fresh water, he settled for coffee and found his seat.

Joy wasn't waiting for her swampy porridge. She couldn't bear much more of this prima donna policeman. Now that the irksome man had vacated the drawing room, there would be another chance to have a dip inside, face down the past, that is if the manor was willing and if the spirits had breakfasted in more ease than the current incumbents.

Joy made her excuses and ignored Prim's piercing gaze tracing her as she left the room. She was certain, more than ever, that the passing scenes that she'd witnessed had some connection to these horrid crimes of the present.

The drawing room smelled of men; that sweaty dampness with a snuffle of shaving lacquer. Joy's timing was flawless. Two minutes to nine. She waited a bit, but then the clock chimed and the two scurrying figures came gambolling out. This time they stopped abruptly, frozen in their tracks.

The room became bathed in a glowing light as if somebody had whipped open the curtains with a flourish, and the atmosphere was suddenly heady with tobacco.

'Hem!' At this point, I have to be honest, at least with myself, as it would have been more than deceitful to claim that I had totally allayed my fears. This novel and exacting fortitude that had been enforced upon me in a hurry-up was actually screened by the flimsiest veneer. The proof of this was immediate, and harsh. As the past opened up before me, my heart began to bound like a lolloping dog, and directly my hands became wetter than a courting schoolboy's.

But I most earnestly yearned to know more. This invisibility, being masked from these figures from the past, was not quite the fun game that I continually tried to kid my brain into accepting, although it did give me the most wondrous buzz; a grasp of almost godlike power.

I was well aware that there was a danger of these dips becoming compulsive. They were too much like my sphere, a heavenly haven from the dread of the everyday.

With the exception of the fear of the sergeant's ability to engage with me, which both titillated and petrified me in equal doses, I felt increasingly mollified. I spoke aloud, but only a murmur – 'Courage, Joy! Stand tall and don't dither so!'

But any angst I had on that front somewhat dropped away. Mainly due to the fact that the sergeant wasn't actually present. The tall inspector was, sitting back in his chair and puffing contentedly. He appeared satisfied, almost blasé, and in no particular hurry either to speak or concentrate on anything other than this pipe.

The young woman squirmed opposite him. She sniffled and I was immediately overtaken by a sagging headiness, as if a lack of sleep was yanking at my eyes.

Again, my faculties were enhanced. The inspector's sucking on his pipe, the tock of the clock, the young woman toying with her buttons, were all hugely amplified.

The pungent rankness of a stale coffee mingled with the sweet richness of beeswax hit me and brought about a muffled sneeze. No one heard or noticed.

Bubbles burbled once more as the young woman's emotions awoke inside me. I felt her dismay, her fatalistic acceptance, and overriding everything a sense that this abysmal tragedy was spiralling out of control and was only going to get worse.

I immediately wanted to cry and run from the room. In fact, run forever and never come back, but the inspector's solemn glance held me to my chair and chastened my rebelliousness.

Finally he spoke. 'Do you recognise this, miss?' He pulled an attaché case from beneath the desk, and unbuckling the clasp like a magician, produced a pink scarf with a flourish. 'Well?'

'It's the scarf … the one Ceccy was wearing on the day she went missing?' I heard herself reply mechanically, but again the voice was not my own.

'You will most likely know where we found this?'

I was cross; thoughts of mutiny were rising again. 'No. I have no idea. But by your grave face I'm assuming you're no closer to locating the whereabouts of the child that should be at the centre of all our thoughts?'

'Miss Celia's whereabouts remains a mystery. Perchance not to us all.'

I felt more fury welling.

He continued, 'but a picture is emerging. A relationship. A desire to whisk a lover away from his family. And this scarf? You yourself admit that the little girl was wearing it on the day of her disappearance. Well, it was discovered hidden on top of your wardrobe. What do you say to that?' The inspector leant in and opened out his chest.

Shock. A spasm ripped at my heart. No. That's not right. It can't have been.

The Inspector seemed poised to quiz me further, but then his form blurred, his lips moved, but his words were lost as he began to evaporate into a weblike mist. Giddiness came in a hurry and then dissipated in seconds.

'Joy! What are you doing in here?' Clarice's face was rumpled in annoyance. 'You are wanted next door. Those policemen have been asking for you. We are commanded to assemble in the dining room. I'm afraid there's been another death.'

The chaos in the dining room centred around Drabble, who was doubled-over in a chair and blowing hard. Gloss handed him a tumbler.

'Now, slow down, man, and stop gibbering like a gibbon. Get him some more of that stuff.' Prim was in charge. 'Nouse, note this down.'

Drabble nodded thanks to Gloss and gulped down another glass, cuffing his mouth.

Mrs Pomp sniffled as if something unwholesome had been thrust under her nose.

'It was horrible. I was at Normandy and have seen some things, bodies blown apart, but this was a thousand times worse.' Drabble's cheeks had sprouted a pimpliness and he held up his glass for another refill.

'All in good time,' said Prim, batting away Gloss's hand.

'It was the expression on his face. All screwed up, agonising pain, and another thing – surprise! Those lifeless eyes and his lids were frosted open. It was ruddy awful.'

Nobody spoke.

'At first I thought he may have had a fall, banged his nut, but then I saw it. Savage thing, vicious contraption,' Drabble went on. 'Shouldn't be legal. And all around his feet this pinkish tinge like somebody had dropped a glass of port in the snow.'

'Contraption. Have you got that, Nouse?' Prim bent close and stared into Drabble's zipping eyes. 'Now stop blathering man, and be concise. Yes, bring him another.' Prim motioned to Gloss.

'It was some sort of animal trap, it had snapped around his shin right to the bone. He wouldn't have had a chance, out there in the dark even with a torch.'

'In the dark?' Grauler quizzed. 'I thought he went out at first light.'

'Yes. That's what we were told,' Barasch said.

'Let him finish,' demanded Prim. 'Now, don't omit anything, man, but for the sake of the Lord, do get on with it.'

'That was Mister Monckton all over,' said Drabble, shaking his head. 'Said he really needed this position, and although it were only temporary, he would do his utmost to prove his worth. Said you never know where it may lead.'

'Right. We are getting exactly nowhere,' said an exasperated Prim.

Drabble said, 'the thing is, Mister Monckton went out last night!'

'Last night!' a few of the guests echoed.

Joy recalled the torch, the bobbing light from her window.

'He said he'd remembered something the professor had said. He wanted to have a looksee. It was on his mind.'

'The butler was traipsing about in the dark?' Prim's face furrowed.

'The storm had given up for a bit and he said he wouldn't need half an hour to double-check.' Drabble fingered the rim of his glass, licking his tips. 'He reckoned it would go down a storm, you know, speed things along in the morning. We could rouse a few to help so when the ladies woke up they'd be able to have hot water to beautify themselves before breakfast.'

Miss Biddle grunted.

'What time was this?' asked Prim.

'Not long after the last of 'em had gone up for the night.'

'Which was?'

'Begging pardon, but that was Mister Grauler and Miss Royce. I was aching for my bed. It had been a whopper of a day. I checked my watch just before they made their way up. Was just about a quarter after ten.'

'Nouse?'

'Got it, sir.' Nouse made a face behind his superior's back.

Joy grinned. He seemed a good sort.

'Then what did you do?'

Drabble looked to his feet.

'Well, come on, man?'

'I went up to my bed and lay down for a bit. Just for a minute or two, you understand. I had meant to wait for Mister Monckton to return, but I was that pooped …'

'You fell asleep?'

Drabble's chin dropped to his chest and he nodded slowly.

'So you wouldn't have known that Monckton hadn't come back?'

'No, sir. I feel so bad, but I woke up fully clothed around five-thirty. I went and knocked him up, but there weren't no reply. I went down to Cook, but she said she hadn't seen him neither.'

'Then what did you do?'

'I figured he'd been up and about already, early doors. So I brushed myself up a bit and went out after him. Searched everywhere I did. I had almost given up when I had a hunch to try over by that tunnel that leads to the sea. I would have missed him, but for the smudge in the snow.'

'But whereabouts exactly?' Gloss asked.

'I followed the trail of pink stuff to those large boulders that poke out from the heath. Behind them, a few yards in, was this craggy path, sort of enclosed either side by overgrown ferns and stuff, suffocating like. And there he was face down with these metal teeth clamped to his leg. I nudged him, then turned him over and … poor Mister Monckton, he didn't deserve that!' Drabble wiped away the beginnings of a tear.

'Was he still warm? Did you notice any prints?'

'Frozen stiff. Could have knocked a nail in with him.'

Mrs Pomp hung her head. 'Oh my!'

'So it's likely he had the accident last night and with the loss of blood …'

'Froze to death.' Barasch shivered. 'The shock. As you say, the loss of body temperature. He wouldn't have stood a chance.'

'I'm sorry,' said Drabble, a whimper slipping out. 'If I hadn't fallen asleep he'd still be alive. It's all my fault.'

'A terrible accident, old fellow. You shouldn't blame yourself,' consoled Gloss.

'Now then, I want you all to remain in this room.' Prim's eyes were full of vigour. Likely another death, and on his watch it didn't sit well. 'I'm assuming breakfast has been prepared so you may as well eat. Nouse, make sure nobody leaves. Doctor – if you don't mind, you come with me as I would value you opinion. Drabble you can lead the way.'

A ruby-faced cook loaded up the buffet with steaming dishes. This latest tragedy hadn't appeared to have dummed-down people's appetites, plates piled high and trips back for seconds. This was excepting, Rebecca Royce who just sniffed and sipped at her coffee. 'Look here,' she said. 'We cannot just carry on, sail through this atrocious experience as if nothing has happened. Somebody knows something. And I have no confidence in these British policeman. I'm not hanging around until it's my turn to be zipped up in the mortuary.'

'But my dear, it is all easily explainable,' said Mrs Pomp with false cheeriness. 'As the Brigadier would have established by now …'

'As if you would know,' said Miss Biddle under her breath.

'The professor found his treasure,' suggested Mrs Pomp unabashed. 'But our German is on to him. The unfortunate Slack witnesses a scuffle, then is attacked …'

'Yes, we've heard this story.' Rebecca Royce pushed her plate away in a petulant show of irritation. 'And now Monckton unfortunately walks into a man-trap. Coincidences abound.'

'*Stille Nacht* …' Kosik murmured.

'I wish you'd stop with that tommy-rot,' growled Gloss.

'The thirteenth man, or woman, strikes again!' Perry Scanner exclaimed.

Joy wished she'd brought her knitting down with her. She began to squirm.

Clarice noticed. 'Come on, ants-in-your-pants! If we can't vacate the room, at least we can get down from the table.'

Cushions sat on the deep windowsills providing extra seating and a wonderful view of that side of the house: they faced north and overlooked open ground which stretched to the main gate, and in between Gloss's crater, the would-be skating rink. Slightly east, as the land rose to the sea was the disused alum works and the track through the heath where, sadly, Monckton lay.

Joy sat with her nose close to the pane. Prim and the others would return this way and then at last she'd be able to escape all this prattling. Why did everyone need to be so shouty?

Gracie joined them, taking a seat next to Clarice. Perry Scanner hobbled over.

'Any sign yet?' he asked.

They all stared into the folds of whiteness. Sprays of mist splurged low over the heathland and hung menacingly in nests up and over the rocks.

'Bleak, but somehow beautiful, don't you think?' Rebbecca Royce joined them.

'Distant memories?' asked Scanner.

'Not really I was too young to recall much of my time in the old country. We have plenty of snow in Canada, of course, and this time of year it never leaves us – it's so brutal, but it's part of life and one almost takes it for granted.'

'What brought you back?' asked Scanner.

'A death of a relation, a Will, family duties, loose ends, and perhaps some closure.'

'Sounds complicated. And to Misenlake, and this tragic gathering?'

'As I mentioned. This part of the world is my country. I was told about the advert by my agent. He thought it might be fun for me and nobody likes to be alone at Christmas.'

Joy winced inside. Why was everybody so afraid to be alone? She would give anything to be bolted up in her room at home.

'And your war?'

'You are persistently inquisitive, Mr Scanner.'

'I beg your pardon. It's my job. I find it hard not to always want to round the circles.'

'I was living alone in a big spread back home in Canada when I heard of that horrendous catastrophe, you know the *Benares?* Those wretched children, it was all over the Canadian news. I immediately volunteered to house as many refugees as I could take. Children of the Blitz and other unfortunates – welcome one and all. I figured it was my contribution to the country of my birth. Doing my bit!'

'The *Benares*?' queried Clarice.

'SS *City of Benares*,' explained Scanner. 'You are unaware of the calamity? I guess most are. It was hushed up at the time – bad for morale.'

'She was bound for Quebec and Montreal,' said Rebecca Royce, her tone muted.

'A passenger ship torpedoed in 1940,' Scanner carried on. 'Which in itself, at that time was not unusual, but unfortunately amongst the civilians aboard were ninety child evacuees. All but a handful died either drowned or from exposure in the freezing sea.'

Rebecca Royce eyes filmed. 'Easy not to mourn the death of our resident German.'

A considerable pause followed that dragged and dragged as they all stared out at the tranquillity of the forlorn landscape.

'Are you going to hang around? Perhaps settle back in Yorkshire?' Scanner asked Rebecca Royce.

'What do you think?' Rebecca Royce said sarcastically, her painted fingernails fumbling inside her overladen handbag. 'Where are my blasted cigarettes? Fuzz? Where is that fool Yank?'

Joy had seen Grauler leave the room a bit earlier in the company of Miss Biddle. The two of them had been arguing on the stairs before breakfast and she'd hung around on the landing until the American had finally bounded past. His face had been plum-coloured, a fevered look rising in his features.

'And you, Mrs Sands?' Scanner hadn't quite taken out a pocketbook, but the questions were without end.

Gracie twiddled with a brooch, a golden butterfly with aquamarines dotting the wings.

'That's an unusual piece – antique? I think you said you were a nurse? Any family to speak of?'

Gracie left off with the brooch and broke away to an adjacent window. 'Dead. Killed in Italy during the war,' she answered over her shoulder as she trundled away, ending the conversation.

'Italy? Really that's where I bought the bullet that crippled the old leg,' Scanner hollered after her. 'The Anzio landings, was it? Idiotic American, General Lucas dawdled and was responsible for the death of a lot of good men.'

But Gracie didn't reply. She had sidled towards the tea and coffee pots on the dresser. Scanner's persistence was met by the tinkle of teaspoons on crockery.

'You doing the honours?' Miss Biddle had joined Gracie. 'Don't mind if I do.'

Prim, fresh with snow, had mustered them all in the drawing room. The hearth whooped up to the grousing chimney stack as the wind outside, tired of whipping up the sea, had now set its sights inland.

The drifts of winter whiteness were being plucked at by the gusts, feathery corkscrews flustering skywards like a flock of spooked birds. From the window, the once picture-perfect gardens were now peppered with a furious flurry. Another storm was stirring.

Prim peered out over Kosik's shoulder as the airman seemed entranced by the ferocity of the elements.

'It appears the forecasters have again called it right,' said Prim with a downcast look. 'We are stuck here, and with this continuing dirty spell, I'll be unable to get word out to my superiors.'

Kosik turned away from the window.

'Well, it appears you are all in my hands, but we will manage, never fear,' Prim announced.

'We'll have to make the best of it,' said Mrs Pomp.

Somebody tittered.

'Make the best of it? People are going down like flies,' cried Rebecca Royce.

'Just a figure of speech, miss. We all need to stay calm,' said Nouse from a corner.

'Tell that to Monckton,' grumbled Grauler.

'Well, at least the butler didn't do it!' Scanner was immediately accosted by sharp tones.

'What about Slack the gardener? Nobody mentions him. Reckon it's 'cos he's the lowest of servants!' Miss Biddle sat deeper in her chair with a shimmy, appearing happy to have made her point.

'Monckton is dead,' said Prim plainly. 'Loss of blood coupled with exposure.'

'Horrible!' exclaimed Mrs Pomp.

'Death is never kind,' Barasch muttered.

'Now see here, Gloss, you were saying that there's a store of those deadly contraptions in the outhouse?' Prim quizzed.

'That's right. Those SOE chaps, auxiliaries collected all kinds of primitive weaponry, best they could find.'

'But they've been gone for years.' Grauler was, yet again, overly loud. 'Holy cow! Are you telling me they just left some of these deathtraps lying around the grounds for some guy to fall on? What a crummy country!'

Prim said, 'I do not believe that to be credible. Considering the events over the past few days, we have to assume that the trap was placed there deliberately.'

'Deliberately? But why would they do that?' Grauler was becoming as rowdy as his curls. 'How could anyone know some fella would take a hike in the woods? A hidden trail – hell of a long shot, don't you think?'

'I agree,' answered Prim. 'But consider for a moment, the pathway where he was found was overgrown with foliage and the track cramped. A perfect place for a booby-trap. Somebody, somehow, knew where Monckton was heading.'

'Or it was meant for somebody else,' said Kosik.

Prim flashed him a look.

'But why? Where does the trail lead to?' Gracie asked.

'The ruins of a disused alum site,' Gloss replied.

'But why go there?' Grauler yapped. 'This makes no sort of sense.'

Prim's gave him a schoolmaster's disdainful stare. Grauler looked for support before giving up and eventually slumping into a chair.

'Drabble told us Monckton had been studying Professor Melville's maps,' Scanner observed. 'Potentially looking for the hidden well out that way somewhere.'

'Maybe the prof planted that story to protect what he really was up to?' suggested Grauler, perking up.

'What do you mean by that?' asked Mrs Pomp.

Grauler hesitated. 'I don't know. I'm not the detective.'

Prim sighed. 'Either way, if the snare was set deliberately, then it's clear somebody didn't want anyone poking about out there. Nouse has had a good ferret around, but says there is nothing of note. Until the snow thaws any further investigation isn't likely to be fruitful.'

'So, we just sit around and wait for another of us to be picked off?' Grauler was back on his feet again.

Silence followed. Each of the guests faces seemed to crease in unison, finally coming to the appalling conclusion that there may be a murderer among them.

'But where has the professor got to?' questioned Barasch.

'Yes, we do seem to keep forgetting about Melville,' Scanner interjected. 'Possibly out there somewhere hellbent on some manic rampage. Perhaps his mind …'

'Please do not be flippant, sir. This is police work and we need to be methodical and as is usually the way, when we are, the solution reveals itself. I always get there in the end, don't I, Nouse?'

Nouse offered a limp salute.

'In the end! There won't be anybody left if you don't get a move on,' Miss Biddle shrieked.

'Excepting the murderer of course,' Scanner pointed out.

Again silence dropped over the group.

Joy's eyes were rooted to the clock. She'd been studying it for fifteen minutes. It was nearly midday.

'Constable Nouse would usually take further statements from you. Routine stuff, your whereabouts, the times you retired for the night, etc, but I see little point as I suspect you will all claim to have been abed when Monckton left the house.'

'Claim?' Mrs Pomp retorted.

Prim sighed and carried on. 'Drabble confirmed that Monckton went out after the last of you went up.'

'That's correct. That was me,' Rebecca Royce asserted in a bothered tone. 'It was a quarter after ten. We've done this bit.'

'We have a similar issue with the demise of our deceased gardener. Again nailing down the time of his death, it is probable it would have occurred not long after he arrived that morning.'

'After speaking to Miss Crabb,' Nouse offered.

Prim threw him a scowl.

'Either way. Before breakfast, certainly, which makes it hard for any of you to have an alibi. And again, with Herr Claube, nobody seems to have seen him leave the house and he could have been killed at any point during a dozen hours or so.'

'So you're saying that as none of us can provide a comprehensive account of our fellow guests' movements during these times, then any of us could be the culprit?'

'Correct!'

'How dare you!' Mrs Pomp cried.

The room erupted in fury and indignation.

'Please refrain from bickering. I would add that if anybody saw anything unusual then my door is always open, and obviously it will be treated in the strictest of confidence. We will be tracking down any leads with the utmost vigour …'

Nobody was listening.

Joy heard the clock strike twelve.

'Hem!' The fuzzy feeling came again and this time it was coated with a hot stickiness as if a fever was trying to grab me and weigh me down. Then came the splodges that screened my vision. I thought I could predict, if not pre-empt these signals, but this transformation appeared more random, as if Misenlake was playing me like fly-fisherman tempting a trout gulping for its fly.

The room felt airless. The atmosphere rotten, as if something was decaying, as if the house was in need of new blood. The trembles inside me did not come, though I continued to brace myself against the onrushing invasion, but as the picture unfolded, I was surprised but also thankful that Miss Ines was not present this time. I would be spared her grief at least.

He was there as was usual; the tall inspector, his features forming, and beside him was the sergeant and he was pressing a point. 'But, sir, something isn't right here. I can feel it. I'm certain that …'

And then the words began to drift and were replaced by a sogginess on my cheeks, tears and such ungovernable heartache, hollow and empty, sensations as acute I had hitherto never experienced.

And rumbling in my head, her words. 'How could he forsake me? How could he believe I would be capable of such a thing? Oh, why won't he come? If only we could be together. When he holds me, I'd make him see. I don't want a life without *us*. And now as my baby grows inside …'

And then I spied the governess over by the window, staring back with a bewildered look etched on her face.

Everything went blank. I was falling – and then thump!

'Miss! Miss, lie still.' Barasch was gaping down as Joy lay prone.

'I assure you, Doctor, she'll be fine.' It was Clarice's voice. 'She has just fainted. This has happened before. Sometimes she does not drink enough. Dehydration is the curse of us all.'

'But her head made such a terrible thud. I should examine her. Are you certain it is not some sort of fit?' Barasch pulled his small leather case from his inside pocket.

'No, Doctor. It's just a bump. A cold flannel and rest is the ticket. She won't thank you for all this fuss. I will take her up to her room and she can rest this afternoon. It's been a hellish few days for all of us.'

'As you wish.'

Gracie took one arm and Clarice the other and supported Joy as they ascended the stairs.

In Joy's room, the bed was starch-cold, but its clean cotton smell reassured her, reminded her of home.

'I will call Drabble to bring some firewood,' said Clarice.

'Don't worry. I will sit with her for a bit,' Gracie reassured her.

Joy groped for her medals.

Gracie beamed as she sat on the solitary chair beside the bed. 'You're going to have a bit of a lump, I'm afeard, my dear. It was a proper fall.'

Joy prodded the egg rising on the top of her forehead.

'This is a cute little bolthole,' Gracie said.

'It was a child's room. Two, I think,' said Joy without thinking.

Gracie followed Joy's gaze to the window.

'There was another bed over there.'

Gracie walked over to the window and looked out.

Joy stacked her medals.

'Drabble will be up soon. I'll see you at dinner.' Gracie said, and left.

Joy sat up and started to knit.

After a time, her eyes drooped. Jolting herself awake several times, Joy smelt the tangy smoke from the fire and the vague memory of a figure shuffling about and stacking wood. And then she drifted off.

It was so hot. The fever that had taken over her in the drawing room had ratcheted up, and as Joy's head twisted right and left as sweat prickled her moist body. Sounds came. Ricocheting around the room like a caged bird. There was singing, then laughter. The searing clamminess slid up and down her back. A soft voice whispered. But Joy's breath gagged in her gullet. Naughty giggles – childlike – over and over and then tripping footsteps.

'Can't catch me!'

A whoosh of cold air snapped Joy awake. Clarice was standing over her waving a towel. Behind her the open window was dragging in the freezing night and vomiting the smokiness from the room.

'JOY! Wake up!'

Joy coughed up tickles and swept sweat from her temples.

'That fool man might have killed you. The fire has been piled far too high and the coals have escaped the grate. If I hadn't come in when I did, the rug may have caught and lord knows what then.'

Joy staggered out of the bed. The flames were indeed dancing in the hearth and were almost kissing the wallpaper. But it had been just a game. There'd been no danger. A child's mischief.

The room was bathed in an orange glow and it dimmed as Clarice emptied the flowers and poured the vase-water onto the fire with a hiss. Joy noticed the scratches in the floorboards again and wondered.

Gracie poked her head in the door. 'What on earth is going on?'

Clarice hastily explained as she attempted to wrestle Joy into her dressing gown.

'I'll call for Drabble,' Gracie said. 'A shovel or two of snow will dampen down those flames for good.'

Clarice scrunched up her face. 'Don't bother. The worst is over.'

Joy yanked herself away and pulled her dress over her head, slipping on her shoes. 'I'm thirsty,' she said.

Clarice lowered the window a little and grimaced. 'Yes, I'm not surprised. You slept through lunch. Tidy that mop and we'll join the others. There's to be drinks and then an early tea.'

Gracie led them out into the corridor.

'What are we to do with you?' Clarice asked Joy linking arms. 'This near disaster, and the fainting fits. It's most peculiar and unlike you, although, of course, understandable, I suppose, with all these horrors going on.'

Joy extricated herself and rushed back to check on her medals.

'And what was all that singing in your sleep? Over and over?' asked Clarice.

Joy tapped her nose. She recalled tunes and ditties reverberating around her head. 'Little children!'

'Huh?'

Of course Joy hadn't really slept just lived in a little girl's dream. 'Hem!'

ELEVEN

JOY FOUND LEMONADE in the library. Prim had once again taken up residence in the drawing room, but had padded in to ask some routine questions.

To Joy, it seemed the crowd, like her, had little faith in this policeman. But the unkind words and harsh jibes froze on their lips as Prim entered.

'I have news.' He skimmed the room. 'But wait, are we not one short?'

'Not another?' yelped Mrs Pomp.

'It's Gloss,' explained Perry Scanner. 'He had some eureka moment and has dashed off out. Said some gibberish about having been so stupid.'

'Gone outside?' Prim shook his head. 'Alone? He had no business leaving the manor unaccompanied.'

'Are we under house arrest?' asked Rebecca Royce fixedly.

'Not exactly. But it's for the best that you stick together.'

'For safety's sake,' chipped in Nouse.

Prim sighed. 'Thank you, Nouse. Perhaps you could try and hunt our Mr Gloss down before we have any more disasters.'

Nouse didn't look convinced, but was rescued by the door swinging open and a harassed-looking Gloss tumbling in.

'Where've you been? You're a bit grubby. You look like you've been rolling around the floor.' Rebecca Royce crinkled her nose.

Prim gave Gloss a stern look. 'Yes, where have you been?'

'Well, actually, the lady is almost correct.' Gloss helped himself to a glass and topped it up with soda. 'I've been a perfect fool. The handy laundry that the army boys set up, it's still in place. As Crabb said, they laid some new pipes here and there. I suddenly thought maybe they're connected to the casks in the stables. Would have made sense. And also, if they had, they'd possibly lagged them or buried them sufficiently deep that they may actually be still serviceable. Nobody had tried the taps out there. Anyway, I was half right. There's a steady trickle, although at it will take hours to fill those huge vats. But beggars and all that, better than nothing. In the morning I intend to light up the burners and we'll have some hot water at last.'

'Thank God!' exclaimed Rebecca Royce.

'I don't want to steal your thunder,' Prim interrupted, 'but if you take a peek the weather is finally turning. The downpour should warm the ground and unfreeze our pipes.'

Gloss looked crestfallen. 'You're right. But if they've cracked, anyway we will see.'

The room as one turned to the panes. Sure enough, the leaded glass was alive with spattering water.

'Going to stay bitterly cold apparently, but Nouse tells me that's almost all year round on this coast.'

'Small mercies,' said Miss Biddle.

Lots of chattering and nattering followed.

Prim put up a hand. 'If I could have one more word. With the roads and drifts clearing, Nouse is going to head for the village shortly.'

'I am?' Nouse replied with a look of surprise.

Prim frowned. 'Hopefully he can get word to the Yard and they can send some help, forensics and the suchlike.'

'If the roads are serviceable, I am going to skedaddle,' Rebecca Royce declared.

'Yes, all that's holy, we'll all be glad to be away from this dive,' Grauler added.

'I am afraid that cannot be,' Prim decreed. 'You are all to remain here until we get to the bottom of this, or until I receive a conflicting command from the Yard.'

A brief babble of dissent, but it appeared the group expected as much and as soon as Prim left the room, the guests all split into conspiratorial hives.

Barasch huddled deep in his chair, was flanked by Kosik and Scanner.

Mrs Pomp as usual, was beside the fire and Rebecca Royce had nabbed the armchair opposite.

Miss Biddle was being talked at by Fuzzy Grauler, who'd beckoned Gloss over.

'You're a swell fella, Gloss, but I don't get you.'

'Get me?'

'Yeh! You're a resourceful guy, so why hang about this dump during the war? I won't pry into your affairs – as to why you weren't re-assigned – we all have our secrets, but I still don't get it.'

Gloss coloured. 'It's true I was brought up in London, but for reasons I'd rather not delve into the Yorkshire air suited me and we all need to earn a crust, do we not?'

Grauler clutched Gloss's shoulder by the way of apology.

'He's right,' said Biddle. 'We can't all be born to riches and even those that are can sometimes be on the rough end of it.'

Gracie and Clarice were at the window peering into the fading light and sniffing at the rain.

Joy found a chair quite removed, with a dainty side table alongside that held a globe. She began to knit.

Once more, the door swung open and Miss Crabb glided in.

'On behalf of Miss Gwynne, I have come to apologise for these unforeseeable and appalling events. It is a godsend that the police were at hand and I have been informed that the plan is for Scotland Yard to send others and hopefully that will put an end to this unfortunate episode.'

'Unfortunate – you said it!' Grauler exclaimed.

'How's our hostess?' Scanner asked.

'Miss Gwynne is still too weak to leave her bed and in the circumstances prefers to keep to her room.'

'I bet she does!' Again Grauler.

'I suspect she wishes she'd never invited us,' Mrs Pomp reflected.

'What there's left of us,' added Kosik.

Scanner said, 'Yes, hardly the twelve days of Christmas. At this rate more like the twelve corpses of Yule.'

'Or thirteen,' said Kosik.

Miss Crabb's face hardened, and seemingly tired of the gallows humour, she blinked and turned to leave.

The music in Joy's head suddenly found voice. The melodic tones of her fevered dream came forth, and she began to murmur to herself.

'Rock-a bye baby, on the tree top … when the wind blows the cradle will rock.

'When the bough breaks the cradle will fall – and down will come baby, cradle and all.'

A faint whistle from someone cut the room to instant silence. Not even a quiver of breath broke the stifling hush. A tangible fear held the moment as if a murder had been announced. All eyes slid to Joy, who instantly took up her knitting, and they all turned as one as the door gently closed and Crabb was gone with a click.

Supper again had been a strained and crotchety affair. Nobody seemed too eager to share their thoughts or fussed with the obligatory turkey curry. Mrs Pomp moaned about Indians, the mutiny specifically, and how they would soon be welcoming Britain back after the chaotic disaster of independence. The Brigadier had never trusted foreigners. That Indians in India weren't the interlopers seemed immaterial.

Perry Scanner had whinged about the novelty of this newly formed Welfare State. Miss Biddle was certain that free health care would be a bad thing; doctors being paid by the state would show less interest, less bang for your buck, Grauler had added.

Grauler had also complained about the television programmes in this godawful country. What was the point in buying the new-fangled sets if the shows were so crummy?

Rebecca Royce added that these sets were oversized intrusions, great boxes of wood and glass, ugly affronts, and took up way too much room.

Gloss commented that nothing would replace the dear old wireless. It would not be the same without having Dick Barton to entertain the family, huddled together, enjoying the moment.

Barasch and Kosik fenced about Berlin and the blockade by the Soviets. Kosik was sure the communists would eventually take over the entire city.

Gracie said barely a word, which was normal, but she seemed unsettled and had fretted that she hadn't waited around to check that Drabble had safely stacked Joy's hearth. And had joined Rebecca Royce's questioning as to why they still hadn't set eyes on the hostess.

Clarice had ploughed through her food as if she were afraid somebody was going to steal it, whilst Joy had people-watched, storing material for her jotter.

Although the atmosphere was testy and subdued, once again Joy could not comprehend why they would not discuss on who could have committed these atrocious acts of savagery – let alone the motive. Perhaps it was human nature, denial better than confrontation.

To Joy's mind, it was clear that almost everyone had suffered at the hands of the Nazis and therefore all had a motive for the killing of Claube.

It appeared that most thought that the professor had had a fatal accident – Joy thought not; it was too convenient.

The circumstances of Slack's death were so bewildering that to speculate would only spawn bizarre and outlandish theories. However, to Joy it was obvious that he'd met his end because of something he'd seen; something he wasn't supposed to have stumbled upon.

Joy straightened her cutlery and for once struggled to clear her mind, but it would come if she waited. And if it didn't, Misenlake's past would surely come for her again, and soon.

After dinner the tone had altered again. The alcohol flowed readily and stiff lips had begun to slip; people's thoughts and fears began to surface.

'Are you trying to suggest that Claube's wound to the back of his neck was a figment of Prim's imagination?' Grauler raised his eyes to the ceiling.

'I am just suggesting that this nastiness may have been a series of ill-fated happenstances.' Mrs Pomp's rouge got redder. 'The gardener's demise – it is clear none of us can explain, but it is possible the other incidents were an unfortunate series of accidents.'

'Doctor?' Kosik looked to Barasch. 'How about our German friend?

Could that have been an accident?'

'It's possible … I'm not sure,' Barasch stammered, pulling his glasses down onto the crown of his nose.

'Hang on here,' interrupted Grauler. 'You've changed your tune.'

'It's just …' said Barasch.

'What sort of doctor are you?' quizzed Scanner.

'Yeh, what kind of phoney quack are you?' Grauler's brashness was steadily increasing.

'I was training to be, but, well … the truth is that I am really a dentist,' Barasch eventually spluttered in reply.

'A dentist!' Grauler cried.

'There you are.' Mrs Pomp seemed vindicated.

'But I did start to train to be a doctor.' Barasch gulped. 'But then changed course, and well that was some time ago before the war and …'

'Oh my God.' Rebecca Royce held out her glass to Grauler for a refill. 'So you are not a doctor at all? And our German airman could have fallen foul of that spiteful bog?'

'I'm not saying that,' said Barasch.

'So why say you're a doctor? Fishy to me,' demanded Grauler.

'I thought I might be able to help, that's all,' said Barasch with a resigned air.

'Indeed. You just wanted to help,' Kosik said with a sardonic smirk.

'Well I have a rotten toothache that you could …' Scanner chortled to himself.

'So it is therefore possible Melville was taken by the sea. Claube another reckless accident. Monckton traipsing down a rarely used walkway. As I said, this could be just be …' Mrs Pomp was interrupted by Scanner.

'And Slack whilst clearing the snow suddenly decided to bash his own brains in!'

'There's the rub,' said Grauler with a whistle.

'But don't you see. That is the crux of the matter.' It was Gloss. 'Prim is perplexed, potentially out of his depth, but in his defence can any of us explain the riddle of how Slack could have been slain and who had a motive?'

'There wasn't another footprint within a hundred yards of him.' Barasch spoke up.

The conversation halted. Eyes wandered. Nobody moved.

Until Mrs Pomp suggested, 'Some sort of missile?'

'There was blood on the shovel.' Barasch cut her short.

'A flying shovel. What next, the Wicked Witch of the East?' Grauler guzzled another whisky.

'Two tyre tracks. A set of the gardeners prints. If only somebody had been looking out they may have seen something,' Miss Biddle offered from the corner, her nose hovering over her cup.

'But as Prim said, it would have been not long after dawn. We were all tucked up,' Gloss observed.

'Why would anyone want to kill Slack? He was known to none of us or so it is suggested.' Kosik thrust his hands in his pockets.

'He's right,' agreed Rebecca Royce.

'So Slack's killing, although inexplicable was most probably unrelated to the others. A local feud … or what about his apprentice?' Mrs Pomp suggested. 'And then there's this man Drabble? We know nothing of his past.'

'Always the servants, ain't it? Thank gawd for our new Labour government,' Miss Biddle sniped from her chair.

'I didn't mean …' Mrs Pomp began.

'She has a point. We don't know this guy, and well, I'm just saying ...' Grauler tailed off.

'But then, we don't really know the slightest thing about any of us, do we?' Rebecca Royce was high on bubbles, her face glowing. 'Who can guarantee that any of the backgrounds that we have presented are authentic?'

'The agency?' Kosik stated.

'Of course, with Nouse heading to the village we could finally clear up the mystery of our thirteenth guest.' Scanner eyed Gloss.

Rebecca Royce sloshed some champagne on the rug, narrowly missing Mrs Pomp who shrieked and moved her handbag.

'When and if they return to their office,' Kosik observed.

'Or are we back to our initial and only solution. Melville was tracked by Claube. Slack was a witness to the German's dirty deed and paid for it with his life.' Gloss made an aggressive sweeping movement with a hand as if to bat away debate. 'If our doctor … dentist Barasch can now be unsure about the wound to the neck, or that he didn't sink to a muddy death, the theory now holds water.'

'And yet,' said Prim who had quietly entered the room. 'Motive is all. And although none of you were too cut up by our German's demise, we always end up with the gardener.'

'But if Herr Claube was murdered, you could lay the blame on any of us,' said Mrs Pomp, bridling. 'The Nazis will never be forgiven. The Brigadier always said Herr Hitler should never have been placated.'

But Prim had puffed himself up. 'It is clear that you all had the opportunity. It's the motive that needs uncovering. Assuming Nouse has success, I suspect a senior officer will be amongst us shortly. However, I have begun to form my own theory. I have said before now that this professor, who crucially still hasn't been located, has to be the most obvious suspect. That and the fact that your gathering became thirteen I believe, are the integral pieces of this puzzle.'

Prim picked up a china figurine and studied it closely. Then, laying it down, he continued, his speech deliberate. 'There are others here who clearly know more than they're letting on.' Prim gave Joy a pointed look. 'But back to our professor. I propose that he was not a professor. I submit that in fact he was some get-rich-quick shyster, a mercenary seeking the aforementioned treasure.'

Scanner snickered.

Prim ignored him and went on. 'Having infiltrated the household, and with the aid of stolen maps, he made for his booty. But unbeknown to him he was tracked by our German, who was on to him. A struggle ensued and Claube was done away with. Then, this Melville lays doggo in one of the outbuildings, and whilst dumping Claube's corpse in the field at first light, was spotted by Slack, who has just arrived to rescue you all from the snow. Melville batters Slack to death with his shovel and then races away to the nearest port, where he catches a ship to the scrum that is France or Northern Europe. He's likely counting his filthy lucre as we speak and congratulating himself that he is home and dry. That is not allowing for the long arm of the law or the wit of modern policing.'

Gloss stared open-mouthed.

Kosik had the beginnings of a smile on his lips. 'And how do you explain Slack's demise? Was Melville an eccentric genius inventor who in the short time he was here designed some sort of pulley system on which he levered himself up and then hovered over the unfortunate man before braining him with his own spade?'

Prim plucked an eyebrow and ambled to the window. 'That is the part I cannot explain. But you should not underestimate the force's ingenuity or relentless pursuit of the truth. We will get there, we always get...' He looked for the absent Nouse for reassurance, but just met bemused faces.

'When do you think your superior will be here?' stammered Mrs Pomp.

Somebody choked back laughter.

On returning to her room, Joy noticed a difference. She hated things being shifted about. It upset her balance, her safeness.

The stench of woodsmoke still hung in the room despite the bellowing wind that was clamouring attention as it raced in and out of the partially opened window.

But it wasn't the smell or that the storm had sullied the drapes or that the rain-filled blackness that now was able to peep inside, it was everything else.

The dressing table was a mess. The door constantly banged. The slate around the hearth was a battlefield of ash. And the most offensive of the cobbled lot was one of the watercolours hanging limply askew, like a pathetic pooch looking for a treat.

Joy tutted and straightened the frame, standing back and studying her handiwork – good enough!

The crudely brushed scene, a rolling stormy sea, was just a little too precise, the waves daubed crustily like a coiffured lady's hair-do. Their thundering tips were much too white, cleansed of any real substance, and then there was this hopeless splindly speck in the foreground, a body too defined, with spidery arms and legs. Joy reached out and traced the craggy waves. A tic like a straggle of hair pricked her eye. She took a step back. The fleck in the foreground appeared to have grown, and with a jiggle it suddenly fizzed across the sand as if a flea was racing across the canvas.

'Hem!' For a moment, I thought it was the after-effects of the smoke and fire. Blotches in front of my eyes were now not a novelty. So, I rubbed them a bit, squinted a bit more, and was satisfied when the plain old picture just stared back at me.

But then something else. The haunting sensation I had experienced before only down in the drawing room crept over me. I felt a growing dread, an alarming impression that someone was standing right behind me. And then came that same pungent hanging staleness like somebody had taken the lid off a dustbin.

I heard shuffling feet and spun around. There was the sergeant. He was on his hands and knees and appeared to be sniffing the floorboards, poking in nooks and sliding his palms under a chest of drawers. Lifting the curtains, he then snooped in a wardrobe and then he was under a bed. After a time, he stretched to his feet with a groan, and rummaged in his whiskers.

It was my room, yet it wasn't. The dimensions had altered marginally and the pieces were all diminutive, a nursery.

I stood as still as I was able, conquering my urge to cough. But of course, he turned and saw me, and this unsettling eruption of alarm flared in his eyes. I wanted to say something but the words wouldn't come. I stepped back and collided with the door as the sourness was sucked from the room. And with outstretched hands, pointing out my figure, the sergeant was powered backwards, and despite his best attempt to battle the current, was sucked into a flurry of dust.

'I'm sorry, love,' said Clarice, barging in. 'I wanted to check everything was hunky-dory.'

Joy massaged her sides for warmth.

'Still smells of smoke in here and it's a bit parky. Best I put another blanket on the bed for you tonight.'

But to Joy the nippiness had been expelled along with the latest phenomenon, thrown back into the tucks of time, and with it another layer of the smog that had been dimming her reason.

TWELVE

DESPITE THE VISION, Joy had embraced sleep and, as always, awoke abruptly. The shadowed corners of the room seemed to suck in the shrill wind as the fireplace blew a smokiness into the air.

Through the window, a crinkled dawn was waking the countryside as the dreary heavy sky, browbeaten by the sea gusts, goosed the clinging snow high into the trees. The torrent of rain had left a muddy slush, but some white globs still held the red brick walls, and thawing pocked holes revealed nature's shades here and there.

Joy stared at the three paintings. Possibly by the same unpractised hand. An immense rock plonked in the sea, although the roughly plastered brushstrokes made all uncertain. The other similar to the first, a stormy seascape, but this time framed from a window, a clifftop retreat.

As she padded back to the bed, the faint strains of childish songs crept into her head, echoing around the walls and ceiling of the room. The light above swayed slightly as a rush of wind buffeted the window.

Joy almost wagged a finger, admonishing the past for toying with her, and attempting to lock it away, busied herself with her coins.

The house itself, the guests and their stewing fusses appeared to be still snoring away happily. But Joy's ears picked up a noise down on the patio: a squeak then a creak. Again, a squeak then a creak. She ran to the window and drew back the curtains expecting to see a winter robin chirping in the day, but there was nothing visible just the snow and the wind.

Immediately below, the terrace was mottled with clumps of icy sludge and as the path stretched around the side of the house, Joy spotted something she might have missed, it wasn't of much import, but perhaps…? She frowned and pinched her nose.

Huddling back into the warmth of the bedsheets, she passed up on her knitting and took out her notebook. Adding to her list, she then did some scratching out. The soft pencil felt good on the paper. And contentedly setting it aside, she propped herself up on her pillows and waited for Clarice and the clamour of another day at Misenlake.

Perry Scanner welcomed them to breakfast. 'Morning ladies, you've missed all the excitement.'

'Really?' answered Clarice distantly.

Joy sat down to her porridge. The table was full of absent spaces. Beside Scanner, there were only Kosik and Gracie.

'Mrs Pomp was the first recipient of hot water and has closeted herself away in her room, presumably cleaning and preening,' said Scanner with his usual casualness.

'And the others?' asked Clarice.

'Gloss is supervising the laundry, stacking wood, and making himself busy with his inexhaustible home-grown expertise. Our American is assisting, or so he says, and dear Miss Royce, resplendent in a spectacular bathrobe, informs us that she intends to bathe in one of the vast tubs.'

'Oh my!' said Clarice.

'Oh my, indeed!' replied Scanner. 'A washbasin insufficient for our resident beauty it would seem.'

'And Barasch,' announced Kosik in a quiet voice, 'has lost his wits and has fled the manor.'

'What?' cried Clarice, choking on her toast.

'Ah yes, our doctor impostor took umbrage at the snooping policemen and clumped up the stairs, and returning with his case, made haste and trudged out into the elements exclaiming some nonsense about being a prisoner before, and vowed never to be again.' Scanner lit a cigarette.

'Dearie me!' Clarice said, wolfing her food.

'Prim didn't seem too concerned. Said he wouldn't get far as the snowbanks were the size of Everest and the paths impassable. Seems our policeman was out detecting very early this morning.'

Gracie smiled a hello at Joy and addressed Clarice. 'I intend to let the sea blow away all my cobwebs today. I've been cooped up too long with all this fuss. I've not come all this way to not take a peek at the coastline.'

This was quite a statement for Gracie, thought Joy. The woman had barely said two words in company since she'd been here. But this was good news – to see the sea at last!

'Is that wise?' asked Clarice. 'Or even safe?'

'Aye,' she answered. 'I've spoken at length with that helpful Mr Gloss. He informs me that there's a pathway beside the rail tunnel that leads up to the headland. It's quite steep, but manageable. He even offered to accompany me and suggested if you were to join us he would enlist the help of young Ernest, the gardener's boy.'

'A boy!' exclaimed Joy involuntarily. It had become an annoying habit. 'And the sea. You did promise, please?'

Clarice looked uncertain.

Gracie turned her eyes on Clarice. 'What do you think? Will you take a turn with me?'

'We will!' cried Joy.

Clarice smiled. 'If Mr Gloss says it's safe, and we're careful, then let's give it a go. As you say, gets us away from this place for a bit and if the boy is willing to scout for us – I'm sure it must be safe enough.'

With perfect timing Gloss entered the room and immediately loaded up a plate with scrambled eggs. 'A right to-do out there,' he said in between mouthfuls. 'Miss Royce is at full throttle. Grauler is insisting he stands guard outside the laundry. She's been accusing him of all sorts. But he's not for budging. Banging on about her not being left alone, undefended. I left them to it.'

'No sign of Barasch?' Kosik asked.

'No, unfortunately not. But Prim's out and about sleuthing, so I shouldn't worry. For once I suspect our policeman's right. The roads still look the devil of a muddle.'

'And the telephone?' Gracie asked.

'Yes, I had thought of that. Prim tells me Miss Crabb says the darned thing is still out of order. Presumably they've been unable to get out and fix the lines.'

Kosik pushed his chair back and bowed to the table. 'A cigarette and some air I think.'

'You won't join us up on the coastal path?' Gloss questioned.

Kosik shook his head and vanished through the patio doors.

'You'll have to count me out,' Scanner said. 'Gammy leg not up to hiking. Anyway, I'm going to see if Prim will allow me a nose at Melville's maps. I can't help but think perhaps there's a clue among them.'

'Well, ladies. All set? Wrap up warm. I'll dig out some capes and wellies and chivvy up young Ernest. Sea air will do us all the world of good.'

They tottered out into the sogginess. Gloss and Gracie led the way, with Clarice taking Ernest's arm and bringing up the rear.

Although frayed and glum described the outlook, and the air was icy fresh with still sniffs of swirling snow, Joy felt overwrapped. It wasn't anywhere near as cold as it had looked from within the cooking mansion.

She'd never been a ready walker. She didn't see the point unless you had somewhere specific to get to. Clarice's cries had ended her daydreams and she'd been forced to slosh through the field to catch up.

Gloss had halted ahead of them, and stood waiting. Joy huffed, her chest heaving.

'Right,' explained Gloss. 'See those crags over there? Beyond them is a gulley of worn steps. Then the land rises quite steeply up to the coast, and another path snakes down into a man-made disused rail tunnel that leads to the apex of the cove, a sort of platform. That's where the alum works had a pulley system to bring up the whiffy loads. Come on, I'll show you. Shake a leg.'

They reached the slash in the land and began to struggle upward. The pathway to the cove forked to the right. Gracie poked a nose and almost slipped.

Gloss grabbed her arm. 'Steady there! That's why we won't be heading that way.'

Gracie seemed a bit peeved, but soon cheered up when Gloss pointed to the crest of the hill where a more gradually sloping path opened out onto the tufty shoulder of the clifftop. 'You'll have to mind your step a bit. Gracie, no more near misses. You grab a hold of me, and the rest of you ladies, please take one of Ernest's arms. His young legs will steady you.'

'Where was Monckton found?' Gracie asked, glancing back.

'Monckton? Why? We've passed his spot.'

Joy turned and stared.

'Just there, at the foot of this incline.' Gloss pointed out two boulders. 'Those ferns you can see, they hide the pathway onto the ruins of the alum factory. Just through the scrub there, although it's grown over quite a bit.'

'Bad business, miss,' Ernest remarked, blowing breath on his cupped-hands.

'Indeed. Now everyone – are we set?' Gloss grinned, and hugging himself for warmth, made a circle of his arm for Gracie to grasp and off they set at a brisk pace.

Joy shivered. The ferocious salty wind watered her eyes and the gusts made it intolerable.

In the distance, propped on an outcrop, there was a run-down-looking hut, and below that a seaweed-strewn strip of shingle.

Gracie was all for making for the cabin, but the snow was packed tight, clumps of ice proving almost impossible to judge. Gloss was having none of it and had soon turned them back.

The sea had waved them on their way. It had seemed almost gladiatorial as it goaded them to stand and fight its titanic gusts, the waves smashing and bashing at the rockface, spray spurting up almost turning to icicles as it twisted in the air.

Gracie had grumbled a bit, grousing all the way back. 'I'm Scottish. I'm not afeard of the weather,' she'd said. But Gloss had been adamant and they'd soon been shepherded back to the steaminess of the manor.

Wet things and damp socks removed, they all met in the library where they found Mrs Pomp at a desk writing a letter. She hastily slid off her pince-nez as they entered.

'Been out for a jaunt?' she observed. 'Rather you than me. I'm sure the air must have been quite refreshing for you all, and indeed I feel most invigorated myself now that I've been able to spruce up a bit.'

They all smiled at Mrs Pomp's sunny face.

But Joy suddenly felt sad for her. She was alone in a world that had always been her husband's to forge; follow the regiment, ensure Brigadier Pomp was never without a clean shirt. It was not a lot unlike Joy's existence in reality. Order and routine ensuring a safety of spirit.

Kosik ambled by and within moments Gloss came blustering in. 'Two drowned rats in the hallway. Best come and see,' he said.

With a scraping of chairs, they all hurried out.

In the hallway, a ruddy-faced Nouse was gurning as Barasch was kicking off his boots.

Prim was suddenly amongst them. 'Nouse, glad to have you back. And it appears like one of the wisemen, you have come bearing gifts.'

Barasch growled and cursed under his breath and marched off up the stairs.

The other rat was Grauler. He was swathed in towels and an oversized dressing gown. 'All very well you gaping, but some goon has just had a pop at me.'

Everyone looked bemused.

'You not hearing me? Some clown has just tried to kill me!'

'Kill you?' Prim screeched.

Grauler was ushered into the drawing room by the policeman. The others huddled in behind him.

'Explain to me what happened, Mr Grauler,' Prim demanded.

'Somebody tried to drown me, simple as that.'

'Drown you?'

'Yeh, out there, in the tub – you know, in that damned fool limey laundry.' Grauler towel-dried his hair. 'I was enjoying the warming water, sitting nice and pretty, albeit Miss Royce's dregs, you know, when some maniac tried to clout me with one of those paddles – the ones they use to spin the dirty washing with.'

'Did you get a look at their face?'

Grauler almost exploded from his armchair. 'Of course I didn't, Sherlock god-damned holy Holmes. I was three feet under fighting for my life.'

'No need to get upset, sir.'

'Upset. I came here for a festive British Christmas, not a real life *Agatha Christie* novel'

'What's all the commotion?' Rebecca Royce sashayed in, her hair in a turban, her make-up immaculate.

'Was it you that clumped me? Some sort of whacky British broad caper?'

'I've no idea what you're talking about,' Rebecca Royce replied icily. 'After the rather crude ablutions, I made straight for my room. Anyway, you said you were bolting the door when I left.'

'That's right. And I did!'

'Then how, sir, did your assailant gain entry?' Prim pointed a finger.

They all looked at Grauler, whose face twisted in puzzlement as he dredged his brain for a solution.

'Unless your attacker was already in the laundry, hidden away?' Prim suggested.

'Most unlikely,' answered Rebecca Royce. 'I don't want to quibble, but my gallant protector here stood guard while I bathed, or so he said.'

'Is that true?'

'Well that's where he was when I left him,' volunteered Gloss.

'I had a cigarette. Waited my turn. Nobody could've got by me,' said

Grauler grouchily.

'You didn't leave the door even for a second?'

'Hey, what do you take me for? Some kind of Peeping Tom or something?'

'Perhaps our murderous professor can glide through solid walls as well as brain gardeners from above.' Scanner cringed theatrically as Prim shot him a dark glare.

The room simmered.

'Exactly,' said Prim fingering his pencil moustache. 'If Mr Grauler is able to spare us a few minutes more, let's see if we can't explain where we all were when this latest affair took place.'

'Barasch is still upstairs,' Kosik remarked.

'Well, he was most probably with me,' said Nouse. 'Waist-deep he was, but I soon pulled him out. Lips were as blue as my uniform. Was in poor shape.'

'But that's hardly an alibi, Constable.'

'Suppose not.'

'Miss Royce?'

'As I said, I went directly to my room.'

Miss Biddle and Kosik also confirmed that they were alone in their bedrooms.

'I was in the library,' Mrs Pomp informed them.

'Alone?' queried Prim.

'Well, I was until the three ladies joined me.'

'And you three?'

'We were in our rooms drying off,' Clarice said.

'So was I,' said Gloss.

'And finally, Mr Scanner?'

'I was taking a peek at Melville's maps. So, I was alone in here until I heard all the commotion.'

Prim stood tall and thrust his hands in his pockets. 'So, yet again, nobody has an alibi. It could have been any one of you.'

'Or our mad professor,' Scanner quipped once more.

And then the clock struck eleven.

The steaminess of the broiling room dissipated, and a stiff chill summoned a vaporous curtain as the burbling chuntering of Joy's fellow guests slipped to a murmur. The tock of the clock, the rustle of papers, and a nebulous imprecision pawed at the room as Joy felt herself being carried along as if on a ghoulish fairground ride. The mugginess began to clear as did the netlike ether, and yet again Joy found herself plonked down in the past.

'Hem!' I must say, this time I felt more than a little bit manhandled. Taken directly from the furore of the present and launched into the past without the gradual easing. And I can't say I was getting the hang of it, but then, how could anyone? In truth, this enervating spontaneity was beginning to wear a bit thin. I was starting to struggle both physically and mentally. But I just knew I had to withstand it, persist; it was too important to think only of myself.

Here I was again, as if an usher had settled me down for the second half of a play, short of the customary choc-ice, of course. The light-headiness propelled me forward, and staggering, I groped for the refuge of a nearby chair. I scarcely knew what I was doing.

And there was the inspector shuffling his papers and stuffing them into his briefcase. With a sigh, he batted away the protestations of his sergeant.

Again the young woman appeared to be absent.

'Look, Coupar. Believe me, it's over,' the tutting inspector began. 'This case is now closed, and however heartrending, which as we both know this horrible episode has truly been, Miss Ines will stand trial and potentially be found guilty of the crime.'

'But sir …'

'Please, Coupar. We have worked together for too long. If you are once more about to regale me with your pronouncements about there being no body to confirm the crime or bombard me with your interminable entreaties of your legendary gut instinct, I may well throw you out of the window.'

'Sir. There's more to this than we have been shown …'

'Coupar!'

'But, sir. I'm certain of it. What about this disgraced tutor and the former governess?'

'Ah, that again. It's all been corroborated. After their … liaison and they were both dismissed, the former governess, a Madame Dalliante, fled to America to start a new life. So she will have an alibi. The tutor involved, a Mr Wolfe, relocated to London along with his wife, and I'm told started a family. They have also accounted for their whereabouts.'

'And this other local girl that's gone missing?' Coupar persisted. 'There might be a link there.'

The inspector sighed. 'I admire your diligence, Sergeant, but that girl left a note. Run off to her mother's for a bit. You know how these young things can be these days.'

'But she's barely sixteen, sir. All I'm saying …'

'Enough of this. That's a job for the welfare. We were brought here to solve this case, and by my reckoning, we have done so beyond reasonable doubt.'

'With that the inspector pushed past Coupar. 'We have a train to catch. A carriage will be outside in five minutes.'

Left alone, Coupar went to the window. He stood silently for a bit staring into the distance. 'She's innocent. I know it,' he muttered.

'You're right,' I blurted out.

Coupar twisted around, but the light dimmed and a sucking miasma engulfed me. The sergeant's words drifted into a distant hum. 'I need to prove it. I need …' But his voice was drowned out by a raucous din. The room came back. So did the light.

The past had slipped away and Joy was once more in the midst of chaotic panic.

Everyone was in a funk and getting louder and more animated as they attempted to make themselves heard. It was hell.

Prim brought a halt to the hysterical outrage. For once he managed to say something that held everyone's attention. 'So, Constable Nouse. How was it in the village?'

Everyone turned to the PC, who doffed at his forehead and gabbled a bit. He appeared to be saying that the trek to village had not been for the fainthearted, or words to that effect, and something being a reet bugger that had given him a proper monk. And aye, the telephone line had been restored. And never fear, he'd managed to get on the blower and make a call to those clever folk down at the Yard. They'd send forensics, for certain. And plain-clothes fellows, and most definitely, a senior detective.

Prim winced.

And no, he hadn't been able to get an answer from that Frenchie agency, but had given their details to Scotland Yard.

With a jabbing finger, he was definite that there was a chance that the roads beyond the village were passable, but he had been told by those that know these things that both north to Whitby and south to Scarborough, the byways were caked in the filthy stuff, deep snowdrifts everywhere.

He'd made it back after stowing away at his ma's and seeing she was all set and cosy, and after a good feed, had high-tailed it back to Misenlake where, in passing, he'd come across Doctor Barasch stuck up to his kegs like a ratter in a hole.

Nouse tailed off with a vague waft of his hand, and a mirthful simper which nobody really understood, but seemed to evince hilarity for the likeable constable.

Grauler was first to leave, god-damning Limeys and swearing nobody gave a fig for his safety. 'Somebody just tried to kill me and I have an idea who it was. I will be taking my own precautions from now on,' he shouted rather too exuberantly from the hall.

The stunned room emptied in dribs and drabs. Joy wandered to the window and peered out into the grounds. More flutters of snow had begun to fall. They were in for another smattering.

Lunch and late into the afternoon the assembled gathering debated their situation. Nerves were frayed and arguments sparked up around the library like fresh kindle on the dying fire. One thing they all appeared to be agreed on is that they all wanted away.

That is excepting Joy and Gracie and rather surprisingly, Miss Biddle.

Miss Biddle appeared to be one of the more remote of the group, excepting her huddles with Grauler. The odd couple had really chummed-up and their trysts had prompted Mrs Pomp to speculate that Miss Biddle was 'setting her cap at him,' which to Joy sounded bizarre as it was obvious the American's only paramour was hard cash.

Miss Biddle, bombed out in the war, as she tirelessly pointed out, was left with little more than what she was wearing and the contents of her case. And unless there was an inheritance adrift somewhere in the background, Fuzzy Grauler was lost to her.

Joy did notice that the unlikely companions managed to find moments to slip away, but there had to be another explanation – some common interest. The comforts of the manor were a relief to Miss Biddle, and murders or not, she wouldn't be in a rush to head back to the rebranded rubble that was now the East End of London.

Gracie was similar. She seemed a bit of a loner and definitely embraced everything Misenlake had to offer. Joy had captured her sniffing around the corridors, peering at the paintings, and wistfully eyeing the grounds. Their trip to the cliffs had been her invention, and the way she caressed the buffed furniture showed a sort of reverence to the past. Despite the events, she appeared to be relishing her stay.

Joy sat with her knitting, switching off her mind to everything bar the music of the needles.

Dinner came and went. Rabbit or so they surmised. Rebecca Royce had almost immediately pushed away her plate and sauntered off to the library.

Barasch had locked himself in his room despite Kosik's polite knocks at his door.

Gracie was next. A book and an early night.

Mrs Pomp was pooped.

Prim had dipped in and notified them that the telephones were still out of service.

So in the library, a stifling fire saw Rebecca Royce smoking with Kosik. Perry Scanner poring through the old family photographs, and Joy and Clarice on the sofa.

Having sized up the porcelain like a bored window-shopper, Grauler had indulged in a throwaway chat with Gloss at the window before grumbling that his perilous situation was being ignored, and grabbing a brim-full decanter, he announced that he was off to the safety of his room.

Miss Biddle made her excuses and followed on behind.

Kosik thumped down another drink. He was on a mission and had been drinking at a furious rate all evening. His eyes were glassy, but other than a glistening sweatiness, he seemed unbothered.

'So, what's next for you, old boy?' asked Gloss. 'Home to Poland?'

'Home? This is not how I would call it. The Soviets have installed a puppet government and our own politicians remain in exile here in England. The Bolsheviks steal our land, shrink our borders. The Nazis murdered our people and yet now they are defeated, we remain at war, just with a different, but equally merciless foe.' Kosik refilled his glass.

'So you going to hang around in Blighty?' Gloss quizzed.

'For what? The likes of our Miss Biddle to insult me and wish me gone? Your people have short memories. Too many of my comrades lie dead in the English Channel for me to even recall all their names. But their faces never leave me. And yet, some of the Nazi scum remain at large. It seems the spoils, they are not for likes of us.'

Clarice coughed. 'Shall we go up, dear?' she suggested to Joy. And not waiting for a reply, made her way out of the room.

Joy dipped her head and followed.

But once in her bedroom, Joy found that she wasn't tired. She set down yet another train of thoughts and also a range of things she had in mind to do when, at last, they finally returned home. She shuffled her coins and set them straight. Repeating this four times, she stole in and out of bed and reorganised the dressing table; the brush at a right angle to her scent, the music box pushed back against the mirror, then pulled forward an inch.

Snores boomed through the wall from next door, a proper symphony. A rasping rattle offered respite for a second before, again, the horrendous snorting and wheezing continued. Hoping for the chorus to come to an end, and that there were no demands for an encore, Joy dumped her head into her pillow, willing sleep upon her.

But it was hopeless. One thing for sure, if Grauler was really in fear of his life, he certainly wasn't allowing anxiety to interrupt his sleep. A proper racket!

In the end, Joy resorted to putting her hands over her ears. The snoring grew worse. She then tried a pillow.

Out of bed, she perched on the solitary chair and drew her knees up to her chest. She was now fully awake, and unsurprisingly her mind was jabbing at her reason. Usually for her, classifying stuff was easy. Dump one in undivided and file the other as nuisance.

But these unworldly experiences had destroyed her normal steadiness. It had made her feel lopsided as if in deep water with no comfort of sand sifting between her toes. She was becoming niggly, but only within herself. What if this freshly acquired specialness was going to continue forever? Was it just this spooky house that had awakened her senses, or more worryingly, had she suddenly developed some sort of second sight? It was as if a spot test had been thrust upon her, and she knew she hadn't done the revision.

Knitting had always been the answer, and she needed its grounding more than ever. But searching around her bed, Joy realised that in Clarice's hurry to depart the library she had left her bag of wool behind.

She could nip downstairs, but what if she came across another guest in her scruffy dressing gown? Clarice was always nagging for her to buy a replacement, but Joy loved the reassurance of the tatty and bobbled veteran, and despite it being almost indecently short, she wouldn't give it up. It was as if the fleecy cotton was part of her, had somehow recorded her past, folded it neatly, gave certainty, like returning to a familiar book as opposed to daring something new.

Joy huffed and puffed a bit, but was unequivocal. She couldn't do without. Listening at the door, she was reassured by the noiseless corridor, and had just steeled herself to trot down and retrieve her needles when she heard footsteps tripping towards her from the far end of the corridor. She pulled back and waited. A squeaky floorboard somewhere near Clarice's room was soon followed by a soft padding nearby. A faint tap, then a whisper. Absolutely a woman's voice, then, a sagging sigh followed by steps slipping away.

Calming her breath, Joy opened the door an inch. But closed it again in a hurry. More tip-toey treads this time coming from the other end of the passage. Softly trod, like stockinged feet. Another light knock on wood and this time the creak of a door opening and closing.

Joy dashed back to her bed and huddled into the covers like a naughty child up too late. She listened to her breath. An ominous stillness hung over the house. It was as if she could almost hear Misenlake slipping its ball and chains, ready to torture its unwanted intruders, reveal what they'd let themselves in for.

Grauler's barks and rasps broke the silence. He sputtered, then chuntered unintelligibly, and with another croak seemed to finally settle.

Joy slipped out of bed and went to the door. She waited a bit. Shivering, she pulled her dressing gown cord tight and ventured into the passage. A dim glow of light stretched to the stairway.

Joy bit her lip. Her chamber held the corner on the south side of the house, above the library, annoyingly the furthest from the staircase. She made a dash. Past her aunt's room, she skirted the gallery and hot-footed it down the stairs.

The library was in darkness, barring a barb of moonlight that speared through a slit in the drapes. Joy soon found her bag under the settee and was just on her way back when the light was flicked on.

'What are you doing up?' It was Prim.

'Getting my knitting. I couldn't sleep,' Joy responded hastily.

Prim looked unconvinced. His eyes were pinholes, and his hair was ruffled. It was as if Joy had just woken him.

She tried to pass, but an arm barred her escape.

'No hurry.' Prim gestured for Joy to sit, but backing up a step, she set her eyes on a fixed point on the wall beyond him.

'As you wish, but it's time for you to be brought into the real world, a few home truths, young lady,' he began. Straightening his waistcoat, he then fashioned his hair. 'Policing isn't easy. I make a point of always seeking to engage with my adversary. That is what makes a proper copper and ensures results.'

Joy groaned inside. This could be a long drawn-out monologue. She tried to pass by again.

He waggled an admonishing finger and stood firmly in her path. 'Over the years, and particularly when I was in the military, I came across a lot of your sort.' Prim smoothed his sprouting moustache and came a little too close. Joy could smell a nasty tang on his breath.

'Deserters, shirkers, malingerers and even some of the officer class who had had their fill of war and could no longer bear the constant stench of death.'

Joy gripped her bag and tried to curtail a whimper of frustration.

'But this so-called mental frailty, battle fatigue – shamming I called it, and the doctors … well, don't get me started.'

Joy marbled her eyes and tried to hide within herself. It was unclear when this would end.

'You're just like them really. Of course, you plead your sex, your age and of course your particular vulnerability. But Prim is no numbskull. You may fool others, but I sense that you're hiding behind this act of yours, this piddling whimsy. You feign being some sort of ninny, a half-wit? Pah – Prim won't have it!'

Joy skirted the furniture, seeking another way past.

Prim danced in front of her, cutting her off. 'I will be honest with you. While I haven't quite got your measure – well, not as yet anyway – I will get there. And that, young lady, is a promise. I always do in the end. It is evident that you know more that you're admitting. I just don't know what it is that you're keeping back, and even more bemusing, is I can't comprehend why.'

Joy fought back forming tears. 'Were you upstairs just now?' She hit back.

Something caught in Prim's throat.

'I thought you were supposed to …'

'Constable Nouse and I are sharing shifts. I err …'

'I can go now?' Joy asked. 'You're done?'

Prim waved her away with a flourish of his hand and headed to the window.

As Joy left the room, she looked back. Prim was staring out into the darkness. The man was clearly fighting a rear guard against his own demons. Until he could confront these torments, his own prejudices, he would never achieve all that he wished. It was really up to him.

Joy scooted up the stairs and sped back to her room. Panting and listening to the grumbles of the house as it settled for the night, with a puff, she took up her knitting and brushed away thoughts of Prim. This detective didn't deserve further thought. She felt sorry for him, but only a little.

The rhythmic clicking banished the ructions of the night and Joy began to doze. A thud sent her bolt upright. Her door, always wedged open an inch or two had slammed. Possibly the wind. Joy slipped out of bed and readjusted the card, propping the door open an inch.

Her eyes caught the watercolours once more. Thankfully the jigging speck was no longer running and the shingly beach held no phantoms. But the sea seemed to holler, the waves roll and the rocks spatter. Joy shook off a self-indulgent shudder and slipped back into bed, thrusting the sheets up under her chin.

A murmur piped somewhere from the shadows, followed by a hissing sound followed by a distinct giggle. Again the door swung open, slamming on its hinges, and a honeyed scent sprang up and a lick of wind feathered her face, and then close by, she heard the sound of a child singing.

'Little Bo Peep has lost a sheep and doesn't know where to find her. Leave her alone and she may come home, wagging her tail behind her.'

Another titter followed and the sound of running steps and yet more childlike laughter whistled out into the hallway.

'Hem!' This time I was absolutely terrified. This capricious house just would not let up. Steps in the corridor, the whistling flue and clanking pipes, and now these ghoulish voices. I sat helplessly peering into the dancing shades. The ghostly echoes came again, hanging in the eddies, slipping around the walls and gliding on the drifting draughts, willing me out of the safety of the bedclothes.

But these lurking phantoms, unlike the others, seemed loath to show themselves. I held myself together, I just had to. Another disclosure was brewing, and with it again the strong feeling that Misenlake was insistent that I bear witness.

All of which sounds a darned touch braver than I felt. In fact, another titter from under my bed sent me shuffling further into the covers. The temptation was there – pull the blankets high and shut your eyes and ears.

But Misenlake wasn't done. It rumbled again. The windows rattled and the doors shifted and groaned. Rather than wait, I cursed myself and leapt up.

Slippers and dressing gown and a gulp of courage and I was in the corridor. It was freezing. I could see my own breath. I realised I was panting like a mad thing.

A streak of light zipped past me and fizzed around the corner of the passage. I grunted in annoyance, but hurried after it. Then with a swish, the light reappeared, and with it, a child's snickering, taunting me again, before tripping away into the gloom as if to lure me into a game of catch-me-if-you-can.

I stopped for a second as the appealing ripples seemed to roll over the ceiling and race back past me and towards my room. But then I heard a whisper close by, beckoning, and yet again the sound of scurrying feet moving ahead of me in the murk.

The corridor tapered, a slip of a passage leading to a dead end. I was now at the back of the house. I snooped to my right and spied the most solid of mahogany doors. Its sturdy timber seemed out of place in all this flimsiness; walls of Essex board presumably slung up by the army stretched either side of me. Opposite was a shuttered door, a concertina effect, potentially a servants' aid.

The sniggering and giggles had now disappeared, and the skipping steps were no more. I stood for a second, and then decided to turn back, but paused, drawn by a burr of voices; harsh words, a fencing argument. I nibbled a look over the bannister and eyed the reception hall below. But there was no Prim, no Nouse; the hallway was empty.

Again murmurs hummed and rose close by. Then somebody shrieked angrily. A softer tone remonstrated. I strained to hear, but the words were unmanageable.

The floorboard creaked beneath me, and the chat momentarily ceased. I felt for my nose, prodding it thrice. Temptation rose in me and for some reckless reason, I reached out for the heavy door, revelling in the smoothness of the wood.

The voices re-engaged and then the sound of tapping feet drew near followed by a series of squeaks and a carping tone.

Something told me it was time to leave. The past had done with me for now and I had no compulsion to confront the present. Whoever was inside the room wouldn't welcome my snooping. I ran away like a coward chasing a custard.

Back in bed, the cold sheets smelt fresh bringing reality back. The room was back how it should be, the sickly-sweetness that had coated the air had gone, and with it the past had thankfully retreated.

Lying back, Joy found some courage again. She whistled a tune to herself, a rhyme from school as she dared herself to summon the naughty child. But the giggling and the melodies would not return. The crimp in time had melded into the darkness once again.

THIRTEEN

THE POLAR BLASTS prickled Joy's cheeks as she stepped out into the awakening morning. As the darkness lifted, the sky had more of a fluffiness to it, paler, more hospitable than the unforgiving gloom they'd been subjected to since they'd arrived.

The terrace had been partially cleared, but compressed snow had turned to ice, making walking a tip-tappy affair to avoid a heavy fall.

Joy's brogues slipped and slapped as she tottered around the side of the house.

To her left, she noted a concreted slope, perhaps once a set of steps now moulded flat. It led down to the path where Slack had been found. It was icy and precarious, but Joy was still tempted to have some fun, a bit of a slide. Vague murmurs from the house changed her choice. She was inclined to have a poke around the rear of the manor before the house totally awoke. There was something she needed to see.

The walkway, as Slack had told her, wrapped itself around the side of the house and led to much denser snow. Thin tracks formed hillocks of ice that halted at the back door, which was locked.

Further on, the snow rose, deeper drifts lay piled up, holding a wooden fence and beyond that a timber structure, possibly a storeroom or the wall of the stable block. There was no way through. She'd seen enough, but her stockinged feet already soaking, Joy decided to use her freedom to take a look at the disused alum works, and crunched onward over the frosted grounds.

Glancing back, she could see the manor was now bathed in a mustardy haze which grew smoggier as lights began to burn at some of the windows. Misenlake was stirring itself.

Reaching the set of boulders, Joy spotted the remnants of a stain, a pink tinge to the slush. She halted a moment, but steeling herself pushed on through the scrub. The track was uneven and overgrown and the wishy-washy sun filtering through the shifting clouds did little to smother the chill as the glistening greenery flung its dripping wetness about her.

There were no mantraps here. No pincers ready to snap her ankles, just a path leading to a clearing filled with partially-fallen flint walls and a sunken impression, the markings of a building, the alum works as once was.

Beyond was another rather forlorn structure, the rotting remains of a mill staggering like an old man groping for his walking frame.

Joy skirted the ruins and prodded a toe at some rusted iron. There was nothing here; a worn-out workhorse, its energy long spent, no use to anyone and left to moulder. All the industry that had once filled this place had long gone, leaving just a haunted set of carcasses open to the ruthless and unrelenting elements. The whole area held a grimness like a Christmas tree dumped after the celebrations were over.

A gull squawked and a sudden saltiness on the wind reminded Joy that the sea was near at hand. She tracked back and took the trail up to the headland and was soon staring down at the foaming torrent. The tide was low and the brownish waves rushed over the silty pebbles below before retreating into the froth.

Joy tramped over the undulating hillocks until she reached the cabin that Gracie had been so anxious to explore. There were no panes in the windows, and a door hung limply on rusted hinges. Inside, the once stout wooden floorboards were damp and sagging and the lightest of steps roused gripes and whines.

A chair had been left, but little else other than a chest with sullied sheets, a few brushes and some folded drapes.

Joy went to the window and stared into the distance where the rolling surf met the sepulchral slashes in the sky. The bucking waves held Joy in the moment, an indulgent trance as she let her eyes meld with the haze.

A fancy of delight, as if the first spring sunshine radiated up and over her, and inside a blissful glow spread as tingles flickered down her arms to the tips of her fingers.

Joy hugged her shoulders, then massaged her arms. A pin-edge caught her finger, a sharpness on her chest, shining metal, a gift of love – and then she was interrupted by a knock and a voice.

'Hello? Is anybody there?'

Joy jerked and shrank back into the harsh shadows of the cold winters morning.

Gracie's head popped around the door. 'Oh! Thank the Lord, it's just you, Joy. I was worried – you know – with all these goings-on. Anyway, great minds, it would appear.'

Joy flinched a hello. 'I was just heading back.'

'All right then. Don't be afeard of Gracie. I'll come with you, if you don't mind an old 'un for company?'

Joy looked blankly at Gracie. The woman half-smiled and hesitated, as people did, expecting a reply.

'Well, I'm sure your aunt would want me to see you safe,' Gracie added, filling the gap. 'She's not aware you're out for a stroll?'

Joy hid again behind glazed eyes. It saved awkwardness.

'Beautiful up here in a rugged sort of way, don't you think?' said Gracie after a while. 'A place where mebbe your soul might settle and these mighty winds purge all the bad things from the past.'

'I like the sea,' Joy eventually replied.

Gracie face brightened. 'I do too.'

At the mouth of the tunnel, Gracie stopped. 'I fancy a peek at the mysterious cove. You care to join me?'

Joy sniffed the briny breeze. 'No. There's nothing for me there.'

Gracie tilted her head to one side as if confused, but Joy dodged her gaze and was gone, striding back to the manor.

Joy made her way into breakfast wearing her slippers and suffering from a proper telling-off. Her shoes were drying by Clarice's hearth and the ruined stockings were in the bin.

Gracie was already there, the cove presumably a brief spectacle even for her unbounding enthusiasm.

A rapid glance around the table confirmed an almost a full house; only Grauler and Rebecca Royce, who rarely made it down before mid-morning, were missing.

'The way he was whacking down the fiery stuff last night, I'd be surprised if we see him before supper,' remarked Perry Scanner.

Joy recalled the cacophonous snores and endorsed his view.

'Do you suppose he was earnest about that drowning incident?' asked Gloss.

'Why would he make it up?' Miss Biddle said, pouring herself another cuppa.

'Attention most likely,' suggested Mrs Pomp.

'Or to divert suspicion,' Kosik speculated.

'I suspect he had a fright. It can happen. Stress, and being cooped up can do strange things to the mind,' Barasch muttered. He looked unwell. His flirt with freedom had shaken him, his eyes were dull, and black blotches sagged behind his bug-eyed glasses.

'Well, it's hardly a holiday camp, is it? Guests and servants dropping like flies,' Gloss said, munching on a sausage.

'Spare me,' said Mrs Pomp. 'How anybody would want to spend a night in one of Mr Butlin's hellholes is stretching belief.'

'What's wrong with 'em?' yapped Miss Biddle. 'Everyone needs a break and a bit of fun after the last few years. Rationing was supposed to end, but it's just got worse. You'll be telling us next that it's only the upper classes that should be allowed to go out for their tea. Well, this Labour government will shake some vim into this blinkin' unfairness. Lah-de-bloody-dah!'

Mrs Pomp kept her eyes on her eggs.

'Ninety-eight per cent income tax is certainly going to shake out something,' Scanner said.

Miss Biddle's glowering face returned to her teacup.

Nouse's jovial features surfaced at the door. 'Sorry to interrupt, ladies and gents. But DS Prim would like you all in the drawing room at ten. Inspector Dunkley from the Yard has arrived with a couple of plain-clothes and he wanted to do the necessaries – if you get my meaning?'

Then with a tap on the side of his nose he was gone.

'Well, heaven's praise, Scotland Yard has finally arrived,' said Rebecca Royce as she swanned in wearing a skimpy blouse and infeasibly high-heeled sandals.

Joy yearned for the shoes instantly.

'Dunkley of the Yard. It does have a sort of reassuring ring to it,' Scanner said.

'Let's hope he relieves us of this preening Prim and his horrendous hackneyed phrases.' said Rebecca Royce. 'Possibly one of us might actually make it through this most catastrophic Christmas.'

Prim's tie was tight to his collar and his hair was combed back neatly.

Joy sniped at the clock. Just after ten. Unless this was a lengthy interview, she'd be spared another kidnapping.

A closer look showed that the wooden pendulum had become stuck. The tick-tock had halted as if time had been frozen. The last hallucination had almost lacked energy, a funereal atmosphere of finality, wearisome; something told Joy that this room was done, that the events from all those years ago had moved on and Misenlake was now drawing Joy toward the winsome singing above the stairs.

The tall inspector had wanted to be away, was in a hurry, possibly to get to his next case, as if he'd been sullied by the happenings here.

Dunkley of the Yard unlike Prim, was as one would expect. A drawn complexion with the hue of greasy dishwater, but dogged attentive eyes that beamed like sapphires from beneath his thorny grey hair. Joy relaxed a smidge. This lawman's whole demeanour rumbled solidity, exuded order and radiated imposing confidence, and an earnestness within his beleaguered world.

His speech was mellow and measured, and during his understated introduction Joy got the impression he wouldn't be flustered even by the most desperate of predicaments; she instantly felt safer.

The rest of the gathering appeared to melt before him also. Suddenly a reassurance and growing notion of resolution washed over the room.

Unfortunately, that changed in a second. Miss Crabb hurried in. 'It's Mr Grauler. He's prone on his bed and still fully clothed. I fear he's dead!'

All eyes swept to Dunkley, who absorbed their stress with barely the hint of a blink.

A howl and a screaming fit halted the fretful hiatus.

Miss Biddle had collapsed sideways on the settee and buried her head in a cushion.

Gracie and Clarice hurried to comfort her.

'Nobody move!' said Prim, melodramatically.

Dunkley speedily raised a hand. 'On the contrary,' he said. 'Miss Crabb if you could ask the servants to arrange some tea. Constable Nouse if you could track down Graves and Stillwell and accompany them upstairs and check on Mr Grauler.'

Gloss jumped in. 'He's been murdered? But how …?'

Miss Biddle wailed all the more.

'It will obviously be necessary to examine the body.' Dunkley looked steadily at them. 'It is self-evident that the chances of all these deaths being accidental and unconnected is slimmer than remote.'

Prim coloured.

Dunkley's voice sharpened. 'Nouse, hurry, man. I will be up shortly. And ring for the local doctor.'

'You don't subscribe to the theory that Melville had something to do with all this?' asked Perry Scanner glaring pointedly at Prim.

'Unfortunately, from what I have thus far heard, I believe the professor was the catalyst for this litany of death and savagery, not the perpetrator.'

'But then where has he got to?' Mrs Pomp asked with a break in her voice.

Dunkley peered at the clock then studied his watch and frowned. 'If you will excuse me,' he said and duly clomped out of the room.

'Shall we all stay together, Inspector? Or possibly lock ourselves away? Hello – Inspector?' Mrs Pomp shrieked after him. 'The Brigadier would never have left us to fend …' But Dunkley had left.

Drabble entered with a tray of tea and the room smouldered to an edgy whisper. Miss Biddle managed a watery smile and blew her nose mightily as she sipped on her brew. Joy gagged back a smirk. Tea, the medicine of the masses.

'Well, this proves one thing,' said Kosik. 'Grauler was right. Somebody was out to get him, and after that failed attempt in the laundry, eventually he or she got their man.'

'She? You can't mean you believe …?'

'Unless he drank himself to death,' Scanner interrupted and offered Rebecca Royce a light. Her hands trembled as she blew blusters of smoke from her nostrils.

Joy's memory ran to the broken sleep in the night. Somebody had been about. She was certain it hadn't been Prim. His dishevelled appearance in the library had suggested twenty winks, snoozing on the job. And had Grauler paid the ultimate price?

Whoever had rapped on Grauler's door first, their knock had been unanswered. But it had been a woman. But had she returned? Or had there been two people padding about during the night? And when the snoring had thankfully abated, had that been the moment Grauler had been murdered? Joy's heart turned over. This she had to tell the new policeman. She could trust him. He would see the truth. Prim could fight his own rear guard.

Joy patted her nose three times. The child's eerie lullabies she would keep to herself for now. This chap Dunkley would hold no truck with tales of ghosts and spectres. And what if her mother had been right all along? Would this new policeman help them lock her away? Joy pummelled her fears into a ball and reached for her knitting. Pray that this Dunkley would resolve this mess; if not they were all doomed.

Miss Biddle had taken to her bed despite the obvious misgivings – her room being next door to Grauler's. Thankfully, Dunkley had steadied the ship. Grauler was to be removed to the ever-growing temporary mortuary, the now redundant tack room at the stables.

Nouse had been ordered to monitor the corridors and lock the door behind Biddle. The group were relieved. Miss Biddle's hysterics had finally brought a sense of reality to the houseguests. Another murder. Fear and dread had boiled to the surface and Dunkley's assured intimation had scraped away the last vestige of gallows humour and fatalistic bonhomie.

Barasch was deteriorating and had taken to grousing, muttering to himself and keeping clear of the others despite Kosik's attempts at reassurance.

The fire in the library having been once again plumped up, Mrs Pomp had likewise and had snivelled a request for company. This was duly obliged by Gracie and a tempering Rebecca Royce.

Scanner accosted Gloss and nudged him toward a desk, smoothing out some scrolls – Melville's maps.

'Let's get you out of those slippers and tidied up a bit,' said Clarice as she led Joy by the arm up to their rooms.

Their timing was unfortunate. The sheeted corpse was being lifted into the passage by Nouse and two others, presumably Graves and Stillwell. Prim was dithering alongside. They froze as they spotted Clarice.

A fussing Miss Crabb appeared from nowhere. 'Not the main staircase!

There is another way. You men, please follow me.'

She led them past the corner tower and toward the rear of the manor. Joy snooped after them, but was prodded into Clarice's room.

This room was definitely smaller than her own, poky in fact. Both their boltholes held a corner of the manor. They were berthed in an L-shaped set of chambers with the skinny bathroom in between. But whereas Joy's room had a sweeping view of the grounds to the front, Clarice only had a high window that gave a glimpse of the stable courtyard below. It was a cosy enough spot, but quite stifling as the fireplace was overly large for the space. As a consequence Joy's shoes had dried and were toasty to the touch.

As Joy bent to reclaim her brogues the heat seemed to catch up with her and she nearly swooned. A vague choke of nausea rose up and another sensation welled, a disheartening hopelessness. The walls wobbled, blinking in and out of focus and sent Joy tottering to the bathroom to wash her face. But the unsteadiness and the angst still wouldn't let up.

She stumbled back into her own room and a glaring ray of sunlight speared in through the drapes, blinding her eyes. She shaded them with an arm and almost fell as her leg thudded into wood. A toybox from nowhere. And adjacent were two miniature desks with chairs. There was also an easel, some teddies and dolls sprawled everywhere. The wallpaper was now pink dotted with yellow buttercups. Chalk crunched underfoot, smudging the whitewashed boards. Joy spun round, her eyes searching for children.

And then he was there; emerging through a shroud of haze: the sergeant. Again he appeared to be frantically hunting for something. Rustling through drawers. Poking in cubby-holes. He stopped suddenly and raised a finger and glanced to the door. This time it wasn't Joy's presence that had startled him, but another, a dowdy-looking woman wearing servant's garb. Her words wouldn't come, but her face was dark and her stance formidable. The sergeant stiffened, and dusting himself down, marched past her. He murmured in passing, 'Something is hidden here, I can feel it. But the Lord knows where!'

The door closed behind the two fading apparitions and Joy's world tipped back to the everyday. Her bedroom was as before, the fire extinguished, a cold dampness holding sway.

She sat on the edge of her bed and gripped the coarse linen tightly. So the room had been a child's bedroom come nursery after all. But why was the police sergeant searching through the drawers? And the young woman who had lived next door in Clarice's room was the governess. Two small children had been her charges. And one of them, a little girl, had somehow been abducted or disappeared and it was clear that she'd been held responsible. Joy opened her door an inch and rewedged the card. She corrected her coins and adjusted the hairbrush.

This tragedy was gradually being unfurled in front of her, and with it, the onus to stay with it was being ramped up. If the past was somehow responsible for this recent butchery, Joy had to allow the house to show her the way. No one, not even the redoubtable, Dunkley would find it easy to behold that which Misenlake was determined to uncover.

FOURTEEN

AN AFTERNOON WALK was Gracie's proposal which was not really a wonder. More of a surprise was that the majority of the gathering went for it.

Miss Biddle was tucked up and Barasch had locked himself away, but the rest were welly-booted and draped in capes and ready to slog around the marshy grounds.

Mrs Pomp looked slightly odd, a definite masculinity to her tweed walking trousers and long woollen socks. Rebecca Royce, in contrast, rather fetching in a multi-coloured silk headscarf and tight pants. Scanner hobbled, Kosik ambled, and Gloss took the lead, aided by high-spirited Gracie. All they needed was a set of gun dogs and the scene would have been set.

Joy's elfin feet slopped around in her boots, but Clarice kept badgering her to stop complaining. They had brought up the rear along with Scanner, who unfurled one of Melville's maps that flapped in the wind like an injured bird.

'Where are we going?' Joy had huffed.

'Nowhere in particular, I would think,' Scanner replied. 'Now if I could just work out this scale.' The map had almost been lost on an up-draught.

The sloshing and tramping brought them to the main gate, and swiftly after they had braved an ill-conceived poke about in the wood. Circling the great crater, it shone like frosted glass, the ice looking thinner than crystal and Gloss's suggestion of a festive lark-about revived longing looks back at the manor.

Gracie again advocated the coast. Joy volunteered, but they were both outvoted, and before any argument could ensue, a waving figure in the distance gestured that they were wanted back at the house.

It was Prim, and as he counted them in, his eyes narrowed, tracing two figures on the horizon. Joy followed his gaze It was the two plain-clothes coppers sniffing around over by the west wall. A slip of sadness lapped in Joy's head. They were searching for Melville. What if he was never found? Would he be left to lie unmolested through eternity? Joy shook off the thought and caught up with the others.

The library had been deemed more comfortable and Inspector Dunkley regarded them closely as they all filed in, standing room only by the roasting fire.

Miss Biddle was still absent, cooped up recuperating in her room. Barasch had been dragged down, but his features were sapped of colour and his eyes sorrowful.

Nouse was still patrolling the corridors and had saluted them in with his usual tap of his hooter. Prim had buttoned his coat and donned a hat as a taxi arrived. Without a word, he was gone.

Dunkley held the room with a steady gaze. 'Enjoyable ramble? Good.'

Tea cups clattered as people settled.

'I thought I would update you with the latest developments,' Dunkley began with a cursory glance around the room. 'I have to explain that I am not of the school of the average bobby that finds it necessary to keep information close. On the contrary, I have often found that sharing intelligence produces swifter results. It aids the corroboration of events and helps verify crucial timelines that are generally integral to all cases. My intention is not to wantonly unsettle you, or indeed to harangue you with a persistent and power-crazed frenzy of questions as that would obviously be unfair and foolhardy.'

Scanner nudged Gloss playfully.

'However, this method has in the past often exposed anomalies in the pre-determined suggestions of events and also the decided whereabouts of specific witnesses.'

Joy sighed. Why did these policeman talk so much?

The group quietened. Most looked impressed, if not a touch wary.

'Sadly, Mr Grauler is dead,' Dunkley went on.

A few shuffled and fidgeted, but overall there were limited coughs of surprise.

'But how?' asked Perry Scanner.

'A puncture to the heart.'

'A puncture?' Gloss queried. 'Like a knife wound?'

'It is unclear which particular weapon was used. But Grauler has without doubt been murdered.'

'In his bed?' Mrs Pomp held a hand over her mouth.

'That is where he was found.'

The room started to prattle, murmured disquiet and quizzical spats.

'Whilst it is understandable there will be speculation among you, and undoubted trepidation, you should be reassured that although DS Prim has left us for the time being, two men from the local constabulary will soon be reinforcing the police presence here at the manor. Before this day is out, there will be six of us on duty.'

'But if Grauler was murdered in his bed …' Rebecca Royce began.

'It is fortunate that all the upstairs apartments are equipped with both bolts and lockable doors. I suggest you avail yourselves of that precaution at all times.'

Joy's stomach cramped. She hated being shut away. She wouldn't sleep. She would have to find another way.

'I will now leave you to your evening. My two plain-clothed officers will have finished their exploration of the grounds by now, so we will be in and about the house should we be needed. Tomorrow, I will want all of you back here after breakfast … shall we say ten-thirty? I will explain then how I intend to take things forward.'

Dunkley got as far as the door, but lingered for a moment, 'A word, if I may, miss?' he enquired of Joy

Joy flushed.

The room instantly fell silent and Joy could feel the other guests staring as she hurriedly got to her feet.

'If you will?' Dunkley motioned to the door, gesturing for Joy to lead him out.

Clarice struggled up from the spongy sofa and followed.

'What is it, Inspector?' Clarice questioned.

'Don't be alarmed, madam. I have a question that I thought better asked in private, away from prying eyes.'

'Well? Joy is a simple soul. What can you want of her?'

'Knitting, miss.' Dunkley directed his reply to Joy, turning his back on Clarice.

'Knitting?' Clarice elbowed her way to Joy's side.

'I am told,' Dunkley persisted, 'that you are fond of knitting. Would it be possible to examine the needles and your other bits?'

'The bag is in my room,' said Joy.

'I will fetch it,' offered Clarice.

'No need. I will walk with you.'

Joy stood staring out of her bedroom window as Dunkley rifled through the bag and pulled out the clump of woven yarn, and two needles stuck into the ball of wool.

'Are these the only needles you have with you?' he quizzed.

Joy shook her head. 'Spares are in the zipped pocket.'

Dunkley pulled them out and lifted them close to his face. 'Would you mind if I borrowed these for a bit?'

'No,' Joy replied. She would have to do without. But she still had her notebook and other fidgets.

'Please take the bag, Inspector,' Clarice stammered with an uncertain smile.

Dunkley nodded, then smiled pallidly, and left.

'How odd,' said Clarice stoking the fire. 'What on earth can he want with your knitcraft?'

Joy wasn't listening. That moment was over.

She turned to her music box, and twisting the key, watched the ballerina swirl and twirl. She had faith in this policeman, but as the dancer stuttered to a halt, an iciness washed over her. For the first time since she'd been at Misenlake, she was frightened. The sensation of a stalking terror was all about her. It did not matter how many policeman guarded the doors. All those left assembled for this most savage Christmas were at the mercy of this heaving house and Joy feared that they were all in the most terrible danger.

Dinner was gammon, but Joy barely tasted the food as flutters constantly cramped her insides. This feeling of oppressive foreboding wouldn't leave her. She wanted to act, to help, but felt completely at the whim of Misenlake and these sporadic windows to the past. She was at a loss how to take things forward and her fear was curdled with the guilt of remaining idle and being so timid.

Excepting Miss Biddle and Barasch, who were again absent, Joy and Clarice had been the last to dinner. Clarice had slept forever and Joy had soaked and bathed as the pipes had thankfully come back to them.

As they entered the dining room, the chatter had ceased and a disturbing silence had followed. All eyes were on her. It was awful. She buried her eyes into the rug and almost stumbled as she attempted to take her seat.

Clarice had tried to break the ice with nodding smiles and some small talk with Gracie who'd taken Claube's place to 'cosy-up' as she had called it.

But for once dinner was taken in a laboured hush. The thirteen had become eight; the empty settings a stark pictorial of the lost and the infirm. Joy sneaked a glance around the table. One of these faces held a secret that linked them to the happenings many years before. It was this coupling that had spawned this murderous spree. She shuffled in her seat. If she could just hurry forward time. If she could just knit together the strands trailing around her mind, sew together the vital fragments of this most perilous riddle.

'Well, at least this Dunkley chap seems to know his business,' remarked Gloss trying to ease the mood.

Kosik said, 'Let us hope so.'

'What happened to our delusional Detective Prim?' asked Rebecca Royce as she pursued an errant pea around her plate.

'Chasing up the agent,' answered Gloss. 'It seems our new chap also thinks this baker's dozen could be important.'

'I wouldn't hold your breath,' said Perry Scanner. 'Nouse told me that the outfit in York that Miss Gwynne engaged was a one-woman band. A French lady, it would seem, and she's hopped it for Christmas.'

'Then why send Prim on a fool's errand?' Gracie quizzed.

'If the cap fits!' Scanner joked.

Joy was done. The cold blancmange gave no comfort and it was clear the other guests had discovered that Dunkley had confiscated her knitting. A rupture to the heart, he'd said – it didn't take much of a sleuth to expose the inference.

'Claube's body had a minute aperture to the back of his neck,' Scanner reflected.

Mrs Pomp clattered her cutlery.

'What are you suggesting?' Gloss glared at the newsman.

'Although our would-be doctor did dither a bit on that diagnosis,' Scanner continued.

'He did indeed,' said Kosik, his eyes glinting. 'And the American, Mr Grow- Lay, died of a single puncture wound to the heart.'

Rebecca Royce's skittish eyes wouldn't settle, but finally found their way to Joy.

'What are you all trying to say?' Mrs Pomp asked, sucking in her lower lip.

'His insinuation is clear,' Gracie butted in. 'Whoever killed Claube used the same weapon to kill Mr Grauler.'

Scanner tilted his head. 'And Kosik, old man. What happened to that famous parachute-ripping bayonet of yours?'

Kosik, for once, stumbled over his words. 'It … it's in my room. It is my safety valve, but I don't always …'

'Away from the eyes of our snooping inspector,' Scanner seemed to be enjoying fencing with the Pole.

'I had no thought to conceal it. It didn't cross my mind,' said Kosik his voice again faltering as his eyes burned into the newshound.

'But what about this girl and her infernal clicking? Such a bore. And what of her knitting needles?' Rebecca Royce stared frigidly. Joy kept her eyes on her bowl. 'They could easily have been used as a weapon, primitive undeniably, but then the police must have some reason …'

'How dare you!' Clarice growled, her eyes blazing. 'To implicate Joy just because … well it's just not …'

'Cricket, as you British say.' Kosik finished her sentence. 'As I'm too often reminded, I am Johnny Foreigner in this land, am I not? I did not start these recriminations. I am not the one who should have fingers pointed at.'

'The facts cannot be denied,' Scanner said plainly. 'One of us is a murderer. One of us either has a good reason for this butchery or else we have a lunatic in our midst.'

Mrs Pomp spluttered.

It was too much for Joy. The accusing glares and drumming fingers. She fled the room.

Upstairs Joy almost collided with Nouse.

'Ow do, miss. Best steady on or you'll have us both over.'

Joy gave a slippery smile and bolted for her room. But once inside realised the door would have to be shut on the inspector's orders.

The striking barbs had settled a flush on her cheeks. She could hear raised voices from below and a door slamming.

Peeking into the corridor, she met Nouse's animated face.

'Getting to folk, is it? They're proper mardy by the looks of things.'

Joy's frown relaxed into a grin. 'They think me the killer.'

'You, miss? I wouldn't say that. How could anyone think that of thee?'

Joy detected Nouse's Yorkshire twang. She hadn't noticed it before, but then again, Nouse was a dab hand at indecipherable sign language.

Joy stood awkwardly prodding the skirting with a toe. Then she asked, 'Are you from these parts, Mister Nouse?'

'I am that, missy. Born and bred in the village, but been away ever so many years now. They stuck me down in the smoke and grime of London, but needs must and duty calls and all. But now I'm nearly done, it's almost time to make my way back home. I'm due to retire in a few years, God willing.'

'Are you very old, Mister Nouse?'

Nouse chortled and tipped an imaginary cap. 'No drill here, miss, please call me Nouse, everyone else does.'

Joy gave him her best grin.

He sighed and began his potted history. 'I was born in the year of 1888.'

'That's a long time ago.'

'Popped my head out just as Jack was ripping his last in Whitechapel.'

Joy had heard of the infamous East End murders.

'Appropriate really as I only ever wanted to be a copper.' Nouse sniffed.

Joy had a thought. 'You knew this house, all those years ago?'

'I did that, miss.' Nouse's features creased into a fretful series of expressions as if he was dredging up hazy memories. 'No flies on you, is there? You would have thought some others whose position it is might have asked me the very same question.'

Joy leant against the wall of the passage. 'Was this a happy place?'

Nouse's eyes became guarded, the frown transforming into a distant look as if dimly aware he was sharing too many confidences. 'Was decent for scrumping, I'll give it that.'

Joy gave Nouse a bemused smile. 'Scrumping?'

'Stealing fruit. Not a proper upright beginning for a career in policing. We meant no harm. Freddie Slack used to let me bunk over the wall.'

'Slack? The gardener?'

'That's right. We weren't really what you'd call pals. He was a mite older than me. Had a cushy job here at the house as a stable lad. Suited him as he was a bit of a loner and loved the nags.'

'You knew the people who lived here then?'

'Not likely, miss. Too grand and lofty for likes of me. Used to get chased off by the gamekeeper, Miss Crabb's old dad.'

'You knew Miss Crabb when she was a girl?'

'Knew of her. She was another odd one, another who never liked to mix.'

Joy pushed at the door of her room, letting it swing back before nudging it again. 'Were there any children living here?'

The skin on Nouse's face relaxed. 'It was a bad time. Those wee girls. I saw them playing from time to time. Running around the grounds and the woods. Special place for kiddies. Lots of fun with nooks and camps, and trees to climb into. Not like our old street, no fuss, no bother and full of soot and hungry bellies.'

Joy prodded the door. One-two-three.

'After that little 'un went missing, the family shut the place up. Went away. I was long gone before they came back. That would have been … in the twenties most like.'

'This girl who went missing? What happened? Did they ever find her?'

Nouse scratched at his neck. 'Not that I knows of, miss. Reet mournful it were. A proper horror flick. I remember Fred searching night after night. I went with him at first, we all did, but then it became so hopeless. She had gone and nobody knew where, until …' Nouse's words drifted in tune with his mind. He was suddenly somewhere else.

'Old Fred was fond of Miss Celia,' he babbled on. 'She owned a pony. Fred used to dote on it. Was called Saffie or summink like that.' Nouse leapt up from his chair as steps sounded on the stairs.

'Nouse? You there?' It was Prim, back already.

Nouse ushered Joy into her room. 'Now lock the door and don't you fret. House is gonna be full of uniform tonight. You sleep well now.'

With that he scuttled off. Joy bent down, and leaving the tiniest of gaps, jammed the card. She would have words again with Nouse.

To Joy, it was akin to prison. Doors crashed and thumped, keys rattled and even Clarice, after pointlessly trying to reassure Joy that nobody really suspected her of these crimes, had bounded back to her room and secured both her bedroom and the bathroom door.

The house was firmly tucked up. Policemen's size-nines pounded the corridors and even the pipes had taken a rest from their persistent gurgling. If a murderer lurked tonight, he'd need to be invisible or a cat burglar.

Joy took to the window and scoured the grounds. It all looked so bleak, so sullied, stained with quaggy blotches that smudged dirtiness over what was left of the snow. Christmas was truly over. Within days she hoped to be away. But would this constant sense of fretfulness chase her home, force her to continually spar with the shades of the past?

Fortunately, and rather surprisingly, sleep was swift. The simmering quandaries that raged in her head were finally becalmed. Dunkley was a wise man – he'd get there eventually. And if he didn't, Joy would end this, drag the past kicking and screaming in front of him. It helped her to consider her specialness had been born for a reason. And although impatient for this dread to end, it would only be a matter of time before Misenlake invited her to its final reckoning.

Joy woke extra early by design. The persistent tinkle of her alarm clock signalled dawn was at hand. Dressing swiftly, she peeked out the window.

The easy bit completed she now needed to wait and possibly part-climb out of the window to ensure the requisite view. The charging wind almost blew her back into her room, swirling the leaves about in gusts like manic wasps disturbed from their nest.

A din in the corridor erupted. Shouts and shrieks. Bumps and judders. Somebody had taken a tumble and there was a cry of pain.

Joy peeped into the corridor. As one, other doors opened. Clarice pulled her dressing gown close and yawned. 'What on earth?'

Beyond the bend in the passage, a policeman was prone, clasping Barasch's leg. The comedy was complete when the dentist kicked out, but only sent himself off balance and crashing to the floor.

Rebecca Royce, with a cream lathered face stood with a hand on her hip like a teapot looking down at the fracas.

From nowhere, Prim in a smoking jacket was prancing and shouting for handcuffs. From behind Joy, Kosik arrived, along with Mrs Pomp whose hair was meshed in a net.

'Let me go,' grunted Barasch trying to break free of two policeman. Prim hovered purposelessly. 'I tell you, I cannot be held here,' Barasch growled. 'I have been prisoner before and I vowed I would never be again.'

Gracie shuffled around the corner. Joy watched her take in the scene, and with a flustered glance greet Dunkley as he double-leapt the stairs.

Something occurred to her. This was as good a time as any. Joy backed away from her aunt and dismissing Kosik's stare, she dodged past and made her way down the corridor away from the rumpus.

The scuffle became muffled as Joy hurried to the end of the passage where the boards were thin and where her route tapered. The dead end loomed large, but something was drawing her on.

'Hem!' I felt a bit of a truant, sneaking away from kerfuffle with Mr Barasch. But it wasn't a place for me. These blusters in my mind appeared determined to befuddle me, but I suddenly had the strongest notion that now was an opportunity not to be missed, a chance to snoop a bit. This time I wasn't drawn by some ghoulish apparitions or by ethereal voices, just the impression that it was important to do my own digging while this window allowed.

If I was being manipulated, Misenlake's marionette, then it was being as supple as a snake and about as subtle as a tank. I needed to try and meet it halfway and hurry on this horror before somebody else carked it.

My assertiveness was abruptly extinguished by the sound of a creaking whine piercing the hushed passageway. I halted as I tried to drown out the shambles I'd left behind. I listened. The squeak came again, rhythmic, over and over, but rapidly diminished and followed by a clang and a door closing. Then a whirring sound and a clunk.

Faint voices chattered somewhere ahead. I ran faster and drew to a halt at the shuttered door. At once, I rattled it aside and peered down into darkness. A series of pulleys jiggled in the half-light. It wasn't a dumbwaiter it was a lift, or an elevator as Grauler would have called it.

I pressed the button and with a jangling jolt it jarred into life and out of the gloom the top of the lift juddered upward. It stopped with a thud.

Footsteps sounded from across the hallway, jangling keys and a curse. I slipped speedily into the storeroom next to the shaft. I carefully pulled the door to.

Standing in the hushed darkness, I could hear huffing and tutting and the shutters being pulled shut. With a whirr, the lift was then sent whining back to the ground floor.

There followed a breathless silence and an inkling that somebody was close at hand. I backed further into the pitch and yelped. My ankle had bashed on something metal. I squeezed my yell into a ball and grimaced, throttling down the shooting pain. Then a floorboard groaned beneath my feet. I cursed, well, it was more of a pathetic whimper, and like a frightened child shut my eyes praying not to hear the sound of the door opening and the inevitable flash of blinding light.

But nothing happened. Just a faint whiff, a distinctive smell that I'd come across somewhere before. Then after a second or two there was a rustle, followed by a door being gently pulled to.

I opened my eyes. Light wandered in and partially illuminated the metal contraption that had accosted my ankle. I bent to take a closer look, but immediately shot upright as a wisp of breath tingled my neck and a high-pitched voice from somewhere within the gloom piped up, '*Goosey goosey gander, whither shall I wander? Upstairs downstairs and in my lady's chamber …*'

I reached for the door. But it slammed shut on me. I yanked at the handle, but found it locked. I started to panic and the voice came again. '*So I shook her by her left leg and threw her down …*'

And then with blast of wind the door was swept from my hands, and crashing on its hinges banged open. I rushed out, determined to flee the demons inside. Spinning around with my palms waving in defensive mode, my chest thundered, then I sagged as I found the passageway empty.

My heart began to steady, but rolled again as muffled moans rumbled from somewhere close. And padding feet, a rattling key followed by a creak.

I lost my nerve and bolted back toward the melee with my dressing gown flapping around me. Belting around the turn in the passage, I skidded to a steady walk.

I rejoined the scrum, feeling safe for now. It was clear that Dunkley had restored order. Disentangling Barasch from the uniformed coppers he'd ordered everyone back to their chambers.

'Hem!'

As Joy nudged past, she saw Barasch's wasted face. The man's mind had been overtaken by fever. Joy could sense his despondency and desperation. Thankfully Dunkley was sensitive to his distress, and offering Barasch an arm, helped him up.

'Let's get you a hot drink and we can sit and rest up a bit. Nobody wants to keep you against your will, but let's see if we can find a way.'

Barasch gave Dunkley a resigned look and tramped almost in a trance down the stairs as the constables righted themselves and took an arm each.

Prim glared at Nouse and followed on behind. Miss Crabb belatedly made an appearance swaddled in an overly large dressing gown.

Joy sat on her bed for some time and twisted the cotton sheets between her fingers. Barasch was yet another with a secret buried deep. Something his soul couldn't bear and wouldn't banish. She felt it. This man needed to be away from Misenlake before his memories ate him up. They all did.

FIFTEEN

BLEARY EYES charted the Dunkley as he entered the library after breakfast.

'Good morning to you all,' he said, slurping on a mug of tea.

Joy had again jammed herself between Clarice and Gracie on the sofa, a comfort blanket of sorts.

'Are we all here?' Dunkley enquired as he regarded his audience over the bridge of his stippled nose.

'Miss Biddle and Barasch …' Perry Scanner began.

'Miss Biddle is to keep to her bed. Doctor's orders.'

'How is Barasch?' Kosik asked.

'We've had quite a time of it with our Mr Barasch. He is sleeping off his dawn dash and hopefully may join us later. The doctor said he's mentally exhausted. His list of patients is growing with Miss Gwynne in a similar predicament.'

'It's understandable with all this ghastliness,' Mrs Pomp said.

'Indeed. Ah, here is Miss Crabb. We are complete.'

Miss Crabb's lips were tightly-set. She looked unamused. Being bundled about by the police was not sitting well.

'Well, I shall begin. Firstly, I hope that at least some of you got a few winks of sleep last night?'

Dunkley shuffled some papers and studied his notes. They all waited.

'Written here, I have the basic outline of the events as they unfolded here at the manor over Christmas. I also have some bland background details, bits and bobs on most of you. DS Prim has been more than thorough.'

'He's back? Prim, that is?' Gloss probed.

'Yes. After making enquiries it appears a Miss … now where is it,' Dunkley scanned his notes. 'Edith Sauvage, a French lady, has rather inconveniently returned to her homeland, and our enquiries have been fruitless. We simply have no idea when she will be arriving back.'

'Edith who?' Rebecca Royce piped up.

'Sauvage. She is 'Sauvage Hospitalitie,' the agency that Miss Crabb engaged to organise this gathering.'

Miss Crabb nodded her assent.

'According to DS Prim's notes, only Mrs Pomp had the foresight to keep her letter of invitation. The rest of you have either lost, burned or discarded your paperwork. That is correct?'

Mrs Pomp beamed and played with an earring.

'It is of no matter. Although peculiar, I do not believe the fact that you are … or were thirteen rather than the originally conceived twelve is of particular importance to this case. That it may have a mystery all of its own, I do not deny, but for now I will put it to one side. It's a distraction and we have so many other puzzles that warrant my full attention.'

'But DS Prim …' began Perry Scanner.

Dunkley threw out a shrewd glance. 'DS Prim has gone to the village with PC Nouse to make further enquiries about the possible whereabouts of Professor Melville.'

Dunkley was in command. His eyes assessed the room like a schoolteacher, a raking glare warning that more glib interruptions would not be tolerated.

'Which neatly brings me to the start of this baffling episode.' Dunkley picked up his papers and wagged them like a conductors baton. 'Written here are the bare facts. There is no colour, no substance and therefore as I peruse and reread this chronology of events, there are omissions as there were bound to be. The picture remains cloudy. Now do not get me wrong. I do not blame my colleagues. As I have stated they have done their duty as they were trained to do.'

Scanner tittered needlessly.

Dunkley stared him down. 'So I have a script of sorts. Unfortunately, there were no movie cameras rolling, no filming of the relevant incidents, no time standing still for my edification.'

Joy stared as Dunkley rummaged in his trouser pockets withdrawing a hanky. She did the same, drawing crumpled lace from the sleeve of her cardigan.

'But what I do have assembled, and close at hand, are you – the players.'

Everyone looked bemused.

'Players?' Rebecca Royce enunciated their bewilderment.

'That's correct.'

Mrs Pomp opened her mouth then shut it again.

'What I intend to do, over the next day or two or however long it takes, is to re-enact the circumstances around these murders as they occurred. And as we inch forward, to forensically reconstruct the goings-on piece by piece. Who was where? Who said what to who? At what time did he or she? … etc, etc,'

More than a few sighed.

'And you will find that this method is always more revealing than one would expect. Somebody recalls seeing something they'd forgotten or remembers the events slightly differently to others, and often without malice aforethought, it renders previously written statements either incomplete, redundant or just plain incorrect.'

It made sense. Joy sat up in her seat. This was going to be interesting.

'But what if we can't remember?' Rebecca Royce stirred her coffee.

'Then that would be human and quite natural,' replied Dunkley. He took a moment before framing his next sentence. 'But I assure you, somebody will recall an instance that's possibly been missed or recorded somewhat hazily, or add further snippets that in time prove vital. What I can guarantee you is that you will either dovetail and bring about a fuller, but possibly no more helpful picture, or else, as is usual, illuminate some glaring exclusion that will lift the fog from this conundrum.'

Kosik leaned forward in his chair. 'But what about Barasch and the Biddle woman?'

'And the dead can't speak,' Scanner cut in.

'Very astute, Mr Kosik. It is more than unfortunate that the two you mention cannot be with us. All I would say is that any gaping holes we uncover, anything less than certain that requires their corroboration, I will charge them to fill. Then of course, with the dust clearing, I may come about you individually to substantiate specific instances.'

Dunkley straightened his tie and looked with deliberation at the group.

Joy adjusted her collar, twiddling with the button.

Dunkley frowned slightly. 'Now that is my method. I like to not only be thorough, but transparent and inclusive – it always ensures that we arrive at the correct result.'

Her courage returning, Joy studied what was left of the gathering. Apart from Gloss, who squirmed a bit in his chair as he picked at a shaving scab, the others seemed entirely composed. If there was a murderer among them, he or she was as icy as the settling snow.

And indeed under instruction from Dunkley they did start from the beginning. How they had arrived and in what order? Who had greeted them? How had their rooms been allocated? And during the long drawn-out series of questions, Dunkley did not as much as pick up a pen, let alone call for a scribe. Indeed, a lurking constable, being deemed a distraction, was banished to check on Barasch and Miss Biddle.

Joy had a thought and dashed from the room.

Clarice shouted after her, but Joy had charged up the stairs and into her room.

When she arrived back they all stared. She brandished her notebook.

'She likes to make lists. It's one of her things,' explained Clarice with an uncertain grimace.

Dunkley's pale smile begged Rebecca Royce to continue where they'd left off. She again explained the whole saga of her detour to London. Dunkley didn't seem particularly engaged.

Instead, he turned to Gloss. 'You were employed here during the war?'

'Yes, toward the end of 1941 I took up my position.'

'And you left …?'

'Straight after VE day. A sabbatical. Went down to London to catch up with a few friends who'd I lost touched with during the conflict.'

'And your employment was terminated not long after?'

'That's correct. Bit rich. But there was plenty of work down south and I'd saved up quite a bit, so I had plenty …'

'And you returned on a whim?'

'Yes, with the major dying I thought I'd pay my respects and pootle about the area. It was my home for nearly five years, you see.'

'And you met the butler in the pub, who told you there had been a cry-off. Very handy as it allowed you to sneak in by the back door as it were?'

Gloss coloured, but held his temper. 'Crikey! I was hardly sneaking in. I rang the agent and made sure it was all right and proper.'

'So you say.' Dunkley walked over to the window and stood staring for a few moments. Without turning, he carried on. 'And Miss Gwynne was pleased to see you?'

'I have no idea,' Gloss explained. 'I've not laid eyes on her since I've been back. None of us have. She's kept to her rooms since we arrived.'

'I see,' said Dunkley as he criss-crossed between them. 'One last question and then we can break for lunch. Was Slack the gardener employed here during the war?'

'Slack? No, he wasn't. Plenty of troops coming and going, not all of them lame. Bit of a distraction for them, possibly a payback helping out a bit, so you see we had no need of a gardener as such, with all that latent manpower. And Miss Dotty, as ever, was keen to keep an eye on the pennies and make use of all her recuperating guests.'

'Thank you,' said Dunkley and picking up his papers, left the room

After lunch, Joy fled to her bedroom. Discarding her notebook, she dragged the blanket from the bed and wrapped it around her. It was freezing. The tip of her nose tingled.

She checked the window, but it was shut. The fire was meagre, but even so, it seemed even colder in the room than it had been outside.

Shivering, Joy toyed with the music box. The ballerina tinkled gracefully into her moves. The gentle tune seemed to warm the air. Joy stared rapt in distracted awe as the jingling notes went on and on, the dancer twirling elegantly until, alas she began to slow, the key finally drawing the heavenly music to a halt. But then a melodic tone took up in its place. A childish tune Joy had heard many times before.

'Humpty Dumpty sat on a wall. Humpty Dumpty had a great fall …'

And with a bang the door whooshed open and then slammed with a crash. Joy's eyes spun around the room. But there was nothing. No emerging figures from a tissue-thin fog. But again, giggles cheeped, and a skirt swished. Footsteps ran back and forth in the corridor, followed by more cheeky sniggers.

Joy dropped the blanket and ran over to the door. This time she was determined to draw out this mischievous apparition. She rushed past the tower to the sound of laughter, but the pacing faded, and the voices now seemed faraway. And once again Joy butted the dead end.

'All the king's horses and all the king's men couldn't put Humpty together again …'

This time the words came from behind her. Joy swung around. But the corridor was empty.

Joy heard a clearer voice – it was Crabb's, and it was coming from behind the wooden door. In reply, there was a faint hum followed by a squeaking, screeching sort of noise. Somebody was shuffling, coming closer. The door handle twisted and Joy ran for it.

The sky was leaden and heavy. The respite of the previous two days looked to be over. They were going to get another shellacking.

Clarice and Gracie walked ahead, keeping to the gravel paths as they wound their way around the walled garden. Joy sidled to an archway and stared out over the open land. The grass was slick and dotted here and there were longer clumps of yellowing turf, dead and dying, adding to the drabness of the landscape.

Joy pictured Claube floundering in the mud and shuddered. An itchiness like chilblains spread over her wrist necessitating a scratch and then she remembered something. She would add that to her notes.

On their way back past the fountain they bumped into Prim and Nouse.

'What are you doing, swanning about outside?' Prim grumbled.

'Good afternoon,' Gracie replied frostily. 'I wasn't aware we were under some sort of arrest.'

Prim glared at Joy. 'Knitting, eh? Another easy way out. I've heard plenty about these schizophrenic rages, and if I had my way …'

Clarice strode off. 'Buffoon!' she hissed under her breath.

Nouse saluted them past as Joy hustled after her.

'What a thoroughly unpleasant and rude individual,' said Clarice, scowling.

'Don't mind that numpty, Joy, dear,' Gracie comforted. 'Some people's ignorance knows no bounds. We can take solace a better man has replaced him. Thank God for Inspector Dunkley, that's the last I'll say on the matter.'

'He can't help it,' said Joy, sloshing in and out of the icy mush.

The library was airless. They'd all been cooped up since the break after lunch and once more, Dunkley had corralled them inside, leading them through the happenings of the previous days.

Dunkley nodded and probed, sometimes wandering to the window, at other times examining the books on the shelves.

Joy scribbled. She began to anticipate Dunkley's pattern. He would allow the group to chatter, wittering on about all sorts of stuff until the thread was absolutely lost, then he'd jump in with a pertinent question sending them into a flap, before simmering the ruckus and placing them back on track. Joy liked it a lot. There was plenty to enjoy and much to record.

Melville had been the focal point for what had seemed an eternity. Who had seen him at breakfast? Had he said anything peculiar? Had anybody seen him leave the house? And after a time, again, Dunkley's deliberations shone upon Gloss.

'These maps Melville brought with him. Some were ordnance survey pamphlets, but some of the others he'd acquired privately?'

'That's what he said.' Gloss sat back in his seat, studying his fingernails.

'When was that, sir?'

'I bumped into him after breakfast on that first morning. Monckton had been of little use and I offered my services – to show him the lay of the land, that sort of thing.'

'And he took you up on it?'

'No. He was in a bit of a flutter. Muttered some excuse and told me perhaps later. He then strode out into the snow.'

'And did you indeed meet up, later that day?'

'No. I never saw him again.'

'We did,' Joy piped up.

Clarice's frown softened. 'Yes of course, you're right, dear. On our walk with Gracie. He was over by the treeline, but changed course when he spotted us and headed off toward the gate, near that iced-over crater. He was pacing out the land and taking notes.'

'And you, Mr Scanner. You travelled down with him from Whitby?'

'I did. Didn't offer up much, I'm afraid. I've had a poke around the maps he left behind, though, but to be honest, apart from a few pencilled scribblings, I didn't see any obvious 'x' marks the spot sort of thing.'

Dunkley did not appear to be paying attention, but Scanner continued to blather on about the maps.

Eventually, Dunkley spoke over him. 'So, the last anybody in this room saw of Professor Melville was directly after breakfast on Christmas Eve? Nobody saw him come back to the house after that. And he wasn't present at the carol service?'

They all looked to each other and shook their heads.

'And Herr Claube, it states here,' Dunkley pulled a sheet close to his eyes, 'was noted at lunch on that same day, but he also wasn't present at the carol service?'

A few furrowed brows, but again, they all agreed they hadn't seen him there.

'There was some unpleasantness after lunch,' Kosik advanced. 'He took offence and stormed out. It was close on two p.m.'

'That's right. He cut up rough and marched out early afternoon,' Gloss volunteered.

'I certainly never saw him after,' added Mrs Pomp.

'Miss Biddle was most unkind, I'm afraid,' said Gloss.

'I think we all assumed he was keeping to his room,' Scanner said. 'To avoid further conflict.'

'So at the supper on Christmas Eve was the first time both the Professor and Herr Claube were noted to be missing?'

'That's correct, Inspector. Mister Monckton had me check their rooms and I reported back that they were nowhere to be seen.' Drabble coughed politely having chipped in. 'The two of us then did a quick looksee around the house and Mister Monckton then informed the guests.'

Dunkley nodded. He seemed satisfied. 'And then Mr Gloss, along with Mr Kosik, Drabble and Monckton, went out to search for the two missing gentlemen?'

'That's true, we did,' said Gloss. 'But we didn't get very far. The wind was so fierce and the snow blinding, it became obvious pretty quickly that we had no chance of finding them and a good prospect of further injuries. In truth, we were in poor shape for a search on a night such as that.'

Dunkley huffed deeply. He seemed disgruntled. 'And that was your Christmas Eve? If nobody has anything else to add I will leave you to your dinner and …'

'The capes,' interjected Joy.

'Capes?' Dunkley for once looked off-guard. 'There's nothing in these notes about any capes, miss.'

'They were wet,' Joy explained.

'She's right!' exclaimed Scanner. 'By George, I'd forgotten about them!'

Dunkley suddenly had a second wind and his features sharpened. 'Tell me about these wet macs, miss.'

'And nobody knows why,' Joy added.

Scanner interrupted. 'As she says, Inspector. Hanging in the porch. Three sodden oilskins. At the time we had a bit of an inquest. But with the search and everything, I'd quite forgotten about them.'

Joy bathed in the glow of sudden respect as the other guests' eyes ran to her.

'There were three?' Dunkley quizzed, pulling out a pocket book. He licked the end of a stubby pencil.

Joy licked hers.

Scanner went on. 'There were, and had been only recently worn. As has been mentioned, they were dripping wet.'

'And yet nobody would admit to availing themselves of them? Interesting,' mused Dunkley as he slipped into his thoughts.

Everyone sat in silence waiting.

Dunkley looked up and pulled a face as if surprised they were all still in attendance. 'That'll be all for today. I appreciate your time and energy. It has been most informative. Tonight, as you did last, lock your doors and I will see you all in the reception hall in the morning. I think we may take a little stroll around the grounds.'

After grabbing a hurried breakfast, Joy toddled out armed with a curd tart and joined the rear of the group. She'd slept like a top, thankfully one that had ceased to spin, indeed a slumber that had been so deep that she'd awoken late and hastily piled up her hair in a jumble of tufts.

Dunkley had set off at a decent lick down the earthen path that led to the crater. Here he paused. Turning and looking back at the manor, all eyes followed his as they had flipped from the house to the wood and back again.

Barasch and Miss Biddle were still absent, but Miss Crabb had again been directed to attend.

Dunkley scanned the treeline to the west of the gate, then began to trudge toward the coastal path.

Clarice linked arms with Gracie; their blooming friendship was one of the positive things that had come out of this most wretched week. Miss Crabb completed the gaggle of backmarkers. Her eyes were as frosty as the rutted turf, a woolly scarf swaddling her face, wreathing her features.

'Have you been with Miss Gwynne long?' asked Gracie by way of conversation as they reached the mouth of the rail tunnel.

'Not really,' Crabb replied.

'It must be marvellous to be able to live in such a wondrous house in such a location, especially with you being local and all.'

'Yes,' said Miss Crabb. 'It is.'

'And Miss Gwynne is a good mistress?' Gracie prompted.

'The best,' said Crabb, tugging her scarf higher.

'It's a shame we haven't been able to meet her,' said Clarice cupping her hands.

'A shame – yes,' Crabb said, pointing out Dunkley.

'This is the pathway where Monckton was found.' Dunkley poked in the bushes. 'Can I ask if anybody has visited the disused alum works? Before or since his accident?'

Nobody spoke.

Peering down the leafy tunnel, Dunkley sniffed the air, and seemingly satisfied, spun around, and picking up the pace, started hiking back toward the manor.

'And the coastal path or the cove?' he quizzed after stopping abruptly and waiting for the stragglers to catch up.

Gloss informed him of the trek they'd taken. Joy kept silent and for some reason so did Gracie.

'Good enough.'

'This is insufferable, Inspector. Why have you dragged us all out into the mud?' Rebecca Royce looked down at her encrusted wellies. 'Couldn't you have asked these rather banal questions back at the house?'

Dunkley chuckled, his eyes shining. 'Yes, Miss Royce, that I could have, but it would have been a shame to waste the whole morning cooped up inside, and if you would please be patient, we aren't quite done yet.'

Walking back, Gracie shivered. 'I wish I had a wrap like yours, Miss Crabb. It looks wonderfully warm.'

'Perhaps Joy could knit you one,' suggested Clarice. 'A belated Christmas present.'

'Do you think Miss Gwynne will always live here?' Gracie chattered on. It's an terribly large place to live on one's own.'

Crabb's patience snapped. 'She has me! And of course, I shall remain as long as I'm needed.' Crabb bent close to Gracie. 'You must know that this is my mistress's home. Why would she want to be anywhere else?'

Gracie's eyes fell, as Clarice jumped in. '*Here we are again, happy as can be* …'

Joy cringed.

Dunkley led them up the dicey-looking slope onto the terrace and halted outside the drawing room. He peered in the French doors, and pivoting, snooped over the short wall as he examined the path below. The gravelled walkway ran parallel to the house halting at a set of steps that led down into the walled garden: the spot where the unfortunate Slack had met his death.

Squinting up at the manor, Dunkley studied the bedroom windows, pointedly counting them one by one with a pencil.

Joy followed his gaze and spotted her own room with the yellow drapes bunched. Next to hers would be Grauler's, and beside his was Miss Biddle, where presumably she still lay convalescing.

Dunkley pointed vaguely at the two huge urns that framed the stairway down to the walled garden.

'Slack was found there,' he remarked.

'That's what I understand, Inspector. It was Monckton who discovered the body.'

'Yes, if Prim's notes are correct, he would have been standing about here.' Dunkley braced himself like a skier and stared down at his feet and then back down at the path. Joy did the same.

Dunkley bent over and picked up a cigarette butt and brought it close.

Perry Scanner flexed his knee. 'He told us that he had been seeking out

Slack to ask if he had seen anything of Melville. That's when he found him sprawled over his barrow.'

'Yes, thank you, Mr Scanner. DS Prim's notes are very clear on that point, and he's even drawn a useful diagram.'

Prim – they hadn't seen him all morning. Possibly sent off on another chore. Joy was glad.

'So despite Miss Crabb's express instructions that nobody was to leave the house, Monckton took it upon himself to seek Slack out?'

Mrs Pomp made a chattering noise and shuddered in the wind.

'Correct,' said Crabb.

'Really?' said Dunkley. 'So, if Monckton hadn't popped out then Slack could have lain out here for hours.'

'What about his boy, Ernest I think he's called?' Gloss questioned.

'It was Christmas Day. A day off,' Crabb put forward quietly.

'But as it seems that Slack was killed not long after dawn then none of us can have an alibi,' Scanner said.

'True enough. And that much was obvious to Prim,' said Dunkley, placing the butt into a handy plastic bag.

'I was with Miss Gwynne, of course,' Crabb declared.

'That you were. Sleeping, I would have thought, at such an early hour. Therefore can you really vouch for her and she for you?'

Crabb looked mortified by the insinuation.

'Drabble and Monckton were seeing to the fires. Cook was cooking. Those of you who have windows overlooking this side of the house were questioned, but none of you will purport to witnessing anything untoward, which in all honesty is no surprise given the early hour.' Dunkley paused a second, and then carried on. 'And even more mysterious, despite everybody being in agreement that they awoke to clear skies, and not a fluff of snow had fallen that morning, the only footprints leading to the body were those belonging to Slack himself?'

'That's correct, but we've been through this, Inspector. It's a bit parky out here, can't we go in?' It was Rebecca Royce who was huddling further into her fur stole. Mrs Pomp's lips were blue.

'Not long now, Miss Royce.' Dunkley walked down the terrace, stomping away from them toward the front door of the manor, then again squinted over the wall. 'The only marks along the path were the wheeled trails made by the barrow. Correct?'

Murmured irritation, but eventually rolling into an agreed yes came back.

'Much like these ones that stretch around the side of the house?'

Everyone shuffled back toward the inspector and scrutinised the crushed ice leading past the dining room.

'And according to Prim there was no sign of a scuffle in the area around the wheelbarrow.' Dunkley halted as if something had disturbed his train of thought. 'Monckton discovered the corpse when you were all at breakfast …' His voice quietened and then trailed off as if not expecting a reply.

Joy squinted into the low sun as the last of the cottony clouds dashed over the headland. A rook cawed somewhere, and without a word, a sedate Dunkley scratched his chin and led them back into the house.

Joy wasn't hungry so ducked out of lunch. Dressed for a walk, she jammed on her hat and trudged away from the manor, scuttling through the pathways of the knotted garden, and halting at the frozen fountain.

She had little sympathy for all the blathering and bleating – how Dunkley had wasted everyone's time. Joy rather liked him and understood his methods. She just feared that Misenlake was bent on its own course, and through no fault of his own, the forces within the house were masked to him, but she would be able to help there – indeed she was more than happy to set him straight!

Ambling toward the wood, a scuffling of feet from behind made her spin around.

It was Nouse.

'How do again, miss. Sorry to mither you, but you were spotted from the window by my governor. Told me to keep an eye. Check where you were off to.'

Joy shaded her eyes from the sun and regarded the manor. Prim was probably watching them.

'Orders is orders,' explained Nouse pulling a face.

'I wasn't going anywhere. Just away.'

'Know how you feel. Wish this was all over so I could get back to London and my old routine and a decent pint of mild.' Nouse stamped his feet for warmth as Joy pootled around the triangular rose beds.

'Don't get me wrong. It was nice to see my old ma and I was curious to see this old place once again, but now, like the rest of you, I've had my fill.'

'When you were a boy,' Joy began, stooping and brushing snow from the box hedging, 'you told me, one of the children who lived here went missing. What happened to the other?'

'The other? Well that'll be Miss Dorothy. She's the only surviving member of the family. She's your hostess.'

Joy scraped a toe on the gravel, kicking a dent in the ice.

Nouse went on. 'The major died a few years back. His wife passed back in the twenties, as I said, overseas somewhere. Something makes me think Switzerland or perhaps Austria. Miss Dorothy returned with the major and has been here ever since as far as I know.'

The sergeant's face from the past loomed in Joy's mind. 'So the police never found the missing daughter?'

Nouse fingered a brow. 'It were a terrible scandal at the time. The force arrested the governess on suspicion of murdering the girl. Young lady was said to be in love with the major and wanted him all to herself. Local gossip reckoned that the poor mite was drowned, shoved from the cliffs down by the cove. Miss Dorothy, so they said, wriggled free and got away.'

'Not very likely,' Joy stated.

'P'raps not, miss. But they had nobody else to lay the blame on. There was talk of a tutor that'd had been dismissed – well-known for the ladies. But they hung the governess for it despite her protests.'

Joy massaged her temples as a giddiness broke over her.

Nouse steadied her. 'Best we head back. All this maudlin talk on top of these latest shenanigans will be getting a bit too much for you.'

Joy stared back at the grey flinty manor, smoke spiralling up into the clear blue sky.

Nouse's eyes traced her look. 'It's sounds barmy. But those in the village say this old place is cursed. My old ma says they brought evil in from the sea when they built this house. Tall tales no doubt.'

Joy was only half-listening. Her thoughts were of the young governess. They'd hanged her for the murder of one of the little girls in her care. Coupled with the torment of losing her lover, they'd brutalised her life. Joy could still feel her smothering sadness. It was clear that this tragic woman's soul had reached out, but the child's voice – the ghost of the missing child? Whatever was happening here, Misenlake was screaming loud and clear – they'd hanged an innocent woman.

SIXTEEN

'I CAN ONLY APOLOGISE for my erratic behaviour,' said a rueful-looking Barasch as he took his seat in the library, rejoining the group after lunch. 'Being locked away, it's a bad part of my history, I do not cope well with such appalling memories.'

'It's good to have you back, Doctor,' said Mrs Pomp.

'Yes, you have been missed,' added Kosik, an arm around Barasch's shoulders.

Dunkley allowed the murmurs in the room to die down before starting. 'To begin, we will resurrect this new development, the wetted oilskins.'

'Is Miss Biddle not joining us?' asked Perry Scanner.

'I'm afraid it's a day too early for that lady,' said Dunkley, looking slightly miffed. 'As I have told the other guests,' he said looking fixedly at Barasch, 'this sequencing of events is not to catch you out or accuse any of you of falsehoods – there is no need for that – it is to shake your brains a little, to see if you can recall anything that was missed in your interviews with DS Prim.' Dunkley opened his pocket book.

Joy flicked through hers.

'Where is Prim?' asked Gloss.

'DS Prim has been interviewing Miss Gwynne.'

'And she won't be joining us either?' asked Mrs Pomp.

Dunkley sat on the edge of a table. 'There is no need to trouble the lady. At no point has she been amongst you. She can therefore add little value.'

Joy scribbled it down.

'Now if I may,' Dunkley carried on. 'The oilskins. None of you have any recollection of seeing anybody out in the snow in any of these capes?'

He paused for effect.

A few shook their heads. Others waited for him to continue.

'Therefore, allowing that Miss Gwynne was bedridden and didn't nip down for a stroll, and assuming none of you are holding back the truth, then we are left with the likely trio of Herr Claube, Professor Melville and Mr Grauler.'

'What about Monckton or Drabble or Slack the gardener?' suggested Scanner.

'If you recall,' Kosik interjected, 'Monckton was there when we first noticed them. And he said that they were solely for the use of the guests.'

'And Miss Biddle? What about our pearly queen?' Gloss joked.

'Prim will interview her shortly.'

'Bit unlikely, I suppose. She rarely budged from her armchair or her teapot,' said Gloss, again with a boyish playfulness.

Dunkley banged a paperweight down on the desktop. 'So to the point, unless Claube or Melville came back to the house and removed the cloaks before venturing out again, it remains a mystery.'

'Why would they do that? It doesn't seem plausible.' Perry Scanner said.

'I'm in complete agreement,' stated Dunkley. 'When Claube was found he was wearing his own longcoat. In the professor's case, we obviously have no idea.'

'But these three cloaks had to have been worn by somebody,' Rebecca

Royce reminded them.

'So it draws me to the conclusion that more than one of you, for whatever reason, is hiding something.'

'Now look here, Inspector …' Gloss began hotly.

Dunkley put up a palm. 'It is of no matter. I merely make a statement of fact and at this moment, it would appear further discussion will prove pointless. So shall we press on?'

Joy glanced up from her book, scanning the group. An uncomfortable tenseness had settled over them. Only Miss Crabb had kept her composure, sitting straight-backed in her chair, her hands clasped motionless in her lap. Barasch fidgeted like a cat with a flea, shifting his seat over and over.

'Now listen here, Dunkley,' Gloss red-faced blared out. 'How much more of this dramatic play-acting are we to put up with? We've all just about had enough of this rot. Miss Biddle and Barasch's nerves are shot. If you're not careful somebody else will be joining them in the hothouse. The young girl has been having fainting fits. Lord knows what other maladies this charade will foster.'

'I didn't faint,' said Joy.

Dunkley nodded to her and politely motioned for Gloss to retake his seat. 'Perhaps it will be as well to close things for today. But before I leave you to what's left of the afternoon and your evening, I beg your forbearance for just a few more minutes.'

A tetchy hum rose in the room.

'If I could just back up just a bit,' Dunkley continued unperturbed. 'And get one niggling point clear in my head.'

Shuffling papers, Dunkley traced the writing with his finger. 'Nope,' he muttered under his breath. 'Nope – nope!' Turning to face them, he addressed Miss Crabb. 'Perhaps you can tell me how the bedrooms were allocated on arrival?'

'Of course,' Miss Crabb responded coolly. 'Although, I'm not sure it will be of much help. You see the all our rooms are numbered – a function of the war years. The keys to the bedrooms were left in a box in the reception hall. My mistress, as always, was happy to leave things to me, and I was equally content to defer their distribution to Monckton. So you see it was he who decided who slept where, an allocation of his own haphazard concoction.'

Gloss frowned.

'Excepting Miss Royce?' Dunkley queried.

'That is correct. She was given one of the two spare rooms available on her late arrival and of course ...'

'Thank you,' Dunkley interrupted. 'There is no further need to go into the saga regarding the additional guest. That has been a well-trodden path.'

And with that, Dunkley ordered his papers and left the room.

'I don't have any confidence that the inspector has any idea what's been going on here,' Gloss remarked, jiggling a finger in his ear.

'There must be some logic to his methods,' said Scanner. 'I'm sure he's keeping things back. He'd have to, otherwise he'd potentially prewarn our killer.'

'I still cannot believe that the murderer is amongst us,' muttered Clarice.

'Convenient,' said Rebecca Royce tartly.

'What does that mean?' demanded Clarice, rising from her chair.

Rebecca Royce scowled and flicked ash in the direction of the hearth as Gracie gently restrained Clarice.

'And you chose to keep quiet, Kosik?' Scanner punctured the scuffle.

Kosik levelled his eyes on Perry Scanner. 'You are suggesting what exactly?'

'I'm not suggesting anything. I saw you leave the house during the carol concert. One of those wet capes was worn by you. It's an indisputable fact.'

The air was sucked from the room. It seemed to be holding its breath.

'You are of course mistaken.'

'You had words with Claube. You said yourself that nobody would mourn a dead German.'

'So, you are now accusing me of murder? If you are so certain why did you not run to our policeman with your tale?'

Perry Scanner limped to the fire. 'Because I was waiting to see if you would offer it up. You had motive, opportunity, and with that bayonet you are so fond of – the wherewithal and the experience.'

'Now see here, Scanner.' Barasch was on his feet. 'We all have reason to hate the Nazis.'

Kosik's face had lost all colour and a tic twitched his cheek as he walked towards the door.

'Where are you going?' Scanner yelled after him.

'To my room,' Kosik hissed and running his eyes over them all, said flatly, 'I suggest if Mr Scanner is convinced that I am Claube's killer then he approaches our inspector and makes his statement. Either way, in consideration to the ladies I will be keeping to my room.'

Kosik withdrew, leaving the room smouldering.

'Do we think he's our killer?' Gloss eventually piped up.

Scanner, leaning on his stick, appeared lost in thought.

Barasch plucked at an eyebrow and murmured something incomprehensible to himself.

'As the police have made quite clear, it could be any one of us,' Rebecca Royce pronounced as she replenished her lipstick.

*

Dinner had been consumed in near silence. Neither Scanner nor Kosik had joined them. Miss Biddle was still ensconced in her room, so that left only seven of the original thirteen.

The trimmed-down party took coffee in the library, but Joy was restless and sneaked away, slipping along the passageway into the drawing room.

The room was dark and felt bitingly cold. The fire had been doused and the clock remained stuck at just after ten.

Joy sat for a bit and tried to think up a plan. But nothing came. Voices drifted in from the library. She could hear Rebecca Royce's twang and Mrs Pomp's trill.

Wandering to the window, Joy stared out into the night. Total blackness, not a pinprick above, as if the stars had been blotted out by a heavy slapdash coat of paint.

A snowdrop fell, then another and soon the darkness was blotted with smudges of white and grey. Joy's fingers were drawn to the freezing moistness on the pane. She drew them back as if scalded as from behind her the clock struck. Joy didn't turn, but counted the chimes. Nine! Outside, a sharp light streaked across the sky and like the sweeping brush of an artist the landscape erupted into daylight, fallen leaves gusting on a clear crisp blustery day.

On the edge of the wood, Joy saw two specks and narrowing her eyes could see there were two little girls. Between them they were holding onto the string of a kite and were tugging hard.

Flapping in the branch above was a snagged red slip of canvas and dancing ribbon. No matter how hard they hauled at the string, the kite wouldn't budge. After a moment, one of the girls pointed and motioned to another tree.

A gawky teenager with lank black hair was lurking, and on being spotted, made to scurry off, but she stopped suddenly as the younger girls waved her over.

She came gingerly. The small girls pointed up into the tree. The elder girl shook her head and again began to make her way back into the wood.

The chunkier of the little ones ran after her and grabbed the girl's arms, and with a smile dug into her pocket, and produced something which she offered up.

She then again motioned to the tangled kite above. It appeared a deal had been done, as cautiously the teenager began to scale the trunk and manage her way up into the branches. She didn't falter, and encouraged by the hollers from the girls below, finally inched out onto the offending branch and yanked the kite free. It sailed high into the air.

The girls below whooped and dashed for the string, but it was too late and the kite, free of its pursuers, vanished high into the windswept sky, up and over the wood.

Sliding down the trunk, the bigger girl was accosted and pushed in the chest. The spat continued until eventually the teenager was barged to the ground. With a squeal, the two little girls then skipped off in the direction of the coast.

The clock broke the spell. It chimed the half hour and the sun faded to darkness, clouds churned and the blackness returned. A snowstorm obliterated the wood and the inhospitable night was once more filling the sky. Joy turned to the clock and found the hands were still stuck at five past ten. 'Hem!'

Back in the library Joy found the remnants of the gathering in solemn and reflective mood.

'Joy's condition is exactly that. It's not qualifiable. You can't look it up in a medical journal.' Clarice went on as Joy held fast outside the door. 'Some have mentioned schizophrenia. She tells me she sometimes sees and hears things that others miss. Her mother couldn't cope with her, and with the Blitz and for safety's sake, she packed her off to me. It was either that or have her restrained – sectioned as they call it.'

'How awful,' Mrs Pomp sympathised.

'But although she has her ways, she has been an absolute wonder to me.'

Mrs Pomp beamed.

'But I do find it difficult at this time of year. Joy is such a solitary soul, and I find it hard to press her, but she is not much company. But even so, I do love her, and please all of you try to understand and believe me when I tell you that I have never known Joy have as much as a malicious thought, let alone consider any act of violence.'

Joy pushed open the door, giving birth to a painful silence. She hastily found a chair a bit away from the huddle. Beside her was a globe on a round piecrust table. With her knitting confiscated, she spun the globe. It squeaked as the shiny colours of the world twirled round and around.

Mrs Pomp broke the suffocating hush. 'I suppose we are here for similar reasons. On the death of my husband my world altered more entirely than I would ever have imagined,' she explained. 'Like you, I take solace in my little routines, charities and the suchlike, but at Christmas I find it most testing. Oh, for a chest of the professor's treasure and to live in a house such as this. Some are most fortunate. To be born to this.'

Rebecca Royce idled over to the window, turning her back on the room.

Mrs Pomp gave out an exaggerated sigh. 'If only the Brigadier hadn't been so easy with money.'

'And yet, there are some amongst us who just keep running,' said Barasch. 'The horror of the Nazis. Then in London, no less, these fascists spring up. Will it ever be over?'

'Jeffrey Hamm and his hoodlums are a disgrace, an affront to this country,' Gloss cut in.

'I suppose we're all hiding from something,' Rebecca Royce murmured. 'Once the children left me. Sailed back across the ocean. It left a chasm in my life and made me pine for family, my roots and to understand how it all began. It was to be expected, I suppose.'

'The war enveloped us all. But I know how you feel. The memories that you just can't shift. To make some sense of how it ended in such a way. To able to move on.' Gloss slipped down a glass and refilled his and Rebecca Royce's from a decanter.

'Miss Biddle, she suffers also,' pronounced Barasch. 'The Blitz – such bombs, she tells me – night after night. She may seem a bitter woman, but she is lost too. To return to London would only relive those nightmares. Where does she go with no money to help her?'

Gracie said, 'We all have our tales to tell.'

Barasch blew his nose. 'Like me, we are all still roving, refugees from the war in one form or other.'

A log splintered on the fire as Joy spun the globe again. It whined as it turned. Clarice gave Joy a bright look. Joy twirled it around, again and again, revelling in the melding pastel shapes and colours as it spun like a spinning top, squealing and squeaking.

Joy's fingers reached for the tip of her nose for reassurance, as again a memory hatched.

Dawn arrived at Joy's window revealing a refreshed carpet of white. The snow had fallen in bundles overnight and only the nakedness of the spindly trees blemished the splendour of the unspoiled outlook.

But there was no time for dreaming. Joy had again risen early for a reason. Climbing into her layers, she pulled a mackintosh from its hanger, and adjusting her hat, walked out into the arctic morning.

The air smelled of wet leaves and the fluffy sky looked marginally less forbidding, and the snow-white perfection reflected a mellowness, adding a soft tinge to the budding light.

Joy crunched her way down to the knotted garden, enjoying the cushioned compactness. She halted at the fountain and stared down into the ice-covered mildew. Creaking branches heavy with snow dropped hissing bundles, stirring the birds and sending them rocketing skywards.

Prodding the ice, Joy traced her name, then made a snowball and threw it at a fat pigeon. Shaping the snow, she fashioned a funnel-like volcano. And then, she waited.

Standing in silence, she hummed to herself and took in the manor. The groggy house was still abed, no lights were shining out as yet, and the chimney stacks remained dormant.

Even the sea beyond, with the faint smacking of waves, seemed subdued. The drone of the half-hearted wind as it flicked at the lawns added to the delicious sensation of solitude. Joy's only companions were two pheasants pecking at the snow, divots revealing the gravel, their passion frozen underneath, and an inquisitive robin, bobbing on a hedge, its head jerking as Joy toyed with the icicles.

A door closed somewhere, jolting Joy to attention. A shuffling of footsteps followed and a hunched figure emerged from the rear of the house, picking its way through the drifts on the terrace.

It was Miss Crabb. She took trippy steps as her sensible shoes soon became deluged with slush. Joy could hear her admonishing the elements, crossly tutting and muttering as she lifted a foot and shook it. Then she turned back.

Joy repositioned herself behind the fountain. She had no intention of swapping niceties with the woman. The morning was her own and she wanted to be able to watch and imbibe the moment as Misenlake awoke.

Within minutes, Crabb returned wearing wellingtons. She also had a shovel and was breathlessly sweeping aside the snow, engineering a pathway to the front of the house. Joy wondered where Ernest had got to. Probably too early for him.

A seagull flew down and skidded onto the lawn. The pheasants, taking fright, scooted away, their trill chirps resonating across the grounds.

Crabb's eyes zipped up, and instantly spotted Joy. For a second, they stared at each other. Then Crabb's body seemed to relax and she attempted a half-hearted wave.

Joy signalled back with a lukewarm flap of her own. Crabb stood for a second, then turned and vanished back inside.

An orange glow grew within the manor as first the downstairs windows threw back their curtains. Joy's toes were frozen and her nose was stinging. Lights started to flick on and off on the upper storey, one of which Joy recognised as Clarice's. Drapes swished in another and a face fleetingly appeared, but hastily drew back. Joy frowned; it was time to go back.

Snow slid to the ground as a window slammed shut. Morning had arrived. For Joy her moment was done, and although it had been a tad disappointing, it had been enough.

Miss Biddle made it to breakfast. Her wasted features were a shock to everyone, a dark smear hugging her eyes. Whatever illness had grabbed hold of her body had also told on her mind as she offered up even less than was usual, snivelling into her teacup.

Kosik had been a latecomer and had grabbed some toast on his way, as they all trooped into the library for their daily post-mortem with Inspector Dunkley.

Perry Scanner, who'd been absent at breakfast, was already seated when they entered and the murmur of words between Dunkley and him ceased as people found their usual places.

'Good morning all,' said Dunkley. 'Firstly, despite the overnight storm the telephone appears to be working.'

'Hooray! The twentieth century has arrived in Yorkshire,' Rebecca Royce said, pitching her voice like a Pathé newsreel narrator.

'Further points of order before we commence.' Dunkley began to pace. 'DS Prim and PC Nouse managed to get out before the weather set in. I have sent them to Hull on an errand.'

Again, Joy was glad to be rid of Prim. Whilst he was in the house she could always sense he was ready to pounce.

'As to Mr Kosik, I have accepted his account of his movements. He has apologised for not speaking up sooner, and I will add only this, he has admitted to being one of the wearers of the wet oilskins.'

Somebody whistled.

'But I must inform you that the wounds that were possibly responsible for the deaths of both Herr Claube and Grauler were not inflicted by his bayonet.'

'Then what?' asked Gloss.

Dunkley ignored him. 'Whilst the matter is not entirely closed, these sets of circumstances are, shall I say … shelved for the moment.'

'Shelved? What balderdash! What was he doing out in the snow? Is he or isn't he our …'

Dunkley darted Gloss a warning look. 'I'm satisfied with his explanation.'

Rebecca Royce looked the most put out. 'It's intolerable. Will we ever be allowed to leave this dismal place?'

'All in good time.' Dunkley rustled his papers and produced a wad of white fivers. 'A tidy sum, I think you'll agree,' he ventured, waving the money and laying it in a pile on a table.

They all gaped nonplussed as Dunkley went on, 'It was discovered in a sock amongst Grauler's things. A ripped segment of one of these notes was found in his clenched fist as he lay prone, well, it would seem whoever perpetrated his murder, potentially was in the throes of some sort of lucrative tug-of-war.'

'I wouldn't be so sure,' said Rebecca Royce lighting up again. 'He gave me the impression that he lived for the day and never passed up an opportunity to make a buck. But then easy come, easy go. That's what he told me, anyhow. I'm sure he always had plenty of readies about him.'

'Did he offer up any precise explanation of where he may have come by such a tidy cache of money?' asked Dunkley.

'Why ask me? The vulgar man was no great friend of mine,' said Rebecca Royce, her heavily made-up face creasing into crusty crevices. 'Ask Miss Biddle over there. She was his confidante. They were always squirreled away together.'

Miss Biddle glared at Rebecca Royce and smothered her face in a tatty hanky.

'Miss Biddle?' Dunkley pressed.

'Why pick on me?' she bleated. 'I 'ardly knew the bloke.'

'Then what was all that infernal gossiping about?' Rebecca Royce rested her chin on her hand and hunched forward.

Miss Biddle's face flushed slightly. 'This and that. He spoke mainly of rationing and how he could get hold of things that, well, weren't easy to get. He weren't in a hurry to go back to America. Opportunity knocks – he said.'

Dunkley plucked at his lower lip. 'And money?'

'I've no idea about no fivers,' Miss Biddle blathered. She sneezed and swept away the beginnings of a dribble.

Dunkley let it go. 'Let us press on.'

Joy knew not what was coming next and she wriggled in her seat expectantly.

'The day before I arrived, Mr Gloss contrived a sort of bathing house, out in the disused laundry.' Dunkley riffled through his paperwork and found the page he was searching for. 'DS Prim states that Miss Royce bathed whilst Grauler stood guard outside, and when she had finished, he made use of the water.'

'That's correct,' said Gloss. 'I left them to it once I'd ensured it was safe and the water was warm enough.'

'Did anybody else venture out to the laundry?'

Most shook their heads.

'DS Prim also noted that not long after Grauler re-entered the manor, he claimed somebody had attempted to drown him – crowning him with a washing paddle. He also goes on – here we are – Mr Barasch had absconded, and yet again, none of the guests were able to put forward any sort of alibi.'

Dunkley regarded them keenly as if he expected somebody to contribute. After a pause, he went on. 'The door to the laundry had been bolted. Is anybody aware of another way in?' Again he waited for a reply.

'That's assuming he was telling the truth and wasn't making it all up,' Scanner cut in.

'Miss Crabb?' Dunkley enquired. 'Are you aware of a separate entrance or potential way into the laundry?'

Miss Crabb shifted in her seat. 'No. But then, I do not make a habit of wandering around the outhouses. I am a lady's companion, sometimes housekeeper, and the stable area is the gardener's space.'

'Of course.' Dunkley then addressed Gloss. 'If we accept the late Mr Grauler's word that he made the door secure behind him, would it have been possible for somebody to have been already inside, hiding within the laundry?'

'I saw no one,' said Rebecca Royce.

'I suppose it's possible, Inspector,' replied Gloss.

'So, you believe this was a real attempt on Grauler's life and not some figment of an overwrought imagination?' Perry Scanner probed.

'I do. And I also think that whoever was responsible for Grauler's death had made this earlier attempt on his life, and one has to surmise that this exceptional sum of money had some bearing on the assault.'

'Hem!' I had started to hum. It was an unpleasant feeling, recalling Grauler's snoring and wheezing. After all, they had been probably his last moments. And thinking back to that long, cold night, I had definitely heard someone outside in the passage. Had it been the same person returning the second time, I didn't know. And in this open forum, what if I volunteered that I'd potentially heard the killer roaming the passages? How could it help? I hadn't seen anything. I'd been too afraid. And would such a revelation place my own life in danger, pre-warn the assassin? I scanned the faces in the room. A killer was amongst them, I could feel it. But who and why? And how was it linked to this injustice from the past? Discretion was required. I had nothing useful to add, not as yet anyway. But the time would come when the house burned off this murky haze. The visions had begun to plot a path, but the fragments were all jumbled, crucial pieces were missing. Find them and I would seek out this affable but painstaking policeman. Dunkley would make things right.

Joy scrambled up the path. .The wind had whipped itself into a torrent and pummelled her face and grabbed at her hat as she reached the shoulder of the snow-puckered clifftop. The sea was a heaving torment of grey and frothy peaks, as if a scrum of starving seamonsters were falling over each other in a quest to get at their prey.

Gracie suddenly appeared from a dip in the land. She waved and held onto her headscarf as she approach. 'My goodness, it's a wild one.'

Joy pulled aside some straggles from her own cheeks.

'I wouldn't venture further if I was you, lassie. I've only been along a ways and I'm frozen to the core.' She offered Joy her arm.

A gust of iciness took Joy's breath away. She'd wanted to be alone to enjoy these untamed elements, allowing herself the recklessness of being shaped by nature. But also a moment to clear her head. She needed to be brave. She needed to embrace these visits to the past. The hut on the outcrop was part of the story. Would the lost souls feel her presence there and seek her out once more?

Joy shivered. She'd wished she'd packed her woolly vest and slacks as it was cold as heck. Staring down at the tumbling waves, she became mesmerised by their might as they battered the rocks. The brackish spray stung her face as salty missiles fired up and over the headland.

Before she could pull away, Grace had circled her arm and had yanked her back the way she'd come. 'Let's have a peek at this famous cove, hen!'

And they did. But the trek down was perilous. The rocks skidded under their feet and Gracie almost went over twice. They halted at an outcrop and peered over the edge. Just below was the platform that Gloss had mentioned. It jutted out over the sea like the square jaw of one of the Hollywood movie heroes.

A winding stairway of sorts cut out of the cliff led the way further down, but the narrow steepness looked like a deathtrap, frozen slurry coating the rock.

'I love the seascape,' said Gracie. 'Wouldn't it be wonderful to live somewhere such as this.'

Joy followed her stare as they watched the sea surging on the horizon, the ocean's swashbuckling wilfulness stretching out and leaping into the clouds.

Gracie dipped her face into the wind. 'To settle myself, be done with the past and just exist for moments like these. Don't you think that'd be heaven, lassie?'

A spume of spray exploded around them. A cloven slash in the rocks had created a seawater spurt, hissing salvos erupting into the air as the swell crashed below.

Joy had had enough. She wanted to go back to the house. Gracie seemed a hearty woman and not the type for strong emotions, but as the woman let her hair be buffeted by the breeze a sort of recklessness came into her eyes as if she may at any moment leap into the sea, taking Joy with her, the two of them dragged away by the elements.

Thankfully, with a pronounced shiver Gracie snapped out of it and without warning, coiled her scarf around her face and clinging to Joy said, 'Let's make our way back if we can. Careful now – a cup of tea by the fire is calling me!'

They tentatively scrambled up the cascade of rocks and trudged through the muddiness in silence. The only sound the mewing wind that seemed to be determined to help them on their way. At last the manor hove into view.

'Do you miss your parents, Joy?' Gracie asked, blowing her nose.

Miss them. Joy didn't really understand the concept of missing anything. True, it was sometimes annoying to be without her fidgets or be away from her comforts and the closeness of Clarice's cottage, and of course the steadiness of her routine. She took a minute.

Gracie smiled expectantly.

Joy set her eyes to the right, as far as they would flick. Her dad was gone and that was a shame. Her mum sent her away and then duly died. What more was there? 'I don't know,' said Joy. 'I'm not sure it matters.'

It seemed to be enough as Gracie huddled further into her coat, and with brimming eyes, said, 'Perhaps you are right.'

Prim appeared to be back in the fold as midway through afternoon tea he came striding into the library obliterating the restful drowsiness. Fortunately Dunkley was only seconds behind him.

'I'm sorry to disturb your peace,' said Dunkley, snuffling into a hanky.

'But policing never ceases, even on New Year's Eve,' dovetailed Prim. 'Routine and drudgery are our mistress, and constant bedfellow. It is a chastening experience being …'

'This will be brief, of that I promise,' interrupted Dunkley with a pointed look at Prim.

'How is Miss Gwynne?' Gloss asked.

Prim looked mournful. 'Frail. Sadly laying prone in her boudoir.' He pulled a grave face and lowered his voice to a reverent murmur. 'The dear lady could barely lift herself from the pillow. It's taken its toll, this foul business, coupled with her illness. A class above, that's indisputable. Yes indeed, a very fine lady. She will see out this nastiness stoically, as one would expect, of that I'm sure.'

'But what is exactly is wrong with her?' Mrs Pomp enquired.

'On that I cannot speculate. I am no physician.' Prim had taken over. His speech was gushing with self-importance. 'Rest and tranquillity is what her delicate frame needs most.'

'That's not the Dotty I knew,' observed Gloss. 'Fit as a flea and never still for a minute.'

'We all get old,' Barasch said.

'I think this gathering may be the last of its kind,' said Prim fixated by his inside track. 'She told me that her father had saddled her with too many loose ends, and that the running of this old place is not for the faint-hearted, indeed a pricey undertaking, so she tells me. This Christmas indulgence just adds to the expense.'

Dunkley reasserted his authority thrusting himself in front of Prim. 'Mr Grauler was killed sometime between nine p.m and nine a.m. Twelve hours unaccounted for. We would obviously like to narrow this time frame. Has anybody anything to add?'

Nobody spoke.

'Miss?' Prim pounced. His eyes arrowed at Joy.

Joy flushed. She had been taken by surprise.

'I heard him snoring,' Joy stuttered. 'When I was getting off to sleep.'

'Ah-ha! At what time exactly?' Prim drew so close that Joy could see the prickly greying bristles on his chin.

A noise caught in Dunkley's throat. Prim stood aside.

'Nearly midnight, I think,' Joy replied.

'And the last to bed that evening was …?' Dunkley turned his attention to Drabble.

'Usually it would be Miss Royce,' answered Drabble, 'but I'm unsure.'

'I think I turned in just after ten,' said Rebecca Royce. Her eyes were tinged with red as if she had been crying.

'I was the last, Inspector.' Gloss spoke up. 'Along with Kosik. It would have been around eleven. We went up a few minutes after Scanner.'

Dunkley penned a note. Prim peered over Dunkley's shoulder. 'It should all be there, if Nouse was paying attention,' Prim babbled.

Ignoring him, Dunkley continued. 'Does anyone know why Mr Grauler came to Misenlake this Christmas? Did he mention his future plans?'

'Like our mad professor, I believe he was treasure hunting,' Rebecca Royce let slip tartly.

'He was after the treasure?' Prim stammered.

Dunkley shot him another firm look.

'Of the female kind.' Rebecca Royce tossed Prim a derisive scowl.

'Well, he did quiz me a bit,' offered Gloss. 'Was asking about the Gwynne family and Miss Dorothy, her age, her likes and dislikes, even her appearance. I found it rather distasteful and his presumption, well, he could be a trifle coarse, and more than a tad cocksure.'

Miss Biddle muttered into her tea.

Dunkley turned to her and raised a brow.

Miss Biddle's nose rumpled. 'Well, look at you all. Mighty fine people speaking ill of the dead. Just trying to better yourself don't make you a bad person.'

Mrs Pomp's hand covered her mouth.

Dunkley carried on. 'So again, with this added intelligence, the plain facts are that Grauler was murdered sometime between midnight and nine the next morning. As with the prior assault, and the two other murders, you were all in your rooms. Again, nobody has an alibi. We know that the weapon that killed him was similar to that used on Herr Claube.'

'And you didn't hear anything else?' Prim piped up, again homing in on Joy.

Joy fiddled with her notebook and lowered her eyes.

'If she had, she would have said, wouldn't you, dear?' Clarice came to the rescue.

Prim glowered, his dark weasely eyes lancing Joy with a glare.

'How much longer is this going to go on?' Rebecca Royce enquired, delving into her handbag.

Dunkley said, 'I am sorry for having to keep you here against your will. I'm aware the New Year is nearly with us, but until I get to the bottom …'

'But when will that be?' Rebecca Royce shocked everybody by slipping into a convulsion of sobs.

Mrs Pomp tried to comfort her, but was shrugged off.

'I'm sorry I can't deal with this anymore.' And with that Rebecca Royce ran from the room.

Dunkley signalled that the meeting had ended with a resigned gesture, and opening the door to see them out, fell back into a huddle with Prim.

Everyone drifted in their separate ways except Miss Biddle, who tapped Gloss on the elbow and asked for a word over a cup of tea in the drawing room.

A commotion met Joy's ears as she descended the staircase. Clarice held her back for a moment and then strode ahead. Raised voices came from the library. And then the door crashed open and a red-faced Drabble came storming out, almost knocking them from their feet.

'Beg pardon, ladies,' he said and marched toward the back of the house.

Clarice made eyes at Joy.

Prim sauntered out of the library and pushed past.

'I think I shall treat myself to a small sherry, to help bring in a merrier New Year,' said Clarice through thin lips. 'This house is fit to explode, and if this bother doesn't come to an end soon, Lord knows who'll be next to crumble.'

The library was empty and welcomingly warm with a recently stacked fire.

'What a relief. A haven of peace.' Clarice sighed as she fell into a sofa.

Joy went over to the globe.

'Not now, dear. It makes the most dreadful racket. Now for my sherry.'

Joy sniffed at the decanters.

'That's whisky, dear, and by the looks of that other one, port. Perhaps you could try the bell?'

Joy pulled the chord and within moments Drabble appeared.

His tie was unbuttoned and his hair a mess. He muttered and said he'd be back in a tick.

On his return, with a silver salver laden with sherry, Joy noted that his hands quivered, just holding himself together enough to get some in a glass for Clarice.

'Are you feeling quite well, Drabble?' Clarice asked.

'I'm sorry, madam. It's this place and the police and everything. I need to be gone before I do something we'll all regret.' Drabble muzzled a snivel.

'Joy, dear, please close the door.' Clarice patted the sofa next to her. 'Sit a second. Perhaps telling someone will help – it generally does.'

Clarice glanced to the drinks trolley. 'And perhaps a tot of whisky won't hurt. If somebody comes I'll take responsibility.'

Joy handed Drabble a tumbler. The drink smelt peaty. Joy couldn't understand the fuss with alcohol. It made people talk nonsense and become somebody they oughtn't.

Drabble gulped it down. 'I wouldn't worry about me taking a drink – that's the least of my bother.'

Clarice lifted an eyebrow.

'That know-nothing copper Prim's been poking about in my affairs.' Drabble's eyes fired briefly.

'I suspect he'd be checking on all of our backgrounds,' said Clarice. 'I'm afraid as much as it's unpalatable, that is his job.'

'Well, his digging has had proper awful consequences for me. My old lady is now after her share of my pay. T'ain't fair. Nothing's right anymore. The war – the Jerries – the 'stablishment – the politicians – the whole blinking rotten country.'

Drabble again just about frustrated a sob.

Clarice gestured with her eyes for Joy to stand a refill.

Joy topped him up.

'You served overseas?' asked Clarice.

'Course. Three murderous years. Mates copped it. I've seen things …' Drabble tried to still his shaking hands. 'And you know what kept us going – allowed us to face death every blooming miserable day – the thought of getting back home. We'll meet again and all that. One day to wake up to a peaceful life, getting through the horror and returning to the cosiness of our own castles. Huh! What a bleedin' rib-tickler!'

Joy could almost hear the screams that flared in the man's eyes as he blinked and swiped away tears.

Hunkering back into his own torment, Drabble carried on. 'And when we got back? The relief, the sheer bliss of having survived the war lasts less than five miserable minutes. Everything's changed. It's like we ain't welcome anymore, and all the hardship we've been through is taken for granted and … I dunno … people don't want to know you. They've had their own troubles and we're just in the way.'

'Your wife?'

Drabble cuffed his eyes, but sat upright and began to marshal himself. 'Don't get me wrong. She didn't say anything. But I was a sort of trespasser. A stranger in my own house,' he said, his face becoming red and blotchy.

'So you ran away?'

Drabble's features sharpened. 'It weren't like that. She didn't want me. She'd had a job and been her own mistress and then I come back and expect it to be how it was. It was the right thing to do.'

'Where is home?' asked Clarice.

'North London.'

'You have no other family?'

'Family? No, I'm an orphan like my ma was before me. She brought me up. Never had a dad. When she died in nineteen-forty, I joined up. Due to my age I was next to be called anyways.'

Joy went to fill him up again, but he stopped her, putting a hand over the top of the tumbler. 'Musn't get too tipsy, miss. That'd suit that bleedin' rozzer. I've known plenty like him in the forces – jobsworth! Proper little Hitler. Happy for us squaddies to do the dangerous stuff whilst he wears the uniform and takes his share of the glory.' Drabble's eyes were awash. 'Except there ain't no glory in war. Just death and blinkin' damnation.'

'But you survived,' Clarice summoned a smile.

'Survived? What for? These demons in my head. I just can't get rid of 'em. I figured a job in service. Order and routine and keeping busy would do the trick – just like the army.'

Joy felt a silent accord with the troubled man. The clatter of the world was tearing him apart. He needed to find a shelter within himself. It wasn't easy.

'Then I arrived in this slaughterhouse. And now with my references blown, I'm tempted to run up those cliffs and toss myself into the sea before I do any more mischief.'

The door opened and Gracie walked in.

Drabble leapt up and thrust his glass at Joy. Straightening his tie, he bowed. 'Thank you, ladies. That has helped, but I now better face the music and fess up to Miss Crabb before that Prim proper peaches on me.'

'What was that all about?' Gracie asked after he'd gone.

Clarice swept back a curl and grimaced. 'Another troubled soul.'

The library filled. The other guests drifted in. Dinner seemed to be an inconvenience. This New Year was going to slip in unannounced with most not even attempting politeness or niceties.

'Shall we go through?' suggested Mrs Pomp.

'Best to wait a bit for the others,' Gloss replied.

'Who are we missing?' Gracie asked.

A breathless pause ensued. Twitchy eyes wouldn't settle.

The faces of the dead seemed to float amongst them.

'Miss Royce and Miss Biddle aren't here yet,' said Scanner breaking the impasse.

'Perhaps somebody should give them a knock?' Mrs Pomp suggested.

'I can go,' said Gracie. 'I need a shawl anyway.'

The embittered silence was festering, and chafing Joy's brain. She had to get away. The odd-looking clock emerged from storm clouds in her head. Joy slipped out. Within a moment, she was in the drawing room.

The fire was nearly done. The faded light from a solitary lamp gave the room a sepulchral pallor.

Joy started. Slouched in a highbacked chair with her teapot beside her was Miss Biddle. She was dozing. Tentatively, Joy leant over and gave her a gentle nudge.

Biddle's body slumped, her head lolling to the side, and her teacup slid from her hand, crashing to the floor.

Joy yelped and in seconds Prim was beside her.

SEVENTEEN

'DONT MOVE! Don't touch a thing.'

Prim thrust an arm across Joy's chest, pinning her back against a table. Pulling on a silver chain, he peeped on a whistle over and over.

Joy put her hands over her ears and began to snort, over and over. But it wouldn't drown out the shrill racket. She just wanted it to stop.

Gracie was there in seconds then came the stomping feet of the two constables.

'Keep everyone out,' Prim instructed one of them. 'And handcuff the girl,' he barked at the other.

'What on earth …' Clarice was there and her arms were around Joy.

'It's Miss Biddle,' gasped Gracie. 'I think … she's dead!'

'Oh goodness gracious, not another!' shrieked Mrs Pomp from the doorway 'Oh, Brigadier, that you have left me to this.'

Dunkley barged in. 'Put those cuffs away and get this lot out of here right now – yes, that includes the young lady. And stay with them until I tell you otherwise.' He gave Prim a venomous glare and made himself busy over by Miss Biddle. 'This is my doing. You fool, Dunkley. You never learn. Again you have been too damned steady.'

*

'It's Miss Biddle. I fear she is dead,' said Mrs Pomp, wringing her hands.

'Our lives are fashioned by our choices.' Barasch pinched the bridge of his nose.

'What's that supposed to mean?' Gloss asked gruffly.

'Another silenced,' Kosik murmured.

'For God's sake! I was only with her just now," Gloss blustered.

'Everybody stay where you are.' Prim was all around them. Nouse was lurking. 'Nouse, be alert. Inspector Dunkley will be with us shortly once he's examined the body.'

Joy wrestled herself away from Clarice and found a corner. Prim signalled for Nouse to follow.

Drabble came bundling in, followed by Miss Crabb, both looking hot and flustered.

'Are we all here?' Prim snapped.

'Miss Royce is still upstairs,' Gracie responded. 'I did knock, but there was no reply.'

Barasch cast a grave look and cursed under his breath.

'You don't think – oh my!' cried Gracie.

'You there! Constable whatever-your-name is. Go and check. Hurry, man!' Prim hollered at a loitering copper.

The PC almost collided with Dunkley at the door.

'Steady on, Constable. OK, very good, but be quick about it.'

Dunkley led Prim out of the library by the arm. Raised whispers resonated from the hallway.

'She was slumped in her chair – it was horrid,' said Gracie. 'Joy? How are you doing, pet?'

'I want my knitting.'

Stamps on the staircase were followed by doors slamming.

The constable flew into the room. 'Where's the Inspector? Miss Royce – I can't get her to wake up!'

Within seconds there was more crashing and pounding feet.

At last the house seemed to take a breath, dousing the hullabaloo.

Dunkley reappeared and drew near to Clarice. 'Is she doing all right?' he said quietly, motioning to Joy. 'It must have been quite a shock.'

'She tends to withdraw within herself. Perhaps if she can be allowed her knitting – that usually helps.'

Dunkley nodded to Nouse.

'Miss Biddle – she's definitely dead?' Clarice stuttered.

'It appears so. Preliminary examination suggests death would have occurred within the last few hours, but with no marks on the body, it's impossible to say exactly how it happened or whether it was natural causes or not.'

'A few hours, you say?' Clarice queried. 'Then Joy had nothing to do with it. She was with me all afternoon, tidying our things.'

'Yes, I apologise. DS Prim has been hasty.'

Clarice huffed.

'But what about Miss Royce?' Mrs Pomp reminded them.

'Ah! It appears she has taken some sedatives and has slept through this mayhem quite untroubled.' A grim-faced Dunkley warmed his hands at the fire.

'A few hours, you said?' Gloss pressed.

Dunkley nodded.

Gloss recoiled and loosened his collar. 'Then perhaps I was the last to see her alive.'

Dunkley turned away from the hearth and eyed Gloss steadily.

'She wanted a word,' Gloss continued, unabashed. 'Told me she'd seen something from her bedroom window that first morning.'

'And?' Dunkley bent his head forward.

'She mentioned that she'd spoken to Grauler about it. She was a bit cryptic, but definitely scared.'

'Did she elucidate, shed any light on what she'd seen?'

'She wasn't specific. Just said that morning she had been staring out into the gardens for ever such a time, and it sort of popped into her head. She told me it would have been easy to miss it.'

Joy grunted.

Dunkley shot her a look, but his eyes snapped back to Gloss. 'Didn't you press her further?'

'Of course. I asked her why she hadn't informed the police. She said she didn't want to end up like Grauler. I told her we'd have words after dinner, but it would be best to seek you out and tell you what she knew.'

'Then?'

Everyone waited on Gloss as he filled a glass with whisky.

'Then nothing. She offered me a cup of tea from that infernal pot she carries about with her. I turned her down, was impatient to pen a note to Miss Gwynne to see if she would grant me an audience – old times and all that.' Gloss downed the drink. 'I left her there. I'm afraid quite alone and defenceless.'

For the first time, Dunkley looked shaken. His sausagelike fingers pressed his cheeks like bludgeons.

Joy clicked away. Her knitting seemed to come alive between her fingers. It was cold enough. It would definitely be a scarf, she decided, perhaps a gift for Nouse.

Miss Biddle had also noticed. And she had kept it to herself. A plain woman trying to better herself and now she was dead. It was as stupid as it was sad. Now, Joy's decision had been made up for her. She had to speak to Dunkley.

'You can't finger me for this one,' Drabble stammered.

Dinner had been forsaken. A buffet had been laid out in the dining room, but nobody appeared hardy enough to brave the murky inhospitable corridors.

Inspector Dunkley had retired to the drawing room and was supervising Graves and Stillwell and the forensic chaps, with Miss Biddle's corpse joining the others in the makeshift mortuary. It was becoming popular.

Prim was on the prowl. Nouse was standing by, and the unfortunate Drabble was still on the defensive. 'But I don't make the bleedin' tea. I just took her teapot to Cook.'

'Ample opportunity to slip something inside.' Prim rooted around in a nostril with his finger.

'I'm telling you. I had nothing to do with it.' Drabble's face spun to the guests looking for support.

'Are you certain she was poisoned? Has it been confirmed?' Barasch asked.

Prim bounced back and forth from tiptoe to heel. 'It's obvious. She had her cup in her hand and there wasn't a mark on her.'

'That you could see without examining her,' remarked Scanner.

Prim looked fixedly at Joy. 'To use the same method twice would be more than foolhardy. But experience has taught me that there can be an arrogance to even the most simple criminal. They like to tease the law. They always underestimate our methods.'

'Shouldn't we wait for your colleagues to confirm the cause of death before we speculate further?' Clarice rebuked him.

Gracie nodded in support.

Prim glared at them and left off. After some sort of internal turmoil that twisted his face like mangled washing, he eventually said sharply, 'Nouse, keep an eye on them. I need to see the inspector.' And then he left.

The room heaved a sigh.

'Pain we cannot hide from – suffering we can choose to endure,' Barasch murmured. 'And this house has plenty of both.'

Kosik nudged Barasch's shoulder and pursed his lips as if he was going to say something.

'We all have our secrets,' Barasch went on. 'And perhaps we will all die here with them firmly clutched. Something that began so simply has mushroomed into a duel with the Devil. This place is not for us, not for anyone.'

Gloss was on the offensive. He'd finished the entire decanter of whisky and had sent Drabble for replenishments.

Joy studied his face. The healthy ruddiness he'd arrived with had morphed into a mottled clay-colour. He'd obviously not slept. His eyes were red-rimmed. He was another nearing the edge.

'Drabble? Where is Miss Crabb?' asked Gracie.

'Up with the mistress, I suspect,' Drabble replied slamming another bottle of single malt onto the dresser. 'I heard a constable telling her to lock her door and keep to their apartments.'

Joy pulled out her notebook and read through her scrawl. Something Gloss had said had made her think. She made a decision and asked Clarice if she was permitted to go up.

'I'll check with the governor, miss,' Nouse intervened.

'I think I will join you,' added Mrs Pomp. 'We can't be made to sit here all night. I for one have no compulsion to see in the New Year.'

'Are you all right, old boy?' Scanner prodded Gloss, as his head drooped almost sending him over. He clasped a sidetable and gripped his glass.

'All right? Of course not. This damned house of horrors!' Gloss grappled with Nouse as the policeman re-entered the room.

'His bedtime I think!' said Nouse with a wink.

This time they'd all gone up together. Nobody was left alone. Joy and Clarice huddled into the latter's bedroom along with Gracie. It was quite a squeeze, but with the overly large fire snorting heat, it held an ease that they all welcomed.

'Peculiar little room,' said Gracie, snuffling around the walls.

'I suspect it was converted during the war years,' Clarice observed. 'The wall adjoining the bathroom is thinner than paper, the dreaded Essex board.'

Joy traced their appraisals. They were right. It was an irregular-shaped room, cramped and hoisted onto the end of the south-end corridor.

'Miss Biddle was ill-starred.' Gracie sucked in a breath. 'To survive the Blitz and have her life taken so cruelly. Mr Barasch is right about this place. It's as if we are all being condemned for the sins of our past.'

Clarice frowned. 'You're sure Miss Biddle was murdered?'

'What else? Nothing else seemed to ail her.'

'I suppose you're right. It's just too horrid for words.'

Joy poked the fire, teasing the flames higher. How she loved to bate the ferocity of those untamed talons.

'Do you think you will stay in your village?' Gracie asked Clarice.

'Oh, I don't know. There really isn't anything to hold me – no ties – no history to speak of. But where else would I go. And Joy?'

*

The alarm clock dinged. The New Year, 1949, was slipping in, swiping away the smothering darkness by degrees as Joy peered into the patchiness from her window. A rising mist hung low over the dips like the scalding steam from a witch's cauldron, adding to the feeling that the night was slipping back to its sinister environs.

Joy dressed speedily, yanking the partially-knitted scarf from its bag. The packed snow had slipped to slush, sogginess everywhere. She slid down the slope, once again heading for the fountain, where she paused on the pathway and looked up at the house.

The curtains were drawn in her own bedroom by design. Counting across, she established Miss Biddle's window and peered down at the terrace beneath it. Raking left and right, she shuffled back to the concrete slope and had a snipe around the side of the house.

Joy kicked at some icy clumps. The wind suddenly ripped and Joy shuddered, as head down, she pulled down her hat and pushed on along the gravelled path. The walkway was slippery and dripping and her stockings were again drenched in seconds.

The evergreens had almost shed their snowy capes. Joy watched and listened. The occasional crow cawed, a lone seagull joined in, but despite the air having an essence of being cleansed and ready to salute this New Year in, a layer of foreboding held itself over the manor – a stickiness like an iced Christmas cake that was acting as a barricade barring the warmth permeating from the resolute wintry sun.

Staring down at the stone cherubs and nymphs that framed a circular birdbath, Joy felt a tingle slide over her shoulders. A draught whistled over the powdery deposits and the air was suddenly full of frosty sprinkles. The fogginess lifted, and through the dewy ether Joy caught a glimpse of red, skimming across green lawns.

A child laughed. Footsteps crunched. Joy's head snapped around, but only a vacant-looking pheasant glared back. The fountain seemed to gurgle, then bubbled into life, water cascading over and over.

'Jack and Jill went up the hill…' The child's voice was singing once more.

'Come on slow-coach… over here.' It beckoned.

Twisting this way then that, Joy scanned the grounds, but the gardens were deserted.

Another giggle and more scudding feet.

'… To fetch a pail of water.'

Joy stumbled into a run, following the sounds. Trees seemed to stop and stare as she chased across the swampy field toward the crater.

'Jack fell down and broke his crown...'

Laughter echoed from within the dark rail tunnel.

'… And Jill came tumbling after.'

Falling onto her bottom, Joy tobogganed, and regaining her feet, tumbled over sleepers clawing at rock for balance. Sliding to a stop, she stared up at the nearly blue sky. Down below her the cove was becalmed, the sea for once seeming contented to thud and plop rather than fire barrages at the land.

'Hem!' And there I was. Almost out of my senses. It was as if I had been sleepwalking and drawn to the spot subconsciously. The singing had departed, leaving me alone with the scraps of withered gorse tilting in the gusts.

I let the sea blasts do their worst, ripping at my coat. On a whim, I leant into the wind and let the current control me. I dared to bend further forward, and for a second, I held the pose. My heart soared to the stars. Freedom! Clear-headed abandonment. A carefree screech sang out of me as with a grab for my hat, I flung my arms wide. Furious flurries whistled. A forceful backdraught came from nowhere, almost toppling me from my feet, but it made me even more reckless. I leant further still. It felt as if I could glide up into the sky and lose myself in the clouds. I only had to let myself go!

'NO!' screamed a woman's voice from somewhere within the misty spray.

I jerked awake. The sea below me was raging, its thunderous swell rampaging at the land.

'Up Jack got up, and home did trot…'

Joy gulped back the freezing draughts and shook herself. She was freezing, the icy wind was biting. Clambering back up the cliff face, her knees scraped on the frozen shale.

At last into the respite of the tunnel, her head swayed then cleared as she managed to come back down to earth.

'As fast as she could caper …' ricocheted around the stonewalls.

'Go away! Leave me alone!' Joy screamed.

The child giggled again. But Joy had had enough and began to run, heedlessly streaking through the mud, sloshing and sliding around the crater and almost collapsing onto a wall close by the manor.

Coughing, Joy put her hands to her temples. Somebody or something passed close by. She spun around, but there was nobody there. The voice in her head, the presence, it had stopped her from falling from the cove. It had been the words of the young woman from the past. She had done enough. She had saved her from falling.

Joy shivered and gagged up some acidy bile. All of a sudden she was exhausted and cold and lost. What was happening to her? Misenlake was worse than condemned, it held a curse that needed to be released. And it was way beyond her energies to govern its power. She was nearly spent. She could not cope with this for much longer.

Joy had found a moss-pocked stone bench to rest on. The ornamental garden was casting aside the frost, and scuffs of green were poking through.

A moment was needed. The scent of the stricken governess was everywhere. She appeared to be drawing ever nearer, and these inner body experiences, these invasions, were beginning to leave a void. Not only did Joy feel that she'd been intruded upon, but something else; this overriding sensation of loss and bitter grief. Nothing could have prepared her for this depth of what they described in the trashy Ruby Ayres novels as complete and utter heartache. A rawness had been thrust upon her by the spirit of the lost young woman.

She'd sat for perhaps fifteen minutes as the house had gradually awoken. Then the front door was flung open and Rebecca Royce, swaddled in furs and lugging a case, had strutted to her car. This was not going to end well.

Slinging the case in the trunk, she threw her arms in the air dramatically and swept the snow off the blanketed bonnet. Shovelling it aside with a mania, she slammed the door behind her. She was in a hurry, in a proper funk; it was clear her New Year's resolution had been to fly away from Misenlake at a fair lick.

Clanking it into throttle, the doughty car skidded into gear, and began to slither down the drive. It congered through the slush, its tyres struggling for purchase.

Joy watched. She knew what was going to happen a second before it did.

The woman lost the back of the car. She'd been heavy on the brakes, and the rear was swinging wildly and it had begun to spin round and round.

Despite Rebecca Royce's obvious attempt to right it, the steaming car had nowhere to go. It ploughed off the driveway and bumped and bounced into the field before sliding sideways and sploshing into the frozen sludge of the crater as if it were a sucking plughole. A gurgle and an outrush of bubbles saw the car begin to sink beneath the grungy surface.

Joy sat and waited for Rebecca Royce to come wading out. It was like a scene from the talkies. But the heroine, this time did not emerge, spitting and spluttering. Joy bit her thumb for a bit. Rebecca Royce still didn't appear.

With a mounting flutter, Joy realised the hero wasn't going to come dashing to the rescue, and with no one else in earshot, it was down to her. She leapt up and began to hurtle across the field.

Joy skidded to a halt beside the pit. Only the roof of the car was now visible, and it was surrounded by muddy bubbles – it was sinking further into the gunge.

Joy faltered, but cursing the freezing wind, she removed her shoes and plonked a foot into the icy water, and with an intake of breath, started splashing towards the car. The raping shards sent shockwaves up her body, sucking the air from her lungs. She blew out feverishly, desperately trying to remain focussed.

Wincing, Joy reached below the icy surface and touched metal. Her groping fingers found the handle and yanked hard. But the door wouldn't budge. Her fists pounded the window, but it was useless; the tough glass didn't shatter. But it did bring forward a swirl of platinum curls. Rebecca Royce's panicked face, eyes bulging, appeared before Joy as she frantically shouldered the door. Her cheeks were swollen with breath as she flapped and kicked out. The car was filling up with muck and water and the buoyancy of her partially floating body was sending her crashing around the inside of the car.

Joy yelled. But the chunky window just wouldn't yield. She cursed out loud, and slipped further down into the sludge, almost to her knees. Tracing the glass with her fingers, she found a gap. She wheedled her fingers, levering the window, inch by inch. It juddered and her palms were inside. Then a wrist, next her forearm, and jamming down as hard as she could, the stubborn window budged a bit more.

Rebecca Royce's scrabbling hands joined in, yanking at the window winder, and with a whoosh of water the glass suddenly slid down, sludge spurting up into Joy's face.

Joy tugged hard on Rebecca Royce's clothes, and gripping her collar, hauled with all her power, until like a diver thrusting for the surface, Rebecca Royce kicked out and she was clear.

Arm in arm, they dragged each other through the ice and slopped out onto the bank.

Rebecca Royce was on her knees choking and gagging, her hair straggled all over her face like seaweed. Joy sat down in the mud, her togs heavy and dripping, and began to squeeze out her cardigan.

Suddenly from nowhere, Drabble was all around them. He thrust a cape into Joy's hand and draped another over Rebecca Royce's shoulders. 'Blinkin' 'eck ladies! You two tickety-boo? No, don't try and get up – just take a mo, then we better get you back to the 'ouse before you catch your death.'

Joy struggled up and noticed a growing group assembling on the terrace. She spied Prim among them.

Leaning on Drabble for support, the bedraggled Rebecca Royce wearing a solitary shoe limped ahead as Joy continued to wring herself dry.

'Well done, miss,' Drabble said, glancing back over his shoulder. 'If it hadn't been for you, Miss Royce would have been done for.'

Joy flapped more muck out of her skirt as her teeth chattered.

'What's all the to-do?' Gloss asked the melee as they reached the house.

'Rebecca Royce tried to do a bunk,' Perry Scanner replied. 'And it appears Prim's chief suspect came to her rescue.'

'Clear the way!' Prim strong-armed his way through bodies. 'I'll need statements from both of you. We can't be certain that this is not another attempted murder. The car was likely tampered with.'

Scanner scoffed. 'Well, my dear fellow. This puts a dampener on your theory. The young lady would hardly sabotage the motor and then be on hand to fly to the rescue.'

'Get out of my way.' It was Clarice. 'These two need hot baths and fresh clothes before they catch a chill.' She snubbed Prim's protests. 'Your nonsense can wait.'

After a blissful, scalding bath, Joy had given a full account of her morning to Dunkley as she lay wrapped up in her bed. She'd excluded her scrape with disaster at the cove and the mischievous children's voices. He'd listened, but had appeared distracted, as if through an appeaser's eyes. Joy hadn't experienced any ill-effects from her encounter with the icy water, and in fact, felt refreshed, a smug expectation of the newfound respect that she was hoping to be welcomed with. It felt great being the heroine.

Finally released from Dunkley's questions, despite Clarice's remonstrations, she'd dressed speedily and made her way down to the library.

Only Rebecca Royce was absent. She was smarting in her room, and not a little embarrassed according to Gracie, who'd popped her head in for a moment.

Nodded smiles met Joy as she plonked herself next to Clarice, who handed over her knitting. The deluged scarf had been a write-off, so Joy was starting from scratch. But that gave her a reassurance, like beginning a big fat book that you're intent on enjoying.

The chitter-chatter was interrupted by a grand entrance. Rebecca Royce was once more amongst them. She flounced in wearing an outlandish turban. Her make-up looked hurried and her eyes sore. She forced a phlegmy cough before being offered his seat next to the fire by Kosik.

Mrs Pomp gave her a concerned look, but Rebecca Royce put up a hand to ward off any sympathy. 'I'm sorry to cause such a fuss,' she stated plainly. 'I've been an idiot. But this place … I was just about at the end of my tether. When I awoke I just decided it was time to go before I went off the deep-end. Luckily for me, I wasn't the only early riser.'

Clarice gripped Joy's knee and beamed.

A suppressed purr of acknowledgement, nods of praise went around the room. Joy glanced up as Miss Crabb entered, swiftly followed by Dunkley dampening the freshly fashioned camaraderie.

'A more prosperous New Year to you all,' he began, grimacing as if an old injury was playing him up. 'We expect it to be confirmed, but obviously cannot be sure until we have sent her body for an autopsy that Miss Biddle died from asphyxiation. There certainly was no sign of poison in her cup or the teapot and there were no visible marks on her body.'

'So she was suffocated?' Scanner questioned.

'There were traces of cotton under her fingernails and a faint smudge of calamine lotion on the cushion where she was seated.' Dunkley was suddenly forensic and making no attempt at dampening the horror.

'But nobody heard a thing.' Mrs Pomp broke in.

'I suspect she was potentially sleeping and therefore taken unawares.' Dunkley didn't seem convinced by his own words. His confidence was beginning to wane. Cracks were appearing; his habit of chewing his lower lip had become more pronounced.

The room then descended into a rumbustious rumination of the previous day's events.

Prim entered almost unnoticed with a slip of paper. He thrust it at Dunkley like a dagger. The inspector gave it a cursory flick, and nodded to Prim and they both left the room.

Joy set down her knitting and eyed her notes. She leafed through the pages, almost wincing at some of her scribbles. The police were floundering, but they hadn't seen what she had seen. Dunkley needed her help. But would he believe her? Would he think her unhinged – most did!

Joy thought hard as she hummed to herself, and scanning the room for comfort, her eyes landed on Mrs Pomp. She didn't belong in this grubbiness. The grand old lady had proudly retained her invite, a memento; it was probable that she kept all sorts of similar paraphernalia, birthday cards and such like. Of the original gathering, her attendance seemed the most apt, fitting, attracted to the lure of a splendid and stately Christmas. It matched her profile perfectly. Bereft of her Brigadier, clinging onto and recreating past glories was understandable. But what of these others? Why were they really here?

Kosik an airman used to the banter of his peers, now alone and deciding to descend upon a desolate house full of strangers? Odd!

Barasch the doctor or dentist. A homeless refugee. It was plausible, if not obvious that scarred by the events during the war, he hankered for company. But he appeared such a private man. Why had he come? And to celebrate Christmas? Fishy!

Perry Scanner? There was more to him than the snooping war correspondent. He was here for a reason. His cocksure attitude was a cover. Joy was certain of it. Intriguing!

Gloss's tale of poking around the old country and being fortunate to be in the right place was possible. But like Scanner, his forced jollity was a front. His spick-and-span smile had collapsed into a quiver, tears never far from his eyes. He was suffering greatly. Another with a terrible secret. An enigma!

Rebecca Royce, like Gloss had gone downhill at a canter. Her flippant bravado had all of a sudden fallen off a cliff. Underneath there was something griping at her that had suddenly ruptured. Joy could see it twitching below the surface of her thick make-up. Deceptive!

Melville the treasure hunter held water. Monckton was on to something and Slack was in the wrong place at the wrong time.

Miss Biddle and Grauler both in their own ways had been on the take and Miss Crabb and the enigmatic Miss Gwynne were both cloaked from the drama as if watching a play from the balcony above. Mysterious!

Claube didn't fit. That he would seek shelter amongst strangers wasn't so surprising, but why had he been killed? It didn't match any pattern in Joy's brain. Curious!

Who did that leave, apart from Clarice and herself? Joy wasn't convinced Clarice would have taken the chance to tow her into the company of outsiders. Did she have her own secret – this family history she never offered up? Not impossible!

And of course there was Gracie Sands. Joy was certain she wasn't a nurse. It was not an inkling, as the evidence was there. At no point during this series of deadly chapters had she dashed to take charge. A nurses instinct would have brought her barging to the fore. And these flits to the coast? Did she also hear voices from the past? Baffling!

Dunkley, all meticulous method, hadn't freed his mind and the crucial hidden link was clouded by the deceptions surrounding him. It was as if he had a torn-off scrap of paper, but with the vital words missing, and continued to try to put them together like a cryptic crossword. The manor held the solution not the players within it.

Joy joined Clarice and Gracie by the window. Perry Scanner was again leafing through the family album.

'That's an unusual piece,' said Clarice.

Gracie fiddled with a chain self-consciously.

It was gold and three shiny letters dangled: G.I.S.

'I bet you took some ribbing during the war from the Yanks,' said Scanner, chortling.

'Not too much,' said Gracie with a flush. 'It's my initials, but yes the American GIs did find it annoyingly hilarious.'

The three of them again immersed themselves in the black and white frames. Joy rooted around the edges. The sepia smudges blurred the images, but as the pages turned Joy stared from one dappled face to another and then back again, and at last her mind began to clear.

EIGHTEEN

'THANK GOD, the cook survives!' Rebecca Royce had fully recovered from her ordeal and was again full of acerbic indifference. The sniffles and sobs had been miraculously mastered, and been replaced yet again by a distanced reticence like a child who'd been scolded, and bit by bit was attempting reconciliation without apology.

'They can't keep us here much longer,' she said prodding her food. 'I have business that needs attending to before I return home to Canada. I see now that I was wrong to come to England. I should have left well alone and all that hog's-muddle.'

'The cook has done us proud yet again,' said Miss Pomp shrilly as she dissected her fish, her smile almost as unctuous as the oozing butter sauce sliding down her fork. She was leading the cheer-up charge and was taking people with her to some degree. Rebecca Royce's self-interested whines were no longer holding centre stage.

But in spite of the mock geniality, the stark fact was they were now only nine. The mood appeared to be – perhaps if we pretend enough, the horror will go away.

'I have decided to leave this country,' stated Barasch with a catch in his voice. 'I will go to Israel and find my way. I can help there. It will be perhaps the beginnings of my rebirth.'

Kosik grunted. 'It's obvious Dunkley feels the murderer is among us. Until this matter is settled, we are going nowhere. We remain his prisoners here.'

'I fear Kosik has it,' Perry Scanner said. 'Like the rest of you, I wish I'd never come to this hellish place. This house seems determined to keep hold of us, as if we're in some sort of warped play, determined to shake up our pasts – illuminate our prior misjudgements.'

'Speak for yourself,' said Gloss, his crumbling features beading with sweat. 'But what is it they say, never go back? Old Crabb said it when we first arrived, disclose your secrets – that's up to you! Well somebody here is being mighty industrious to stay undercover.'

'How dare you?' Mrs Pomp slammed down her knife. 'If the Brigadier were here, he'd call you out.'

'Look, we have to get through this,' Gracie interrupted. 'I for one do not believe there's a killer in our number.'

'And exactly, how can you be so sure?' asked Kosik.

'I agree with Mrs Sands,' countered Mrs Pomp, her cheeks burning. 'This is a ghastly business, but I trust in our first-rate police force. They are bound to get to the bottom of it.'

'Prim?' Scanner quipped, again throwing them one of his self-satisfied expressions.

'Well our boys in blue still haven't managed to track down the professor,' drawled Rebecca Royce, holding her glass up for Drabble to refill.

'Are you suggesting he's our villain?' Scanner scoffed with a smile.

Rebecca Royce tossed her head. 'Well, it doesn't instil confidence. That's all I'm saying.'

'So what are we supposed to do?' Gloss wiped his face with his handkerchief. 'Wait until we all cop it – bobbing about like sitting ducks?'

The company sat in a brooding silence. Nobody held a stare.

Joy tidied her cutlery, her frustration beginning to burn. 'This house wants to throw out its secrets – that's all!'

All eyes turned to Joy.

'Can I go up to bed, please? I have finished.'

Clarice threw her a quizzical look, but recovering her smile, nodded and offered her arm.

But Joy was in a rush and sped out.

Joy sat up in bed, captivated again by the ferocity of the clacking fire, and musing at the watercolours on the wall.

She twisted her fingers and yelled at herself – I'm no detective so pray let something happen! It was so infuriating. But her childish pouting brought nothing. No dizzy hallucinations, no chirping voices and certainly no rampaging sergeants. She needed to uncover a murderer. She needed Misenlake's help. And she so wanted it over, and now!

These monstrous seances had brought with them a brooding foreboding – when would the next one would arrive? And in the intervening time? Would more innocents be foully slain while her own dumb-headedness struggled to interpret their pointed messages? It was all too much of a burden. Why her? This house, these ghosts that had summoned up this carnage were teasing her, like a bullfighter drawing away the frayed ends of a red rag.

Stacking her medals, Joy took up her knitting then put it down again. She jumped out of bed and straightened the paintings. She poked at the fire. It spat back. She got into bed, out of bed, sat in the chair. The door was irritating her. It kept sliding to a close. She nosed at the casement and traced her initials on the steamy window.

Sleep would have descended on the remnants of the gathering, but she knew their slumber would likely be a restless one.

Joy felt for them more so than for herself. Sadly, they clung to their baggage like dogs to their playthings. It was too alien for them to try to see through this mist of half-truths. They were mere pawns being posted around the board. And one of them was planning the final mate.

Padding into the corridor on a whim, Joy listened to voices downstairs rumbling as the policeman sifted through their thoughts. The constable had gone. Most probably on a patrol of the house. A fresh draught brought on a shudder and Joy darted back inside.

For once, she closed the door firmly behind her and bolted it before sliding to the floor with her back to the timber. It was as if the house was becoming unstable. The tempests of time were shifting. Although Joy was beginning to see, she had not witnessed enough. The little girl, this stricken governess, were grabbing more and more of her as they attempted to lead the way. But why this latest bloodlust? Was there a bond between the past and present? Were they merging, history taking revenge on the now?

Joy tapped her nose as she stared into the spluttering fire. The cremated embers were pale grey. Drabble, not to be accused of making the same mistake twice, had left her a basket of logs. Joy tumbled a couple onto the blaze and sat mesmerised by the curls of smoke as her mind slipped into a trance.

And the flames leaped higher, growing rowdier, the heat resonating a delicious sultriness as Joy sat hugging her knees. The pipes joined the ruckus, babbling and warbling from the bathroom. The baking room accelerated from toasty to roasting, but Joy was delighting in the frolicking shadows that ran over the floor like a swarm of rodents, nipping this way then that as if fearing an oncoming predator.

Reluctant to douse the beguiling flames, Joy first ditched her dressing gown, and then nipped into the bathroom to fetch a cooling flannel.

Predictably, Clarice's pots and tubs were neatly lined on the bathroom shelf. Joy chuckled to herself. Clarice was a stickler for her aged tonics and creams. The labels were well-worn and barely legible. And reassuringly there was the mottled label 'Calamine Lotion,' her go-to favourite.

Joy sniffed at the perfume – it smelt reassuringly familiar – lavender and rosehip. Then she picked up a compact. She'd never bothered with make-up; her freckles had always won that argument.

But on a whim, this time she dabbed in a finger, but the lid slipped and rolled over the panels like a top, until it finally came to rest against the wall. Bending down, Joy banged her head on the underneath of the sink.

'Hem!' Rubbing my head and cursing like a sailor, I was fascinated by the flickers from the fire next door. They had sneakily slithered beneath the uneven panelling. Little yellow snakes of light spiced up the floorboards, creating a merry jig that briefly became compulsive watching. I don't know why, but I couldn't help stretching out with my fingers to touch these cavorting shapes, tracing their peaks, indulging in the warmness of the grainy wood.

It was, in actuality, a naughty splinter that ended my fun. It smarted a bit, particularly when I attempted to dig it out, and then swearing to myself again, I finally retrieved Clarice's age-old caddie and replaced it beside the others; the compact had settled in a ragged groove just as if it belonged there. And I noticed more ruts and dragging marks running parallel. It was the same set of scratches that I'd spied in my own room; they ran all the way under the flimsy wall.

I'm not sure exactly why, but something echoed in my mind and was so persistent that I just had to investigate. I lay with my cheek to the boards. The grooves felt ancient, but also welcoming as if they'd been chiselled, honed out.

A knot of wood was missing. And the board was splintered around the edges suggesting a man-made hash-job. I traced it with my fingers and as I tried to wake my mind up a bit, I hit on an idea. A clumsy one, perhaps, but nonetheless I couldn't help thinking that this could be a hiding place, a cache of sorts. Coupar had been convinced something had been squirreled away in the nursery. And this bathroom was of course an add-on; these boards would have once been part of my bedroom.

I yanked at the wood. The timber rasped noisily and became loose. I wiggled it, but it was stubborn. I became impatient, then annoyed. Dashing next door, I grabbed a poker, and recklessly jammed it into the gap, making a mess of the floor. But all of a sudden I had to know. With a wrench the wood finally cracked. Groping inside, I was soon smothered in dust and cobwebs. Reaching further in, my fingers found some discoloured ribbon, also some smooth pebbles, and further in a tin box. I strained my arm a little further and touched paper, and drawing it out sniffed at a yellowing scroll tightly bound with a shred of string.

The writing was squiggly, elaborate almost decorative. Despite its bleached appearance, I could see it was some sort of an official document. I brought it closer and squinted at a date and a faded signature; it was a birth certificate. I skimmed over it again, and beginning to understand, I hurriedly replaced the paper back in its hiding place.

As I realigned the cracked board, as best as I was able, I came across some scuffs of wool, caught on the splintered wood. Mere traces of a pink pattern, but tarnished with grime and a faint tinge of red.

'Hem!'

Joy lay back and stared at the ceiling puffing at the enormity of what she'd just discovered. The house had spat out the next part of its guilty past. But what had become of the lost girl? Had she really been taken by the sea? Again, Joy's head ran to the governess and her despair. Misenlake was opening up again, but sadly too late for some.

The north wind was churning up what remained of the snow. The viciously artic squall lashed at Joy's coat.

She'd bypassed breakfast with the aid of one of her limp and listless shrugs. Sitting cross-legged on the floor in her room, under the pretence of sorting her things, she'd finally sealed her freedom. Clarice had huffed, but given up and left her to her stuff.

Finding the back door via the scullery, Joy had taken her life in her hands and yomped up the man-made headland determined to glimpse the sea. But her efforts had not been rewarded. Over the crest of the escarpment there was only a scruffy downslope of bracken, broken rocks stretching down to a sort of a bric-a-brac beach, a crescent of seaweed and untidy washed-up flotsam; not a spectacle to brighten a sightseer's eyes.

The frantic sea was far in the distance, leaving just docile heaves of muddiness plopping almost apologetically against the mildewed shingle, a pongy grubbiness that made her want to turn away.

Joy perched herself on a rock and chomped on an apple. Below was an undisturbed study of Misenlake. Tucked out of the worst of the wind, she scanned the windows. They stared blankly back. A light went on then off. Cook appeared, manhandling an over-spilling bin. Drabble followed with another.

Crabb emerged, sniffing the air like a nervy cat. Then she visibly jumped as Perry Scanner hobbled out of the back door. They spoke for a time. Crabb shrugged her shoulders and went back inside. Scanner lit a cigarette and puffed spirals into the frosty air. Gloss strode into view from the front of the house and bummed a cigarette.

Joy glimpsed a hint of movement at one of the windows on the first floor. A curtain swished. Another light went on and a window was eased open. A head popped out. It was Kosik. Behind him, storming about the room was Barasch. Kosik looked out then drew the curtains.

A curl of smoke caught Joy's eyeline. On the terrace beside the dining room, Rebecca Royce was sucking on another cigarette, her shawl wrapped tight. She threw up her arms and gesticulated to somebody inside, presumably a person at the dining room window. Stubbing her cigarette, she appeared to scream in annoyance, but any words were lost on the wind.

Down below, Scanner had ambled along the terrace, all the time poking at the snow, deep in conversation with Gloss, who laughed raucously and patted Scanner on the back. They continued their jaunt, up and along the path then back again.

Another puff. Then Gloss halted by a timber fence and leapt up, gripping the top, poking his nose over before falling back. Scanner mocked a repeat, and waggling his stick, started laughing again. But they weren't missing anything, only the stable yard.

Scanner suddenly squatted as if something had caught his eye. He stood for a moment and pulled out a notebook, scribbling, then he stretched up and explored the horizon as if searching for inspiration. He tilted his neck and then lit yet another cigarette and watched on as Gloss nudged the fence with a toe. They stood for a moment and then circled back around to the front of the house.

Yomping down, Joy followed in their footsteps and halted by the downslope at the front of the house. The two men had gone. She took out a pencil and, immersed in her notebook, bumped into Nouse.

''Ow do, miss?'

Joy gave him her cheery smile.

'Glad I've caught you. Seems our work here's all done – that is mine and Prim's. Seems daft to me, but been told our time's better spent in London catching crooks down there. Inspector Dunkley will stay and clear up this nastiness. Prim's got a monk on. Reckons he would have cracked it by now if it'd been left to him, or so he says, anyway.'

Joy stared at her feet.

'Less said the better, eh miss? Well, keep thee safe. It's been a horrible business, but now with all these bobbies traipsing about you'll be just fine.'

Joy closed her pad and thrust it into her coat pocket.

'A proper detective, you are. Always with a pencil in your hand. I reckons you notice more than most. That's the problem with our lark – too many questions and not enough thinking.' Nouse shuffled his feet for warmth. 'Why were you askin' about old Fred?' Nouse's face was suddenly attentive.

'Miss Biddle said she saw something from her room. That's all really.'

Nouse eyed her probingly. 'She did, did she?'

Joy looked away. Although she liked and trusted Nouse, she felt self-conscious. Being a grown-up didn't suit her.

Nouse squirmed. 'I won't keep thee. But it's been a real pleasure, miss.' For once Nouse's face held a tinge of regret. Joy hadn't seen that before. 'Keep putting down those thoughts of yours, you never know it may come in reet handy, and perhaps one day our older and betters may pay some attention to those that can see just as well as them.'

And with a tap on the side of his head, off he went.

*

The remaining snow, excepting the odd clod here and there, had been swept away by the increasingly forceful winds from the North Sea. Misenlake appeared to be unbothered by the gale's bullying tactics, and neither were the gulls as they circled, mewing and diving at its singular tower. But inside the atmosphere was sizzling, beyond stifling.

Nouse's news was confirmed by Dunkley, who had finally made a decision. Indeed, he'd been updating them with affairs over coffee: Rebecca Royce's car had been hauled from the mud, and the bodies of the recently departed were being moved to the local mortuary. The subdued silence that ensued was shaken by the shock of his next almost casual announcement. Everyone was to be allowed to leave Misenlake the following morning on the condition that they all hand over their passports and continue to update the police on their whereabouts. That was it.

Uncertainty in Dunkley's eyes betrayed his humiliation; this case had defeated him. And to add to his shame, he was to remain for a day or two, one last haul over the knotted yarns, one last stand-off with Misenlake; an uneven duel.

The reactions of Joy's fellow guests had surprised her. Rebecca Royce, Kosik, and Barasch all welcomed the news and hurried off to their rooms to pack.

But Mrs Pomp's eyes had filmed and Clarice had offered her a understanding and knowing smile.

The forlorn Gloss had turned away, but Joy had spotted the pain flare in his face. Scanner had sighed, consulted a pocketbook, and eventually limped away. Clarice had hurried Joy along, always ready to get on with things, and had chivvied her to get packed and be ready to get back to the real world.

Gracie had almost winced as if somebody had stuck her with a pin. For just a moment, bewilderment had deluged her features and she'd hurried to put down her shaking coffee cup.

Drabble worried Joy. He appeared, underneath it all, to be a kind, but troubled man and Joy pondered on what would become of him. He was lost, just like his comrades who never made it back; out in the fields of Northern Europe, his sense of belonging had died with his brothers in arms. Joy hoped he'd find his way. In the end, it would be down to him to discover a place he could believe in. Lord knows there was little help in this world for those whose minds were set on an alternative bearing.

For Joy, as she ducked Clarice's clucking, her emotions were torn. She had begun not only to dodge meals, but also the other guests. Even Clarice and Gracie's subdued twittering had become distracting and her knitting needles were unable to drown out the nonsensical din. Although frightened not only by what she may find out, but also in doing so being confronted by the evil perpetrator of these vile crimes, Joy also knew that she was so close to achieving what these policeman couldn't, and to her, the manor had appeared to sense it. Whispers and whistles. Echoes and fizzing snippets of what once was came and went in a hurry. The window to the past was opening wider and wider, but now time was against her. The governess was pleading with her to right the wrongs that had sent her to her premature death. How could Joy just up and leave, however tempting the thought?

As she sat in her room waiting for the guests to go down for dinner, Joy crimpled her face in concentration. Coupar had to come back to her. He was the key. He would lead her to the solution to the mystery, possibly unwittingly, she was banking on it.

But however much she willed his presence he wouldn't appear. And the naughty child had also forsaken her. Joy's mind ran to the curious clock. Perhaps if she was bold enough she could give the past a nudge.

The empty drawing room held a coldness. Joy's eyes flitted to the chair Miss Biddle had been found slumped in. If only she'd shared what she'd seen with the police. Grauler had been a bad choice of confidante. Her vanity had been her end.

Joy quivered and buttoned her cardigan high. The clock was again stuck at ten and a bit. Joy went to the window and looked out into the darkness. She gripped the soft leather of Miss Biddle's chair. It held a softness, smooth between her fingers.

The light went on. Joy snapped around and was amazed to see the fire sputter into life, flames instantly warming the room. The clock chimed over and over. Joy lost count and the door banged open. Coupar was there! But followed closely behind by the matronly-looking woman called Chantrey.

This time her voice was clear and full of indignation. 'I allowed you the run of the manor yesterday afternoon, Sergeant. Now, I'm afraid if you don't leave this instant I will have to inform my master, who will likely seek an explanation from your superiors. We're all sad for the unfortunate young woman, but the sentence has been passed. The law is the law.'

Coupar grasped her arm, his eyes flashing.

'How dare you?' Chantrey squealed.

'Just one last look. I'm begging you. I have to be sure.'

Chantrey pulled away, her mouth pinched in annoyance. After a moment she pushed back a stray hair. 'I shouldn't. But be quick. I'll give you ten minutes if you promise you will then leave here forever. I will be locking the house up tomorrow. This has to be your last visit.'

'The execution is tomorrow. I won't be back, don't you fret.'

Coupar then charged from the room.

'Hem!' I shouted after him not to miss my chance. But in his hurry he hadn't spotted me.

I stood uncertainly not sure what I should do. The fire slipped back to black slate and Chantrey evaporated as the light diminished. But there were still clumping feet on the stairs, and hastily deciding that I had to follow. I hurried after Coupar. His vanishing figure bounded up to the first floor, where his form evaporated into a sort of twilight.

I nipped through the dimly lit hall, white dustsheets grabbing at me as I shot through the reception and skipped up the stairs.

There was the most awful din; clattering drawers and scuffling feet, curses and crashes.

My bedroom was altered, the dimensions again enhanced and runners covered the timbers overlapping and brushing up against the skirtings.

And it was in a proper state. Coupar had overturned the children's desks and the dresser had been ransacked. The mattresses were cast aside and clothes were spilling out of the wardrobe.

The hidden certificate. Under the floorboards. He had to find it. I called out. But again he couldn't hear me. I shouted louder still. Coupar halted his rummaging for a second and glanced up. I pointed at the floor, the scrapings! But the marks were partially hidden by a rug.

He shot me an annoyed look that said he'd no time for phantoms and once more became engrossed in the children's boxes. He pulled out scrapbooks and leafed frenetically through paintings and etchings.

Then he stiffened. His hand grasped a particular artwork. Leaping to his feet, he waggled the parchment and made for the door.

I tried to tackle him, to send him back, but he brushed me off, or more accurately walked through my flapping arms. He'd missed the concealed document. It would have told him why. But as he dashed out into the passage, I glimpsed the childish drawing he was grasping. It was crudely etched, but the scene was obvious and distinct. Two girls were playing. They were standing in front of a mill, and to the foreground was a crude sketch of bucket on a pulley: a well.

And then he was gone. Melting into a soupy light which traced his figure as he melted into the stairs.

I stood for a bit. Then started around the room. The turned-over desks, piled drawings on top. One struck me. It was hideous. A child's head substituted by a grotesque-looking vegetable or fruit. There was some illegible scrawl underneath. I could make out a word, but as I studied it more closely, the paper fell to dust, crumbling between my fingers, and immediately the room darkened, a coldness biting at my cheeks. The giddiness came and the past went away.

The music box emerged through the wispy web confirming the transformation back to the present, and I stood frozen as the last pieces of the what once was were wiped clean. I knew where Coupar was heading, and realised that I had no choice but to follow. 'Hem!'

Joy had barely slept. She'd heard steps and murmurings as the last crumbs of the gathering had made their way up for their last night at Misenlake.

Clarice had popped her head around the bathroom door and wittered something about being all packed and being glad to be going home. Not long after, a gentle knock had pushed open Joy's door and Gracie had slipped in.

Joy had waited for the enigmatic woman to speak, but after an edgy moment, she just squeaked a good night and left.

Sitting by the window, Joy clock-watched as the time rattled round and round. It was now three a.m.

Outside the night had turned feral. The wind was hurtling around the woods cowing the trees into a fright, their branches thrown about as if in a fearful lather.

Coupar's discovery was teasing Joy's brain. The now dilapidated mill had once been a playground, a place of fun for the two little girls. But whatever he may have thought he'd discovered, it was now just ancient history. He'd been too late. He hadn't saved the governess. So what could he reveal to Joy that would make a difference? How could his pursuit of the truth in the past help those in the present?

Joy's tired mind was trawling over and over. An endless circle of thoughts and images. Was he the conduit? Misenlake utilising his soul to somehow redeem itself by bringing justice to this latest evil? Or had these phantoms, these people from yesteryear always roamed Misenlake, reliving its secrets over and over, waiting for someone who could see – and then Joy had arrived? Fate? Or was that too conceited, too fantastical?

Joy's eyes blinked and then closed. Tiredness was finally the victor as her head slumped to her chest. The faces of the dead flashed in and out of her consciousness. Grauler then Monckton. Miss Biddle with a teacup in hand. The professor was a hazy fuzz of grey. Claube's hands scrabbling in mud. Miss Biddle came again. This time the tea brought a coughing fit. She hacked and barked, then gagged and coughed again, blood dribbling down her wrinkled chin.

Breath choked in Joy's gullet as she suddenly was at one with Biddle. The air sweeping from her lungs and a bruising pain clamped her windpipe.

A familiar tang woke her from the nightmare. But this wasn't some sort of horror dream, it was actually happening.

Joy kicked back her chair, sending it crashing to the floor. Her head hit the boards and she began to lash out wildly. Cold, vicelike hands momentarily weakened their grip as Joy thrashed at bone. Then the sound of a door slamming and a light being flicked on; she opened her eyes. Joy croaked and wheezed, coughing and spitting.

From nowhere, a constable helped her to her feet. 'What happened, miss? I heard a commotion and came running and found you on the floor.'

'There was somebody in here – they tried to strangle me – you didn't see? Oh God, somebody was in my room.' Joy choked and spat.

'Not that I saw, miss. It was on the hour, so I was just on my rounds downstairs. I should wake the inspector and we'll search …'

'No! Please don't. I must have fallen asleep on the chair … and slipped,' Joy stammered, massaging her throat. But after the policeman had left, a face loomed large in her mind. It was time. Danger was closing in on her. In the morning she'd find Dunkley and tell him everything she knew.

NINETEEN

'DING DONG BELL …'

Joy shook the jingles from her head and hustled into her clothes. Her planned meeting with Dunkley would have to wait.

After the horrific attack, it had been no surprise that she'd slept fitfully. Locked inside, bolted down as if a cell, she refused to bear the suffocating confinement. Panic prodded and poked her all through the night sending her back and forth to the door, her hand desperately hovering on the handle. But the peril had trumped the lure of freedom and Joy had dragged herself back to bed again and again.

Light had eventually begun to seep through the gap in the curtains, and with it, an approaching awareness that these terrible events from the past needed to be played out in front of her all over again. But this time would they bring closure? Impatience had mounted, and a festering fretfulness that she was wasting time tossing in the bedclothes. Then the melodic nursery rhymes began again, relentless, over and over, the flirtatious childlike tunes teasing her from the room.

Predictably, the jumpiness had eventually become too much and scribbling a passing thought in her notebook, Joy tossed it onto the dressing table and scurried out of the bedroom.

The wind was showing no sign of resting. If anything the squall had ratcheted up a notch and Joy's locks swept across her face; the gusts yanking at her hat. Trudging past the crater, Joy winced at the sliding car tracks; Rebecca Royce had been lucky.

Ducking through the ferns, Joy pushed her way through the scrub trying not to think of Monckton. As she entered the clearing, she stumbled as a giddiness suddenly grabbed at her. Steadying herself by a bashed-about wall, the backdrop seemed to shift then freeze as if paused and a wan sun shot up from the landscape.

Squeals and hollers erupted into a perfectly clear winter's day. Two girls were running. One was giggling, the other shouting out, 'Give it back! Give it back, I tell you. It's mine.'

'Catch me if you can!' said the other.

'You're not playing fair, Dotty,' shrieked the shorter of the two as she jumped up.

Dotty had a pink scarf and was waggling it above her head. 'Here we go round the mulberry bush …'

'Chantrey said I could have it. It was Mother's and now it's mine!'

With a burst of speed, Dotty circled the mill, laughing and teasing. 'Ceccy, you'll have to try a bit harder than that. Little Miss Muffet, make an effort. Come on, titch. You're no fun at all.'

Ceccy flapped and missed.

Dotty darted through her sister's flailing arms and skipped down a set of stone steps. 'Ding dong bell! Dotty's by the well!'

Ceccy chased her down, but reaching the bottom step stopped and stared. Dotty was perched on the edge of a circular wall.

'Why would Mother allow you to have her things,' said Dotty. 'It's not as if you belong here. Why should I ever share with you?'

Ceccy's mouth opened. Her face rumpled. 'I don't understand. What do you mean?'

Dotty threw the scarf up in the air and smirked in triumph as it fluttered down into the depths of the well.

'Now look what you've done!' Ceccy howled.

They both stared down into the darkness.

'I see it. There! Look, it's caught on a hook by that ledge,' yelled Ceccy.

Dotty scowled. 'If you want it so badly why don't you climb down and fetch it, you little monkey?'

'I can't … I'll fall,' Ceccy objected.

'Cowardy custard! Go on, I dare you.'

Ceccy ran back up the steps and grabbed a discarded pick handle. Leaning over the wall, she poked and prodded, it trying to hook the scarf like a duck at the fairground. She strained and reached out, swinging the rod, edging further down.

'I'll hold your waist. You've nearly got it,' urged Dotty.

Ceccy bit her lip.

'Chantrey will be cross. She'll give us a proper ragging for losing it. Common people having to do without and all that.' Dotty grasped Ceccy's waist.

Ceccy peered down, and scrunching up her face, leant further over the wall.

'That's it. You can almost touch it. Drop the handle and grab it with your hands,' Dotty pressed.

Ceccy dropped the wooden staff, which bashed and banged against the side of the well, finally landing with a clump somewhere way down in the blackness.

'A few more inches,' Dotty encouraged.

Ceccy stretched, and almost without a sound her feet flew into space and she tumbled over the edge. 'Dotty, get someone! Please, I'm going to fall,' she squealed.

Dotty peered down into the murk. Ceccy's frantic eyes boggled back. Her arm was circling a metal bracket, her toes just resting on the narrowest of ledges.

'Go and find help!' screamed Ceccy again. 'And hurry.'

'We don't have time,' Dotty replied. 'I have an idea. I'll reach down and if you can hurl the scarf up at me, we can use it to haul you up.'

Ceccy looked unsure. But with loosening her grip on the hook she clasped the scarf and flailed it upward. It fell short. She tried again. This time it fluttered over Dotty's outstretched hand.

Third time lucky.

'There. I have it.'

'Now what? Please, I don't want to die. Its horrid in here.' Ceccy started to whimper.

Dotty dangled the scarf. 'Stop snivelling and grab a tight hold. You're such a baby!'

Ceccy lurched, and losing her balance momentarily, snatched the wool. It twisted around an arm as her feet scrabbled for the ledge.

'That's it,' said Dotty as Ceccy levered a foot up onto the metal lever.

'I'll heave and you leap up and reach for the top.'

'But I'm bound to fall.'

'Stop grizzling, it's only a few feet.'

Ceccy peered down and then making up her mind, tangled the scarf around her forearm and sprang. Her hand clawed at bricks, and she slipped back, her shoulder crashing into the wall, and with a horrific shredding sound the scarf began to tear. Ceccy screamed.

As she dangled precariously the torn ends just about held.

'I can't hold you. I'm not strong enough,' a crimson-faced Dotty shouted.

Ceccy yelped as the scarf began to shred some more. But from nowhere, a strengthening heave steadied the ripping yarn and Ceccy began to jerk upwards. 'Dotty?' she cried uncertainly from the darkness.

'Hem!' I watched on helplessly. It was as if I was imprisoned in a sphere of energy. I so wanted to run and help, but again it was as if I was hovering, my buoyancy cocooning me in an unsteady orb. A shining light flashed, eclipsing this horror momentarily, and as my blinking eyes cleared I inwardly cheered as a second pair of hands had joined Dotty's, gripping firmly and hauling Ceccy from the well.

The teenage girl's face emerged through the brightness, and down below fear dropped from Ceccy, her own ashen face suddenly twisting with fury. 'You! What are you doing here?' she brayed through her gritted teeth.

The little girls feet had found purchase and she was now making steady progress, her confidence growing as arm over arm she scaled the walls of the well. 'Get on with it! I'll have your father's job.'

The teenager's eyes flared. She scowled and loosened her grip. Ceccy slipped back. The wool jolted then juddered.

'Don't you dare!' screeched Ceccy.

'Do it! Do it! Do it!' A hysterical song rang out from above.

'If you don't get me out of here right now!' Ceccy's eyes flamed.

But the teenager couldn't hear. She seemed lost in an abandoned rage. And with a violent waggle, she flapped the scarf over and over, thrashing Ceccy into the brickwork.

Ceccy shrieked, as with a chafing splitting, the wool ripped and tore, and finally split in two sending her careering down into the bowels of the well. A horrible thud spiralled up the walls, a faint groan and whimper then silence.

'Ding Dong Bell,' somebody sang excitedly, 'Ceccy's in the well. Who dropped her in …'

And running feet and screeches resonated through the thicket as a faint sound of carriage wheels slid to a halt by the main gate.

A slashing spasm speared across Joy's forehead and brought her back to the world.

The birth certificate. The scarf that had been found in the governess's wardrobe. It all made sense now. But what should she do? And how did this explain the chain of murders that had recently fired up Misenlake?

Joy pulled her coat around her as the sea gusts rocked her on her feet. Skirting the mill, she surveyed the lie of the land. Ragged bricks, piles of rocks, all intermingled with popping weeds and hardy thistles. Ivy snaked over crumbling walls; this was the bleakest of places.

Joy blinked and took in a mouthful of the brackish breeze. Wiping her watering eyes, she tried to rewind the horror show in her mind's eye. The steps down to the well would have been over there, just past that jumble of rubble. Scrambling over a wall, she climbed the mound, but couldn't spot the mini-stairway. There was no obvious scar in the ground, or dip to point the way.

A crest of snow clung to a smaller mound of smashed bricks. There was something too neat in the way they'd been stacked, almost like an ancient burial ground or primitive grave.

Prodding the stones with her foot, Joy tugged a few blocks aside.

Underneath there was a glimpse of rusted steel. Hauling aside the rest of the rocks, she brushed debris from an iron sheet. Levering it up and over it slammed to the ground with a crash of dust. And there was the stairway from the revelation.

Joy took a step back. Recently made footprints were leading down. The musty trapped air had a taint of rottenness, a raw ripeness that rushed out as if eager to escape to the freshness of the sea.

There was the well. Joy spun around. The feeling she was being watched was all around her. A seagull dived, another flew up from the turret of the mill. Was this just fear? The foreboding of what she may find? No, it was more than that. It was tangible. As if the tragic governess was there with her, holding her hand as if she was also finally discovering why her life had been so cruelly and wickedly taken away.

Joy inched forward. It was so cold, and with the darkness deepening, becoming chiller still. She wasn't sure if she could do this.

Again, she glanced over her shoulder. The temptation to go back to the house and leave it all to Dunkley had hold of her. But as if pushed on by an unseen force, she found herself doggedly stumbling down the steps until she reached the rim of the well.

Joy stared down into the pit. She chucked a stone. Then another. She spied the iron hook jutting out from the wall just as it had in the vision. Automatically, she closed her eyes. To summon the past? A plea for help? Or was this just too much for both of them to bear?

The shrill wind showered the stairway with sand, a salty dust flying into Joy's face. She covered her eyes with her arm and staggered forward.

'Hush little baby …' a soft voice murmured.

Joy blinked and held out a hand. From behind, a forceful shove sent her toppling. She yelped and grabbed at air. But cloying blackness clasped at her as her flailing coat flapped and twisted in the consuming pitch. Clawing at air, Joy hurtled down into the depths of the well.

Even in the mere seconds she had to consider, as she plummeted downwards, her brain appeared to be able to freeze the moment and bade her body to brace itself. Then an explosion of pain erupted in her shoulder, wind sucking out of her stomach. Her head thudded on rock and the unmistakable metallic taste of blood flooded her nose and mouth and all around her was dark and wet.

Joy tried to raise her head and groggily peered upwards, but the murk became a haze then a blur, and just before she passed out, she saw a glimpse of a pale face and then metal clanging as the light was taken away.

Water plopped onto Joy's face. She shook it off. But more came. Shaking her head furiously, she instantly regretted it.

Intense pain shot up through the nerves in her left arm, spearing the left side of her neck and sending a stabbing jolt into her head. Gagging, Joy spat out more blood. It appeared to be coming from her tongue, but thankfully her teeth seemed all in order.

Whoever had shunted her down into the well had obviously tidied up behind themselves, concealing the entrance to the steps, as the pitch was fathomless. Not a pin-prick of light escaped from anywhere. Joy trembled. They'd done this before. She'd been trapped and now nobody was going to find her.

She shook off a shiver, but another came and then a tearfulness pulled at her eyes. She should have gone for help. But she'd felt charged, as if pushed on by the temptation to end all this horror. The visions had led her to this.

Joy half-laughed, half-sobbed. That she alone was capable of halting this killing spree. Her self-belief in her specialness had brought on this terrible end. All along the murderer had had her marked out. She'd made it easy for them.

A grinding pain cramped her shoulder again as she attempted to curl into a foetal position. She shivered, then a flame of fever spasmed up her back and over her neck.

The faces of the little girls came to her out of the darkness. A sister's jealousy? More wicked than that? The events from all those years ago had fashioned this latest murderous onslaught. Too many people had died because of an uncovered injustice in the past. And now she was to join them.

Joy touched her nose. Then yelled uselessly into the pitch. Nobody would hear her. How long before Clarice would realise that she was missing? And then, they would likely search the coastal path. Gracie was bound to lead them there.

And after a time and perhaps some tears they would envisage the imbecile child going the way of Ceccy Gwynne and Professor Melville, carried away on the rampaging waves, another victim of the perilous cove.

She cried a bit. Then whimpered, then huddled into her coat. The hotness came and went, but the pain in her head and the freezing chill was always there. She tried to straighten her elbow, but a barrage of pain forced splurges into her eyes as a dizziness again swept over her.

As Joy drifted in and out of a lolling stupor, her mind ran to the past. To her father, her only real soulmate. His benign playfulness brought a smile. He'd recognised what others couldn't see; not to judge, he'd known that from the start. When to coax and when to sound the alarm. And most importantly, when to leave well alone. And her mother had never got it. She couldn't resist the urge within herself to 'make things normal' as she called it, make things better – but always for her, never for Joy.

Joy held some sorrow for her dead mum, but the sad memories of the burdened woman came and went without a shiver of affection. Joy knew she hadn't been as much a disappointment but an embarrassment to her mother. That had to be worse – didn't it?

Joy shouted out again, but her feeble voice just reverberated around the bricks spawning more grizzles.

She sniffed. Damp, and a vague saltiness, but also a sweetish, gamey smell, a foulness. Joy touched slimy stone and pulled her hand away. Was Ceccy's broken body still down here after all these years?

Exhaustion finally engulfed Joy and her eyes, then her brain mercifully shut out the fear and the pain. Remembrances emerged and slipped back into the smog as Joy gave way to a blanketing coma.

'Hem!' I was closer to death at that moment than I knew. What was real and what were dreams, my brain couldn't wade through the smog. I recall the ghastly cold, the petrifying darkness, and random recollections and sliding thoughts that were all meshed in my rambling haze.

I recollect a curtain, a gauze that cleared, homing in and out of focus, and an icy silkiness clutching at my hand. Then a silhouette of a woman, coasting beside me, her outline marked by an intense vividness, an orange hue glittered with golds and silvers.

Tenderness flicked my cheek, a deathly cold caress followed by a cosseting voice, cajoling, and insistent. 'Do not die here. You cannot be another victim as I once was. It isn't your time. Lean on me. I won't let it happen. Keep my angel safe, promise me?'

Then a melancholy lullaby soothed me to sleep and darkness once again closed around me. When I awoke, there was a prickliness in my palm.

Perhaps it was my delirium, but in the gloom I was sure I held a brooch clasped in my fist.

More came to me in a rush. It became clearer than ever. But I remember being more tired than I'd ever been before. And then sleep took me and I recall murmuring to myself in the dark as I drifted off, 'I promise,' over and over until the shadows returned, slipping me back into my shivering fever.

The sky was threatening darkness as Coupar tramped through the mud without a care for his suit and once buffed shoes.

'But where are you going now?' an exasperated Chantrey shouted after him.

Coupar wasn't listening. Across the field he attacked the bushes. The rough trail brought him to the run-down buildings of the alum works. Scouting about, he spotted some steps, and skipping down, halted at the foot of the well.

On his knees, he shouted down into the gloom. But only the echoes of his own cries came back. He shot up as if an idea had hit him and hurried back to the manor.

The stable lad shrank into his jerkin. 'Rope, sir? We have plenty of lead reins, would they do?'

'They would. Good lad! Slack, isn't it? But we must be swift. Bring them with you.'

'Me, sir?'

'Yes, sonny. I'll be needing your help.'

'Help, sir?'

'Yes, it's the missing girl we're after.'

Back at the well, Coupar busied himself with knotting the lengths. 'Now tie that end around your waist and brace yourself.'

And with that Coupar flung one end of the rope into the well. 'Ready?'

'But what if I can't hold your weight?'

'Then, I'll likely break my neck and you'll cop it. So hold steady now.'

Hand over hand Coupar scuffed his way down the well, dissolving into the darkness.

Suddenly the reins relaxed. Minutes passed. The sounds of brick hitting brick and stones crashing about filtered up from the murk.

The length became taut again, and after some grunts and groans, all a tangle, Coupar's arms and legs flopped over the parapet.

Coupar shook brick-dust from his hair. 'Damn! She's not here! But I don't understand. If not here, then where? How can I have got it so wrong?'

The trickles wouldn't stop. Joy held her sweat-soaked head in her hands.

Somebody from above yelled. And a brightness arrowed down.

'Miss? Are you down there? Miss, please answer me.' The shouts held a familiarity; a wonderful, reassuring Yorkshire twang full of eagerness.

A torchlight picked out the bricks, spinning around the walls and finally alighting on Joy's prone body.

Joy put a hand over her eyes and stared up at Nouse's mortified features.

'Oh miss! Can you move? Pray you aren't too broken. I should never have left thee to this.'

'Mister Nouse! Oh, thank you! Oh, thank you ever so much. I don't think I'm too bad. It's just my left side. It hurts a bit. I am so very glad you came back for me.'

The beam circled Joy like a tracer. It highlighted the mildew and filth, creating narrow corridors and patches of light. Joy cried out. A death stare regarded her blankly. Against the opposite wall was a bundle of clothes. A rigid grey frozen corpse of crumpled limbs – Professor Melville! His mouth was agape, his unseeing dead-fish eyes were stuck in their death throe. And sticking out from beneath him was a stick of chalk-white bone; attached was a lady's buckled shoe, the leather shiny and buffed.

Joy screamed and screamed.

TWENTY

'IT'S SOMEWHAT OF A MIRACLE,' said the methodical doctor. 'You say the fall would have been around thirty feet?'

Nouse nodded, and to reaffirm, pinched his conk.

'Well, she must have been a cat in a previous life. As far as I can ascertain there are absolutely no broken bones. A chipped tooth, and yes, this shoulder will be sore, but now I've strapped it up that should ease in time. Some bruised ribs, potentially a crack or two, and as to the cuts and abrasions, they're merely superficial. The ankle seems stable, although will be painful for a bit, but she's an extremely lucky young lady.' The medical man pushed his glasses up his angular nose seemingly satisfied with his prognosis.

Clarice sat on the edge of the bed clasping Joy's hand, a faint look of relief mixed with bewilderment settling on her lips.

Prim and Nouse hovered, and Dunkley towered over the end of the bed like a displeased god restlessly waiting to get at the offering.

'Well, plenty of fluids and a couple of days' rest and she'll be as good as new.' The doctor clipped his bag shut and left with a smile.

Dunkley saw him out.

'I don't understand what you were thinking of,' Clarice remonstrated. She stifled more tears. 'Why were you poking about out there? It's such a dangerous place.'

Dunkley was flicking through Joy's jotter. He waved it at them imprecisely. 'If it wasn't for this, and Constable Nouse's diligence we'd never have found you. Somebody did a thorough job of concealing your whereabouts. If we'd had more heavy snow then, well, we'd likely never have discovered the spot. Lucky for us our villain was in a hurry and left prints leading to the metal sheet, which was fortunately also left partially uncovered.'

Joy pondered.

'That's why the unfortunate professor was never unearthed.' Prim had arrived. 'So much snow.'

Joy winced. Those shocking eyes. Clarice's hands gripped her shoulders. Joy wormed herself free and yelped.

'If Nouse hadn't convinced me we should come dashing back, hell knows what would have happened.' Prim stood as tall as he was able.

Nouse tapped his forehead. 'It was the notebook, see. I knew she wrote all her cleverness down. When I heard she'd gone missing, I had a hunch that we may find it in her room. Just as well. Bit of luck that.'

'Not luck, Nouse' said Prim. 'Just good policing. Well-trained, honest team work.'

'No fuss, no bother, but much obliged, sir, I'm sure.'

'I'll study this further, if I may?' Dunkley asked still poring through Joy's notes. He regarded her piercingly. 'And then, perhaps, when you have rested, we can have a little chat?'

'And don't fear, ladies, Nouse won't leave your doorway. Our killer is almost run to ground. We have them within reach,' Prim said somewhat dramatically.

'I'm going to inform the remaining guests that in the light of new evidence their departure will need to be delayed. One more night should see this seedy business at its end.' Dunkley attempted a wonky smile. Joy just rolled her eyes and looked blankly out of the window.

A knock on the door was followed by a uniformed policeman barging in. 'Sir, I'm afraid another guest has gone missing.'

Dunkley's features sagged.

'It's Mrs Sands, sir. And she's been gone since breakfast.'

'Get back into bed, young lady,' Clarice commanded.

Joy pulled on a cardigan and some woolly socks. Her ribs smarted a bit, but there wasn't a moment to lose.

'But where did you think you're off to?' said Clarice, attempting to wrestle Joy back into bed.

'I think I know where she is,' Joy said, wincing and limping past Clarice.

'Leave the policing to us …' Prim began.

'We're wasting time,' Dunkley growled. 'If what I've already seen in this book has any credence then time is short. Are you sure you are up to it, miss?'

But Joy was already on the stairs. The policemen hurtled in her wake.

Taking up an oilskin and yanking on some wellies, Joy hobbled out into the winter sun.

The coastal path was rutted with ice and they all struggled to make ground. On the rocky headland the vicious wind bit into Joy's face.

At last the hut emerged from the undulating ground. Joy pointed ahead as a terrible scream rang out over the cliffs.

The police charged the door. Gracie's figure was cowering inside. Her hands were covered in blood as she tried to stem a wound in her chest.

Prim dived at Miss Crabb, grabbing her in a bearhug and pinning her arms. Something fell to the ground as she yowled and wriggled, her feet kicking out.

Nouse's handcuffs were out, and with Prim's help, Crabb was bundled to the floor, the shackles pinioning her arms behind her back.

Joy ran to Gracie and hugged her tight. 'Thank God,' Joy gasped. 'I kept you safe.'

'Prim, chase down that doctor, he can't have got far.' Dunkley dragged the only chair across the boards and helped Gracie into it.

'I don't think it's too bad,' said Gracie. 'My hands took the brunt of the attack. Lucky it was just a wee knitting needle. But if it wasn't for …'

Nouse shoved Crabb into the arms of two arriving constables and then offered Gracie his arm. After a moment, they all bundled out of the cabin, Dunkley shepherding them along the cliff path.

Joy hung back and went to the window. The rushing waves, the scraggy strip of shingle; it was the exact same sombre scene as the watercolour in her bedroom.

Letting the wind flick over her face, Joy took a breath. The governess had known love here, and lust and perfect peace until tragedy shook her world and struck her down. Then they'd taken her baby from her, but Joy had vowed that her child wouldn't perish like her mother. It was over. She'd kept her promise.

Miss Crabb was thrust into the drawing room. The other guests were herded into the library, all muttering about broken travel plans. Gracie was in her room awaiting the harried doctor's return and Clarice was with her compressing the wound.

'Miss Joy? If you would join us in the drawing room?' Dunkley requested.

'Bit irregular, sir. Perhaps she should be sheltered…' Prim rumbled.

'Irregular, yes. But deciphering the riddles in this notebook is quite beyond me. I think this time we should allow our junior sleuth the courtesy of perhaps … filling in the blanks as we chug along.'

'But the woman's a dangerous murderess, sir and …'

'Enough, Prim. We have constables aplenty, and by the looks of Miss Crabb she is a defeated woman. I find that tough characters weep the most. It comes as almost a relief to them to be finally caught. Come. Let's get on with it.' Dunkley offered Joy an arm. 'Oh, Prim, would you be so good as to check on Miss Gwynne? From what I understand she won't be going anywhere in a hurry, but it wouldn't look too sharp if we lost Crabb's accomplice.'

'But I thought …' Prim's face twitched.

'Thank you, Prim,' Dunkley said, dismissing the detective sergeant with an indefinite flap.

Crabb, still handcuffed, sat in Miss Biddle's chair.

'I think we can dispense with them,' Dunkley instructed.

Crabb's eyes looked grateful. Her colourless face had aged. Tears were just about being held in check.

Dunkley suggested a chair to Joy.

'Beyond question, without a solicitor being present there is no requirement for you to speak to us.' Dunkley began.

'It is over,' Crabb replied plainly. 'There is nothing left. No reason for me to be obstructive.'

'So you *will* make a statement?' Dunkley gestured Nouse to take notes.

'I will. The only real question is – where to start?' Crabb traced her lips with a twiglike finger and after a lengthy pause began, 'It's been a waste in reality, but to the beginning,' she sighed and carried on. 'I have had no sort of life really. But still, it's ridiculous that it's going to end in such dramatic fashion. But then maybe it was fated all those years ago. Times of hardship and pain, of guilt and regrets, but also redemption, penance even, and always such a duty of love. In our own closeted way, we found contentment and comfort in each other's company.' Crabb coughed slightly into a fist.

'Perhaps some tea?' Dunkley hinted.

Crabb smiled weakly. 'My life became hers that awful, terrible day. Even allowing for my Ceccy's bullying, deflecting her sister's cruelty on to the gamekeepers gawky daughter. Crabb-Apple! She used to tease me. And pinch my arms and twist my wrist and leave such marks. But underneath just an unloved little girl. Her sister, Dotty, such a spoiled bossy one, vindictive, vicious even, but who was I to fight back, and for all their faults, I knew I was not a patch on the misses from the manor.'

Joy hid behind her eyes. Crabb was bringing to life the visions she'd thought were the seeds of a creeping madness, an insanity her mother had predicted. But it had all happened. Misenlake had shown her the truth.

Joy's heart turned over as Crabb gave out a crowing laugh. 'If only I hadn't tagged along on that ill-fated morning. But I was so lonely, and a sponge for punishment, attention I suppose, even if their motives were hurtful ones. I had no one else, I had nothing else. Dad was never there and my blessed mother stricken down, hospitalised. I was very lost and craved something I couldn't have – a family and … anyway, enough of this self-pity.'

Tea arrived. Crabb cupped the warmth and shuddered away an audible chill. 'I always heard their screeching, you see. They were always full of it. And that day, it was nearly Christmas. That was 1898 – so many years ago now.'

'1898?' Dunkley questioned. 'The disappearance of the Gwynne daughter?'

Crabb threw him a rancorous look. 'You see, it was Dotty that made me do it. That hysterical scream, those exhilarated eyes, and Ceccy's jibes – Pruneface and worse! I heard them. They were playing by the old well by the alum works. I held back a bit. I liked to watch them. Then a scream and Dotty had tipped Ceccy into the well. I came forward to try to help and found Ceccy hanging on for dear life, grasping a scarf, a fine pink one all torn and shredded.'

Crabb chewed the tip of her thumb, her eyes somewhere else. It was as if she were alone in the room or back there reliving the agony all over again.

'Dotty's strength was almost done,' she went on in a murmur. 'I grabbed hold and started to pull her up, but then …'

Crabb stifled a sob. 'Instead of being thankful that I'd been on hand to save her, Ceccy just snarled at me. More names. Such horrid words. Demanding and browbeating. I'm ashamed of it now, but then, it was too much. My charity thrown back in my face as if I was some beast of burden to be prodded and poked. The worry of my mum – I just snapped!'

Dunkley refilled her cup.

Crabb smiled her thanks. 'But it was Dotty. It was always her. If she hadn't egged me on so. You see it was *her* laughter, *her* squeals as she begged me to do it. Over and over she screeched – "Do it! Do it!" I can hear her now and see that frenzied and flushed face. And Ceccy shouting up. "Don't you dare or I will see your father is dismissed. I will have you thrown out of your cottage." Two little ladies – tush, what rot! The scarf began to tear, and Dotty yelling, and I just let go. It all happened so quickly. Yet she fell with barely a noise. I turned to Dotty, and do you know, she just yelled and whooped manically, sniggering and laughing over and over. She ran away. Left me standing there, frozen, numbed. I thought I would be in so much trouble. Could I just run away?'

Crabb's shoulders jerked as breathless sobs escaped her. Of course, more tea was called for and Nouse crept forward brandishing a hanky.

'I did run eventually, but I had to duck into the bushes as the damned fool governess and the major, arm in arm were heading toward me. I circled back, my guilt or perhaps my curiosity if I am to be honest, got the better of me. I went back to the well. I had to know, you see. Perhaps it was self-preservation. But I have often told myself otherwise. Then I heard these pitiful whimpers.' Crabb plucked at her throat, leaving red blemishes. 'My mind turned at that moment – what had I done? I chased home and fetched a rope. And with a barrow in tow, I managed to dodge the lady's maid as she dragged Dotty back to the manor. It was a long haul, but I eventually extracted Ceccy from the well. I could hear voices from the wood calling out her name. I just covered her with a blanket and made it home unseen. That's when it all began.'

Ceccy's strangled features loomed in Joy's mind as the girl plummeted into the depths of the well.

'You see,' Crabb went on, 'Ceccy was petrified, first of me, but mainly of that tyrannical madam, her sister. Dotty always wanted me dead, Ceccy told me. She cried and sobbed, and yelped that Dotty would snuff her out. She said it over and over. Then she begged me to hide her. Not to take her back as her parents wouldn't believe her. Dotty was their favoured one, she kept screeching. Dotty wouldn't stop until she'd done away with her. She would try again.'

'Had her sister made an attempt before the episode at the well?' Dunkley quizzed.

'Ceccy was never sure. But she'd been plagued with stomach troubles. Being sick regularly. After this, she'd convinced herself it had been Dotty who'd been trying to poison her.'

Dunkley said, 'Go on.'

'I pleaded with Ceccy to at least let me fetch a doctor, her leg was badly bashed-up. But she wouldn't have it. Said he'd send her back. And for me, I realised that this was the best outcome. I admit that I was selfish. I was so scared that I would get the blame and that they would lock me away. And then who would care for Mother?'

Crabb folded the hanky neatly in her lap. It seemed her tears were done. She was back to the cold fish that they'd become accustomed to. 'Maybe it was the shock, but Ceccy was adamant. She would never go back, that's what she said, the trembling little tyke. At that point, I couldn't imagine it would last as long as it did. For me the future could wait. I just needed to fix her up and to make her better, and then somehow I wouldn't get the blame. I was foolish. I'm not going back, she always insisted. If only we never had.'

Crabb coddled the second cup of tea, her eyes misting over. 'My hatred, jealousy, I suppose turned to love in those tense moments. The fragile mite, all tresses and soft cheeks, she needed somebody to look after her. And I've adored her, and been determined to make up for my spitefulness, ever since. I took her at her word. I could see how frightened she was. I stole money from my father's tin and hid her in our cart. I took her to the cottage that we'd rented in town. It was supposed to be only temporary, you know, for Mum to be more comfortable, nearer the hospital, easier for treatment. But that last time she went in, well, she didn't come out and we … well me and Ceccy never left there, just the two of us. Months turned to years and we never ever spoke of it. We just lived our own way, day after day.'

'If you need a break at any point, just say,' Dunkley said solemnly.

Crabb glowered and ploughed on. 'I suppose I thought over time that Ceccy would miss her privileges and would yearn to go back, back to her family and cosseted way of life. But the fear spawned by that shocking day never left her. I fixed her leg as best I could, although it never recovered properly. That is my one burning regret. But in a way it made her more dependent on me, and that fostered our relationship. You see, I was so petrified that I would be sent to prison. And selfishly, I'd never had anyone, brothers or sisters, even a pet. It was as if she was mine. My mission in life to make up for that ghastly mistake. And as the closeness grew between us, it became a blessing, a reason for my being, to keep our special secret. And dear Ceccy? Well, she was content to be the centre of my world, to be cared for, mollycoddled, I suppose.' Crabb laughed, her eyes gleaming. 'And to boss me about, of course.'

Joy could sense the woman's unconditional devotion.

'When Dad passed I was tempted back here. The all mighty Gwynne's had left in a hurry. The scandal of the execution and all that false mourning sent them overseas.'

'You can't have known that. You had a duty to tell them that their daughter had survived.' Dunkley said firmly.

'Their daughter – huh – so you say.'

Dunkley frowned.

'I was more family to her than they had ever been. Their charity!'

'Ceccy was adopted,' Joy chipped in.

Crabb glared at Joy. 'How did you find that out?'

Joy slid her eyes to the wall.

'You and your snooping. I should have put paid to you when I had the chance.'

Joy choked as she recalled the vicelike hands throttling her airways.

'Well, it's no matter now.'

'Adopted?' Dunkley pressed.

'The grand Mrs Gwynne's whim. If only she'd known what she had brought down on the infant that she'd rescued from the poorhouse.'

'And her true-born found out?' Dunkley was getting there.

'Something like that. Of course, through all those years we never really knew.'

Sadness swept over Joy, her body suddenly chilled as she felt for the young woman, the governess. She hadn't been part of this family feud. She'd just fallen in love with somebody she shouldn't have.

'After Dad went, I rented out the old gatehouse and took in some sewing, mending, and the like. We scrimped and saved and got by. And Misenlake? It lay empty and neglected. Obscene really. Ceccy's home within touching distance and we could never set foot or ask for sufferance.'

Miss Crabb looked to the window. Joy followed her gaze. The clouds were huddling again and the light was being drained from the grounds. It would be dark soon and then would Misenlake finally rest?

Crabb turned down yet more tea and carried on. 'Until one day they came back. Lady Gwynne had died abroad and had been brought home to be buried. Dotty and Ceccy's father took up residence again, and I did wonder whether my darling would soften. But she never did. You see the fear never left her. She never really knew why. And what had Dotty told them had happened? Had they guessed what she'd done and they'd covered it up? How could she go back now after all this time? If only she'd known why Dotty had hated her so.'

Joy picked her nose. She had little sympathy for Crabb. Her thoughts were with the innocent governess. If only they'd come forward, her life would have been spared.

Miss Crabb snooped at Joy. There was uncertainty in her eyes, a wariness that she couldn't quite pin down. 'We found out by accident in the end. A local hack digging into the past. Reliving the story. Ceccy's adoption written bold in the centre spread of the *Herald*.'

Dunkley lowered his eyes.

Crabb sneered. 'Yes, you can imagine. It all suddenly fitted. Ceccy was distraught and then furious and particularly scathing of her late mother.'

Joy pictured her own mother, her bridling glares and snappish sighs.

'We also learned that Miss Ines was having an affair with the major. And subsequently worked out that not only had Dotty's malice attempted to do away with her sister, but she'd also framed her governess. She'd taken care of them both and kept her mother and father for herself. And of course, even at that tender age, the scheming vixen had at one stroke guaranteed her birthright. What she hadn't known, and neither had we was that Miss Ines was carrying the major's lovechild.'

'Until you were approached recently?' Dunkley asked.

'Correct. We were sent a note begging an audience.'

'And you arranged a meeting?' Dunkley prompted Crabb.

Joy went cold. Not a thought for Grace Ines. Not one flicker of remorse.

'Yes, you are right again. I suppose that's why I did what I did. All for her. All for my Ceccy.'

Nouse made a face. He'd run out of paper.

'A break, perhaps,' Dunkley suggested.

Prim bashed in through the door. 'It's Miss Gwynne!'

They all gaped at him, excepting Crabb who kept her eyes low.

'She's dead!'

'It would have been indecent, don't you think? To be executed in a wheelchair. At least I spared my darling that,' Crabb stated frankly.

It all fitted. Miss Biddle's shrill words echoed in Joy's brain. She'd noticed what others couldn't fathom.

'You murdered Miss Gwynne?' Prim shrieked, open-mouthed.

'A mild sedative eased her pain. I have Miss Royce to thank for those. And then her softest pillow to lay her to rest. She knew nothing of it and certainly there were none of the uncouth struggles as there had been with the money-grabbing spinster.'

Joy's hands instinctively massaged her throat.

Crabb glared at her and gave out a low tinny laugh. The skin on her face seemed to tighten.

'Are you certain, Prim?" asked Dunkley, a tic twitching at the corner of his mouth.

'I left the doctor there. He's confirmed the worst.'

'I suppose you will now expect a further statement regarding the goings-on here at Misenlake?' Miss Crabb enquired with a forced smile. 'But first, you have to know, none of this was planned, and dear Ceccy, until she had the gross misfortune to literally bump into that prying gardener, was really none the wiser.'

'But then why murder her?' Prim was deadly pale.

'You think I'd leave her to fend for herself?' Crabb questioned scornfully. 'Like this halfwit of a girl, it is better this way. The Nazis had half an idea.'

The obscene jibe did not jolt Joy. They were words she'd heard before, and from people much closer to home.

Dunkley's eyes flicked to Nouse who motioned that he was ready to continue.

On cue, Crabb resumed. 'It was a momentous day. Major Gwynne was buried and another chip of Ceccy's trepidation fell away. She found some solace that her parents were dead and gone, and her life that was would not come back for her. But of course, her conniving sister still lived, and I knew that Dorothy Gwynne was a terror that my darling just could not rid herself of.'

Again, Ceccy's wretched face swam up from the swells in Joy's mind. The well. The fear. The sickening fall, the little girl's dress flapping around her as she plunged into the black pit.

Crabb wetted her flaking lips. 'I wanted a reckoning. To see Dotty's face as I explained her sister was alive and had come to collect her dues. I figured it would tidy us over nicely, along with the sale of my parents' place, we could then retire quite comfortably. Having worked so hard all these years, some sort of tally-up was only fair, don't you think?'

A reply wasn't required, but nobody met Crabb's gleaming black eyes.

'So after a time, luck wandered our way. An opening was advertised. A lady's maid at Misenlake no less. In actuality, it turned into more of a housekeeper's role. It was a simple enough task to secure the position. Staff were hard to come by. I was on hand. An assumed name, made-up references. It was perfect for my planned grand reveal, but I hesitated. To approach Dotty wasn't as straightforward as I'd hoped. At first she seemed not to notice me. Gloss, the oaf, had just departed and the remaining staff were to be laid off. I penned a cryptic letter to the mistress of the house and slipped it into the mail basket.'

'Ding dong bell …' Joy murmured.

Crabb's eyes raged. 'How could you know?' she hissed.

'I'm sorry, you've lost me,' Dunkley broke in.

Crabb rallied briskly. 'I don't know how, but she's right, of course. *Ding dong bell, Ceccy's in the well. Who pushed her in, little Dotty Gwynne, who pulled her out … ?* I penned a footnote that she was to meet me at the mill. To be honest, I never expected her to turn up.'

Joy threw an involuntary look at the clock. Stuck at 10.05.

Prim found a seat at Dunkley's instruction. His tie was skew whiff and so were his features.

'But she came, and like all women of her class, she brazened it out. Said she didn't believe me. Where was my proof? I told her she'd have testimony enough when the story made the papers or even the local constabulary. And you know, just when I thought that I had her on the back foot, she started to laugh, squealing like a mad thing. The same Dotty. Became quite hysterical. It took me back. Then came the names, Crabb-Apple face, and that I would be sent to prison or worse, hung like the scheming governess. They'd believe her over me and I would be accused of kidnapping. My temper rose and before I knew it, my hands were on her windpipe. I squeezed the life out of her. And you know, I actually enjoyed it. I watched the fear rise in her red bloated face and it finally settled the debt. And as I stared down at Dotty's lifeless body, I said to myself – do it – do it? Well, I had done it and Ceccy had her revenge at last.'

'My God, you are depraved.' Prim's face twisted in disbelief as his eyes darted from Dunkley back to Crabb.

'The thing is that during the entire altercation she'd been so barefaced, so spiteful that she never even asked about her sister. Never showed any remorse or even the merest sign of relief or of interest in how her sister had survived. And that wicked laughter came back to me, over and over and then I knew what I had to do, what would be fitting – I tipped her down the well and covered my traces with an iron sheet. I was glad she was dead.'

'But when did that …?' asked Prim.

'Last summer. Her body has lain there since.'

'But how did you come to live here at the manor?' Dunkley probed.

'Fortune smiled on us. Dotty had arrived for our encounter all helter-skelter, and dressed to the nines. She was en route to London before heading off to the South of France. She had no time for this, she'd said. So when the deed was done it was easy enough. Told the footman he was to forward her luggage. Miss Dorothy had gone on ahead and left me to manage things. I never thought it would work, but it did, and like a dream. I oversaw the manor being locked down for the summer, dismissed and paid up the staff as Dotty had planned. I then made a few alterations, some adjustments for the wheelchair, and Ceccy came home. And here we would have stayed, and been happy, if it wasn't for this tiresome Christmas gathering.'

'The solicitor had been forthright regarding the stipulation in the Will?' Dunkley answered his own question.

'Indeed. There was no way around it,' said Crabb, her eyes showing a tinge of regret. 'The agency sent a list. A dozen nobodies. We tried to cover our tracks a bit. Hired some new servants. But then a last minute glitch – Simon Gloss slipped through the net.'

Joy was beginning to tire. The revelations that would follow she already had rehearsed in her head. It was as if she was reading a book repeatedly, hoping the tragic ending had been erased, and a happier one written in.

'Ceccy so loved the grounds, fonder recollections of her childhood. And of course, I found a way for her, early morning rambles in her chair. The lift the army had installed was invaluable. That's why we took the rooms to the rear. That almost tripped us up. Gloss was too familiar with Dotty's ways, and yet, the irony was that for all our nervousness, he never really troubled us. It wasn't Gloss who discovered our deceit. It was the gardener.'

Dunkley gave out an uneasy cough. 'I think we have heard enough for now. Constable Nouse, if you would please take Miss Joy next door to join the others. Myself and Miss Crabb can tidy things up here. There's no need for her to be more upset than is necessary.'

And that was it. Joy was escorted into the corridor casting a last wistful glance at the enigmatic clock on her way out.

'How are you doing, miss?' asked Nouse. 'You've been through a lot.'

Joy ran her hand along the wall, tracing the bobbly paint work. This was a new addition and it felt good.

Nouse said, 'If it wasn't for your endeavours, I'm not sure we'd have got to the bottom of this little lot.'

'Thank you for believing in me,' said Joy twisting a button on her cardigan. 'Most don't. And if you hadn't come back and thought to check my notes, think them worthwhile, then I'd be still down that horrid pit.'

Nouse made a comic face and shadow-boxed Joy's shoulder. 'Proper team, us two. Now let's see if we can cadge a brew.'

In the library all eyes shot up. Clarice bounced up from the sofa and ran to Joy.

'What's the latest, Constable?' Perry Scanner enquired.

'Miss Crabb's answering the inspector's questions. He said he'll be along shortly to put you all in the picture.'

'So, by jingo, it wasn't one of us, after all!' said Simon Gloss.

'I never doubted it,' Mrs Pomp added.

Gloss raised his glass to her. 'To think, Crabb was behind all of this and with all the panic we never suspected her or the mistress of the house. It's hard to believe Miss Dotty played a part in it. She was a bit feisty, but murder?'

It was clear they hadn't been told either about the switch of identities or the subsequent slaying. Joy didn't offer up any contradiction. She was done. It was over to Dunkley.

'Well, let's hope we can get the hell out of here before they change their mind,' Rebecca Royce said. 'I've had my fill of this place.'

'Any news on Gracie?' Clarice asked Dunkley.

'She's with the doctor. From what I hear, she'll survive. A nasty wound, but fortunately this time no damage to any major arteries.' Nouse gave Drabble a look, and they moseyed over to the dresser and poured tea.

'It appears we owe this extraordinary young lady our thanks,' said Kosik. 'Without her, yet another would have been added to this bloody fest and Crabb would have literally got away with murder.' Kosik eyed Barasch who began to tinker with his natty leather case.

Clarice bent her head and stared into Joy's face. 'Are you all right, dear?'

'Oh yes, I'm fine, and just glad that they got there in the end.'

Uncertain glances rolled around the room.

'Hem!' said Joy, and took up her knitting.

As promised, it was not long before Dunkley came trudging into the library. On the threshold he dismissed Prim and also sent Nouse packing. 'Please see if Mrs Sands is now stable enough to be able to give a statement,' Dunkley called after them. 'I will see to these and be up in a jiffy.'

'Can we go, Inspector?' Rebecca Royce enquired as she twiddled with her gloves.

'I thought we might convene one last time. There are a couple of details I would like some help tidying up.'

'But Crabb has been arrested?'

Dunkley nodded as he accepted coffee from Drabble. In a tired tone he then informed them of the recent murder of Celia Gwynne and explained briefly about the woman's turbulent history and the lurid motive behind all the killings.

'Good God!' Gloss exclaimed. 'You're saying Miss Dotty was done away with months ago? Thrown down the well like dead vermin? I can't believe it. It's worse than barbaric!'

'Yet it is true,' Dunkley affirmed. 'And that's where this bloodbath began.'

'I now see why she kept to her room. My arriving must have been quite a shock.' Gloss paused as if losing his train of thought.

'So, old Melville signed his own death warrant by tracking down the location of the well and, presumably, would have had a nasty surprise when he discovered what lay down there.' Perry Scanner offered his thoughts to the room.

'I'm afraid so.'

'I suppose it was no secret he'd been poring over those maps,' Scanner said. 'We all saw him from the windows pacing about out there.'

'Yes, that is so,' said Dunkley. 'Crabb was onto him. She couldn't allow him to find the body. I believe it was an instinctive thing, much like the murder of Dorothy Gwynne. The professor's torchlight picked out the corpse and he paid for it with a shove in the back.'

'Oh, how horrible!' Mrs Pomp's hand quivered over her mouth. 'To stare down into the darkness and make sure the life had been sucked out of the poor professor. How callous!'

'And she almost succeeded for the third time,' said Clarice.

Joy kept to her knitting.

'But what about Claube? Why do away with him?' Gloss queried.

'Yes, what about our swamp-drowned German?' asked Kosik, his lips teasing a smile.

'Err ... we will come to him in a bit,' replied Dunkley peering at his watch.

'And Slack the gardener?' asked Perry Scanner. 'His death has confounded all of us.'

'It seems Miss Gwynne was a martyr to her constitutional,' Dunkley continued with a heavy sigh. 'She went out that morning, as was their habit, albeit a lot earlier than was usual. Crabb left her alone while she went to check on Melville's body. Her mistress wheeled along the terrace as was her wont. I don't know if you noticed the ramp at the side of the house – a wheelchair aid.'

Joy mentally ticked a box in her head.

'The lift at the back of the house was a lifeline for Miss Gwynne.' Dunkley seemed in a hurry to get this over with. His eyes held no sense of accomplishment. 'They both thought if they went out before anybody had stirred, the house would be asleep, and that it could be managed without prejudicing her identity.'

'But that was the day Slack came back first thing to help clear the snow,' Drabble muttered.

'That's right, of course, he was up with the larks,' said Scanner.

'Poor fellow braved the elements at dawn to get back to us,' Gloss added.

'But why kill him? And who ... and how?' Scanner yapped.

A few frowned. He'd turned into an excited schoolboy.

'Miss Biddle saw the tracks of the wheelchair,' Joy broke in. She couldn't help clearing their fogginess.

'That is right, Joy,' Dunkley agreed. 'Slack used to work as a stablehand at Misenlake as a boy. Although our two ladies were cautious and dismissed the staff when they moved back into the manor, they then took on a gardener. Sadly for all parties, they omitted to investigate Slack's history. Perhaps Miss Gwynne had forgotten him, or had never imagined him the same stableboy from her childhood. Either way, that fateful morning she trundled around the front of the house, and literally bumped into him.'

'So Miss Celia murdered Slack?' Gloss's features furrowed.

'We will never know what truly happened. I assume Slack recognised her, and told her so.'

'After all these years?' Rebecca Royce quizzed.

'Possibly so. Or perhaps he was just startled by meeting a stranger in a wheelchair. Either way, we have to assume Miss Gwynne was already apprehensive about being found out and lost her head. She probably dropped her hanky or the suchlike, and then brained him from behind.'

'From her wheelchair?' Scanner queried.

'According to Crabb, Miss Gwynne wasn't totally incapacitated, but had come to rely on her chair over the years.'

'So that's what Biddle saw? The wheelchair traces? The rest of us assumed they were from the barrow.' Gloss's eyes were bright.

'I think so. Perhaps she'd risen early and spotted Miss Gwynne taking her stroll on a prior morning.'

'The tracks would have been a tad narrower, and there surely would have been returning marks?' Gloss argued.

'Sometimes the human eye only sees what it expects to.'

'Excepting Miss Biddle.' Barasch spoke up. 'Too much time to sit and stare, supping her tea, I presume.' His voice matched his mood – gloomy. He couldn't seem to drag himself out of his darkness.

'And Miss Biddle told Grauler about what she'd seen, of her suspicions?'

Rebecca Royce asked.

'Unfortunately, yes. She trusted in him instead of coming to us.'

'And he saw an opportunity to get rich quick.' Rebecca Royce again.

'He did.' Dunkley wandered to the window, squinting out at the thin sunshine. 'Whether Miss Biddle was in on his caper, of that we are not totally sure, although Miss Crabb has suggested so.'

'That's why Miss Biddle kept the information to herself?' Clarice observed.

'And the money you found was a pay-off?' Gloss followed on.

'Indeed. Grauler confronted Crabb after uncovering the secreted wheelchair. I tend to think he really had no idea about the professor or the others, but after his discussions with Miss Biddle there was only one feasible explanation for Slack's murder.'

'And they paid him off?' Kosik suggested.

'They did, but he wanted more. Crabb was to go to his room with a further payment. Potentially Miss Biddle's share.'

'And she stabbed him with a needle? He wasn't the puniest of chaps,' Gloss advanced dubiously.

'I suspect he was drunk. The attempt on his life in the laundry tub had shaken him. I imagine he was going to grab the money and run.'

'I'd forgotten about that. How did she manage that?' Clarice sat forward.

'I believe I know the answer to that,' said Scanner. 'There's a loose panel on the terrace at the back of the house. It would have been simple for her to go down the back stairs and let herself in without being seen.'

Dunkley nodded his agreement. 'Miss Joy told us of Grauler's loud snoring. I think Crabb bided her time. He passed out. And she slipped into his room and skewered his heart.'

'A needle? Not the most efficient of weapons,' Gloss said.

'It depends on whether you know what you're doing, where to penetrate.' Kosik crunched his knuckles.

'I suspect it was a hasty decision. Also, perhaps in order to implicate Joy.' Dunkley choked a cough back. 'It seemed a few fell for that ruse.'

Joy was glad Prim wasn't in the room. She'd had enough of him to last forever.

'But what about poor old Monckton? You all seem to have forgotten about him,' Drabble stammered from a corner.

'Miss Crabb set the trap on the morning she'd checked on Melville. An insurance policy. I don't think she meant to kill anyone, but it would be enough to ward off prying sightseers. Monckton's late-night decision cost him his life. It's possible that if he'd seen the sense to wait until daylight, he might have spotted the contraption or been found before he had lost too much blood.'

'Poor Mister Monckton. He meant to be so helpful. This post meant a lot to him. And he was slaughtered and left to perish out there like an animal.' Drabble was on the edge of hysteria once more. The man was all-nerves. His guilt palpable.

'That still leaves Claube,' Rebecca Royce reminded them.

'It does, madam.' Dunkley slurped his tea and swallowed hard. 'That's the main reason I held you back.'

The gathering hushed as if sensing a revelation.

'Our Herr Karl Claube was of course an assumed name.' Dunkley paused allowing the words to sink in. 'He was not a POW or an airman in the Luffwaffe.'

'That much I suspected,' said Scanner. 'Cave Castle is more of a manor house, much like Misenlake, than a medieval castle. He clearly had never set eyes on the place.'

Dunkley regarded them with a stern stare. 'His real name was Claus Karbe, but I suspect some of you were well aware of that.' The policeman looked squarely at Kosik.

Kosik inclined his head and smirked.

'Detective Sergeant Prim dug around a bit when down in London and it appears that Karbe was a senior officer at the Dachau concentration camp.'

Barasch let out a yelp.

'And those that hunt down these war criminals were on his tail.' Dunkley went on. 'Possibly he thought he'd be safe, squirreled away in this backwater – a particularly British Christmas.'

Joy shook herself out of her zone. This was new news.

'Mr Barasch, you were interned at Dachau, were you not?' Dunkley's voice had grown firmer, more policelike.

Barasch looked away. 'It is true. I survived that horrific camp of death.'

'And Mr Kosik. Have you not volunteered your services to Nakam?'

Kosik's features sharpened, his steely eyes holding Dunkley in a glare. 'What if I have? Should these Nazi scum be permitted to flee their crimes? Get off scot-free, as you British say.'

'But those at Nakam take the law into their own hands,' Dunkley countered.

'Retribution!' Barash muttered. 'Nakam is our revenge.'

Dunkley turned away. 'Our Herr Claube, or more properly Karbe's body was found with the minutest wound at the nape of his neck. Our divisional surgeon has pored over the aperture, but cannot be certain, and is unable to certify that this was the injury that caused his death. It is possible, and perhaps considering the mud in his lungs that he took off fearing his identity had been uncovered and fell into the bog and drowned. But the one thing that is incontrovertible, his blood is not on the hands of the murderous Miss Crabb.'

'Then you think it's possible it was an accident?' asked Gloss. 'And his death had no connection to the others?'

'What I think and can prove are two different things,' Dunkley said. 'What I know is that he was a convenient scapegoat, similar to Miss Joy and that his demise unwittingly added a level of confusion that concealed the real motive behind these other crimes.'

'So what are you going to do, Inspector?' asked Barasch in a resigned tone.

'Do? I'm going to do exactly nothing. But what I can prove is who it was that left the house on the night of the carol service.'

Barasch's face drained of colour.

The oilskins! Joy sat further forward in her chair.

'Three capes. Mr Kosik has owned up to taking one of them, but strenuously denies he was responsible for the death of Karbe. On the basis he has confessed that he was here to capture Karbe and bring him to justice – why would he lie? And even if he had, I suspect our legal system would not have been able to hold him. Politically it wouldn't wash. Of the other two coats, one was worn by Miss Crabb. She was out seeing to Professor Melville and managed to return unnoticed, replacing the mac in the porch before returning to her rooms. And the third cape … was worn by you, Mr Barasch.'

Mrs Pomp strangled a screech. 'He wore one the wetted mackintoshes?'

'You can prove that?' Barasch stammered.

'I can. Both Mr Kosik and more vitally, Miss Crabb saw you.'

'Then?' asked Barasch.

'Then nothing. That you may have found Claube drowning and did him to death as some sort of revenge or execution? Or had you actively pursued him? I have no witnesses, and as I have stated, the divisional surgeon cannot with any confidence point to the single factor that killed him. I have told you I can prove nothing, so I intend, as we all hope to over time, to leave the war years behind. I will write it up as death by misadventure and we will await the coroner's verdict.'

A stillness hung over the room. Dunkley buttoned his jacket and walked to the door.

'That's it? We can go at last?' Rebecca Royce asked. 'No more intolerable questions?'

Dunkley turned as if recalling an afterthought. 'One final thing. Those that wish to leave, are free to go. However, I am bid to inform you by the new mistress of this house, that any of you who wish to remain a little longer at Misenlake should consider themselves thoroughly welcome.'

TWENTY-ONE

A BUFFET of cold cuts proved ideal for a most-welcome casual dinner. The dining room held a cheer that had been missing during their visit. It was as if Christmas had been put in the deep freeze and now, as relief washed over them all, it allowed a respite to warm their spirits as the festive season always should.

Gracie was the centre of attention. Dunkley's revelation as he exited Misenlake had ignited a buzz around the library. Prim had entered to affirm that they would need to stay contactable as witnesses, first for the inquest, and thereafter, at the forthcoming trial. He also shocked them all by stating that Gracie Sands was to be confirmed the new mistress of Misenlake Manor pending a blood test, but that documents she'd produced made that a formality.

'So you were the mysterious thirteenth guest?' asked Simon Gloss as Gracie joined them.

Gracie gave the table a spreading smile. Six remained from the original gathering. Mrs Pomp had been in no hurry to leave the splendour of the manor and curiosity had ensnared Perry Scanner and Simon Gloss.

Gracie nudged herself into a chair. She was flanked by Joy and Clarice who'd had a preview of the enigmatic woman's secret. Grace Sands had been born Grace Ines, the orphan daughter of the executed governess, and christened after her mother. Her necklace that had brought such a ribbing, Grace Ines Sands – G.I.S!

'But how and why?' asked Perry Scanner. 'And were you the person who thought to engage me to sift through Misenlake's past?'

Gracie nodded, her cheeks turning from pink to ruby-red. 'Yes Mr Scanner, that was me. That was before I had the courage to come to Misenlake myself. At that time, I considered it the best way to find out about the place. Perhaps uncover some facts about my mother that had never come to light.'

'What on earth?' Mrs Pomp broke off as Scanner filled them in.

'I was a correspondent during the conflict,' Scanner informed them, 'but found employment hard to come by on my return. What I did notice was the amount of folk who wished to trace loved ones. People who had moved on, some coming back from the war who weren't of a mind to resume their old lives.'

Drabble throttled a cough.

'So I set up my own private detection service. And a few months back, I received a letter from an anonymous person who wished to engage me to find some background information about Misenlake. Its grounds, and history, to dig into the riddle of the missing child. It was a bit off-chart, but also supremely tempting – a bit more diverting than tracking down errant husbands. And as fortune would have it I found out about the gathering that was to be held here at the manor, and managed to snaffle a place, courtesy of the old gammy leg.'

'My mother was killed by the state for a crime she didn't commit,' said Gracie. 'They didn't even have a corpse, Lord forgive them.'

Coupar's face jumped into Joy's head.

'When my adopted parents died they left very few details of my past,' Gracie went on. 'But I had some letters, my birth certificate and crucially, a letter she'd penned to my father from hospital begging him to visit his newborn bairn – returned unopened.' Gracie sniffled, but rapidly recovered her poise. 'Also some personal bits and bobs that my mother left me.'

The brooch. Joy remembered.

'When I discovered exactly whose daughter I was, I just had to find out more about this supposed crime. What was she like? About my father's life and his … my family.'

Clarice smiled encouragingly as Gracie stuttered.

'I saw Mr Scanner's advert,' she went on. 'and thought it was the best way to root out what really happened here at Misenlake in the run-up to Christmas all those years ago.'

'But what changed your mind? What made you decide to find out for yourself?' Scanner quizzed.

Gracie blushed like a beetroot with excitement, gabbling her words. But there was also something else, a resilience in her tone, a reverence for her wronged mother whom she'd never had the chance to love and the horrendous memory of her appalling plight. 'I came upon the idea when I received your letter detailing this most peculiar Christmas. I realised that I'd lost a chance, an opportunity to see where she'd lived and worked. As fortune would have it, I was hunting down an employment in York – you see, I am actually a seamstress by trade.'

'Not a nurse?' Clarice asked uncertainly.

'I'm sorry, hen. It was all a bit breathless when I arrived and until I was certain I hadn't been exposed as an impostor I wasn't sure what to say or do. I had no real right to be here. Being a nurse was the best excuse I could think of.'

Joy knew she'd been right. She'd always sensed something was wrong about Gracie.

'You see, perhaps it was fated. I bumped into this twitchy wee chappie coming out of the Sauvage agency,' Gracie said. 'I asked him on the spot whether he was going to the gathering. He told me he was fortunate enough to have nabbed the last place. His good luck was my bad or so I thought. But as I sized him up, I immediately knew that he was the sort of fellow who lived on his nerves. I had to try. So I took a gamble and asked if he'd like to share some tea. It emerged that he'd been an air raid warden during the war, enough to shred anyone's spirit, I would have thought. I'm afraid I wasn't at all honest. I'm ashamed to say that I made up a sorry tale about Misenlake – about my being a local – and its terrible past. When I added some stuff about the harsh weather and lack of modern conveniences, he visibly shrank before me. I felt rotten, but he thanked me and said his plans had changed.'

'So, that's where I came in?' asked Gloss.

'Yes, I suppose so. My luck ended there. I went straight to the agency, but they'd just closed for the day. And when I went back the following morning your call pipped me at the post. Indeed, I was there when the call came in, sat in the waiting room. I was mortified when the lady informed me that I had been just a few minutes too late. But whilst she apologised, and offered me a consoling cup of tea, I noticed a copy of the guest list lying on the desk, contact details and so on. I hid my disappointment and made myself pleasant asking to be put on reserve. And when the French lady went off to refill the teapot, I filched the paper and ran out. What she thought I'll never know.'

'It was you that tried to put Miss Royce off?' Scanner asked.

'Yes. She seemed the most likely candidate. A stranger to these shores, and she'd fortuitously given the agency details of her solicitor in London, along with her arrival date, the vessel, and so on. The rest, along with the weather forecast, was straightforward enough. I then made sure that I was one of the first to arrive at Misenlake and hastily made myself comfortable in a bedroom. I must admit I never thought I'd get away with it. But everyone was so reluctant to offer much about themselves – it was far easier than I imagined.'

Gracie restlessly rubbed her palms together. 'I held my breath when Miss Royce arrived, but Monckton and Miss Crabb did not appear to notice an extra guest and so I went with it. Mr Scanner here nearly gave me a heart tremor when he noticed the presents under the tree. But I braved it out. I suppose I was lucky that the French lady had travelled home for Christmas, but as they say, fortune favours the brave!'

'That's all very informative,' Mrs Pomp broke in. 'But how can you be mistress of this great house?'

Perry Scanner held up a hand. 'If you'll allow me, Gracie.' He took a moment for effect. 'I think I can explain that for you. Miss Grace Ines was hanged for the murder of Celia Gwynne, but months before the execution she gave birth to Major Gwynne's lovechild. When Dorothy Gwynne attempted to murder her adopted sister and frame her father's lover, she obviously had decided she needed to protect her birthright and at the same time avenge her beloved mother. So Gracie is the major's last living heir. Bit of a long thread, but I think that's right?'

Gracie blinked in agreement.

'So the house is yours?' Mrs Pomp spluttered.

'What will you do?' Clarice asked.

'I have some ideas. We can take some air a bit later, dearie, and I will fill you and Joy in with my plans. If Mr Gloss would care to join us?'

*

'Hem!' So this tale of this most murderous Christmas is almost done. You know, they still say that it was an impossibility, that it was all in my mind, and that I didn't see or hear anything strange or out of place. They insist that I made things up; but I saw them all the same. Maybe it helps people to be so foolish and disbelieving, and bury their own self-doubt by poking at the unreal and abnormal. But you know, that seems particularly silly to me.

I felt for Inspector Dunkley. A fine man and an honest policeman. But he didn't have my advantage. The help from the clouds of the past. And the voices? The ghost of Dotty Gwynne leading me to her killers? I suppose I will never be certain. Of Grace Ines, and that she was with me, of that I'm sure. Misenlake? This grand old house heaving with the ruptures of the years gone by? Redemption at last?

Sergeant Coupar saw me as I saw him. And as I close this tragic chapter, will these phantoms now be able to go on their way? Perhaps, but you see, I have proven that I'm not quite as wanting as they'd have you believe and maybe my peculiarities in any form they like to label them are rather more prevailing than they'd like to imagine.

Take Miss Biddle. If others had taken the time to see what she had noticed, could that have been an end to it? And my having been lured to the lift at the rear of the house, had I not banged a knee on the wheelchair, and heard the mutterings from Miss Crabb's apartments, would it have come to me that there could only be one who had slain the hapless gardener?

I didn't know enough at that point, of course. Pure luck and those flicking flames from the fire that had pointed out Dotty's hideaway, the birth certificate had finally cleared my smog. It confirmed Sergeant

Coupar's suspicions. And it gave me a warm satisfaction to know that his intuition had finally led to the solution to this ghastly mystery. A terrible tragedy that he never managed to unravel in time to save that condemned young life. That is the sadness that will never leave me and presumably never left him either.

But once Miss Crabb was taken away, and Miss Ceccy had settled with her maker, I saw no more of Coupar or Chantrey or the misted apparitions. As Gracie put it, the house needed to wake up and throw off the miseries of the past. Too much hurt had passed under the roof for the old house to bear. Could it recover? Would the phantoms finally settle? Gracie was going to give it a damned good go.

You see, she proudly informed us that she was going to make Misenlake her home. She was full of golden ideas, renovating the beach hut where her mother had spent such happy hours and of course, to level the alum works and fill the dreaded well. The cove still seemed to hold a fascination for her; the focus of her mother's death. And there, she talked of erecting a solid-fenced gallery where the beauty of the sea could be enjoyed in safety.

I liked that idea very much.

Simon Gloss was to stay on as estate manager. His great love, Gladys, had worked as a nurse for a time at Misenlake before her bravery at Dunkirk had done for her. So the house held both sweet and sourness for him, just as it did for Gracie, but to leave would feel like an abandonment. Indeed, Gracie suggested a particular rose garden named in his truelove's memory. Mr Gloss had blubbed a bit, but we all pretended we hadn't seen.

The biggest surprise was revealed to Clarice. Gracie and she had become such pals that Gracie asked her to stay on. Clarice hesitated. But I know it's what she wanted; a life of her own. So I agreed for her sake. My only quandary is when to tell her that I have my own ideas, my own outline for my future. I won't be locked away anywhere by anyone anymore, especially by my own insecurities.

And although Misenlake is a special place, it is for Gracie and Clarice and no longer for the spectres of the past. If I stayed, would I continue to conjure up these long-forgotten ills? And would my bond with Clarice take something away from this newfound friendship? I wouldn't want that. Perhaps the house has helped me see my way. It's time I started to be more self-assured and write my own future, in my special way, and stop feeling like the world is warring against me. But I will come back to Misenlake one day.

I will miss some of the thrill, meeting the phantoms of yesteryear. And I do so wish Sergeant Coupar could have found out the truth. But ghosts and ghouls, if that's what they are, are no more frightening than the horrors of the present. To me, they are just kinks in time, shaded from those who don't want to see. And perhaps, just maybe, I will meet others in the future and get better at embracing this most peculiar and supernatural world. I have I may have gone on too long. 'Hem!'

At Easter, I was still pondering the way forward and how best to tell Clarice that I was going to be off soon, when Perry Scanner came calling. In the drawing room, Clarice and Gracie fussed over him with tea cups and cake, and interfered as Drabble attempted to get on with his job. Nouse had popped in from the garden, his gimlet eyes twinkling. Having retired from the force, he'd taken up the vacant post of gardener, well, botherer of Ernest in reality.

'Good to see you Nouse,' Scanner had said. 'I suspect Prim's missing you.'

Nouse's face had contorted. He appeared to be struggling to coax out his words and eventually settled for a mumble and a tap on his forehead.

'So you said you had some news for us, Mrr Scanner?' Gracie enquired, offering more cake.

Perry Scanner stretched out his lame leg with a look of pain. 'No fresh news as such, just some intelligence to fill in some gaps. I was passing and thought it might be good to put an ending to our tale, and obviously I was champing at the bit to see how you all have settled.'

'We are all ears,' said Gloss, who'd tramped in from the grounds.

'I have kept up with some of those that managed to survive our most extraordinary Christmas gathering. I thought there may be a book in it, but I will discuss that with Gracie in a bit.'

Gracie's eyes sparkled.

'I know that you're determined that the truth is known about your mother's past, hopefully an exoneration and possibly a posthumous pardon.'

'To begin,' he started in his usual self-satisfied and slightly jocular tone. 'Barasch is in Israel. A new country and fresh opportunities. He has set up a dental practice there. Kosik has also arrived there. There is talk of a formal organisation for the apprehension of war criminals. It's in the formative stages, but possibly will be named Mossad. He's a cert apparently.'

Drabble offered Scanner a refill.

'Something a bit stronger?' Gloss asked taking up a decanter.

Scanner accepted and swilled the cognac breathing in the fumes. 'Mrs Pomp, it appears has found God. Or at least according to the personal column in the *Times*, an eligible vicar who would have her. Primrose Pomp is to marry Augustus Rufus Makepeace on May 8th, 1949. Let's hope she lives up to her new name.'

'I'm pleased for her,' Clarice declared.

'That leaves the divine Miss Royce,' said Gloss. 'And then me, I suppose.'

'Now she is almost worth a book herself,' Scanner remarked. 'As to your past, your secrets are safe with me.'

'Secrets, Mr Gloss?' asked Gracie.

Gloss's face had a relaxed resignation around the eyes, furrows smoothing as his mind seemed to wander. 'I met Gladys here. That much you all know. But that I was one of the first patients is a fact that I have never disclosed.'

'A lot of men were injured fighting for their country.' Clarice said soothingly.

'That's just it. I fell at the first hurdle. Leftenant Gloss of the Irish Guards. A regular soldier. Sent to Norway May 1940. We were bombed and blasted as we landed. I lost friends and my nerve. I wasn't prepared for such wanton carnage. Whether my mind was affected, or possibly it was the shame. Anyway I was sent home to recuperate and Gladys was there for me.'

'There's no dishonour in that, old man,' said Scanner.

'Possibly not, but dodging the draft thereafter – feigning mental frailty, a bit shady what?'

'I wouldn't be too hard on yourself, sir,' Drabble cut in. 'Battle does it to all of us. Some aren't brave enough to show it, that's all.'

Gloss half-smiled gratefully.

'Now to Miss Royce?' prompted Gracie hurriedly.

'I'm surprised none of you spotted it in the newspapers. There was a piece in the *Sunday Express*. It seems as a child she was sent to live in Canada with her aunt and uncle. That much we were aware of. What nobody had told her, and she had been ignorant of, until a letter she received recently, was that her parents had been murdered way back then.'

'Murdered? Poor thing!' Gracie exclaimed.

'Yes some sort of botched burglary. As a toddler she'd slept through it and had no recollection. She told me all this when I stood her lunch in Leeds a week ago.'

'She's still in England?' Clarice enquired.

'Hanging about for the trial. As you're aware, it's scheduled for the back end of May. She said she'd been taking the time to wheedle out bits of her history that were still uncoverable.'

'Did she find out the grisly news whilst she was here?' Gracie looked concerned.

'Yes. On arrival in England, she'd addressed a letter to a distant cousin who until recently had been living in her childhood village. Now in a hospice, this note had finally reached her relative. Unfortunately, in the reply this age-old tragedy was divulged, how Miss Royce's parent's died. If you recall, Miss Royce's mood altered considerably one night, and probably initiated the irresponsible dash for freedom. Thank the Lord for Joy once again.'

Joy caressed the arm of her chair three times and licked her upper lip. Another fresh fidget, albeit on probation.

'Quite a story,' Gloss observed. 'What a rum lot we were. It's no wonder we chose to keep our secrets.'

Scanner grinned. 'I see you've taken Nouse on? Prim's been made up to inspector. It was his diligence that uncovered Claube's true identity and began to demist Dunkley's eyes.'

'That and Miss Joy's notebook,' added Drabble.

'I still don't understand how Joy came to know so much detail about the manor all these years ago …' Gloss began.

Gracie flustered a reply and changed the tone. 'No one for fruit cake?'

'Ah! I'm with you old chap,' said Scanner, not to be put off. 'Which brings me to the last little bit of information I came upon. Its rather a coincidence, I think.'

Joy buried her head in her cocoa cup.

'The police chaps investigating the disappearance of Celia Gwynne all those years ago were an Inspector Ponder and his Sergeant, an Angus 'Crombie' Coupar.'

Joy glanced up.

'Coupar – not with a 'u'?' Clarice queried.

'That's right. The thing is …' Scanner began.

'That was your mother's maiden name!' Clarice declared to Joy.

'I was coming to that. Rather bizarre, but this chap appears to be Joy's maternal grandfather.'

Joy avoided their stares and squinted at the quirky clock.

Gloss followed her gaze. 'You love that old clock, don't you, Joy?'

All eyes turned to Joy's burning face.

Gloss prodded the little doors and fiddled with the hands. 'Shame really. Such a fine piece, but it hasn't worked for years.'

'Hem!' said Joy.

Joy watched the waves tumble over one another, up and over, and then over again. The breeze for a change had a warm tinge that cuddled her face and made it wondrous to be there, alone and free. The tang of the sea was tart, and the moist smell of newly shooting grass was rich in the air as she kicked pebbles over the cliff edge.

Arriving at the hut, she pulled out her jotter. It was the first time she'd been back since Gracie had brought her on that typically biting and early grey January morning. Everyone else had gone. She'd stood beside Joy as they stared out at the sea, and Gracie had ventured her own tale of a distant voice, a young woman singing so sweetly, a lullaby of sorts, and when Joy had turned to her, Gracie had swept away a tear and perhaps hid more behind her fluttering hanky.

Gracie confided in Joy that on that murderous morning, a slamming door had temporarily halted Crabb's murderous intent, possibly the gusting wind, but again she swore she'd heard a scream and sensed that they had not been alone. When the police had barged in, the sensation had left her and she later thought perhaps it had been the gulls, but whatever had happened, whoever had intervened she had been truly grateful for her life.

Gracie had looked into Joy's eyes and asked if she perhaps had imagined it all. Joy had not replied. But then, with a misted eye, Gracie had sung flawlessly; lyrics she'd said had only recently come into her head:

'Do the angels smile in heaven
When thy happy smile they see
While in slumber at my breast
On my bosom peacefully?'

'Hem!' was all I could offer. And as hard as I tried not to show it, I had also heard these words before, way down in that horror-filled well, they brought with them a rushing shiver. That Gracie had found her mother if only in snatches was enough, I think, for her if not for me.

I had hoped sitting alone in that cabin would bring me closure and rid me of the dreadful desolation that had plagued me for so many days. And in truth, I could no longer feel Grace Ines's love or her anguish, or the dread and appalling resignation, but what I couldn't bear was not being sure that she had finally found her peace. Had she seen that I'd kept my promise? Or would this place be forever hers? Well, either way, that's how it felt to me.

I began to ponder my future and wondered about my parents. My mother's face wouldn't come. But my father's smile brought the beginnings of a sob that was halted as a pouring of sunlight pierced the clouds and dazzled through the glassless pane. Dappled boards, patterns that an artist would have been proud of. These dancing kaleidoscope of buoyant colours were the most perfect epitaph of my dad and his indomitable spirit.

I again lost myself in the thrusts of the sea and for no reason sang that young mother's words again, exorcising her lost hope and attempting to wave farewell to the woman that I'd promised so much.

For my sanity, I said my goodbyes there and then to the governess whose idealised dreams of love were shattered by hatred, jealousy and wickedness. I was done with Misenlake and hoped it was done with me, but as I turned to leave, the haunting echoes returned once more. Shameless giggles ran around the walls and up and over the ceiling. Footsteps creaked on the timbers and a swish of a dress flicked at my leg. I stood for a moment, waiting, so sure I would see them again.

But as I hugged myself for comfort, the two girls wouldn't come. But then their teasing voices arose from nowhere, squealing and yelling, hollering and whooping. The door whooshed open, trailing the lyrics of a rhyme over the clifftops, a verse I'd heard before, mesmeric mischief tempting me back to Misenlake:

'Ding dong bell …'

ABOUT THE AUTHOR

Stephen Begg lives in Essex with his wife, Lydia, and their five cats: Lord Lynx, Lady Minx, Twinks, Master Binks and the new addition, Dinks, the little cat.

COMING SOON

JOY

&

THE BOY ON THE BEACH

Printed in Great Britain
by Amazon

63771671R00193